MW01119719

STUDIES IN
CLASSICS

Edited by

Dirk Obbink
Oxford University

Andrew Dyck
The University of California,
Los Angeles

A ROUTLEDGE SERIES

Studies in Classics

DIRK OBBINK AND ANDREW DYCK, *GENERAL EDITORS*

Aphrodite and Eros

The Development of Erotic Mythology in Early Greek Poetry and Cult

Barbara Breitenberger

Routledge
Taylor & Francis Group
New York   London

Routledge
Taylor & Francis Group
270 Madison Avenue
New York, NY 10016

Routledge
Taylor & Francis Group
2 Park Square
Milton Park, Abingdon
Oxon OX14 4RN

© 2007 by Taylor & Francis Group, LLC
Routledge is an imprint of Taylor & Francis Group, an Informa business

Printed in the United States of America on acid-free paper
10 9 8 7 6 5 4 3 2 1

International Standard Book Number-13: 978-0-415-96823-2 (Hardcover)

Library of Congress Cataloging-in-Publication Data

Breitenberger, Barbara M.
   Aphrodite & Eros : the development of erotic mythology in early Greek poetry and cult / By Barbara Breitenberger.
      p. cm. -- (Studies in classics)
      Includes bibliographical references (p.) and index.
   ISBN 0-415-96823-2 (alk. paper)
      1. Greek poetry--History and criticism. 2. Aphrodite (Greek deity) in literature.
3. Erotic poetry, Greek--History and criticism. 4. Eros (Greek deity) in literature. 5.
Aphrodite (Greek deity)--Cult. 6. Eros (Greek deity)--Cult. I. Title: Aphrodite and
Eros. II. Title. III. Series: Studies in classics (Routledge (Firm))

PA3015.R5A734 2005
884'.0109--dc22   2005013364

Visit the Taylor & Francis Web site at
http://www.taylorandfrancis.com

and the Routledge Web site at
http://www.routledge.com

Contents

Preface

This book is a revised version of my doctoral dissertation, written at St Hugh's College, Oxford. Naturally the concept has undergone many changes since its initial stages as a DPhil project. Its development into an interdisciplinary study would not have happened without the expert guidance and encouragement of my supervisor Dirk Obbink, who, during many illuminating discussions, taught me to view literature within its contexts. My first thanks must go to him.

I have been greatly helped by the comments and suggestions of several scholars. The work as a DPhil thesis was examined by Stephanie West and Ian Rutherford, from whose suggestions I greatly benefitted. In addition, I wish to thank Laetitia Edwards, St Hugh's College who read and commented on early drafts, and helped and encouraged me in many ways. I should also like to acknowledge the assistance of Peter Parsons, Robert Parker and Simon Price who read and commented on individual matters, and to the anonymous reader at Routledge for constructive criticism and comments. I am very grateful also to my colleagues in Cincinnati who offered valuable help towards the end of this project. My thanks also go to Hellmut Flashar who has continued to provide support in various ways.

I would not have been able to undertake research without the financial support from the following institutions: the DAAD (German Academic Exchange Service), the British Academy and the Fritz Thyssen Foundation all of whom have granted me a period of study without financial worries. I am also grateful to the Department of Classics (Cincinnati) for a Summer Research Grant and to the University of Cincinnati for a Research Counsel Award.

I have been greatly assisted by the staff of various libraries, especially of the former Ashmolean Library in Oxford, of the Burnam Library in Cincinnati, and of the Institut für Klassische Philologie in Munich.

For granting me permission to use their photographs, I am particularly grateful to the following institutions: the National Archaeological Museum of Athens, the Antikensammlung, Staatliche Museen zu Berlin, the British Museum London, the Staatliche Antikensammlungen Munich, the Staatliche Münzsammlung Munich, the Martin von Wagner Museum Würzburg and the Hirmer Verlag Munich. I am especially indebted to Erika Simon who kindly allowed me to reproduce photographs from her book.

My editor at Routledge, Max Novick, has been extremely considerate. My thanks also go to Andreas Müller for his diligence in formatting the manuscript, Catherine Lomax, Linda Sutherland and Christine Jackson-Holzberg for proof-reading the manuscript and improving my style of written English.

A word of special thanks must also go to my parents for making so many things possible in my life, to Inge, my sister, who proof-read several chapters and provided the charts for the Appendix, and to Ken for various reasons, above all, for his patience and understanding.

Finally, the book is dedicated to the memory of my mother who was the first to tell me stories about the ancient Greeks.

B. Breitenberger
Cincinnati, Fall 2003

Abbreviations

Anth. Pal.	*Anthologia Palatina*
ARV	Beazley, J.D., *Attic Red Figure Vasepainters*, Oxford ²1963
CEG	Hansen, P.A., *Carmina Epigraphica Graeca Saeculorum VIII-V a.Chr.n.*, Berlin 1983
CIG	*Corpus Inscriptionum Graecarum*, Berlin 1828-77
D.-K.	Diels, H., Kranz, W., *Die Fragmente der Vorsokratiker*, 3 vols., Berlin ⁶1952
DNP	Cancik, H., Schneider, H. (eds.), *Der Neue Pauly. Enzyklopädie der Antike*, Stuttgart/Weimar 1996-
ED, EV	Peppa-Delmousou, D., Rizza, M.A., (eds.), *M. Segre. Iscrizioni di Cos*, 2 vols., Rome 1993
EGF	Davies, M., *Epicorum Graecorum Fragmenta*, Göttingen 1988
FGrH	Jacoby, F., *Die Fragmente der griechischen Historiker,* Berlin/Leiden 1923-58
G.-P.	Gow, A.S.F., Page, D.L., *The Greek Anthology: Hellenistic Epigrams*, 2 vols., Cambridge 1965
IE	Engelmann, H., Merkelbach R., *Die Inschriften von Erythrai und Klazomenai*, Bonn 1972-74
IG	*Inscriptiones Graecae*, Berlin 1873-
LfgrE	*Lexikon des frühgriechischen Epos*, Göttingen 1955-
LIMC	*Lexicon Iconographicum Mythologiae Classicae*, Zurich/Munich 1981-99
L.-P.	Lobel, E., Page, D.L., *Poetarum Lesbiorum Fragmenta*, Oxford 1955
LSAM	Sokolowski, F., *Lois Sacrées de l'Asie Mineure*, Paris 1955
LSCG	Sokolowski, F., *Lois Sacrées des Cités Grecques*, Paris 1969
LSJ	Liddel, H.G., Scott, R., rev. Jones, H.S., *A Greek-English Lexicon*, Oxford 1996 (9th edn. with a rev. Suppl. 1996)
LSS	Sokolowski, F., *Lois Sacrées des Cités Grecques* Suppl., Paris 1962
M.	Maehler, H., *Pindarus*, ii. *Fragmenta, Indices*, Leipzig 1989
ML	Roscher, W.H., *Ausführliches Lexikon der griechischen und römischen Mythologie*, Leipzig 1884-1937 (repr. Hildesheim 1965-)
M.-W.	R. Merkelbach, M.L. West, *Hesiodi Fragmenta Selecta*, Oxford ³1990

OCD	Hornblower, S., Spawford, A. (eds.), *The Oxford Classical Dictionary*, Oxford/New York ³1996
PCG	Kassel, R., Austin C., *Poetae Comici Graeci*, 8 vols., Berlin/New York 1983-95
PEG	Bernabé, A., *Poetarum Epicorum Graecorum. Testimonia et Fragmenta*, vol. 1, Leipzig 1987
Pf.	Pfeiffer, R., *Callimachus*, 2 vols., Oxford 1949-51
PGM	Preisendanz, K., Henrichs, A., *Papyri Graecae Magicae: Die griechischen Zauberpapyri*, Stuttgart ²1973-74
PMG	Page, D.L., *Poetae Melici Graeci*, Oxford 1962
PMGF	Davies, M., *Poetarum Melicorum Graecorum Fragmenta*, vol. 1, Oxford 1991
RAC	Klauser T., Dassmann E. (eds.), *Reallexikon für Antike und Christentum. Sachwörterbuch zur Auseinandersetzung des Christentums mit der antiken Welt*, Stuttgart 1941-
RE	Wissowa, G., Kroll, W., Mistelhaus, K. (eds.), *Pauly's Real-Encyclopädie der classischen Altertumswissenschaft* (*RE*), Stuttgart 1893-1972
SEG	*Supplementum Epigraphicum Graecum*, Leiden 1923-
SH	Lloyd-Jones, H., Parsons, P.J., *Supplementum Hellenisticum*, Berlin 1983
SIG	Dittenberger, W., *Sylloge Inscriptionum Graecarum*, Leipzig ³1915-24
TGF	Nauck, A., *Tragicorum Graecorum Fragmenta*, Leipzig ²1889 (Suppl. by B. Snell (1964))
TrGF	Snell, B., Kannicht, R., Radt, S., *Tragicorum Graecorum Fragmenta*, 4 vols., Göttingen 1971-85 (vol. 1: Göttingen ²1986)
V.	Voigt, E.-M., *Sappho et Alcaeus*, Amsterdam 1971
W.	West, M.L., *Iambi et Elegi Graeci ante Alexandrum cantati*, Oxford ²1989-92

Abbreviations for journals are given as they appear in the list of *L' Année Philologique*.

Introduction

FACTORS HELPING TO DEFINE A DEITY: CULTS AND MYTHS

There are several ways to experience deity. Among the most important, one would certainly count the cults and rituals in which gods and goddesses are venerated and receive sacrifices from their worshippers. Since the Greeks were not a homogeneous cultural unit, the range of regional (and temporal) variation has to be borne in mind: different regions have different preferences for different gods. Men would address them on various occasions, depending on which specific aspect of a deity's capacities was required at public festivals and sacrifices, or they would do so privately, as many preserved dedications indicate. In many cases one would also experience deity through a cult image which represented or was even considered to be identical with the actual god in question. Another criterion would have to be the myths which define a divine personality by illustrating genealogy, province, exploits and possibly also relationships with other gods. It is these myths which make deities like Aphrodite the protagonists of their particular stories. Artists seem to have been particularly inspired by such myths when they chose gods as the subject of their art. If we consult modern dictionaries of Greek mythology, first of all we will find a portrait based on an account of these stories and their illustrations in ancient or even modern art. Myth and art exert a particular influence on our conception of the Greek gods, but a deity was always first and foremost an object of cultic veneration. Moreover, there are deities who, unlike Aphrodite or Apollo, are not surrounded by stories as these are, but nonetheless enjoy cultic veneration as, for example, cult personifications such as Peitho and the Charites, which occupy a particular place in the Greek pantheon. Finally there is Eros who is undeniably a god even without cult and specific story. It will be one of the main objectives of this book to explore the role and relationship of some of these personified deities with the Olympian deities against the background of myth and cult.

APHRODITE AND EROS: TWO DISTINCT DIVINE CONCEPTS

It seems to be a unique phenomenon in mythology that, for the Greeks, the province of love is represented not just by one deity, but by two: Aphrodite and Eros. Modern mythological dictionaries refer to them as forming a whole, implying that they have always been related to each other. However, they do not seem to have featured as equally established figures in a myth before the 3rd century BC. The popular image of the mother Aphrodite and her little son Eros, which has inspired artists and poets, particularly in Rome, for centuries, does not occur before the Hellenistic period, being first presented in Apollonius Rhodius' version of Medea's love for Jason in *Argonautica* book 3. That they were not related to each other from the very beginning is all the more surprising because both have their roots in Eastern cult and myth, although here they were never related to each other. Could this be because Aphrodite was perceived as a goddess in cult and also on account of her particular stories, whereas Eros, it seems, had no cult and was not featured in myths like other Olympian deities? Eros can be grasped only if one considers his origins in cosmogonic tradition, his identity as an erotic personification, and his links to a specific phenomenon of Greek society. These components seem to have prepared the ground for Eros' mythologisation by the poets.

   This book examines the different features of Aphrodite and her entourage in myth and cult, and analyses the different origins and nature of Aphrodite and her personified companions, Eros in particular. It will explore why and how they finally became related to each other as a pair, as mother and son. The other members in Aphrodite's train—the Charites and Peitho in particular—will also be examined. Their role in myth will be considered as to how it reflects their relationship to Aphrodite as cult-personifications, i.e. personified deities with a cult. This characteristic is common to the Charites and Peitho, and distinguishes them from Eros, whose peculiar character seems to emerge even more sharply by this juxtaposition.

A NEW APPROACH

In classical scholarship no attempts have been made so far to analyse the interactions between Aphrodite and her train, specifically Eros. Normally, scholars have treated each deity separately under a specific aspect or within a certain discipline. Aphrodite's early mythical representations in Hesiod and Homer have been examined against the background of her origins, for example, by D. Boedeker, who in *Aphrodite's Entry into Greek Epic* (1974) infers the goddess's Indo-European origins from the formulaic epic language. P. Friedrich (*The Meaning of Aphrodite*, 1978) analyses Aphrodite's literary representation from Homer to Sappho and, in a structuralistic approach, interprets Aphrodite as a female symbol of love. He identifies her as an Indo-European sky goddess. V. Pirenne-Delforge's monograph

(*L'Aphrodite Grecque*, 1994) consolidates the literary and epigraphical sources related to Aphrodite's cults throughout Greece, but does not give a comprehensive interpretation of cultic, epigraphical and literary evidence. A more universal approach to personified deities with a cult has recently been undertaken by R.G.A. Buxton in *Persuasion in Greek Tragedy* (1982) and B. MacLachlan in *The Age of Grace* (1993). The goddesses Peitho and the Charites are examined in their varying erotic, social and political contexts, but are virtually ignored in their function as goddesses of cult and in their relationship with Aphrodite. In the monograph *Eros. La Figura e il Culto* (1977), S. Fasce combines the examination of Pausanias' references to cultic evidence with Eros' literary representation, whereas other scholars have directed their interest specifically towards Eros' conception in poetry. This is also the case in the first extensive monograph on Eros, F. Lasserre's dissertation *La Figure d'Eros dans la Poésie Grecque* (1946). H.M. Müller's mainly philological study *Erotische Motive in der griechischen Dichtung bis auf Euripides* (1981) examines the implications of the pre-personified Eros, without taking into account mythical and cultic contexts. C. Calame's monograph *L'Eros dans la Grèce Antique* (1996) focuses on the literary features of Eros. Some recent publications, *Eros the Bittersweet* by A. Carson (1986) and *Eros. The Myth of Ancient Greek Sexuality* by B.S. Thornton (1997), are contributions not specifically to the divinity or mythical figure Eros, but rather to Eros as a concept of Greek love in a broader and more general context.

This study takes an approach that is new in comparison with the works of these scholars in two main respects. Firstly, it investigates not only one god, but the Olympian Aphrodite and her train of erotic personifications, with a special focus on the love-goddess herself and Eros, who emerges as her most prominent and individualized companion. Secondly, a more interdisciplinary approach than has so far been used is called for in order to elucidate the different nature and specific character of these deities and the way they interact with each other. This approach takes into account the deities' representation in their literary and mythological features, their functions as cult deities, and also their iconographical representation. It will emerge that for Eros the poetry in which he is represented as well as the social background from which the poetry emerged has been crucial. While Aphrodite's identity as a cult goddess manifests itself in many myths depicted in various literary genres and remains fairly consistent throughout the centuries, Eros is not a cult god, but a myth created by the poets. His nature and image vary according to different genres and contexts, and his complex identity is also reflected in different parentages.

OBJECTIVES

On a more general level this book also examines the relationship between myth and cult and considers how poets combined these in creating their mythological figures. It hopes to contribute to the discussion of whether the representation of deities in myth and cult practice are related to each other and if so, how. While they have been considered as two separate incompatible units, the discussion of Aphrodite's different appearances will show that mythical representation can never be entirely separated from cultic experience. On the other hand, cult realities usually find their explanation in mythical features.

A further objective of this book is to illuminate the complex structure of what we call Greek mythology today by distinguishing between myth and poetic invention. It will be shown that Greek mythology is not simply a collection of stories of the same kind, but a conglomerate of various elements: of myths in the original sense, i.e. which define the roles and functions of deities (in Burkert's terminology "traditional tales"), of cosmic myths, and also of literary mythical figures and their stories, which subsequent poets created by imitating the structure of deities and their "traditional tales". The emergence of the male love-god will demonstrate that the poets' artistic innovation as well as their social and historical background played an important role in creating Greek mythology.

SCOPE AND SOURCES

Since the evidence relevant to the topic ranges widely, the framework of this book has to be limited. It will therefore focus on the early, i.e. Archaic period. Of course, the absence of a satisfactory account of religion in Athenian tragedy and its implications for the conception of Aphrodite and Eros is particularly regrettable. But a satisfactory treatment would overreach the compass of this book. I will, however, include the choral lyric of the poet who wrote on the threshold to the Classical period and whom most scholars count among the early poets: Pindar (see e.g. H. Fränkel, *Poetry and Philosophy. From Homer to Pindar*). He is the poet considered to have perfected the art of choral lyric and therefore marks the peak of the genre whose main representatives thrived in the Archaic period. Although occasions for the performance of choral lyric did not diminish in the 5th century BC, the genre had certainly lost its former significance as poetry of praise with the downfall of aristocratic or tyrannic structures, at least within this particular environment. Pindar is not discussed here in order to throw light on earlier attitudes, since in some cases he is actually the earliest preserved source for erotic lyric motifs relevant to our topic (the role of Peitho, for instance). For this reason he is part of the subject. Although Pindar sets the final point of the period under discussion, this study cannot dispense altogether with works of Classical and Hellenistic poets. They are cited only where they show earlier Archaic features and help to illuminate them (as, for example, the image of the winged Eros appears in Anacreon and then again in Euripides and Aristophanes—in different contexts which are relevant to our topic).

A homogeneous corpus of contemporary literary, iconographical and epigraphical documents is not available for the Archaic period. Whereas literary and iconographical evidence from the Archaic age is comparatively abundant, epigraphical evidence from this period is not sufficiently dense. Problems particularly arise in defining Aphrodite as a cult goddess—the role that is highly relevant for our argument since it marks a distinctive feature in the demarcation from Eros, who had no cults at that time. It would be impossible to produce an account of Aphrodite's cultic role in Archaic religion based solely on contemporaneous documents. Wherever possible, the earliest inscriptions are adduced. When later sources are cited, they appear for purposes of comparison only, not as a claim for continuity. Such later evidence has to be handled with care. Continuity of practice cannot be projected back into the Archaic age, and there are certainly typical Classical and Hellenistic phenomena which cannot simply be postulated for the preceding periods. In some particular cases, however, it seems helpful to refer to and interpret inscriptions of a later date as parallels, since sometimes they are apt to illuminate earlier stages. This is especially the case when inscriptions are related to a cult which is attested to have been established in the Archaic period. Although new gods were introduced in the 5th century BC and changes in practices occurred, the stability of the cultic and religious system from the Archaic down to the Classical and Hellenistic periods seems to have been the norm in several respects. This has been pointed out recently by modern scholars (see e.g. Price (1999), 7; Mikalson (1998), 4).

The popularity of foundation myths, which is well documented in so many genres in Greek literature, may indicate a conservative Greek attitude in matters of religion. So, for example, the cult of Aphrodite Πάνδημος at Athens, together with its political implications, is already attested by traces of an Archaic sanctuary and also by myths going back to this period (see ch. 2). Therefore Classical and Hellenistic inscriptions indicating those functions are considered here as parallels for earlier cult phenomena. Renewed interest in Aphrodite Πάνδημος is documented by an increasing number of dedicatory inscriptions made by magistrates after Athens' liberation and the restoration of democracy in the 3rd century BC. This, however, does not simply mean that the cult of Aphrodite Πάνδημος at Athens experienced a revival, but corroborates that a particular function which already existed in an earlier period gains importance again at a given moment in Greek history. Thus a few epigraphical documents, even if they represent developments peculiar to a later period, may provide some insight into earlier stages of the original cult even though the nature and the degree of importance among existing cults change over centuries. Later inscriptions from colonies can also sometimes throw light on the earlier stages of the cults in the mother city. Even though they perhaps developed their own idiosyncrasies, it was the cults and religious activities which shaped the basic ties between the new colonies and the cities of mainland Greece. What supports the idea of a certain conservatism is the fact that, for the colonies, an important means of self-definition and confirmation of origin was to preserve the traditional cults of their homeland. This does not mean that individual practices relating to cults remained static. Thus we cannot take for granted that a phrase such as κατὰ τὰ πάτρια ("in the ancestral way") attests an ancient tradition, but it shows a positive attitude towards religious conservatism: in religion, ancient ways are best. This formula occurs for example in an inscription (dated to 287/86 BC) indicating civic practices (i.e. the bathing of a statue) in the cult of Aphrodite Πάνδημος, which may go back to an earlier period. Although we know that the cult did exist at that time, we cannot conclude that the formula proves the existence of a ceremony of a cultic bath already in the Archaic period.

Our literary sources include not only poetic texts, but also, where appropriate, the geographical writings of Strabo and, in particular, Pausanias' travel guide through Greece. In his *Description of Greece* Pausanias describes the cults and sanctuaries still in existence in his own day, together with their historical background, festivals and local stories about the gods worshipped. Although himself a traveller during the Roman epoch, he depicts the religious culture as central to Greek cultural identity. We cannot take for granted that a cult is as ancient as Pausanias claims it is (see, e.g., ch. 7 for the allegedly Archaic cult of Eros at Thespiae), but in those cases where he adduces a mythological tradition or where he is corroborated by non-literary evidence, his testimony can certainly illuminate phenomena of previous epochs. It was much earlier in the 5th century BC that the investigation and collection of tradition became a literary genre. Our oldest surviving historical source, however, Herodotus' *Historiae*, has to be handled with caution, since the historicity of Herodotus' source citations has been questioned (Fehling (1989)). In his view, they are attached to Herodotus' own free literary creations, a product of Greek thought bearing the spirit of Ionian historiography and geography, and do not represent genuine local tradition. Therefore passages relevant to our topic will be reconsidered in the light of other literary, archaeological and epigraphical evidence, and will be reexamined in view of their possible fictional character role.

Chapter One
Aphrodite: The Historical Background

1.1 INTRODUCTION

Like other deities in the Olympian pantheon, Aphrodite is not of Greek origin, but was introduced from the Near East, probably during a period of intense exchange.[1] Cult-related iconographic manifestations seem to have played a significant role in this process of transmission. By this means the Greeks came to know the Eastern Ishtar-Astarte[2] as a fully personified goddess who enjoyed cultic worship. Although the Greek Aphrodite inherited many of the characteristics of her predecessors in her mythical representations and also in cult as regards her province and attributes, she was given a typical Greek varnish which distinguishes her from her Eastern forerunners. This chapter will look briefly at the discussion on Aphrodite's possible predecessors in general and then explore how Greek manifestations of the goddess in early cult, iconography, and myth reflect her Eastern origins, but also modify them so that her Greek character becomes clear. Aphrodite will be seen to be a "composite figure whose Greek configurations are different from the originals".[3]

1.2 THE ORIGINS OF APHRODITE

Over the past hundred years Aphrodite's origins have been discussed intensely.[4] L.R. Farnell was one of the first to claim that she was originally an "oriental divinity".[5] Other scholars such as D. Boedeker and P. Friedrich argued in favor of an originally Indoeuropean predecessor,[6] some in addition emphasize a Hellenic or specifically Minoan-Mycenean character.[7] These views are not generally accepted, and the more correspondences between Aphrodite and Ishtar-Astarte are discovered, the less convincing they become. However, since our evidence of Indoeuropean mythology is from a stage when it had already been amalgamated with motifs and traditions from the Near East, it cannot be excluded that the Greek Aphrodite may be a complex combination of both origins.[8]

More recent scholarship has limited Aphrodite's provenance to Phoenicia. This view has recently been supported by a possible Semitic etymology in which her name is interpreted as the Greek rendering of a local title of the Semitic goddess Astarte ("she of the villages") and thus related to the phonology and morphology of the Cypriot Phoenician language.[9] W. Burkert emphasizes many significant parallels on the basis of cult traditions and iconography. Ishtar-Astarte is the Queen of Heaven, and this title is reflected in Aphrodite's frequent cult epithet Οὐρανία in Greece.[10] Aphrodite is the only deity in Greece worshipped with incense, altars and dove sacrifices, which are also offered to Ishtar-Astarte.[11] She is a warrior goddess, and Archaic *xoana* of an armed Aphrodite are documented in Sparta and Argos as well.[12] One of Aphrodite's most frequent epithets, χρυσέη, together with its compounds (e.g. πολύχρυσος), has been interpreted by W. Burkert as a reflection of artworks made of gold representing the Eastern goddess.[13] And, of course, both goddesses are associated with sexuality and procreation.

However, during the last few years correspondences in another area have attracted the attention of scholars. Striking similarities in the structure of mythological contexts and in their representation of deities seem to affirm the parallels in cult and iconography. A recent publication by M.L. West gives the impression that most of the significant contexts and characteristics of Aphrodite, not only in Hesiodic and Homeric epic, but also in the *Homeric Hymn to Aphrodite*, are inspired by oriental models.[14] The parallels of Aphrodite's complaint in Heaven with that of Ishtar in the Akkadian epic of Gilgamesh have been discussed extensively by W. Burkert and more recently by M.L. West.[15] I will argue later that, in spite of clear parallels, there are modifications in the *Iliad* which indicate Aphrodite's separation from her predecessor and confirm her own Greek identity.[16]

Support for a Phoenician origin gains ground the more one learns the extent to which many different fields of Greek culture, not only literary structures and motifs, but also trade and art, magic and medicine have been influenced by the Near East.[17]

1.3   CULTIC AND LITERARY EVIDENCE FOR THE NEAR-EASTERN ORIGINS OF APHRODITE Οὐρανία

There is in fact good evidence that the key role which Cyprus and Cythera played as mediators between the Near East and Greece in general was vital for Aphrodite's entry into Hellas.[18] The customary use of Κύπρις, Κυπρογενής, and Κυθέρεια in the preserved Archaic epics suggests that at the time of their composition these epithets were so well known that Aphrodite can be identified by them. Furthermore, they are likely to reflect a historical development during which these islands became Aphrodite's earliest cult places in Greece.[19]

That it was the Phoenicians who established her cults there is not only suggested by their traditional role as sea-trading intermediaries between the Orient and Greece, but endorsed by archaeological findings.[20] The Phoenicians' first settlement *en masse* in Paphos on Cyprus becomes evident at the beginning of the first millennium.[21] Recent research dates Aphrodite's famous temple there back to Mycenean times, around 1200 BC.[22] However, this does not disprove the assumption that it could have been founded by the Phoenicians. It is quite possible that smaller Phoenician communities were present there already before their actual main settlement. We have evidence from historical times that the adoption of foreign deities does not require a proper settlement of their original worshippers.[23] Furthermore, votive offerings found in another Archaic sanctuary of Aphrodite in Paphos show distinctly Phoenician traits and can thus accord with Aphrodite's Phoenician origin.[24] In this context it is important to note that later, in 333 BC, Phoenician merchants received permission to establish a sanctuary of Aphrodite at Athens. They were from Kition on the island of Cyprus which had become a Phoenician city in the mid-9th century BC.[25] However, the foundation of the cult at Athens cannot attest a continuous worship of the Phoenicians' ancestral deity in Greece. Early Phoenician traces have been found on Cythera too. According to G.L. Huxley, the most important cult in Cythera was Aphrodite's, and it was for her worship that the island was famous. He deduces from the evidence of purple industry there that the Phoenicians whom he assumes to have founded the cult settled on Cythera by the beginning of the Middle Bronze Age.[26]

This evidence finds confirmation in historiographical writings. Although Herodotus' testimony, his source citations in particular, have to be considered with care, as D. Fehling has shown, the historian's view concerning Aphrodite's early cult places and her provenance does not seem to be a product of mere speculation.[27] The goddess's epithets Κύπρις, Κυπρογενής and Κυθέρεια, which indicate her special relationship with these islands, are attested as early as Hesiod and Homer. Furthermore, Phoenician influence on Cyprus and Cythera is corroborated by sources other than Herodotus, i.e. archaeological evidence.

Herodotus (1,105,2) mentions the pillaging of the sanctuary of Ἀφροδίτη Οὐρανία in Ascalon by the Scythians and says that he learnt (ὡς ἐγὼ πυνθανόμενος εὑρίσκω) that this was the oldest of all shrines of the goddess.[28] He does not clearly say who his informants were—he probably means the people in Ascalon. Of course, we should not take this statement literally. Certainly, Ascalon in Syria was a Phoenician settlement, and that Phoenician merchants played a role as mediators of the cult of Aphrodite is, as we have seen, otherwise attested. But whether the sanctuary at Ascalon was the oldest ever cannot be proven (cf. Pausanias' statement, see below). It is doubtful whether Herodotus is referring to a real source here; maybe he is just putting a story into the mouth of a Phoenician local whom he need not even have met in Ascalon. One of the numerous Phoenician settlers in Greece could have told him the story as well—or some locals in Cyprus or Cythera. One can imagine that if he real-ly had gone there and asked the Phoenicians, they would very possibly have claimed their own sanctuary to be the earliest ever, simply out of local patrio-tism. Considering the maritime expansion and lively exchange with Greece, one can assume that they were aware of their own cult foundations there.

In the same passage Herodotus mentions the tradition, allegedly narrated by his Cypriot informants, in which the Greek sanctuary of Cyprus was also founded from Ascalon, and adds (without indicating a source) that Aphrodite's temple in Cythera was established by the Phoenicians from Syria. We have seen that Aphrodite's links with Cyprus and Cythera are attested as early as Hesiodic and Homeric epic, and thus in this respect Herodotus' statements are certainly correct. We may, however, wonder whether Herodotus really would have had to question these informants to be able to tell us what we read in his work. It is very likely that these things were common knowledge in Greece at the time of Herodotus.[29]

Six centuries later Aphrodite's early settlement in Cythera is reaffirmed by Pausanias.[30] His testimony alone, however, cannot back up Herodotus. Pausanias is much later and may in certain aspects have been influenced by Herodotus. Interestingly he diverges from Herodotus' account on one impor-tant point. While the latter says that it was the Phoenicians who established Ἀφροδίτη Οὐρανία's oldest sanctuary ever, Pausanias emphasizes their role as mediators. He says that the Assyrians were the first to venerate Ἀφροδίτη Οὐρανία. Then, he continues, the Paphians from Cyprus and the Phoenicians in Ascalon took over the worship of the goddess, and it was from the latter that the people from Cythera learnt how to venerate Aphrodite.[30] Elsewhere he says that the "oldest and most sacred sanctuary" of Ἀφροδίτη Οὐρανία in Greece is the one in Cythera, where she is represented by an armed *xoanon*.[31] While in Herodotus the cult in Cyprus is said to have been founded from Ascalon, Pausanias claims that it goes back to the Assyrians. This would actually mean that the cult in Cyprus, since founded by its original worshippers, is earlier than the one in Cythera which was established by Phoenicians, who then represent an intermediate stage. Pausanias stresses the function of the Phoenicians as mediators of the cult rather than as the very first worshippers of this kind of goddess. This is certainly correct, since other peoples also venerated a love-goddess or Queen of Heaven (Inanna, the goddess worshipped by the Sumerians in the 3rd millennium, for instance).[32] One can imagine that some traits of the Phoenician goddess may go back to features of an even earlier predecessor. Nevertheless, one can still consider it likely that it was the goddess's specific Phoenician idiosyncrasy with which the Greeks became acquainted.

Herodotus and Pausanias usually refer to the goddess's cults as those of Ἀφροδίτη Οὐρανία.[33] The assumed provenance of the cult title certainly sug-gests that one should relate it with Ishtar-Astarte's title "Queen of Heaven" which is attested for example in the *Old Testament*.[34] That Οὐρανία is an inheritance from Ishtar-Astarte in the sphere of cult is indicated by the fact that Οὐρανία is Aphrodite's most frequently documented cult title in Greece, but never seems to have been used as a literary epithet in mythical accounts about Aphrodite.[35] We know that Phoenicians, when expressing themselves in Greek, identify their goddess as Aphrodite Οὐρανία in 4th-century BC inscriptions.[36] In addition, a dedication is made to Aphrodite Οὐρανία at Piraeus by a Phoenician woman, Aristoklea.[37] The cult epiclesis Οὐρανία is almost uniquely Aphrodite's and is by far her most widespread cult title all over Greece.[38] But these later epigraphical testimonies cannot be taken as a proof that Aphrodite Οὐρανία has always been considered as identical with the Phoenician goddess of love. The other frequent cult title of Aphrodite, Πάνδημος, which signals the goddess's civic and political function, seems to be a distinctly Greek phenomenon: it has no Eastern parallel and is instead related to the Athenian city hero Theseus.[39]

What are the functions and implications of Aphrodite in cult when she is Οὐρανία? Her cult at Athens demonstrates that she is, like her forerunner, associated with procreation, specifically with having children. It emerges there that she is also a goddess to whom women make offerings before they get married. If the monumental altar in the Athenian agora has been correctly identified as part of the sanctuary of Aphrodite Οὐρανία, whose cult is mentioned by Pausanias (1,14,7), public veneration for Aphrodite Οὐρανία would be attested around 500 BC in Athens.[40] According to the myth attached by Pausanias, the foundation of the sanctuary is (unlike that of Aphrodite Πάνδημος,) not linked with the civic hero Theseus himself, but with his father Aegeus. Also, here we see the tendency to relate a cult to Attic mythological tradition: Aegeus is said to have founded the sanctuary since he feared that he might not have children and that Procne's and Philomela's misery—in particular that Procne killed her son Itys—was caused by the rage of Οὐρανία.[41] That Aphrodite was appealed to in this cult for the purpose of having children is supported by two archaeological and iconographical finds. Near the sanctuary, archaeologists have found a fragmentary relief dating from the end of the 5th century BC. It shows a young woman with a veil, looking at a vessel. Behind her, one recognizes pieces of a ladder. The ladder has been noticed on various scenes related to marriage, and C.M. Edwards has interpreted the ladder as the means by which the young bride receives access to the bedroom in the house of her groom.[42] If this interpretation is correct, it would be justified to see in this relief a dedication made to Aphrodite Οὐρανία by a young woman on the occasion of her wedding, probably for the sake of having children. That this is the goddess's main function in the cult is also indicated by a more recent discovery in this area: a box with premarital offerings dedicated to Aphrodite Οὐρανία dating from the 4th century BC.[43] We do not, however, have any information about forms of worship in this cult.[44]

Considering these two pieces of evidence, together with the Attic myth that Aegeus founded the cult for fear of not having children, it seems justified to interpret the function and province of Aphrodite Οὐρανία here as similar to that of Ishtar-Astarte: sexuality and procreation. In the case of the Greek goddess this includes marriage, the ἔργα γάμοιο which Zeus attributes to her in the *Iliad* (5,429). Yet this is a role which she, the notorious seductress and adulteress, cannot fulfil in her myths, only in cult. Also, in Sparta the epithet Οὐρανία has a connection with Ishtar-Astarte: it is one of the few cults in Greece in which Aphrodite's worship is linked with warfare.[45]

1.4   THE MYTH OF APHRODITE Οὐρανία

Although Οὐρανία does not seem to be a current epithet in literature, it has certainly provided the basis for a Greek myth.[46] Hesiod mythologizes Aphrodite's epithet in her birth story in a famous passage of the *Theogony*, where she is born from the genitals of her father, Uranus. It is interesting that Hesiod, unlike what we find in some of the *Homeric Hymns*, does not simply recount the famous cult places and parentage of the deity. He seems to presuppose that his audience is acquainted with what was presumably her most famous cult epithet, around which, without specifically mentioning it, he mythologizes her birth and creation from Uranus' genitals. The myth, as featured in the *Theogony* (190-200), does not seem to have a direct parallel in any Eastern culture, but its Eastern connection has never been denied.[47] We can expect Hesiod, who probably invented this myth, to have been familiar with the different elements necessary to create the story: Aphrodite's cult epithets and cult places, the folk etymologies of her name and also the relevant succession myths.[48]

Aphrodite came into being in the foam which was formed around her father's genitals after Cronus had cut them off and thrown them into the sea (188-192). When Hesiod calls her κούρη here (191), a significant characteristic of the Greek Aphrodite is already implied. After the amorphic primeval entities (such as Chaos, Earth and Tourtarus), and the hardly imaginable gods such as Cronus, she emerges as the first deity to be given clearly anthropomorphic characteristics or, what is more, a detailed female identity. Her description resembles that of a hymnic epiphany: Aphrodite is a young and "beautiful goddess" (καλὴ θεός 194), with "tender feet" (ποσσὶν . . . ῥαδινοῖσιν 195), but her character is rather like that of a "shy girl" (αἰδοίη 194). As one would expect in a hymn, the goddess's favourite cult places are also integrated into the birth story.[49] After her birth she swims directly to the "very sacred Cythera" (Κυθήροισι ζαθέοισιν 192), and from there she approaches "sea-encircled Cyprus" (περίρρυτον Κύπρον 193), where she goes on land. Cyprus and Cythera were certainly already at the time of Hesiod famous for their Aphrodite cults, and the epithets derived from them (Κυθέρειαν 198 and Κυπρογενέα 199) were probably already traditional.

Hesiod also integrates another central hymnic element: the deity's sphere of influence. When the grass starts growing immediately after she has put her tender feet on the earth (194-95), we are reminded that Aphrodite, as the oriental Queen of Heaven, is linked to reproduction and fertility. In the subsequent context of the *Theogony*, however, her responsibility in this sphere seems limited to the sexuality of the anthropomorphic gods, as the formulaic expressions with which her name is connected seem to indicate.[50] It is a plausible assumption that the first "historical condition" that inspired the birth myth is her actual cult epithet Οὐρανία, which was already common in Greece at the time of Hesiod. It could have been easily linked to the Hittite version of the succession myth which underlies the section preceding Aphrodite's birth myth in the *Theogony*. There, Uranus' equivalent, the King of Heaven, is deprived of his genitals.[51] As Aphrodite is Οὐρανία by cult reality, Uranus could easily become her father and thus link her to the old generation of gods. An additional factor which may have inspired this birth story is the folk etymological interpretation which links her name to ἀφρός, "foam", alluding to her emergence from the foam around the cut-off genitals.[52]

Aphrodite's earliest attested epithets in literature also seem to confirm that Cyprus and Cythera represent the first stages of Aphrodite's entry into Greece. Not only does Hesiod refer to her as Κυθέρεια and Κυπρογενέα, but Homeric epic and the *Homeric Hymns* frequently also simply call her Κύπρις[53] and Κυθέρεια.[54] This suggests that they belong to an established mythological and epic tradition which an Archaic audience apparently could be expected to know: they would thus identify Aphrodite on the basis of her epithets Κύπρις and Κυθέρεια.[55] Hesiod explains the epithets by describing how the goddess immediately after her birth arrives first in Cythera, then in Cyprus (*Theog.* 192f.).[56] In the *Odyssey* (8,362f.) Paphos in Cyprus is her home, the place to which she flees, awaited by the Charites, after her affair with Ares had been discovered.[57] In the *Homeric Hymn* she is addressed as "Cypriot Aphrodite" (*Hymn. Hom.* V,2) and the temple which she enters to receive her beauty treatment for the seduction of Anchises is located in Paphos in Cyprus.[58]

We have already seen that these mythical features, together with Aphrodite's traditional literary epithets, may be taken as a proof that the origins of those cults of Aphrodite, which were also the most important ones in Greece, were on these islands. Archaeological finds corroborate these assumptions; moreover, Herodotus and Pausanias also indicate that the cults were associated with the Phoenicians.[59] These testimonies confirm firstly that Aphrodite Οὐρανία is directly related to the Eastern love-goddess; secondly that her earliest and probably most important cult places were the islands of Cyprus and Cythera;[60] thirdly that it was the Phoenicians who brought her to Greece. There is epigraphical evidence that, in 333 BC, it was Phoenician merchants from Kition on Cyprus who gained permission to found at Athens a shrine of Aphrodite, whom they presumably looked upon as their ancestral deity Astarte.[61]

1.5   ISHTAR-ASTARTE AND APHRODITE IN ICONOGRAPHY

None of our historical sources records that the Phoenicians brought a cult statue or any other images of the goddess to Cyprus or Cythera. Pausanias (3,23,1), however, mentions an ancient armed *xoanon* of Aphrodite which was set up in her most ancient sanctuary at Cythera.[62] It is not surprising that she, armed like her predecessor, is Οὐρανία.[63] One would expect iconography in general, not only cult images, to be one of the most important media by which the Greeks came to learn of Ishtar-Astarte. Maybe also Aphrodite's epithet "the golden" was inspired by early Eastern artworks. It has become more and more evident how much the East influenced not only archaeology and arts, to which the term the "orientalizing epoch" was originally applied, but also all sorts of crafts, as well as religion, literature and science.[64]

The beginnings of trade and interchange between the Near East and Greece can be dated back to the 10th/9th century BC, but the contacts must have increased immensely in the mid-8th/mid-7th century BC, as one can infer from the number of imported objects which were found not only on the Eastern islands Cyprus, Crete and Rhodes, but also on the Greek mainland.[65] This interchange was not limited to the trading of goods and products of all kinds, but included also the artistic skills and techniques which Eastern craftsmen brought to Greece, and the Greeks' imitation of certain oriental motifs, including religious iconography. Such reproductions are preserved from the 8th century BC onwards.

One of the frequent motifs which the Greeks were acquainted with through different media was that of a naked, upright standing goddess, sometimes holding her breasts in a significant pose: Ishtar-Astarte.[66] This type was conveyed for example by clay plaques, such as those which have been preserved from North Syria, where they had been produced since the 14th/13th century BC.[67] This image of the goddess had a crucial influence on Greek art and was imported, and imitated from the 9th/8th century BC onwards in various ways and places, sometimes just by using the same moulds (See Plate 1).[68] Other media could be bronze plates and all kinds of minor arts and objects, such as jewellery and golden pendants which, among other reasons, may lie behind Aphrodite's being called χρυσέη in epic.[69]

Eastern influence also becomes palpable in the ivory figures which imitate the Ishtar-Astarte type.[70] They were found in a tomb at Athens and date from the third quarter of the 8th century BC. Their material points to Phoenicia which was at the forefront of the production of ivory and bronze statuettes.[71] They are, however, not just imported objects, as their style reveals new features in comparison with originally Eastern models.[72] Whereas the latter show the typical nutritive maternity in their full waist, the Athenian model is more refined in detail and has a significantly slimmer waist. Also, Ishtar-Astarte's most prominent characteristic, the position of the hand on the breast, is missing. Perhaps we see here already the beginning of a development during which the Greek Aphrodite diverges in distinctive points from her predecessor and establishes her own Greek idiosyncrasy. The Greek Aphrodite is never a full and maternal type. These features tend to be displayed instead by goddesses like Demeter. In the case of Aphrodite it is always more the aesthetic aspect, her rather pre-maternal beauty and attraction, as admired by later Greeks, which is emphasized not only in iconography and art, but also in myth, as we will see later.[73]

However, the small gold-leaf figures which were sewn as ornaments on shrouds found in the third shaft grave in Mycene may give an early impression of the image the Greeks became acquainted with. They date from around 1600 BC and display a female figure accompanied by birds, probably doves. As this type of female figure, especially its nudity, is very rare in Mycenean-Minoan culture, one assumes that this figure is the unique imitation of an image of the Eastern love-goddess.[74] These figures have been connected with Aphrodite, although it is agreed that she was added to the Greek pantheon not before the post-Mycenean period. Her name does not appear in Linear B documents, but in Greek epic, she becomes the "golden" one.[75] The doves, as the birds with which she is depicted are usually interpreted, are attributes and sacrificial animals of both Ishtar-Astarte and Aphrodite.[76]

1.6 APHRODITE AND DOVES

In Ascalon doves were sacred to the love-goddess as well as in Aphrodisias, where for this reason it was forbidden to hunt them.[77] Doves are attested on the coins of those places in Greece which have important cults of Aphrodite, for instance Sicyon, Corinth, Cythera, Cassiope, Eryx and Paphos.[78] This shows how closely related doves are with the veneration of Aphrodite.

There is also archaeological and epigraphical evidence to attest Aphrodite's relationship with these birds. In Aphrodite's sanctuary in Argos vessels of the 2nd century BC have been found which bear a dedication to the goddess.[79] In the same place, female votive figurines from the 6th/5th century BC have been discovered. As well as different kinds of fruits and flowers, they carry animals, most frequently birds, which have been interpreted as doves.[80] Furthermore, the birds depicted on Attic reliefs, together with birds made of marble found in the sanctuary of Aphrodite at Daphni, look like doves.[81] It is hard to judge whether the dove is a direct inheritance from the Eastern cults or whether it had developed its own meaning, because our extant evidence for the dove as Aphrodite's animal does not go beyond the 6th/5th century BC. Besides, it is amusing that Apollodorus of Athens makes the doves' notorious propensity for mating the reason why they are Aphrodite's birds, and thus he relates them directly to the province Aphrodite has in myth. He corroborates this with an etymology which relates the Greek word περιστερά to περισσῶς ἐρᾶν .[82]

We do not know with certainty what the meaning of the dove was in cults of Aphrodite before the Hellenistic period, but we know from a Hellenistic *probouleuma* at Athens that the *astynomoi* had to provide a dove for the purification of the sanctuary of Aphrodite Πάνδημος there.[83] Presumably the dove, originally being the sacrificial animal of Aphrodite Oὐρανία, was transferred to the cult of Aphrodite Πάνδημος at Athens around which votive doves and decorative ornaments have also been found.[84]

To sum up so far: iconography in its various forms had a key function in the transmission of the goddess's cult and image and also of her sacred animals. It will have been these concrete visualizations with which the Greeks first of all became acquainted. Therefore it seems that Aphrodite-iconography shares at least some common features with her predecessor.[85] The three cult statues of Aphrodite at Cythera, Sparta and Corinth, which Pausanias describes as carrying weapons, are influenced by Eastern models. Also, the doves occur in the cult and iconography of both. Therefore it seems that the Greeks, when they came to know Ishtar-Astarte, received immediately a relatively clear idea about her personality and appearance. Since aniconic portraits of Aphrodite in Greece seem to have been an exception, it is clear that, in cultic contexts, worshippers conceived of her as a clearly defined anthropomorphic goddess.[86]

However, whereas common characteristics between Ishtar-Astarte and Aphrodite are documented in early iconography,[87] the more recent portraits which are familiar to us show that Aphrodite developed a distinctively Greek character. While the aesthetic element of the oriental love-goddess does not seem to have prevailed in Greece, pre-maternal beauty and femininity become peculiar to Aphrodite in Greek art and literature.[88] This development towards a Greek conception of the love-goddess finds expression in subsequent iconography. Generally speaking, naked goddesses disappear from art in the late 7th century BC,[89] and from then on Aphrodite is presented in significantly lavish robes and adornment, which are also paralleled in Hesiod's and Homer's descriptions in epic. When the type of the naked Aphrodite re-emerges in the Hellenistic period, it becomes evident that she is being more associated with the Greek concept of pre-maternal feminine beauty than the fertility or nutritive maternity characteristic of her predecessor.

1.7   APHRODITE AND DIONE

Although iconographical parallels and the ancient historical tradition suggest that Aphrodite is of Phoenician origin, Ishtar-Astarte, when she came to Greece, did not enter a "religious vacuum". Aphrodite also has early connections with the Charites which are reflected not only in iconography, but also in myth and cult. This will be discussed later. The other Greek deity with whom Aphrodite has early connections is Dione. The depiction of Aphrodite's relationship with this Indo-European goddess in Homer's *Iliad* (5,370ff.) is unique.[90] I suggest that Dione's role as Aphrodite's mother in this episode is not only based on a possible mythical model—Ishtar's complaint in Heaven as featured in the epic *Gilgamesh*—but may also be motivated by cultic similarities between the two goddesses.

It has been argued by W. Burkert in particular that Homer's version of Aphrodite's complaint about Diomedes, who had hit her hand in battle, is modelled on an episode of the Akkadian epic of Gilgamesh.[91] Ishtar, not physically hurt by Gilgamesh, but rejected, retreats to Heaven and complains about the mortal to her parents Anu, the God of Heaven, and Antu, the Goddess of Heaven. Then she seeks revenge. Apart from similarities in the narrative structure, another parallel between the Akkadian and Homeric version has been seen in the fact that in this episode Aphrodite has a mother, Dione, and a father, Zeus.[92] In the same way as Antu is the feminine form of Anu, Dione is the feminine form of Zeus; however, she is not called his wife.[93] This role is taken by Hera. Considering the Homeric tendency to give gods individual names, this is certainly a unique case in Homeric mythologizing.[94]

The question now is whether the Akkadian epic, as a possible narrative model, was the only inspiration and motivation for the poet of the *Iliad* to make Dione the mother of Aphrodite. How should one interpret the fact that Aphrodite, who is herself Goddess of Heaven, Οὐρανία, and traditionally motherless, becomes the daughter of Dione? It must be considered whether this mythical relationship could reflect a cultic phenomenon.

The only cult place where Dione was worshipped conjointly with Zeus as his consort in Greece was at Dodona, at the same time one of Zeus' most important and ancient cult places. There he had a famous oracle.[95] That this cult place was already familiar to Homer emerges from Achilles' invocation of the "Zeus of Dodona, where the Selloi live, the prophets who never wash their feet and lie on the ground".[96] There is no direct epigraphical evidence to define Dione's role and her relationship with Zeus and Aphrodite there.[97]

Homer's early mythical connection suggests that Zeus, Dione and Aphrodite were linked in a cult at an early stage as well. Since the mythical model for the episode in the *Iliad* required a mother for Aphrodite, Homer may have referred to the cult association of Zeus and Dione in which the name of the female deity is a derivative of the god. Moreover, Hera would not have been the right goddess to sympathize with Aphrodite, by whom she was beaten in the beauty contest.

Zeus' epithet at Dodona is Naïos, which has usually been interpreted as referring to Zeus as the god of "flowing water", since the environment of Dodona has always been famous for its abundance of springs and fountains.[98] Pausanias (10,12,10) mentions a hymn in which Zeus is related to the Earth who "makes the fruits grow" at Dodona.[99] Thus Dione's function and association with Zeus will have to be seen in this context of fertility and reproduction—and this province belongs to Aphrodite as well. And there is another interesting feature in this cult at Dodona which one may relate to Aphrodite. Doves, an important attribute and sacrificial animal in the worship of Ishtar-Astarte and Aphrodite, as has been shown above, appear in this cult too: a bronze figure representing a dove was found at Dodona and dated to the 7th century BC. This date suggests that the animal could have been associated with the cult already in Homeric times, but its meaning is certainly different from that in cults of Ishtar-Astarte and Aphrodite, since the dove has an oracular function at Dodona.

Together with the oak the doves are traditionally associated with stories of the foundation of Dodona. This tradition went back at least to Pindar. In one of his *paeans* he mentions oracles in Libya and Dodona which were founded from the same origin in Egyptian Thebes, as well as Egyptian doves or priestesses as their founders.[100]

This myth is strikingly similar to the two mythical variants Herodotus was told by his informants in Egypt and Greece (2,54-7). According to the priests of Ammon at Thebes, Phoenicians had carried off two of the Theban priestesses and sold one of them to Libya, the other one to Greece. The former had founded the oracle of Ammon at the oasis of Siwa, the latter the oracle of Zeus at Dodona (2,54). His Greek informants, the priestesses of Zeus at Dodona, however, told him that it was not abducted priestesses, but two black doves (πελειάδες) who founded the oracles. They had both flown from Thebes, one coming to the oasis of Siwa in Libya, the other to Dodona, where she sat on an oak tree and announced that an oracle of Zeus was to be set up at there (2,55).[101]

Herodotus, in a γνώμη, harmonizes the two diverging accounts by rationalizing the Dodonean version through the Egyptian variant: if the latter is correct, the woman was sold to Thesprotia (near Dodona). Enslaved, she established a sanctuary of Zeus under an oak, remembering her god in the foreign country. Of course, the inhabitants were unable to understand her language, which they perceived as the cooing of a dove. As soon as the Egyptian priestess had learnt the new language, she installed the oracle of Zeus there (2,56-7). That Herodotus distinguishes between the foundation of the sanctuary and that of the oracle can probably be explained by his assumption that the priestess had to learn the language first. We may have expected Herodotus to refer to his informants as Πελειάδες so that the story they had to tell could be expected to explain their strange cult-title. Instead, he tells us their individual names (2,55: Promeneia, Timarete, Nikandra), and adds that their account was confirmed by other people who were affiliated with the sanctuary. Perhaps the priestesses only adopted the cult-title later.

The two variants of the myth are reflected in Sophocles (*Trach.* 171f.) where the two πελειάδες on the oak are the source of the oracle.[102] The ambiguity of the phrasing there leaves it open as to whether the oracle is meant to be announced by birds or priestesses who were called Πελειάδες as well.[103] Perhaps Sophocles' phrasing is deliberately vague. The priestesses' name may suggest that they were to interpret the animals' voices.[104]

The idea of links between Thebes, Libya and Dodona, of oracles of the same origin, of Egyptian priestesses or doves as their founders already existed at the time of Pindar.[105] However, if these motifs were common knowledge, Herodotus' information did not necessarily depend on the priests at Thebes and the priestesses at Dodona, and Herodotus may well have been acquainted with these motifs through literary sources.[106]

As it turns out, the presence of doves in the oracle of Zeus at Dodona, which is of interest to us, is well attested by several Greek versions. Independently from any foundation myth, the doves can be assumed to have a long-standing tradition going back to the Archaic period, since literary evidence is corroborated by a 7th-century BC bronze figure of a dove found there.[107] The ambiguity of whether doves or priestesses established the cult could have its roots in two different Greek mythical versions. The double version, together with the two locations implied in them, may have inspired Herodotus to attribute one to a source in Egypt, the other to a source in Greece, the origin and target of the doves or priestesses. Whereas an archaeological find proves the presence of doves in the cult, the excavations at Dodona have not uncovered any evidence to indicate a connection between the oracle and Egyptian Thebes.[108]

The appearance of doves in this cult does not seem to be directly related to its deities, but rather to the fact that there was an oracle. It has been suggested that the doves here may be considered mediators between the divine and human world.[109] It may be coincidental that doves, Aphrodite's animals, are also connected with Dione's only cult place in Greece. Perhaps it helped to suggest to the Homeric poet this special relationship between Dione and Aphrodite, i.e. as mother and daughter.[110]

The reasons why Aphrodite is shown with a mother in *Iliad* 5 (and only here in epic) have been debated. G. Kirk argues on aesthetic grounds that Homer tends to avoid "carnal extremes" and therefore "wished to gloss over the savage old tale of her birth in the sea".[111] Of course, he may have known the story. Some scholars see in the parentage of Zeus and Dione an indication of Aphrodite's Indo-European origins.[112] It can be argued, however, that the tendency in Homeric epic to subordinate deities supposed not to be originally Greek to Zeus as his children corroborates Aphrodite's Near-Eastern origins.[113] Thus Aphrodite's unconventional individual birth story (which makes her one of the oldest deities in the *Theogony*) would not have suited her less outstanding role in the *Iliad*.[114] Given that the Homeric poet was acquainted with the epic featuring Anu and Antu, it can be expected to have influenced his choice of Zeus' and Dione's parentship. That he could relate the Akkadian mythical couple to a cult reality in Greece where the God of Heaven and his female equivalent of the same name were venerated together, may have facilitated the borrowing, as well as the choice of Dione rather than, say, Hera. The cultic link need not have been the primary motivation.[115]

1.8   CONCLUSION

It was the aim of this chapter to map out the main directions in the discussion of Aphrodite's origins. In defending the idea that the predecessor of Aphrodite Οὐρανία is to be sought in the Eastern goddess Ishtar-Astarte, the most important similarities in mythical, iconographic and cultic features have been considered against the background of ancient historical sources, which include (apart from the testimonies of Herodotus and Pausanias) epigraphical evidence. The Phoenicians played a crucial role in transferring the cult of Aphrodite Οὐρανία to Greece, and the islands Cyprus and Cythera were Aphrodite's first and later most traditional cult places. Her literary epithets seem to reflect a historical development. The Greek Aphrodite diverges from her predecessor in certain respects (the aspect of feminine, pre-maternal beauty seems to be more important for Aphrodite). In the two following chapters, the evidence of myth and cult will show how Aphrodite's typical character and functions are modulated in different contexts.

Chapter Two

Some Aspects of Mythmaking and Cults of Aphrodite

2.1   INTRODUCTION

The image of Aphrodite depicted in literature and art is that of an irresistible seductress. She is perceived as the embodiment of ideal female beauty, and the sphere of activity attributed to her is the "joyous consummation of sexuality".[1] These are without doubt her most common mythical features and would be verified in any mythological dictionary.[2]

It is probably on account of this conception of Aphrodite that it has been considered surprising and paradoxical that the goddess of love also appears in civic contexts.[3] A great number of votive inscriptions made by different magisterial colleges in many places in Greece suggests that Aphrodite was worshipped as patroness of various magistrates.[4] This phenomenon, which is documented from the 5th century BC onwards, is less astonishing considering the public and political functions of Aphrodite which are prefigured in cult, since the epithet Πάνδημος ("of the whole people") is well attested already in the Archaic period.[5] This aspect of Aphrodite, which seems to have been so present in real cultic life, is hardly reflected at all in mythological accounts. No poet seems to have ever made this facet the theme of his work.[6]

The alleged paradox can be illuminated by an approach which tries to analyze the identity of Aphrodite from different perspectives, such as myth and its literary representation, cultic, and epigraphical evidence. For the idiosyncrasies of the Olympian deities cannot simply be grasped by the contents of their specific myths, which are displayed particularly in epic and bound to this genre.[7] It is still true that our idea of the Olympian gods (their names, myths and provinces) is particularly shaped by the roles and functions given to them by the two poets who, according to a famous passage in Herodotus (2,53,2) gave the Greeks their gods: Hesiod and Homer.

In this chapter I will take Aphrodite as an example to demonstrate that, if we considered only these mythical accounts of the Greek deities, which have almost become clichés, we would receive a very limited perspective. An examination of cultic evidence, of epigraphical documents, combined with an analysis of cult epithets, conveys an important insight into the complex aspects and intricate functions of individual gods.[8] It helps us to understand that they are more intricate than their literary portraits can convey, and that there are additional factors which have to be taken into account in order to understand the various facets in which the Greeks perceived a divine personality.[9] It has been pointed out by A. Henrichs that myth and religion (cults, rituals, festivals) are never identical.[10] I will try to demonstrate how they are normally related to each other, with each modulating different aspects of a deity. This becomes particularly clear if we consider the various occasions and genres in which myths were recounted, as well as their different intentions and uses. These considerations determine how directly cult realities are related to mythical stories.

2.2   DIVINE MANIFESTATIONS

That it is possible to isolate and define the essence of a god or goddess, and to find a unifying principle behind their various appearances has recently been denied.[11] Other scholars, however, by comparing different manifestations, have made attempts to isolate certain factors which help to shape a core of the image of deities. Among these factors, there are activities and phenomena of cult, such as the sanctuaries and the festivals, sacrifices and rituals related to them, the names of the deities, and particularly the epithets applied in cult, which supply important information about the function a god or goddess performed in a certain cultic environment. Iconographical evidence may be taken as an indicator of how deities were perceived and to which mythological or social contexts they were related. Finally, myths and stories seem to have shaped the idea of a deity.[12]

The following sections will take into account the complexity of elements which define a deity, focusing on the relationship between Aphrodite's cultic and mythological representations. It will emerge that the myth in its regional peculiarities prefigures the way in which a deity is perceived, according to respective cult practices and their historical implications. Moreover, myth bears in itself a "collective importance", a meaning that is related to a particular occasion and audience.[13] This is essential for the portrait of a god. Therefore the genre in which a myth is conveyed is also relevant for the representation of a divinity, and there is always a significant link between context and contents.[14]

Epic, for example, shows a less direct link to cult and ritual, but revels in the frivolity and all-too-human character of the Olympians when the pleasureable aspect of a myth is emphasized. An important task of the singer is, after all, to give pleasure to the audience.[15] When myths are performed within hymns, the cultic character is stronger, since we get information, *aitia* and explanations, about the worship of the gods, for instance.[16] Certain Attic myths are taken as examples that myth can also be used in order to establish political identities, and that images of gods are, consequently, very closely related to local cult.

2.3 CULTIC FEATURES AND EPIC NARRATIVE

The idea of Aphrodite as goddess of beauty and sexual pleasure has been inspired particularly by her early epic representations, namely in the works of Hesiod and Homer and in the *Homeric Hymn to Aphrodite*. I shall explore the ways in which ritual is reflected and integrated in the narrative.[17]

It has been argued by W. Burkert that Homer, when he represents the Olympian gods in an unheroic and all-too-human way, follows a traditional form of narrative which had been developed in Greece under the influence of Oriental models, and that this purely narrative representation has nothing to do with traditional ritual and the seriousness of religion.[18] Thus he emphasizes the apparently exclusively amusing character of epic narrative. However, the Homeric representation of Aphrodite is not merely the Greek version of an Oriental model. Nor is it simply an imitation of a similar scene in the Akkadian myth of Gilgamesh, whose main features Homer may have become acquainted with via tradition.[19]

Beyond its narrative function, it seems that the Homeric version of myths of Aphrodite also reflects the historical development of contemporary cult. The account of Diomedes wounding Aphrodite (*Il.* 5,311-430) demonstrates that the spheres of narrative and cult must not be considered separately, but as interlocking: Homeric mythologizing seems to comment on realities of cult. Within this context, Aphrodite's definition as being purely a goddess of love also means a restriction of her warlike facet, which is present in some cult places.[20] I shall argue that the poet exploits the absence or disappearance of a cultic phenomenon for narrative purposes. By depriving her of her warlike function through the mouth of Zeus, he portrays a goddess who is exclusively responsible for love matters and thus contrasts her all the more with Hera and Athena.

In this episode Aphrodite, while rescuing her son Aeneas from the battle, is recognized and wounded in the hand by Diomedes. Supported by Ares, she removes herself to Olympus and complains to her mother Dione. When Athena and Hera make fun of her failed war activities, her father Zeus, with a slight reproach, puts her in her place by limiting her activities to the ἔργα γάμοιο.

It has been claimed that this all-too-human family scene of a daughter complaining to her parents shows striking analogies in its structure and ethos with a famous episode in the Akkadian epic *Gilgamesh* (VI iii 11ff.). Here Aphrodite's equivalent Ishtar has also been enraged by a mortal, Gilgamesh. She had offered herself to him, and he had hurt her psychologically by scorning her love, recalling her previous lovers' unhappy ends. She also retreats to her parents, the god and goddess of Heaven, and complains about the disgrace she has suffered from the mortal against whom she is now seeking revenge. Like

Zeus, her father is at first not very understanding, but finally agrees to let her have the Bull of Heaven to punish Gilgamesh.[21]

There are certainly some analogies in the narrative structure and the style of these episodes. In each version, the goddess of love is hurt by a mortal and, as a child would do, complains to her parents in order to seek revenge. Even if the tone and the staging of the gods look un-Greek, one should not overemphasize Homer's dependence on Oriental models; we do not know whether he was acquainted with the epic *Gilgamesh* in such a way that he would have been in a position to reshape an episode of it point by point. Perhaps he did not have any literary model at all, but had observed girls running to their fathers in real life. The motif of a goddess assaulted by a mortal and then complaining to her parents is also a motif in Greek literature. In Hesiod's *Works&Days*, Dike, personified as a girl, comes to her father Zeus, complains about human beings who have violated her (i.e. what she stands for: justice), and seeks revenge.[22]

More tempting, however, is the idea that Aphrodite's parentage in the *Iliad* (only here is Dione her mother) has been inspired by *Gilgamesh*.[23] Dione is derived from Zeus' name with a feminine suffix, in the same way as the name of Ishtar's mother Antu is formed from her father's name Anu. However, even in this respect, direct dependence on *Gilgamesh* is not inevitable. I have argued earlier that the parentage may have been inspired firstly by the cult which Zeus shared with Dione at Dodona (see ch. 1.7). The poet knew this cult-association, as it is mentioned elsewhere in the *Iliad*. The second source of inspiration was very probably certain cultic features which were common to both, Dione and Aphrodite. Thus the presence of Dione in the *Iliad* need not be purely literary mythologizing of the Akkadian goddess of Heaven.

In any case, one should not overlook distinctive alterations in the Homeric episode. I will argue that Zeus' benevolent words concluding the episode are to be interpreted as a reference to Aphrodite's sphere of activity in Greek cult—a feature which is not presupposed in its model.[24]

In the Akkadian epic Ishtar is presented as goddess of love who is defeated in her own realm because Gilgamesh has rejected her offer of love. In the end, divine power remains victorious over the mortal since her father agrees that the Bull of Heaven should strike Gilgamesh down. In the *Iliad*, Aphrodite becomes active not, as one might expect, in love, but in the business of arms and war. The result of her complaint to Zeus is not, as in Ishtar's case, support in taking revenge on the mortal Diomedes who has wounded her physically, but gentle mockery (*Il.* 5,428-30): "My child, you are not given the works of war, but participate in the lovely works of marriage; all that will be the business of swift Ares and Athena."

"οὔ τοι, τέκνον ἐμόν, δέδοται πολεμήϊα ἔργα·
ἀλλὰ σύ γ' ἱμερόεντα μετέρχεο ἔργα γάμοιο,
ταῦτα δ' Ἄρηϊ θοῶι καὶ Ἀθήνηι πάντα μελήσει."

Aphrodite's failure in the works of war and her being reprimanded by Zeus do not come as a surprise in the literary context of the *Iliad*, considering the poet's ironic tone throughout this scene. One may well ask whether Diomedes' words, which mock Aphrodite's incompetence in the use of weapons, need to go back to a model.[25] Perhaps the poet himself innovated here in making fun of Aphrodite whom he later (*Il.* 24,30) portrays as the giver of μαχλοσύνη, a "madness for sex". But neither is the love-goddess's defeat in the business of war unexpected in the context of the society depicted in the *Iliad*, where war was the affair of Greek men. Hector's advice to Andromache, πόλεμος δ' ἄνδρεσσι μελήσει, is indicative of the role women played in wartime.[26] Thus, unsurprisingly Zeus finally summons his daughter, who has an all-too-human image in the *Iliad* anyway, to refrain from the works of war, although she is, after all, a goddess herself. In addition, these lines concern the interaction between myth and cultic features.

Homer's placing of Aphrodite on the battlefield may give an aetiology for armed portrayal of Aphrodite or her predecessor in cult in some regions and places, and Zeus' reproach seems to draw attention to this. It is entirely consistent with Aphrodite's image as goddess of love in the *Iliad*, when Zeus' rebuke finally denies her association with weapons and war. This, however, had been a typical quality of her Oriental predecessor Ishtar, who was worshipped as a warrior goddess in cult.[27] The cult association of Aphrodite with Ares, which clearly implies her affinity with war business, is well documented.[28] A mythical reflection of this relationship is attested as early as Hesiod (*Theog.* 933f.), where they appear as a couple. The myth in the *Odyssey* (8,266-366) is about their illicit affair.[29]

Thus it does not seem to be mere coincidence that an armed Aphrodite can also be found at Cyprus and Cythera, Aphrodite's earliest cult places, where Oriental influence is strongly felt and where a close affinity with Ishtar is most likely.[30] Literary sources know of Aphrodite Ἔγχειος ("with a spear")[31] in Cyprus, and Polycharmus of Naucratis records that as early as 688/5 BC a statuette of Aphrodite, nine inches high, was brought from Paphos to Naucratis.[32] Pausanias (3,23,1) mentions that "the goddess herself is represented by an armed image of wood" (αὐτὴ δὲ ἡ θεὸς ξόανον ὡπλισμένον) on Cythera and at Corinth (2,5,1)—a place which also had affiliations with the East. It has been suggested that the cult of the armed goddess Aphrodite came via Cyprus from the East to Sparta.[33] Of course, these sources cannot prove that Aphrodite was worshipped at Cyprus and Cythera as a warlike goddess in the 8th century BC, but since these were the earliest cult places of Aphrodite most strongly affected by Eastern features of the love-goddess, it seems likely that one of her most prominent facets was represented here as well.

There is also later evidence that in certain regions, namely at Argos and Sparta, Aphrodite's inherited warlike facet survived, and that she was in fact worshipped as an armed goddess who could grant victory.[34] It is again Pausanias (3,15,10) who mentions an armed wooden image of Aphrodite in an allegedly "ancient temple" (ναὸς ἀρχαῖος), veiled, with her feet tied together.[35] There her cult name is Aphrodite Μορφώ.[36] Elsewhere in Sparta (Paus. 3,17,5), she had a temple where her cult epiclesis was Ἀρεία. Pausanias points out the antiquity of the cult images there, but of course we cannot take their great age for granted.

Besides, there are later sources which provide *aitia* in order to explain this strange phenomenon. Lactantius (*Inst.* 1,20,29-32) tells why the statue of Ἀφροδίτη Ἐνόπλιος was erected. While the Spartans were besieging Messene, a part of the Messenian army slunk away and attacked Sparta. In order to defend their city, the Spartan women armed themselves and fought successfully against the enemy. When the Spartans realized that part of the Messenian army had disappeared, they sent their soldiers after them; these then attacked their own womenfolk, assuming they were Messenians. The women revealed their identity by taking off their weapons and clothes; this was followed by a wild sexual orgy. Thus, although the story itself lies in the realm of myth, it is likely to refer to a ritual involving a role reversal of male and female, which could also explain the paradox of an armed female goddess. F. Graf suggests that Aphrodite's Eastern provenance cannot alone account for the fact that an armed Aphrodite has been preserved for centuries at Sparta. He therefore assumes that there must have also existed a ritual during which the norms of daily life were changed and women took over the roles of men—as was the case at the festival called Hybristica in Argos.[37]

Beyond our literary sources there is iconographical and epigraphical evidence to endorse the idea that Aphrodite kept her affinity to war and weapons as an inheritance from her Eastern predecessor in certain places in Greece, particularly in those regions which were under a strong Eastern influence. The actively performed rituals suggest that an armed Aphrodite is not just an imitation of an iconographical feature, but part of cult. How do we interpret Zeus' statement regarding the warlike activity of the goddess of love which probably goes back to Aphrodite's predecessor? Could his mocking of Aphrodite really be just an inherited narrative element, as Burkert and M.L. West claim?

It is clear that Aphrodite's failure in war-matters as depicted in the *Iliad* is not only a narrative mythological feature invented by the poet in order to put a very unheroic Aphrodite in her place as a love-deity.[38] Beyond its narrative qualities, the myth could also be meant to refer to a cult reality: it may give a witty *aition* as to why Aphrodite had no function as a goddess of war in the cultic environment of the Homeric audience, although they may have known of her or her predecessor as warlike elsewhere. Ionia was not among the traditional cult places of an armed love-goddess, but Athena and Ares are the gods responsible for weapons and war. We might consider whether the image of Aphrodite as a war goddess was regarded by Homer's audience as something foreign and ancient. If so, the episode—by narrating Aphrodite's failed mission on the battlefield from which she is subsequently called back by Zeus—may be a humorous comment on a historical process during which Aphrodite has in fact lost one of her or her predecessor's accustomed spheres of interest—warfare—in the cultic environment of Ionia.[39]

Thus the myth can be interpreted in several ways. Apart from its narrative function, it also gives an *aition* to explain a limitation of activities of Aphrodite which seem to have survived in other places, while it separates her from Eastern equivalent goddesses. It defines "love" as the Greek Aphrodite's one sphere of interest. How influential Homeric mythologizing was in this respect becomes clear in several Hellenistic epigrams: these show how paradoxical the armed Aphrodite at Sparta was perceived to be throughout antiquity, how exclusively she was related to love matters, and how present the epic feature of golden Aphrodite, the goddess of love and beauty, was in the literature of the Hellenistic period.[40]

On the other hand, Aphrodite's association with war did not only survive in armed portrayal in cult, since we also have much evidence from the Classical period that Aphrodite received special offerings and dedications, particularly from magistrates who, in some cases, were concerned with weapons and war. It is interesting that Aphrodite's association with Ares in the mythological version, as displayed in the *Song of Demodocus*, shows her as a love-goddess who has to submit to her own influence.[41]

The sphere which Zeus assigns to Aphrodite generates a paradox concerning a possible reference to cult within the narrative: Zeus reminds his daughter that her true business is not works of grim war, but the lovely ἔργα γάμοιο (*Il.* 5,429):

ἀλλὰ σύ γ' ἱμερόεντα μετέρχεο ἔργα γάμοιο.

The interpretation of ἔργα γάμοιο has caused puzzlement. Scholars sway between "lovely works of marriage" and "lovely works of love".[42] The problem lies in the discrepancy between the actual meaning of the term γάμος and Aphrodite's true field of activity as displayed in the *Iliad*. Γάμος, at least in epic, does not seem to mean simply "love" or "affair", but is usually linked to the institutionalization of love, normally indicating an event which takes place on a particular day. Sometimes, however, it cannot be decided with certainty whether it refers to "wedding" or to the ceremony of the actual "nuptial rite".[43] γάμος also refers to marriage in the sense of a long-term relationship.[44] It is only later in Euripides (*Tro.* 932) that the unlawful wedlock of Helen and Paris is called γάμος.[45] In any case the ἔργα γάμοιο imply that Aphrodite is meant to have a particular function concerning the wedding and all that follows, i.e. sexuality within marriage. Presumably this is with a certain emphasis on the wedding night, as one could infer from Aphrodite's invocation in some *epithalamia*.[46] This diverges from her factual role in the context of the *Iliad* where she, instead of fostering legitimate marriages, supports seduction and illicit affairs. In a passage towards the end of the *Iliad* (24,25-30), the only allusion to Paris' judgement, Aphrodite is said to have brought to Paris μαχλοσύνη, "a grievous madness for sex" (*Il.* 24,30).[47] Since this term is exclusively applied

to women in early literature, it is unlikely that Aphrodite struck Paris himself
with μαχλοσύνη, in spite of his effeminate character.[48] Instead, it makes more
sense to relate the term to Helen whose "lewd" character it describes.[49] In this
context μαχλοσύνη clearly indicates something sent by Aphrodite as a punish-
ment rather than as a reward.[50]

Whereas myth illustrates Aphrodite within contexts of more adventurous
sexual encounters, her role in cult often relates her to marriage and children.
For this aspect, we have to consider later material, since we have no epigraphical
material dating from the 7th and 6th centuries BC. It is likely that Aphrodite, by
her nature, was early on related in cult to legitimate marriage and reproduction
(as was her predecessor). There is no evidence that Aphrodite could have been in-
voked for the sake of giving sexual pleasures in public cults. We know of sacrifices
and offerings that were made to the *xoanon* of Aphrodite Hera by mothers on the
occasion of their daughters' wedding in Sparta. There is evidence that there were
cult rites linked to the marriage ceremony.[51] We have already seen that the pre-
marital offerings, προτέλεια γάμο found in the sanctuary of Aphrodite Οὐρανία
at Athens provide clear evidence that she was venerated as a deity related to mar-
riage at least as early as the 4th century BC. However, the myth associated with
this cult suggests that Aphrodite was already worshipped as a goddess of mar-
riage and children by the time of its foundation at least circa 500 BC.[52]

At first sight it may appear surprising that Aphrodite Πάνδημος, who, as
we shall see below, is mainly concerned with civic unity and harmony, can also
be associated with marriage. A recently discovered public decree from Cos (ear-
ly 2nd century BC) provides the evidence that Aphrodite Πάνδημος received
compulsory post-nuptial sacrifices from wives—whatever their status—within
one year after their marriage according to their financial means.[53] The decree
after a preamble (lines 1-5) and instructions for the auctioning of and payment
for the priesthood (5-6, 8-15) says:[54] "In order to increase the honours for the
goddess and that manifestly all married wives—be they citizens, *nothai*[55] or *pa-
roikoi*, honor the goddess according to their financial means, all those whoever
got married, they are all to make sacrifices to the goddess after having sworn
an oath [that they were sacrificing to the best of their financial ability?][56] in the
year after their marriage"(15–20):

> ἵνα δὲ ἐπαύξηται τὰ τίμια τᾶς θεοῦ
> φαίνωνταί τε ταὶ γαμοῦσαι πᾶσαι τάν τε πολιτίδω–
> ν καὶ νό[θ]ων καὶ παροίκων κατὰ δύναμιν τὰν αὑτῶν τι–
> μῶσαι τὰν θεόν, ὅσαι κα γαμῶνται, χρηματισθείσας
> εἰσωμοσίας θυόντω πᾶσαι τᾶι θεῶι ἱερῆον μετὰ τὸν
> γάμον ἐν ἐνιαυτῶι·

We do not know what type of offerings these were. It is interesting to note,
however, that as far as we know, in Athens Aphrodite was to receive premarital
offerings only, whereas in Cos she was to be given offerings when the marriage

had already been performed.[57] It also seems striking that these marriage offerings in Cos were decreed by the state, whereas elsewhere they were made by custom not only to Aphrodite, but also to other gods.[58] It will be discussed later why the more politically oriented Aphrodite Πάνδημος was suitable to receive these compulsory marriage offerings.

The most famous mythical context in which Aphrodite seems to be traditionally linked to sexuality within marriage is the myth about the Danaids who refuse to marry their cousins. In Aeschylus' *Supplices* they frequently refer to Aphrodite as the goddess whose worship they refute.[59] There is one choral song (probably performed by the Danaids' handmaidens) in which the institution of marriage is defended: here Aphrodite presides together with Hera and Zeus over wedlock.[60] The myth presumably reflects an actual Argive cult in which Aphrodite, together with Zeus and Hera, was worshipped as a goddess of marriage. On this point there is no archaeological evidence. Pausanias (2,19,6) records an allegedly ancient myth according to which the *xoanon* of Aphrodite Nikephoros was dedicated by Hypermnestra, who had spared her husband from death and was acquitted with the goddess's help. That Hera, who actually presides over marriage, had such a prominent role in Argos makes it, however, all the more likely that Aphrodite had only a shared or subordinate function in cultic life in this respect. In any case she obviously had a traditional role in this myth.[61]

That Aphrodite is supposed to be responsible the ἔργα γάμοιο is in fact paradoxical, considering Aphrodite's own image and her activities as displayed in the *Iliad*, the *Odyssey* or the *Homeric Hymn to Aphrodite*. She does not appear at all as a matchmaker of legitimate marriages, but rather as an agent of illicit relationships (in the case of Helen and Paris) and of spontaneous passion in the *Dios Apate*, in which Hera manages to seduce Zeus by applying Aphrodite's magical κεστὸς ἱμάς.[62] Thus the function which she performs in those mythical accounts is well defined in the *Odyssey*[63] when the name Ἀφροδίτη itself represents the pleasures of love the maids enjoyed with the suitors. Accordingly, when she becomes active herself in her own sphere, she seduces and even commits adultery as in the *Song of Demodocus*, joyously indulging in a god who is more attractive than her husband. Moreover, in the *Homeric Hymn* she is perfectly in her element when she gives in to her sudden passion for a mortal, Anchises. Here the depiction of Aphrodite's beauty seems to be particularly emphasized.[64] The ἔργα γάμοιο, interpreted as the works of seduction rather than wedlock, correspond to what Hesiod in the *Theogony* already mentions as her realm: whispering, smiles, deception, sweet joy and love.[65]

This discrepancy between Aphrodite's attributed and factual role in the *Iliad* can be explained if we look at the way in which a possible cultic feature and narrative intentions interfere with each other. If we consider the authority of Zeus within the context of the *Iliad*, ἔργα γάμοιο as sexuality sanctified by marriage are an appropriate and serious province for a father to attribute to his daughter, and they may have also been among Aphrodite's functions in cult. But the point is that Aphrodite's behavior in the epic myths is distanced both from the propriety of Zeus' intention and from an appropriate and serious cultic function. I suggest that the mythologizing of Aphrodite's role as patroness of wedlock would have been far too prosaic to satisfy the requirements of the audience to whom mythical narrative was related. Illicit affairs are much more exciting and entertaining than any display of works of wedlock for which the goddess is responsible in other contexts. The fact that she does not obey her mighty father in the *Iliad* offers additional confirmation. In the *Odyssey* and the *Homeric Hymn* her own love stories provide the best way of presenting a deity in a most anthropomorphic and unheroic way. In the *Song of Demodocus* she herself embodies μαχλοσύνη, the "lust" she imposes on Paris in the *Iliad*.

The mythical representation of Aphrodite either defeated on the battlefield and put in her place by her father, or caught red-handed can in no way be separated from one of the aims of epic performance, which is to amuse the audience. This objective is even made explicit by the epic texts themselves, for example, when Achilles "delighted his heart when he sang of the glorious deeds of gods and men",[66] or when we are told that the Phaeacians and Odysseus found Demodocus' song delightful.[67] Consequently the account of Aphrodite's love affair with Ares is related to, but not meant to illuminate the deities' cult association. Its intention is rather to amuse by putting Aphrodite in a context in which she is in her element. The irony is even heightened when, paradoxically, her partner is the god of war, because he is her opposite.[68]

It would seem, then, that the narrative function of the sometimes humorous myths within epic was quite influential in shaping the mythical representation of the gods, which can be very different from cultic experience and "serious" cult-*aitia*. The Homeric image of Aphrodite shows the favourite facet of the Greek goddess: love and beauty. Therefore her ancient cult relationship with Ares also has to be turned into a love affair not only in order to amuse an audience, but also to depict the favourite mythical feature of the goddess of love—in love. Moreover, the epic representation of Aphrodite appears to reflect the poet's desire to contrast her as much as possible in order to give her a clear personality. Particularly in the *Iliad* she needed to be differentiated from Hera and Athena, her opponents in the war—and losers in the beauty contest. Thus she had to be dissociated from military and matrimonial concerns, aspects with which Athena and Hera were chiefly associated.

2.4   APHRODITE Πάνδημος IN ATTIC MYTH AND CULT

In what follows, I offer a detailed discussion of Aphrodite's role in Attic mythological tradition and related cults which is in many ways different from that in epic tradition. An analysis of the meaning of Aphrodite there shows how mythical themes and cult practices vary within Greece.[69]

Some important aspects of Attic myth which seem to have determined the function of Aphrodite in Athens have been pointed out by R. Parker. He argues that Homer and Hesiod showed very little interest in Attic myth. One reason why Attic mythology can hardly compete with other regional mythologies is that its themes are mainly public and concerned with politics. This explains why in the 5th century BC, in the process during which the Athenians defined their identity as a people, myths about Athens and the Athenians receive a privileged position in art and literature.[70]

As Attic mythology is distinctively political, it is not surprising that there seem to be only three erotic myths which received attention from the tragedians.[71] One is about Cephalus and Procris,[72] another tells of the tragic triangle involving Procne, Philomela and Tereus.[73] The third one narrates the story of Boreas and Oreithuia.[74] Can it thus be surprising—considering the public and patriotic nature of Attic myth—that Aphrodite is less prominent here than in Trojan mythology, in which it was her victory in the beauty contest which provoked the great war? Whereas there are many myths which show Aphrodite in an erotic way, we do not have a myth, taken up in literature, which features her active in a political way. Nonetheless, our evidence suggests that Aphrodite did not play a wholly insignificant role in Attic myth, since she was involved in the deeds of the legendary Attic king Theseus, who embodied qualities the Athenians thought important about their city and was considered the founder of democracy. Theseus is associated with distinctive changes in Athenian self-definition and becomes the mythological figure who is most related to Athenian democracy. Thus the myth in which Aphrodite appears is aetiological.[75]

Theseus' abduction of Helen, the journey to Hades, the Cretan adventure, or the Centauromachy were all familiar stories before the 6th century BC. But Theseus' prominence in Athenian tradition does not seem to predate this time.[76] Thus the cult of Aphrodite Πάνδημος need not originally have been linked to the tradition of the myths about Theseus, but was perhaps related to them as a result of Theseus' importance as a hero in Athens. This conveys an important aspect of the nature of myth and the gods who are represented in it: myth is partly determined by the socio-political context in which it is performed.[77] In what follows, I will look at the type of myth in which, Aphrodite is featured, and also at the archaeological and epigraphical evidence of cults of the goddess in Athens. There is in fact good evidence that Aphrodite enjoyed cultic veneration in many places in and around Athens. However, she does not seem to have belonged to the main group of deities worshipped in this area, since festivals in her honor played a minor role in Attic and Athenian cultic life. The reason for this may be related to Athena's particularly strong role as a city goddess.[78]

On the Acropolis, there were two different sanctuaries of Aphrodite, in which she was venerated under different epithets. These sanctuaries have been well documented through excavation. They are considered ancient, but the archaeological evidence does not go back further than the late Archaic period.[79] There is, as we have seen, a sanctuary in the agora in which Aphrodite Οὐρανία was worshipped (dated circa 500 BC). The foundation myth and the recently discovered premarital offerings suggest that at some point Aphrodite was associated with marriage and reproduction there (see ch. 1.3). Furthermore, there is also the ancient cult of Aphrodite Πάνδημος (in association with Peitho) in the Athenian agora which has been dated to the last quarter of the 6th century BC.[80] This widespread cult epithet indicates a specifically Greek political interpretation of an aspect of Aphrodite's traditional sphere of influence. It is significant that neither the cults nor any myths related to them have been mentioned in any of our literary sources from the 5th century BC—possibly because this "political myth" was not considered as particularly attractive for literary elaboration.

Plato's distinction of two Aphrodites in the *Symposium* (180c1-185c3) reflects these institutions of Aphrodite's worship on the Acropolis. But his philosophical interpretation does not seem to reflect the nature of the actual cults. It is indeed paradoxical and, in a sense, a reversal of the cult reality that he interprets Aphrodite Οὐρανία as the "Heavenly" responsible for the spiritual aspect of love, and Aphrodite Πάνδημος as the "Vulgar", presiding over sexuality. In cult, however, Οὐρανία is worshipped under the aspect of reproduction, whereas Πάνδημος is associated with a rather abstract, political principle civic harmony.

Two literary sources interpret Aphrodite's epithet Πάνδημος: Pausanias explains it with a mythical political *aition*, whereas Apollodorus gives a more historical interpretation. In Pausanias' version (1,22,3), the cult of Aphrodite Πάνδημος is linked with the deeds of the legendary city hero Theseus who is said to have founded the cult of Aphrodite Πάνδημος and Peitho on the occasion of his *synoecism* of the demes.[81] Aphrodite is normally associated with Theseus on his expedition to Crete where she was his special protectress and leader. In gratitude for her help he dedicated an image of her at Delphi on his return. Ariadne's tomb in Cyprus was allegedly situated within the *temenos* of the sanctuary of Aphrodite-Ariadne (Plut. *Thes.* 18; 20; 21).[82]

The myths about Theseus seem to be a product of the "invention of tradition"; therefore it cannot be excluded that the cult of Aphrodite Πάνδημος goes back further and that Theseus was given a role in its invention when he was so popular in Athens.[83] The cult epithet may therefore have been reinterpreted by a political myth that referred specifically to the history of Athens. Whereas Heracles, for example, symbolizes the panhellenic hero, Theseus, from the late Archaic period onwards, emerges as the national hero of the city who claims the political and cultural leadership of Greece. It is then that Theseus becomes a specifically Athenian construction.[84]

Just how far Theseus is linked with self-definition in Athens becomes clear in the artistic and literary culture of the Archaic and Classical periods.[85] Scenes showing Theseus in the fight with the Minotaur reach a peak in popularity on vase painting around 540-530 BC. In the last two decades of the 6th century BC numerous representations of Theseus suddenly appear on Attic vase painting showing him as a civilizer and benefactor of humanity. This cycle appears fully developed on vases after 510 BC, while the first attested representations of individual scenes date from around 520 BC.[86] The treasure house dedicated by the Athenians at Delphi displays Theseus: he secures the way from Troizen to Athens by eliminating enemies who were threatening the people's safety.[87] The civic aspect of his deeds is contrasted with the depiction of Heracles' exploits: the latter fights against wild animals and foreign monsters.

Literature also shows an increasing interest in myths about Theseus. Since poetry tends to inspire artistic representation, the emergence of vase paintings showing Theseus as a civilizer has often been interpreted as illustrating an epic, the *Theseid*, intended to present a national hero to the Athenians. In that case it would be datable before 510 BC, probably before 520 BC.[88] However, the testimonia are few and a secure date cannot be established.[89]

In the works of Bacchylides and Pherecydes, contemporary politics under Cimon are brought into a relationship with Theseus. Bacchylides' 18th dithyramb, which was composed 476/5 BC, is about Theseus' labours, with reference to the festival of the Thesea. At the climax of the poem, Bacchylides' description of Theseus undoubtedly contains allusions to Cimon's father and mother, and to all of his three sons. The message of the lines must be that Cimon is a second Theseus.[90] The monograph *Attica* of the historian Pherecydes focused on the legend of Theseus as the inventor of democracy.[91] It has been argued from fr. 149 that this work was composed under the influence of the statesman Cimon, who intended to trace his ancestors back to Theseus.[92] How much Cimon identified himself with the hero becomes obvious when in 476 BC, no doubt close to the date of Bacchylides' poem, he arranged that Theseus' alleged bones be transferred from Scyrus back to Athens. He reinterred the hero's relics in a marvellous shrine, the *Theseion* which was decorated with murals painted by leading artists of his time. By locating this monument in the agora, Cimon proclaimed Theseus the founder of Athens.[93]

Pausanias' political myth of Theseus' *synoecism*, reflects a process rather than a heroic exploit of an individual. However, Theseus certainly symbolizes the model of a democratic politician[94] and thus it is no surprise when he is linked to the cult of Aphrodite Πάνδημος, whose epiclesis and location are so much associated with political and democratic principles.[95]

An interpretation of the cult epithet which seems to contain a historical element and also implies a strong political connection is provided by Apollodorus

(180–after 120 BC).[96] He explains the title "Aphrodite Πάνδημος" by relating it not to a specific function of the goddess, but first of all to the location of her sanctuary: "In Athens they called the goddess (whose sanctuary was) established near the ancient agora Πάνδημος, since it was here that in ancient times the whole people met in assemblies which they called 'agorai'."[97]

> Ἀπολλόδωρος ἐν τῶι Περὶ θεῶν Πάνδημόν φησιν Ἀθήνησι κληθῆναι τὴν ἀφιδρυθεῖσαν περὶ τὴν ἀρχαίαν ἀγορὰν διὰ τὸ ἐνταῦθα πάντα τὸν δῆμον συνάγεσθαι τὸ παλαιὸν ἐν ταῖς ἐκκλησίαις, ἃς ἐκάλουν ἀγοράς.

It is likely that the establishment of the cult took place in the Archaic period, in a "spirit that was in a broad sense political." There is a possibility that the cult was founded by Solon. In any case Solon's ties with the cult, which are mentioned in other sources too, indicate that the cult was considered to have been established or to have existed in Solon's lifetime.[98]

The 2nd-century poet Nicander of Colophon (floruit 130 BC), says that "Solon had purchased good-looking slaves and had established them in rooms because (of the sexual needs) of the young people. With the money earned by the women he is said to have founded the cult of Aphrodite Πάνδημος since Πάνδημος means 'common to all'."[99]

> Νίκανδρος ἐν ς Κολοφωνιακῶν (III) Σόλωνά φησι σώματα ἀγοράσαντα εὐπρεπῆ ἐπὶ στέγης στῆσαι διὰ τοὺς νέους, καὶ ἐκ τῶν περιγενομένων χρημάτων ἱδρύσασθαι Ἀφροδίτης πανδήμου ἱερόν. ἔστι δὲ τὸ πάνδημον πάγκοινον.

In this version Aphrodite is associated with common and venal love. Nicander's statement may have been influenced by a work of the 4th-century comedian Philemon. He too refers to Solon's sexual politics, but does not relate them to the foundation of a cult of Aphrodite Πάνδημος.[100]

Instead of interpreting both institutions (the cult and the public house) as a monument to Solon's socio-political regulations of public sexuality, I would rather see the passage in Nicander as a reflexion of Plato's philosophical explanation of Aphrodite Πάνδημος as "vulgar", which does not seem to be associated with the actual meaning of the cult. After all, it is only Nicander who refers to this cult of Aphrodite in her function as goddess of love.[101] The two other versions, the more mythical as well as the more historical one, have a strong political connotation. Much is in favor of Apollodorus' explanation relating the epithet to the location of the sanctuary in the agora, as Jacoby has convincingly demonstrated, the place of the historical *synoecism*, which was, subsequently mythologized as an exploit of the Athenian city hero Theseus in Pausanias' version.[102]

2.5 CULTS OF APHRODITE Πάνδημος AND THEIR WORSHIPPERS

The cults of Aphrodite Πάνδημος were widespread on the Greek mainland and the islands, so for example at Elis, Megalopolis, Thebes and Erythrae, and on the islands of Paros, Thasos and Cos.[103] According to our epigraphical evidence, they are not documented before the late 5th century BC. The cult of Aphrodite Πάνδημος at Athens is the earliest one attested. An inscription which has been dated to 480/70 BC records the offering of a first-fruit gift to Aphrodite.[104] E. Simon has identified Aphrodite Πάνδημος on even earlier evidence: coins of the last decade of the 6th century BC. This would indicate that the cult existed at least as early as the Cleisthenic period.[105] H. Shapiro relates the emergence of these coins to the political circumstances and tradition. He suggests that the minting shows how the cult flourished under Cleisthenes, whose reorganization of Attica was likened to the *synoecism* under Theseus, commemorated in the cult of the civic goddess Aphrodite.[106] Thus it is clear that Aphrodite's area of responsibility as Πάνδημος is not love. That she plays a prominent civic and political role, with her relation to the "whole people", is confirmed by inscriptions from all over Greece. Some of these identify the donors and worshippers as magistrates.[107] Although these inscriptions are mostly Hellenistic in date, they document and illuminate the political implications of Aphrodite Πάνδημος which are prefigured in the Archaic and Classical periods. The dedications of the magistrates help to explain how the specific role of Aphrodite Πάνδημος was realized in actual political life.

We have already seen that it is this special relationship with Theseus, the founder of democratic Athens that makes Aphrodite an eminent political goddess. Thus it is not surprising that she is venerated by Athenian magistrates, in subsequent periods and especially at times when Athens is in danger. Aphrodite's realm, which has been defined as *concordia civium* ("civic harmony"), is indicated in those Hellenistic inscriptions.[108] I suggest that this civic or political harmony can be considered an extension of the private harmony Aphrodite brings to lovers. This interpretation is corroborated by the inscription from Cos cited earlier (ch. 2.3). It refers to compulsory post-nuptial offerings from wives to Aphrodite Πάνδημος. There seems to have been a synchronic coexistence of both functions of Aphrodite, as providing a more public and a more private harmony. Despite her prominent political role, Aphrodite is not attractive for mythmaking in Attica apart from the example of Theseus.[109]

While Apollodorus explains the cult epithet by relating it to the location of the sanctuary rather than to Aphrodite's function as Πάνδημος for the "whole people", we have evidence that, at least circa 400 BC, Aphrodite was related to civic administration and revenue. In 1977 a decree about the building of a temple for Aphrodite Πάνδημος was discovered at Erythrae (North Ionia). The introductory formula includes the *demos*. Where preserved, its frequent references to the *demos* are conspicuous (see lines 2;5;7;9;12): The Erythraeans had sent ambassadors (θεοπρόποι) to consult the oracle and were told to build a temple for Aphrodite Πάνδημος and various instructions were given:[110]

> [.........]το[— —
> — — — — — —]
> [. εἶπ]εν· ἀγαθῆι τύχηι τοῦ δήμου· ἐ[πειδὴ οἱ ....]
> [. . . κ]αὶ οἱ θεοπρόποι ἀπ[ήγγειλ]αν ὑπὲρ τοῦ ἀ[γάλμα–]
> [τος κ]αὶ τοῦ ναοῦ τῆς Ἀφροδίτης τῆς [Πανδή]μου ἐ[πὶ σ–]   4
> [ωτηρ]ίηι τοῦ δήμου τοῦ Ἐρυθραίων οἰκοδομῆσ[αι να–]
> [ὸν κ]αὶ ἄγαλμα ποιήσασθαι, δεδόχθαι τῆι βουλῆι [κα–]
> [ὶ τῶ]ι δήμωι, ἀποδεῖξαι ἄνδρας πέντε, οἵτινε[ς ἐπιμ–]
> [ελή]σονται, ὅπως ὁ ναὸς οἰκοδομηθήσεται κα[ὶ τὸ ἄγ–]   8
> [αλ]μα ποηθήσεται κατὰ τὸ ψήφισμα τοῦ δήμου· τὸ[ν δὲ]
> [ἱ]εροκήρυκα κηρύσσειν [.]ευδ........ κ..τριδι[. . .]
> [..]τας.ε.[...... ἄ]νδρας πέντε ἐπ’ ἱεροποιοῦ Ἑ[κατω–]
> [ν]ύμου· εἴ τις βουλήσει τῶν πολιτῶν ἢ τῶν ἐνοικ. [..]   12
> [. . .].............. τὸν ναὸν τῆς Ἀφροδίτης τῆς Πανδ[ήμ–]
> [ου
> omit 15-27
> [τὸ] δὲ . γηρ .... τῆι Ἀφροδίτηι τῆι Πανδήμωι εἰς [τ –]   28
> [ὸν] ναὸν κα[ὶ τὸ ἄγ]α[λμ]α ἐπ’ ἱεροποιοῦ Ἑκατωνύμου vacat

The circumstances which led to the consultation of the oracle do not clearly emerge from the preserved passages of the inscription. Merkelbach inferred from these lines that the consultation of the oracle was about the establishment of concord among the citizens.[111] Although not given explicitly by the text, I think that this interpretation can be supported if we consider the implications of (i) Aphrodite's political and administrative role as cult goddess bearing the epithet Πάνδημος and (ii) the numerous, predominantly Hellenistic dedications to Aphrodite offered by various corporations of magistrates who were responsible for securing civic harmony. They throw light on a cultic phenomenon which is already attested in the Archaic period.[112]

(i) Πάνδημος in its most general application means "related to the whole civic body".[113] About the exact function in which Aphrodite is related to the whole people one can only speculate, since no inscription mentions an exact incident. There is no explicit evidence to confirm that Aphrodite in a political context as Πάνδημος was chiefly linked with the concepts of concord and civic harmony and was responsible for them. One would, however, infer from the meaning of the epithet that she was considered as bringing and keeping the whole people together. This function could be interpreted as the public or political dimension of her role as a goddess of love (as such she brings lovers together).

The post-marriage offerings which, as we have seen earlier, had to be made to Aphrodite Πάνδημος according to public regulations in Cos seem to explain particularly well the public and more private aspect of the goddess.[114] That women made these dedications to Aphrodite after marriage is, as in the case of the offerings made to Aphrodite Οὐρανία in Athens, to be associated with her function as goddess of reproduction and therefore with children. Moreover, the fact that Aphrodite's veneration seems to have been better represented on Cos than that of Artemis for example, may explain why she, although being Πάνδημος, receives marriage offerings.[115]

I would suggest that the sacrifices made to Aphrodite Πάνδημος by the wives of Cos also point to her specific role as a unifier of the *demos* and donor of civic harmony, of which harmony within marriage seems to be a reflection. This is probably what the wives requested from her. Just how important harmony within marriage was valued by the community may be inferred from the fact, that unlike in Athens for example, the offerings for Aphrodite Πάνδημος were required by the state. Moreover, the additional regulation that "all wives of Cos" (γαμοῦσαι πᾶσαι 16) have to make the sacrifice appears to suggest that private harmony promotes civic harmony within the *demos*.[116] The cult in Cos provides the first epigraphical document expressing the idea of love in a civic or political sense and may help to illustrate and to explain earlier attitudes. This idea seems to be a familiar one at least in Classical Athens, since Pericles in the funeral oration (Thuc. 2,43), when describing the citizens' relationship towards the institution of the *polis* in erotic terms, admonishes the surviving citizens to become "lovers of their *polis*". Presumably Thucydides makes Pericles imply that a common love for the *polis* keeps the people together. Aphrodite in her function as Πάνδημος could be seen as a patroness of this.[117]

(ii) Aphrodite's role as Πάνδημος seems to become more prominent in certain political circumstances, i.e. when her function as unifier of the *demos* is required. We have seen earlier that this role is already indicated in the myth about Theseus. The coins that were minted when Cleisthenes restructured Attica in the last decade of the 6th century BC commemorate Aphrodite Πάνδημος and her link with Theseus' *synoecism* of the demes. New interest in the goddess in this specific function emerges during and after the liberation of Athens from the rule of Cassander and Demetrius of Phaleron and the restoration of democracy in the 2nd decade of the 3rd century BC. Mikalson relates this interest to her ties with Theseus in his function as unifier of Attica and founding father of Athenian democracy.[118] An inscription dated to 283/2 BC has been interpreted as reclaiming the deity for democratic and nationalistic purposes.[119]

Thus it is not surprising that Aphrodite comes to the fore again when, in 229 BC, the Athenians established their freedom from Macedonian domination. An inscription (215-02 BC) records that the Athenian βουλευταί dedicated an altar Ἀφροδίτει ἡγεμόνει τοῦ δήμου καὶ Χάρισιν.[120] This document is interesting in two respects. Firstly, the epithet can be considered as a specification of Aphrodite's epithet Πάνδημος, making her the "leader of the *demos*"; secondly, it explains why magistrates worship her. The goddess is described as assisting the magistrates in their own duties, since they are "leaders" of the people as well. Thus it is from the same perspective that Aphrodite protects the civic body and the body of the magistrates. It is probably justifiable to connect the dedication of the altar with the restoration of the independence of Athens, which had been achieved by the concord of the people.[121]

Defeated in the war in 262 BC, Athens had for many years been under Macedonian rule and then in 229 BC, after the death of King Demetrius II, was re-established as a free republic.[122] Given Aphrodite Πάνδημος' political implications, which she seems to have had at all times, it is no surprise that in such a situation she is the goddess addressed by the people. We have evidence through decrees of the assembly that the decisive role in the initiative for independence was played by two brothers, Eurycleides and Micion, and in addition to them, by the *demos*. It was the two brothers who dedicated the cult to Demos and the Charites on the North slope of the agora-hill and Eurycleides was probably the first priest.[123]

I conclude that the civic and political role of Aphrodite Πάνδημος, which is indicated in the myth about Theseus" *synoecism* of the Attic demes, becomes more prominent in political crises when the welfare of the *demos* is in danger. There is good evidence that at such times Aphrodite functions as the guide and leader of the *demos*, including its magistrates. This function is implied when she is called ἡγεμόνη τοῦ δήμου or Πάνδημος. In this context it is interesting that in a myth Apollo admonished Theseus in Delphi to take Aphrodite as his leader (καθηγεμόνα) on his way to Crete and to invoke her to be with him (Plut. *Thes.* 18). I would interpret this as an attempt to mythologize a cult reality by relating it to and making it an exploit of the city hero Theseus.[124] The unifying aspect of the goddess suggested by her epithet Πάνδημος is presumably a political interpretation of her function of bringing lovers together: she makes the people cherish their common love for the *polis*.

2.6   APHRODITE Πάνδημος AND THE MAGISTRATES

The role of Aphrodite Πάνδημος as protectress of the civic body and its harmony embodies just one aspect of her political and administrative function. Given this, it seems only natural that she is also considered as the patroness of those who are actually in charge of it: the executives of civic harmony. This new phenomenon being a consequence of the goddess's political function may throw light on how the political aspect of Aphrodite is to be interpreted. In the same way in which she keeps the people united in a kind concord, she is responsible for friendly harmony among the magistrates and their relationship with the people they govern. Usually they make their dedications as a whole magisterial college. I will consider this phenomenon since it is related to an Archaic function of Aphrodite. Her political meaning is closely related to the founder of democratic Athens, and thus the worship of the magistrates of the *polis* seems to be a subsequent development of this.

While documents indicating that magistrates were among Aphrodite's worshippers are comparatively rare in the Classical period, epigraphical evidence increases considerably in the Hellenistic age on the Greek mainland as well as on the islands, particularly in Thasos. Aphrodite's political implications, in varying manifestations, are recognizable over three periods in different locations. This shows how important this facet was, even though it was not a feature current in literature.[125] The earliest datable inscription to confirm Aphrodite's protection of magistrates goes back to the 2nd half of the 5th century BC and was found at Carthaia on the island of Ceos. A certain Theocydes makes a dedication after having been an *archon*. Unfortunately, it is not explicitly stated why and in which function Aphrodite was addressed.[126] That the magistrates' dedications were to Aphrodite as donor of civic unity and harmony, is not only to be inferred from the actual meaning of the cult titles, but also suggested by the category of magistrates who particularly worshipped her; for these magisterial colleges concord and harmony were essential when they carried out their duty. As with every other deity, Aphrodite is related to a specific class.[127] In what follows, I will examine the various magisterial colleges and investigate, according to their particular competences, why they were worshippers of Aphrodite. I suggest that this has to be explained by the special relationship these magistrates have with the people and Aphrodite's function as Πάνδημος. In the same way as Aphrodite effects peaceful harmony among the people, she also ensures concord among the magistrates within their college and their cooperation with the people.

The magistrates who worshipped Aphrodite were mainly entrusted with supervisory functions, controlling the (moral) conduct of the people. Since they often had to deal with crime, they possessed penal capacities:[128] among them were for example *agoranomoi*, a sort of police committee controlling the markets, and aspects of trade like weights, measures and prices,[129] *epistatai* who also dealt with crime and justice,[130] and even *strategoi*, a reminiscence of Aphrodite's not unimportant association with war which, as we have seen earlier, has survived in some places in Greece. Whereas these magistrates also honoured other deities, there was only one college which dedicated exclusively to Aphrodite: the so-called *gynaikonomoi*. Their function in its relation with Aphrodite was remarkable. They were a subcommittee of the police with particular powers over the regulation of women's lives and conduct in public.[131] They controlled their dress (εὐκοσμία),[132] as well as their participation in festivals and cult or funeral ceremonies. Thus their service also had a civic and religious character.[133] Aristotle in *Politics* criticizes the *gynaikonomoi* as an undemocratic and aristocratic institution, since they imposed restrictions upon women of poorer social classes.[134] One group of magistrates seems to have been particularly concerned with the public regulation of sexual matters, namely with the *hetairai*. According to Aristotle (*Ath. Pol.* 50,2) the *astynomoi* at Athens and Piraeus ensured that the girls who play the flute, the harp or the lyre were not hired at more than two drachmas.[135] We would have expected them also to make dedications to Aphrodite, but there is no epigraphical evidence for that.[136]

In the Hellenistic period, these magistrates appear in different places of Greece, at Athens only under Demetrius of Phaleron who was noted for his sumptuary legislation.[137] Although the responsibilities of the *gynaikonomoi* were not, as the title may suggest, restricted to women, they controlled mainly the appropriate female conduct in public, in general and in particular situations and events. This relevance to public life may be the reason why Aphrodite, in her role as Πάνδημος, is the goddess worshipped by the magistrates, and not Hera, as one could well imagine: the legislation seems particularly to concern married women. I suggest that Hera, in contrast to Aphrodite, presides strictly over the private aspect of marital life, whereas Aphrodite often has, as we have seen, a strong reference to public issues, in this case how women are seen in public.

A dedicatory inscription from Thasos offered to Aphrodite by *gynaikonomoi* is a good example of how the goddess, in her political and administrative role, is considered a mediator to the people as well as to their magistrates.[138] The *gynaikonomoi* supervised celebrations, political events as well as religious festivals, and so it is obvious that they were omnipresent and involved with the people in many contexts of civic life.[139] In the inscription on a marble block dating from the third quarter of the 4th century BC, the *gynaikonomoi* make an offering to Aphrodite after they have been "honoured with a crown by the people":[140]

Τιμαρχίδα[ς Π]υθίωνος.[141] ΙΑΓΟΝ.Σ..ΙΣΤΟΙ..
γυναικονόμοι Ἀφροδίτηι ἀνέθηκαν
στεφανωθέντες ὑπὸ δήμου.

That the honours paid to the magistrates by the people at the end of their office period precede the actual offering (as implied by the aorist participle) suggests that Aphrodite is considered the authority responsible for the good relationship between the magistrates and the *demos*, and therefore worthy of a dedication.[142]

Aphrodite's patronage over the well-being of the *demos* in public contexts is indicated in a Delian inscription.[143] This function may be one of the reasons why she is a civic goddess, a Πάνδημος and as such related to magistrates. A reason why she is the particular patroness of the committee of the *gynaikonomoi* may be that especially for them—as they interfered with the citizens in many aspects of daily life—a good rapport with the people was desirable for a successful fulfilment of their task. Therefore the *gynaikonomoi* particularly needed abilities that Aphrodite on the grounds of her specific influence on the *demos* oversaw — concord and harmony.[144] It has been argued that the two statues set up on the Thasian marble block were either Aphrodite and Peitho or Aphrodite and Eros. Considering the political and public implications of the two, it is by far more likely that Peitho had a statue there, as Eros does not seem to have had any comparable political significance.[145]

Concerning Aphrodite's role as provider of civic concord it is also interesting to mention that we have evidence that Aphrodite was worshipped as Νομοφυλακίς, as "guardian of the law", by the relevant college in Cyrene. When the same college erected a statue of Homonoia it is likely that she embodied a particular personified aspect of Aphrodite's realm.[146]

The goddess's relationship with magistrates finds its most intense expression when her epithet is derived from the title of the college which she patronizes. In different places in Greece she was worshipped not only as Νομοφυλακίς, but also as Ναυαρχίς ('guardian of the naval commanders'), Ἐπιστασία ('commander'), or, more generally, Συναρχίς ('partner in office') in different places in Greece.[147] The 3rd-century BC epiklesis Στρατηγίς ('of an army') shows the regard of military chiefs for Aphrodite. Aphrodite Στρατεία appears in a calendar of sacrifices of the 2nd century BC.[148] In both cases she was associated with harmony and concord within the army and presumably also with success in the missions. The cult titles need not have been exclusively military. A civic or political function of Aphrodite is also likely to be implied here, since in some cases military commanders were politicians as well. Early examples are Themistocles, Aristides and Cimon. The military aspect of Aphrodite occurs mainly in places where her cult was combined with that of Ares.[149] The dedication of the *eisagogeis* to Aphrodite Συναρχίς in particular confirms her association with concord (this time within the committee itself) which she seems to share with Hermes.[150]

The expression στεφανωθέντες ὑπὸ δήμου in the Thasian inscription cited earlier not only explains the relationship between Aphrodite, magistrates and *demos*, but conveys an additional point of information. The aorist participle suggests that the dedications were usually offered by the magistrates at the very end of their office, i.e. probably after undergoing a formal audit.[151] This assumption is endorsed by an episode told by Xenophon. The Theban *polemarchoi* of the year 379/78 BC, also magistrates concerned with war business, planned to celebrate Aphrodisia "on the occasion of their retirement from their office" and summoned their secretary to prepare the banquet for the college. In fact, this did not happen, since the *polemarchoi* were killed in a conspiracy. But it becomes evident that Aphrodite was the goddess to whom these military magistrates made formal dedications. The expression ὡς Ἀφροδίσια ἄγουσιν ἐπ' ἐξόδῳ τῆς ἀρχῆς also suggests that this celebration was customary and periodically repeated.[152]

The Aphrodisia celebrated by the magistrates were obviously related to Aphrodite's political meaning, as was the procession in honor of Aphrodite Πάνδημος of which we have evidence from a magistral decree of the 3rd century BC.[153] The private Aphrodisia were a different kind of festival: parties arranged for erotic encounters between men and women, as we find them mentioned in Athenaeus and Lucian.

2.7 APHRODITE AND HER COMPANIONS IN CULT

The main cultic associates of Aphrodite Πάνδημος' are identical with the companions related to her most frequently as attendants in early, mostly erotic mythical contexts: Peitho and the Charites.[154] It seems remarkable that the foundation or revival of cults of these goddesses seem to be related to contemporary political circumstances and the needs of the people, "themes of the moment". It would appear to be the case that in times of danger and insecurity people seek to consolidate peace and harmony by deifying these values and ideals and worshipping them in cult.[155]

We have seen that the early cult at Athens associates Aphrodite Πάνδημος with Peitho, and already here Peitho's political meaning becomes discernible, if Apollodorus' explanation that the sanctuary was near the agora is correct. This was the venue for the assembly where persuasion was necessary in order to achieve peaceful concord among the "whole people". Peitho embodies an aspect of Aphrodite which, under the epithet Πάνδημος, takes on a political connotation. Thus magistrates who deal with people also make dedications to Peitho.[156]

The same is true for the Charites, whose cult at Athens had been known since early times.[157] The fact that in the late 3rd century BC the βουλευταί offered an altar to Aphrodite and the Charites (see ch. 2.5) has, rightly, been interpreted within the context of the political circumstances in which the dedication was made, namely the reorganisation of democracy in Athens. To this same historical background may be related the fact that the Athenians dedicated a sanctuary to the personified Demos and the Charites, in order to celebrate the generosity and the reciprocal deeds of the Athenian citizens, as we have seen earlier.[158] The importance given to the Charites at that time is all the more plausible when we consider that in 5th-century Athens χάρις was regarded as a specific quality of the Athenian people. This is documented in Thucydides' speech of Pericles, who says that it distinguishes them from others.[159] In religious contexts, χάρις indicates what was given in return for a divine favour. In an inscription dated 500 BC and found on the Acropolis at Athens, a certain Oenobius sets up a statue to Hermes in commemoration, returning a favour. The χάρις felt by him is reciprocated by an offering which makes the deity well disposed to help in the future.[160]

The dedication of the βουλευταί signifies the revival of these traditional political values and the "gratitude" for the citizens' solidarity within the community during the period of war. Two more political qualities of the Charites are also well documented: Diodorus (5,73,3) says that the Charites, by evoking the people's "gratitude", influence the community by stimulating individuals to support the common cause and therefore the wealth of the whole people. It is probably also the notion of "gratitude" which makes the magistrates honor the Charites or ask Aphrodite for χάριτες. The idea of "gratefulness" which the magistrates expect from the people is certainly implied, but when in the 2nd century BC an Eunomia-college asks Aphrodite to present them with χάριτες and a "life free from harm", it is evident that χάριτες here means that they ask for a certain "charisma" (not "charm" as one would expect in erotic contexts) to please or to win over the citizens for the sake of the harmony of the whole people.[161] Like Peitho, the Charites too embody a particular aspect of Aphrodite's province and, in the same way as Aphrodite is perceived as Πάνδημος, they also receive a political interpretation which is related to the well-being of the people. In this sense the Charites imply either the expected "gratitude" of the *demos* or the "charisma" (or both) which the magistrates need for the good reputation they want to enjoy among the people.

We also have evidence that Eros (even the plurality of Erotes) can receive dedications from *agoranomoi*, but the significance which the male love-god had in civic contexts and related cults is negligible compared with that of the other cult personifications.[162] The cultic environment at Athens demonstrates that Peitho and the Charites are related to civic issues, whereas Eros in his cult association with Aphrodite represents an aspect of her functioning role in fertility and reproduction. That he, in contrast to Aphrodite, Peitho and the Charites, is no political deity, appropriately confirms his different nature and origin.[163]

2.8   MYTHS OF APHRODITE AND HARMONIA

When Aphrodite appears in civic or public contexts, she is automatically interpreted as goddess of civic harmony by scholars. In our epigraphical evidence, however, apart from the two inscriptions from Cyrene discussed earlier, Aphrodite is hardly explicitly addressed as a source of civic concord and harmony. That the scholarly *communis opinio* is nonetheless justified, is not only recommended by the political contexts—since it was magistrates who made the dedications to Aphrodite—but also by the genealogical association of Aphrodite and Harmonia in myth.[164]

Already in Hesiod's *Theogony* (934-7), Harmonia is presented as daughter of Aphrodite and Ares. While her brothers Deimos and Phobos (as depicted in the *Iliad*) become their father's companions, Harmonia joins her mother in dancing with Hebe, the Charites and the Horae in the *Hymn to Apollo* (195). Maybe also in this combination she represents an actual aspect of Aphrodite's sphere of influence.[165] That she could be so conceived is suggested by the fact that Aphrodite is not differentiated from Harmonia, Zeus and Peitho in the *Derveni Papyrus* (col. XXI).[166] But at the same time she probably also symbolizes a mediator between the two extremes her parents stand for: Love and War. Whereas Aphrodite and Ares enjoy rich cultic veneration all over Greece,[167] cults of Harmonia, in contrast to that of other companions of Aphrodite (Charites and Peitho) are rare.[168] It is usually the cults of Homonoia which are linked with the harmony within and between cities.[169]

2.9   CONCLUSION

An approach which seeks to define the character of a deityneeds to take into consideration the complexity of manifestations. One important constitutive element is certainly myth, but the representation of a god or goddess strongly varies according to the mythological tradition of the region in question. I have argued that the genre in which a myth is performed and the audience related to it strongly influence the way a god is represented. Thus a myth which is used for mainly narrative purposes, as in genres such as epic or the narrative sections of hymns for example, emphasizes aspects of Aphrodite's sphere of interest differently from political myths, which are meant to explain political identities. It has become clear that cult realities often convey an image of a deity which is completely different from mythological representation. How intricate the relationship of mythological narrative and cult realities can be in the case of Aphrodite has become obvious in the interpretation of her role in *Il.* 5. Although Aphrodite is shown as anthropomorphic here, we can infer from this divine burlesque indications of her more serious realm in cult, and a possible divergence from her predecessor. The poet gives a clear personality to Aphrodite who, put in her place by her father, experiences a limitation of her sphere of influence. Her warlike facet is denied in the epic narrative, and thus Aphrodite is exclusively a goddess of love.

That Aphrodite's province of love can also be interpreted in a political sense is shown by the cult of Aphrodite Πάνδημος; the epithet, which probably emerged from the location of the old Aphrodite cult at Athens, makes her the protectress of the *demos*. The political function which is associated with Theseus is revived and receives new interest in situations of Athenian history when matters of the Athenians and their freedom are concerned. This particular aspect of Aphrodite makes her a goddess who is worshipped specifically by magistrates in the Classical and Hellenistic periods. The mythologizing of this cultic phenomenon has to be seen within the peculiarity of Attic myth, which has a strong political function in its intention to create a political identity. This explains why Aphrodite was linked to Theseus' *synoecism* of the demes.

Notions associated with her epithet Πάνδημος also link her to those for whom harmony with the people is of crucial importance: the magistrates. Aphrodite's accustomed province "love" receives a political interpretation which exists only in the reality of cult. There is evidence that Aphrodite's political meaning is extended to her companions, preferably to Peitho and the Charites, who are responsible for Aphrodite's adornment in erotic mythological contexts. These also receive a political dimension.

Considering the cults of Aphrodite Πάνδημος, Plato's philosophical interpretation seems all the more tendentious: in cult it is the political ideas related with Πάνδημος which appear as a sublimation of sexual aspects.

Chapter Three
Losing Her Own Game: Aphrodite in the *Homeric Hymn*

3.1 INTRODUCTION

There is hardly any other extant Greek narrative which creates a portrait of the love-goddess as clearly defined as the *Homeric Hymn to Aphrodite*.[1] In a unique way, the hymn narrates the story of Aphrodite falling in love with Anchises. It fully unfolds the nature of the love-goddess by featuring her in a situation where she is most herself and which is appropriate to emphasize the two ideas with which the Greeks most associated her: beauty and sex. Thus in the myth about the beauty contest, Paris decides against Athena and Hera in favor of Aphrodite. Already in the *Odyssey* (22,444), and perhaps earlier in the inscription on "Nestor's cup", her name is used as a metonymy meaning "sexual love".

The hymn, however, has three paradoxes which the following analysis aims to solve: (i) Aphrodite is shown defeated at her own game while performing the activity she actually stands for; (ii) she is not as fully praised as one would expect in a hymn; it seems that the fact that even the love-goddess has to succumb to love emphasizes, in a paradoxical way, the power of her own sphere of influence; (iii) the way in which epiphany substitutes for the expected praise is also paradoxical. I will argue that the epiphanies before Anchises in this mythical narration are peculiar, as they are intended to highlight Aphrodite's main characteristic, her beauty. Further, these literary epiphanies may tell us something about the way in which worshippers generally imagined (or even perceived) divine epiphanies. The related adornment scene, i.e. Aphrodite's preparation for her encounter with Anchises, alone appears to be a narrative feature which is paralleled not only in Greek epic but also in myths about Ishtar and Inanna, Aphrodite's predecessors.

3.2   THE BACKGROUND: CULTIC ELEMENTS IN THE HYMN

The *Homeric Hymns* are intended as praises of gods. Their ancient term προοίμιον hints at their function: they were composed in order to introduce epic songs in rhapsodic *agones* which took place during festivals for the gods.[2] Formally and thematically they are influenced by cultic choral songs, as is for example Sappho's personal prayer to Aphrodite (fr. 1 V.).[3] The hymns' relation to cult and ritual has at times been denied on the grounds that their intention is not to invoke the deities to make an epiphany, but to represent them in epic style.[4] However, it has been conceded that they are most likely to have been performed in a religious context, paying tribute to the deity in whose honor the festival is held.[5] Thus their themes have become of special interest to the historian of religion since they are "the almost unique vehicle of a distinctive and important form of narrative about the divine world".[6]

There is good evidence that the narrative of the *Homeric Hymn* to Aphrodite, although its purpose is obviously different from that of a prayer, relates in several points to the sphere of cult and ritual in the way it incorporates divine epiphany as an important element within the mythical narration. It has been pointed out by Parker that, in spite of close similarities in style and manner, the hymns and heroic epic diverge from each other by putting a different emphasis on describing divine epiphanies. Homeric epic is chiefly interested in the reaction of mortals, whereas for "*Hymn*-writers epiphany is a climactic revelation of divine power, which may lead to the foundation of a cult".[7] Concerning the two protagonists, it seems remarkable that Aphrodite, at different stages of her appearance or epiphany, shifts between a goddess, a cult image and a mortal virgin. In a similar way, Anchises alternates between a worshipper and a mortal lover when he "adores" his visitor. Corresponding elements between mythical narrative and cult, which are briefly outlined here, will be discussed in greater detail in a subsequent section.[8]

Aphrodite's first appearance, her entry into the temple (58-67), may give us an idea of how worshippers in Archaic Greece imagined or experienced a divine ritual epiphany. Aphrodite's preparation for her encounter with Anchises there (61-7), however, recalls descriptions of other epic adornment scenes in which women (see Pandora in Hesiod's *Works&Days* and *Theogony*) and goddesses (see Hera in the Iliadic *Dios Apate* and Aphrodite in the *Cypria*) prepare themselves either to seduce mortal men or a god, or to gain the favor of the umpire of a beauty contest.[9] Furthermore, the motif of dressing is also found in a number of places with Ishtar-Astarte and the Sumerian Inanna.[10] The adornment of a goddess by her attendants in mythical accounts is comparable to the ritual service performed by worshippers. Thus myth could reflect actual ritual procedures.[11] In her second appearance, Aphrodite is recognized as a pure goddess by the wild animals, which immediately start mating (64-74).

The third scene (81-175) is actually the most interesting one: before Anchises, Aphrodite's nature becomes ambiguous—to the eyes of the mortal—when she adopts human height without relinquishing divine beauty in order to achieve her aim. The way she is depicted and perceived while appearing in this half-human, half-divine form may remind the modern reader of a cult statue adorned with jewellery. Consequently, Anchises, impressed by her appearance, first behaves like a worshipper, offering her an altar and adoring her as a deity (100-2).[12] Then, as soon as he has been assured that she is not a goddess by her lie, he adores her as if she were a woman (145-54). When he subsequently undresses her, he removes everything that is connected with her divine identity: here Aphrodite is almost a mortal herself (162-7). Getting dressed again also means that she "puts on" her true nature once more, and it is only at the end of the encounter (which is also the end of the love story) that she is, by revealing her divine nature, presented in an epiphany in a traditional way (168-90). Now, in her fourth appearance, Aphrodite is most clearly a divinity and unmistakably recognized as such by Anchises—not by her lovely clothes and jewellery, but by her height and supernatural beauty. Aphrodite's various epiphanies have a narrative function within the love story. They allow the poet to depict her in all her beauty and power, representing the sphere of influence she stands for. Within the narrative, Aphrodite uses her different modes of appearance to manipulate Anchises' reactions: first a prudish girl in order not to frighten him, then a *femme fatale* to make him desire her, and finally a threatening goddess prophesying his bad end if he does not keep the secret.

In its structure and constitutive elements, the *Homeric Hymn to Aphrodite* follows the other longer hymns transmitted in the corpus, in particular that of the *Homeric Hymn to Demeter*:[13] the welcoming of a guest by a mortal and the final revelation of the guest's true divine identity in an epiphany is a topos in the *Homeric Hymns*.[14] However, in contrast to the hymns to Demeter and Apollo, the hymn to Aphrodite does not provide an obvious *aition* for her particular cult places, temples or festivals, although hints of cult places and, possibly, cult practices are given. The place where Aphrodite goes for her adornment is the temple in Paphos (66f. and 292), one of Aphrodite's most important sanctuaries in Greece.[15] Anchises, assuming that a goddess has come to visit him, immediately offers her what is usually intended, and in fact achieved by the epiphany of a deity: an altar and sacrifices (100-2). Although this offer does not lead to the basic foundation of a cult—moreover, cultic veneration of Aphrodite is already presupposed—,[16] the hymn has some reference to religion also when, for example, at the beginning of the narrative, Aphrodite's epiphany on Mount Ida in Troy (68f.) provokes a mating among all the animals (70-4).[17] This, combined with the geographical setting, is likely to be reminiscent of the worship of the local Phrygian goddess Cybele, the Great Mother, with whom Aphrodite is identified, here as elsewhere, on grounds of having similar functions.[18] Like their common Oriental predecessor Ishtar-Astarte (Aphrodite's Eastern origins are again discernible), they are not only both responsible for sexuality and reproduction, but share also a passion for mortal men, whose punishment by the love-goddess after the encounter is a common element in these myths.[19]

As in other hymns, the mythical story displayed in the narrative focuses on the divinity, relating an important episode of her life and involving a conflict.[20] Nonetheless, in the case of Aphrodite it is different. We learn nothing about her own birth, nor do we get an *aition* explaining why her main sanctuary is at Paphos or why she is called "Cypris" or "Cythereia".[21] The way the epithets are used suggests rather that the cults of Aphrodite are already presupposed as a known fact, just as her beauty trip to Paphos seems to be a habit. Another type of *aition* aims to explain not a cult, but the semi-divine parentage of the *Aineiadai*. It has been suggested therefore that this hymn was composed as an *encomium* of a historical family in Scepsis (Troad) who considered themselves descendants of Aeneas—the same family the poet of the *Iliad* honoured in Aeneas' *aristeia* (*Il.* 20).[22] While this theory has been discredited, most scholars agree upon the early date of the *Homeric Hymn to Aphrodite* and its temporal proximity to the poems of Hesiod and Homer.[23]

However dubious the actual external evidence for a historical family may be, the *Homeric Hymn to Aphrodite* does emphasize in the prophecy the fate of Anchises' offspring (191-291), the upbringing of Aeneas (256-73) and his presentation (274-80) at the end. Thus it is implied in the text that Aeneas and the subsequent generations are accorded great importance as being notable examples of the ἔργα Ἀφροδίτης. It is this offspring which Aphrodite herself has produced in her union with the mortal Anchises, and it is the result of her activity in her own realm. As the hymn focuses on Aphrodite and her epiphanies in particular, one could ask why a noble family should have been glorified in a hymn. One might assume that the divine genealogy for a family of mortals praised in the hymn refers to its actual commissioners within a religious community. It was perhaps they who paid for the statue of Aphrodite and her adornment in the cult.[24] There are certainly parallels for tracing back the parentage of historical figures to divine origins for the sake of political propaganda.[25] Had such a family still existed at the time and the place the hymn was written, it seems quite natural that the poet would have alluded to their origin. The conception of the hero Aeneas and Aphrodite's prophecy about the future lineage of Anchises, both of which are important elements of the hymn indeed, may be seen as tribute paid to the family.

The core of the composition is the praise of Aphrodite's power over sexuality and creation on earth, as is suggested by the introductory lines. This is illustrated by the seduction scene, which is to be considered as a significant episode of Aphrodite's life. It presents her in an epiphany during which she has to succumb to her own power. As a result, Aphrodite and Anchises become the parents of Aeneas, a genealogy already mentioned in the *Iliad*.[26] It is conceivable that the poet, by following the traditional pattern of hymnic narrative, intended to illustrate divine genealogy by showing how the hero was conceived according to traditional epic.

Although the *Homeric Hymn to Aphrodite* does not allude to the circumstances in which it was presented, it is likely that its occasion was a festival for Aphrodite at which the family could have been present.[27]

3.3 THE MYTHICAL NARRATION: A LOVE STORY

The celebration of Aphrodite's ἔργα, her great victory over gods, men and beasts by arousing their sweet desire, commences the hymnic invocation (1-6).[28] The three "negative" examples (Athena, Artemis and Hestia), who alone are untouched by Aphrodite's works, form a suitable transition from the invocation to the narrative: they already allude to certain weaknesses in her authority (7-33). Whereas they are resistent to Aphrodite, the love-goddess herself is not immune to her own power. She therefore suffers a heavy defeat in her own realm, and this is caused by Zeus. Even Aphrodite has to succumb to love. It is paradoxical and perhaps ironic that she herself is conquered by her own weapons.[29] This proves the power of her ἔργα, but, at the same time, weakens her so that she regrets and feels guilty about her encounter with Anchises.[30]

Although not merely a "love story", the hymn is still dominated by the love theme.[31] It is here that, for the very first time in extant literature, those aspects which are so typical of the goddess in Greek thought—her own beauty and love in its various facets—are fully unfolded at one and the same time and become manifest in Aphrodite: she represents the idea of love as a universal cosmic power, and her appearance is responsible for all that grows on earth. This aspect is mentioned in the opening lines, which praise the works of Aphrodite on a general level, and appears again in the narrative section (68-74), when Aphrodite is on her way to Anchises.[32]

She represents the province she stands for by pulling out all the stops of the female art of seduction and deception in order to get what she wants. Since Aphrodite represents both seductress and lover, she too experiences that kind of love which can have weakening repercussions and makes lovers suffer. This is a prominent theme in Archaic lyric poetry and later in tragedy, but is not known in epic, where the idea of "love" is limited to mere sexual desire which is usually satisfied and therefore rarely painful.[33] In the hymn, it is Aphrodite, despite being a goddess, who is the desire-ridden party that takes the initiative and thus plays a role reserved for the male partner. Her "love pain" is, of course, different from what we would expect in comparison with lyric or tragedy. She does not suffer from unhappy, i.e. unrequited love, but from the disgrace of having slept with a mortal man. The action, which was launched as a trip of mere pleasure, takes an unexpected turn with the conception of Aeneas, who is nothing but the result of an accident. Thus Aphrodite unwillingly plays also the role of a mother; but her suffering shows that this is not what she actually wants—presumably the poet, by emphasizing her pain, wants to depict her, in spite of Aeneas, as a goddess of sensuality, not marital love and child-bearing.

Classical scholarship has interpreted the *Homeric Hymn to Aphrodite* in various ways. Thus P. Smith, for example, argues that the incompatibility of the gods' immortality and human mortality is the point of the hymn, "a problem of central importance to the audiences for which it was created".[34] J. Clay in the most recent full-scale interpretation of the major *Homeric Hymns* similarly focuses on the problems caused by sexual encounters between gods and mortals, arguing that the hymn explains why divine miscegenation with men came to an end just before the Trojan war.[35] Of course, the contrast of immortality and mortality is discernible throughout the narrative. It is not a general theme, however, but is one reflected in the concrete example of Anchises, whom the goddess cannot make immortal, but who will live forever through his son and his offspring. Furthermore, the hymn gives no indication that Aphrodite and Anchises are the last such "couple". P. Walcot has compared the "humor and irony" in the hymn with that underlying the *Song of Demodocus*, who entertained Odysseus and the Phaeacian court with the encounter between Ares and Aphrodite (*Od.* 8,266-366).[36] It is certainly true that amusing tales of divine love affairs are very old, and sometimes even appear in epic.[37] Why should they not occur in the narrative of a hymn as well, especially as we also find humorous elements in the hymns to Hermes and Demeter?[38] However, one cannot go as far as Walcot does in assuming that a humorous tone dominates the hymn.[39] Of course, when Aphrodite has to succumb to her own weapons and undergo sufferings which she normally causes in others, this is mildly amusing, in a similar way as is the revelation of her affair with Ares. I suggest that the somewhat tragic element in the whole story lies in the combination of the immortal goddess and the mortal Anchises and the ensuing gap: Aphrodite, overwhelmed by the power of love, uses Anchises, threatens him with death, and suffers as well. This is finally overcome by the prospect of the common child Aeneas. Although his name is reminiscent of his mother's suffering, he is the mediating element and must be given a certain role in the story.

3.4   THE REPRESENTATION OF APHRODITE: ADORNMENT SCENES, EPIPHANIES AND THEIR CULTIC BACKGROUND

For our purposes it is significant that Aphrodite appears in a double role. In the introductory hymnic praise she is represented as the ultimate divine authority and source of desire, responsible for any confusion of the mind caused through that.[40] In the narrative section, however, according to Zeus' wish, she embodies and experiences what she normally metes out to mortals. At the beginning her divine nature is only suspected by Anchises. Although Aphrodite does not quite look like a mortal woman, she convinces Anchises by means of a seductive ἀπάτη, pretending to be a virgin and suggesting the prospect of marrying him (107-42). This scene has been appropriately interpreted as quasi-homeric *aristeia* of the goddess as mistress of beauty and seduction.[41] At the same time, she transgresses mortal female nature by claiming active sexual desire, which is normally exclusively the prerogative of men.[42] That her passion is finally fulfilled, in spite of the reversal of the norm, is a reflection of her divine nature. She must be a goddess in order both to choose and finally to seduce a lover.[43] Aphrodite's divine nature is developed in four different stages or epiphanies, and the metamorphosis which she undergoes is articulated by herself within the narrative when she finally asks Anchises whether she still seems to be the same as before (. . . εἴ τοι ὁμοίη ἐγὼν ἰνδάλλομαι εἶναι / οἵην δή με τὸ πρῶτον ἐν ὀφθαλμοῖσι νόησας 178f.).[44]

Aphrodite's arrival and adornment at the temple in Paphos and her appearances before Anchises have been vaguely and very generally regarded as recalling "traditional elements which suggest a divine epiphany".[45] Brief statements that Aphrodite "looks like her cult image in Cythera",[46] or the observation that her jewellery is Mycenean[47] also need further investigation. In what follows, I will argue that these hymnic adornment scenes and epiphanies, revealing the goddess's power and her attributes, are part of Aphrodite's religious mythology and can be related to a cultic background.

For our purposes, the goddess's epiphany and adornment scene in the temple are significant. Aphrodite makes her first dramatic appearance at the beginning of the narrative. Having just fallen in love with Anchises, she leaves Olympus to embark upon a journey to enhance her beauty, which is depicted in an adornment scene. This demonstrates that the *Homeric Hymns* are indebted to heroic epic not only in their formulaic diction, but also in certain type-scenes. Other famous examples are the adornment of Pandora, where Aphrodite appears as the cause of beauty and desire, without which seductions would not take place,[48] and that of Hera when she prepares to seduce Zeus in a famous episode, the *Dios Apate* (*Il.* 14,153-353). This latter example is the most detailed adornment scene in epic, in which Aphrodite is not yet involved.[49] It is a peculiarity of the *Hymn to Aphrodite* that the adornment scene does not take place in a *thalamos* on Mount Olympos, as in the case of Hera, but in one of Aphrodite's most famous sanctuaries in Greece: "She went to Cyprus and entered her fragrant shrine at Paphos; it is there that she has her precinct and fragrant altar. There she went in and closed the gleaming doors" (58-60):

ἐς Κύπρον δ᾽ ἐλθοῦσα θυώδεα νηὸν ἔδυνεν
ἐς Πάφον· ἔνθα δέ οἱ τέμενος βωμός τε θυώδης·
ἔνθ᾽ ἥ γ᾽ εἰσελθοῦσα θύρας ἐπέθηκε φαεινάς.

In fact, the vivid and detailed description of the goddess's entry into her sanctuary and how she closes its doors (60) does not seem to be intended to give an *aition* for the foundation of Aphrodite's shrine at Paphos. Instead, it leads us to expect an epiphany of the goddess, perhaps as worshippers conceived of it in actual cult, epiphany being what they intend to evoke when they sing cultic hymns.[50] Presumably, the poetic depiction was meant to recall a cultic epiphany of the goddess in the audience's mind.

This is all the more likely since the location where an epiphany happens to be expected and to take place is the temple.[51] Past epiphanies are represented by a cult image of the deity and thus made visible at all times.[52] It is highly probable that a cult image of Aphrodite was venerated in her sanctuary at Paphos at the time the hymn was composed. There is good archaeological evidence in situ that proper temple buildings can be traced back to the 8th century BC.[53] In view of the size and significance of Aphrodite's temple at Cyprus, one might assume that it had even been a regular feature in the oral hymnic tradition. The presence of a cult image there is suggested by the main function of a sanctuary, which was to house the deity imagined to dwell within.[54] As it turns out, the Hellenistic historian Polycharmus from Naucratis (*FGrH* 640 F 1) records that in 688/5 BC a statuette of Aphrodite, nine inches tall, was brought from Paphos to Naucratis. One may speculate whether this statuette, which seems to be an offering, could imitate an original, already existing, Archaic cult image.

Subsequently, Aphrodite was tended to by her traditional companions (see Plate 9): "The Charites there bathed her, anointed her with oil, deathless oil as it shines upon the immortal gods, ambrosial sweet-smelling oil which had been perfumed for her. When she had clothed herself well with all her fine garments around her skin, adorned with gold, Aphrodite the lover of smiles rushed to-wards Troy" (61-6):

> ἔνθα δέ μιν Χάριτες λοῦσαν καὶ χρῖσαν ἐλαίῳ
> ἀμβρότῳ, οἷα θεοὺς ἐπενήνοθεν αἰὲν ἐόντας,
> ἀμβροσίῳ ἑδανῷ, τό ῥά οἱ τεθυωμένον ἦεν.
> ἑσσαμένη δ' εὖ πάντα περὶ χροῒ εἵματα καλὰ
> χρυσῷ κοσμηθεῖσα φιλομμειδὴς Ἀφροδίτη
> σεύατ' ἐπὶ Τροίης.

Before I discuss the special cultic significance of this passage in greater detail, I will analyze other adornment scenes for comparison. It will emerge that there are not only parallels, but also distinctive divergences in wording and motif, depending on the genre, heroic epic or hymn, in which they appear.

Hera's seduction of Zeus in the *Dios Apate* in *Iliad* 14 is motivated by her aim to manipulate the war events in favor of the Greeks; it is preceded by an adornment scene which is, with almost twenty lines (169-87), the longest and most detailed one of its kind in extant Archaic literature. Hera enters her bed-chamber, closes the doors (169) and then makes herself up; having washed and anointed her body with ambrosia, whose scent is emphasized (170-5), she combs and plaits her hair (176f.). The dress which she subsequently puts on has been, as we hear, woven by Athena, who has lavishly embellished it (178f.).

Above her chest she puts golden pins (180), around her waist a belt decorated with a hundred tassels (181); she is wearing earrings in the shape of triple mulberries (182f.) and then she takes her veil shining like the sun (184f.) and her beautiful sandals (186).[55] After this she makes her way to Aphrodite to request her κεστὸς ἱμάς. It has been argued by P. Smith that, apart from three whole verse formulae, there is not much similarity in structure and theme with *Hymn. Hom.* V;[56] one may add that it also lacks allusions to cult and epiphany—a feature prominent in hymns.

The scene in the *Homeric Hymn to Aphrodite* is comparatively short and considerably less detailed than that in the *Iliad*, but the poet delays the full depiction of the effect of this adornment in order to develop it lavishly in Aphrodite's subsequent epiphanies in front of Anchises, which far outdo Hera's performance in the *Iliad*. There is probably no better moment in our literary evidence to prove that "the loves of the goddess of love derive from the very centre of her being."[57] The hymnic adornment differs from the one of Hera in another respect: the place chosen by Aphrodite is not simply her *thalamos* on Mt. Olympus, as in Hera's case. She leaves Olympus and withdraws to her island Cyprus, to Paphos, where she has a shrine, *temenos* and altar (58-60). The hymn implies that Aphrodite's temple is her home. And it is the doors of her shrine that she closes, not those of any profane dwelling. The formulaic verse (ἔνθ' ἥ γ' εἰσελθοῦσα θύρας ἐπέθηκε φαεινάς) is the same as in the *Dios Apate*, but clearly transferred to a religious context.[58]

This feature marks the difference between the heroic epic and the hymn. Whereas Hera's adornment is an element central to the context of the burlesque and has therefore a predominantly narrative function, the one of Aphrodite, by its setting in a temple, may recall a ritual epiphany in which the goddess's specific power is revealed. Here as elsewhere (*Od.* 8,364f. and in *Hymn. Hom.* VI), Aphrodite has attendants who bathe and anoint her: in the *Odyssey*, as in *Hymn. Hom.* V, it is the Charites, in *Hymn. Hom.* VI, it is the Horae alone. In this case one might assume that the presence of attendants and the Charites' use of immortal oil may be related to cultic features, since cult images were anointed as well and the hymnic scene takes place in a shrine. The motif of fragrance, a characteristic element of epiphany (see below), is therefore central and emphasized in the context of the major *Homeric Hymn*. The fragrance, however, does not only exist in distant Olympus as the example of Hera in the *Iliad* suggests, but, as the hymn proves, can also be brought down to the real world i.e. to the temple where the gods are venerated.

Most closely related to the adornment scene of the *Homeric Hymn* is the one in the *Odyssey* (8,362-6) which appears to be an abbreviated version. Perhaps the poet of the *Odyssey* was acquainted with this rendering of the hymn and abridged it to satisfy his own narrative purpose. For a scene such as "Aphrodite's adornment in her temple at Paphos" may well have been a traditional feature in the repertoire of oral poetry.[59] In comparison with the *Odyssey*, it is interesting that a withdrawal to a sanctuary, even for the sake of making up, fits much better in a hymnic narrative where cults, especially their foundations and cult places, are essential elements. Less obvious is the reason for the withdrawal in the *Odyssey* passage: Why should Aphrodite go to her temple for an adornment *after* her affair with Ares has been discovered? I suggest that there her retreat to the temple is simply meant as an escape or flight out of embarrassment, without any further cultic implications. Therefore the author of the *Odyssey* omits details which are not essential here, but are probably only for the more religious requirements of the hymn. Compare the earlier discussed description of Aphrodite's arrival in her Paphian temple in the hymn (*Hymn. Hom.* V,58-60)

> ἐς Κύπρον δ' ἐλθοῦσα θυώδεα νηὸν ἔδυνεν
> ἐς Πάφον· ἔνθα δέ οἱ τέμενος βωμός τε θυώδης·
> ἔνθ' ἥ γ' εἰσελθοῦσα θύρας ἐπέθηκε φαεινάς.

with *Od.* 8,362f.:

> ἡ δ' ἄρα Κύπρον ἵκανε φιλομμειδὴς Ἀφροδίτη,
> ἐς Πάφον, ἔνθα τέ οἱ τέμενος βωμός τε θυήεις.

The hymn explicitly mentions the "fragrant temple", at Cyprus, which is omitted by the poet of the *Odyssey*. Lines 59 and 363 are almost identical: both mention the "fragrant *temenos* and altar." But then the depiction of Aphrodite's entry into the concrete building and the closing of its doors are only to be found in the hymnic version. Then, whereas lines 364f. of the *Odyssey* exactly correspond to 61f. of the hymn,

> ἔνθα δέ μιν Χάριτες λοῦσαν καὶ χρῖσαν ἐλαίῳ
> ἀμβρότῳ, οἷα θεοὺς ἐπενήνοθεν αἰὲν ἐόντας,

it is only in the hymn (63) that a central element of epiphany is emphasized again. The goddess was entirely surrounded by the scent of the immortal oil (ἐλαίῳ) which had been perfumed for her:

> ἀμβροσίῳ ἑδανῷ, τό ῥά οἱ τεθυωμένον ἦεν.

Both versions say that Aphrodite herself puts on her lovely garments; but it is only in the hymn that her golden jewellery is also mentioned, compare *Hymn. Hom.* V,64f.:

> ἑσσαμένη δ' εὖ πάντα περὶ χροῒ εἵματα καλὰ
> χρυσῷ κοσμηθεῖσα φιλομμειδὴς Ἀφροδίτη.

with *Od.* 8,366:

> ἀμφὶ δὲ εἵματα ἕσσαν ἐπήρατα, θαῦμα ἰδέσθαι.

Thus one may conclude that in spite of correspondences in style and wording, a different emphasis on details of content is recognizable in these adornment scenes. The notion of a divine epiphany is much more strongly suggested in the hymn (58: mentioning of the "fragrant temple"; 59: the "fragrant *temenos* and altar"; 60: the goddess's entry into the temple and the closing of its doors; 63: after her treatment, she smells fragrant herself) than in the epic scene, which seems to use the scenery just for the sake of rounding off the love affair. In the hymn, the fully developed epiphanies are postponed and not described until Aphrodite stands in front of Anchises. It is only then that the poet, by depicting her beauty in every detail, reveals her divine power.

The adornment scene of the *Cypria* very probably belongs to Aphrodite's preparation for Paris' judgement at the beauty contest. "She set on her skin the garments which the Graces and the Seasons had made and dyed in the flowers of spring-time, garments such as the Seasons wear, dyed in crocus and hyacinth and in the blooming violet and in the fair flower of the rose, sweet and fragrant, and in ambrosial burning cups of the narcissus, beautifully breathing. Such were the garments fragrant with all seasons that Aphrodite put on herself" (1-5):[60]

> εἵματα μὲν χροὶ ἕστο τά οἱ Χάριτές τε καὶ Ὧραι
> ποίησαν καὶ ἔβαψαν ἐν ἄνθεσιν εἰαρινοῖσιν
> οἷα φοροῦσ' Ὧραι,[61] ἔν τε κρόκωι ἔν θ' ὑακίνθωι
> ἔν τε ἴωι θαλέθοντι ῥόδου τ' ἐνὶ ἄνθεϊ καλῶι,
> ἡδέϊ νεκταρέωι, ἔν τ' ἀμβροσίαις καλύκεσσιν
> αἴθεσι ναρκίσσου καλλιπνόου. ὣδ' Ἀφροδίτη[62]
> ὥραις παντοίαις τεθυωμένα εἵματα ἕστο.

6 αἴθεσι Ludwich, Bernabé: ἄνθεσι A, Davies | καλλιπνόου Ludwich, Bernabé: καλλιρρόου codd.: καὶ λειρίου Meineke, Davies | ὣδ' Ludwich, Bernabé: δ' οἷα A : τοῖ' Meineke olim: δῖ' Ἀφροδίτη Casaubon: †δ' οἷα Ἀφροδίτη† Davies.

The text itself is corrupt, and the recent editors Davies and Bernabé disagree in their editions.[63] The fragment describes the fabrication of Aphrodite's robe by the Charites and the Horae, with a special emphasis on the different flowers in which the garment is dyed.[64] Clearly, the goddess's principal aim is different from the one in the *Homeric Hymn*: Paris needs to be "seduced" only in so far as he is meant to decide the beauty contest in her favour. It is perhaps for this reason that an emphasis is put on her outfit. The fragment gives a detailed, not to say exaggerated, description of her flowery and "beautifully breathing" garments rather than of her divine physical beauty.[65] Presumably the poet of the *Cypria* wants to stress the vanity of Aphrodite who desires the most precious and glamorous clothes, even though she is by nature the most beautiful goddess anyway. Fr. 5 (Davies/Bernabé) probably represents a slightly later stage of the story. In a similar style it depicts Aphrodite together with her attendants plaiting wreaths and garlands which they set upon their heads as they make their way singing down Mt. Ida.[66] As it transpires, not only the context, but also the nature and style of the adornment scene of Aphrodite in the *Cypria* fragment is different from the one in the temple at Paphos. Therefore I cannot agree with Stinton who says that "the preparation of Aphrodite before her visit to Anchises in the *Homeric Hymn* is very like her preparation before the judgement in the *Cypria*".[67]

It is also true that in the *Homeric Hymn to Aphrodite* the garments which the goddess herself puts on are also given a special emphasis (ἐσσαμένη δ' εὖ πάντα περὶ χροῒ εἵματα καλὰ / χρυσῷ κοσμηθεῖσα φιλομμειδὴς Ἀφροδίτη 64f.).[68] The continuation of the mythical narrative, however, shows that the goddess's journey to Cyprus is not simply the preparation of a seduction. The adornment is a physical manifestation of the goddess's individual power and defines the goddess's specific sphere of interest and her function within the Olympic pantheon: Aphrodite is the goddess of beauty, attraction and seduction. Such an adornment scene defining divine identity need not be even linked to a context of seduction. In the minor *Homeric Hymn to Aphrodite* (VI), the adornment is part of her birth story, one of the most essential elements of a hymnic narrative. The goddess is received and adorned by the Horae with dresses and all kinds of jewellery immediately after Zephyrus' breath conveyed her in soft foam through the sea (see Plate 9). Then she joins the gods: "The Horae with golden headbands welcomed her gladly, and clothed her with deathless garments. Upon her immortal head they put a well-wrought crown of gold, a beautiful one, and in her pierced earlobes they hung flowers of mountain copper and precious gold. About her tender neck and gleaming breast they adorned her with golden necklaces, the ones that the gold-filleted Horae themselves would be adorned with whenever they went to the lovely dances of the gods and their father's house."[69] (5-13).

> ... τὴν δὲ χρυσάμπυκες Ὧραι   5
> δέξαντ' ἀσπασίως, περὶ δ' ἄμβροτα εἵματα ἕσσαν,
> κρατὶ δ' ἐπ' ἀθανάτῳ στεφάνην εὔτυκτον ἔθηκαν
> καλὴν χρυσείην· ἐν δὲ τρητοῖσι λοβοῖσιν
> ἄνθεμ' ὀρειχάλκου χρυσοῖό τε τιμήεντος,
> δειρῇ δ' ἀμφ' ἀπαλῇ καὶ στήθεσιν ἀργυφέοισιν   10
> ὅρμοισι χρυσέοισιν ἐκόσμεον οἷσί περ αὐταὶ
> Ὧραι κοσμείσθην χρυσάμπυκες ὁππότ' ἴοιεν
> ἐς χορὸν ἱμερόεντα θεῶν καὶ δώματα πατρός.

Aphrodite's epiphany before the other Olympians reveals her specific realm and attributes in a peculiar way.[70] Her own beauty and attraction are so stunning that the gods who are overwhelmingly charmed by her first appearance want to marry her. What could demonstrate more clearly that beauty and charm are what Aphrodite symbolizes? "And when they had put all the adornment about her body, they led her to the gods, who welcomed her on sight and gave her their hands in greeting. And each of them prayed to lead her home to be his wedded wife, as they admired the beauty of Cytherea who wears a crown of the violet's bloom" (14-8):

αὐτὰρ ἐπεὶ δὴ πάντα περὶ χροῒ κόσμον ἔθηκαν
ἦγον ἐς ἀθανάτους· οἱ δ' ἠσπάζοντο ἰδόντες
χερσί τ' ἐδεξιόωντο καὶ ἠρήσαντο ἕκαστος
εἶναι κουριδίην ἄλοχον καὶ οἴκαδ' ἄγεσθαι,
εἶδος θαυμάζοντες ἰοστεφάνου Κυθερείης.

One may ask whether the application of adornment scenes to contexts of mere seduction is only a secondary development; *Hymn. Hom.* V somehow seems to combine both aspects: preparation for a seduction and also the definition of Aphrodite's role as the divinity of love, the latter being an essential requirement of a hymn.

We must not leave unmentioned, however, the fact that the dressing scenes of Aphrodite's predecessors, the Sumerian Inanna as well as Ishtar-Astarte, are famous and much celebrated in literature.[71] We know of a hymn to Inanna in which a dressing scene—without attendants, however—takes place on the island of Dilmun.[72] In an Old Babylonian hymn, Ishtar's beauty and attraction represent the goddess's qualities of love and thus express her greatness and power:[73]

Sing the praises of Ishtar, the most impressive of all goddesses,
who is to be glorified as the mistress of mortal women,
the greatest of the
        Igigi.
She is dressed in serenity and love,
She is equipped with sexual attractiveness, power and charm.[74]

Those myths and the *Homeric Hymns* use the same motif, the dressing scene, to establish the goddess's specific province and demonstrate her power. The religious elements in the *Homeric Hymn* V have been emphasized by C. Penglase in particular. He concedes that the hymn is a work of literature, but points out that, after all, the mythical narration is part of a religious mythology, since it relates to the activities of a goddess "who is much more than just a woman preparing for an assignation".[75] In the major *Homeric Hymn*, Aphrodite's sphere of influence also becomes manifest on her way to Troy, where the goddess' epiphany on Mount Ida provokes a mating among all the animals (64-74).[76]

It is at this point, I think, that we may turn to the question as to whether there are traces of cultic activities in the mythical depiction of Aphrodite's adornment in her shrine. It takes place in a temple and therefore recalls rituals during which priestesses or temple-servants look after a cult image. The latter was strongly involved in cult practices, since their performers acted as if it were the god or goddess herself whom they were looking after.[77]

In myth, as we have seen, the Charites, less often the Horae, are Aphrodite's attendants and traditionally responsible for her outfit (see Plate 9); thus in the *Iliad* (5,338) they weave her dress. In the hymn, they bathe and anoint her with sweet, immortal oil before she herself finally puts on her lovely dress, over her golden skin (61-5). Since the offering of garments is testified as early as Homer's *Iliad*, it is justifiable to assume that the dressing of cult images is an Archaic rite. In a famous scene in the *Iliad* (6,286-312), which Burkert considers to represent "the developed *polis* cult as it had arisen during the 8th century", it is not the Charites or any other divine beings, but the women of Troy who rush to Athena's sanctuary to offer the goddess a precious woven *peplos* in order to reconcile her with the Trojans. The priestess Theano opens the door of the temple and puts the garment on Athena's knees. The dedication seems to presuppose a seated cult image.[78]

There is good evidence that some epic depictions show certain similarities in procedure, and even in wording with actual cult practices in which images of gods are washed and cleaned in a ritual of purification.[79] But we cannot, of course, decide with certainty whether mythical bathing and anointment scenes and the provision of garments to a goddess reflect cultic activity, or whether the process went in the reverse direction, i.e. that ritual was prompted by mythical descriptions. Contemporary comparative material, i.e. epigraphical testimonies and literary sources recording actual cult practices of the 7th century BC, is unfortunately not extant. Nevertheless, I should like to discuss some later evidence which would seem to suggest that washing, anointing and dressing belonged to cultic procedures and ritual. The following examples can only be cited as parallels.

An example of a possible cultic cleansing is provided by Pausanias (2,10,4). He mentions a ceremony at Aphrodite's sanctuary in Sicyon, during which two women, a married woman and a virgin who was called λουτροφόρος, enter the temple. Apparently it was their task to bring the bath for Canachus' chryselephantine image of Aphrodite.[80] The famous image at least can be dated to the Archaic period;[81] yet the description of the rite as conducted κατὰ τὰ πάτρια, "according to the ancestral tradition", which appears frequently, and mostly in inscriptions, cannot guarantee for sure that a certain activity goes back to the Archaic period, even if there is a tendency in historical and periegetical writing to believe that everything in religion is authentic and Archaic.[82]

The Plynteria and Kallynteria celebrated in the month Thargelion at Athens, for example, were washing festivals.[83] Whereas hardly anything is recorded about the Kallynteria, we are better informed about the Plynteria, during which the old wooden image of Athena Polias was cleaned.[84] Our main sources are Plutarch (*Alc.* 34,1-2) and Xenophon (*Hell.* 1,4,12), who also both state that the rite is at least as old as 408 BC. It was on the very day of this festival of the Plynteria that, in 408 BC, Alcibiades came back from exile to Athens. We learn from Plutarch that the female members of the noble family of the Πραξιεργίδαι removed the adornments, the jewellery, and probably also the robe from Athena's image in the Erechtheion and veiled it (τόν τε κόσμον καθελόντες καὶ τὸ ἕδος κατακαλύψαντες). Then they carried it to Phaleron where the secret rites, of which the washing was part, took place.[85] The noble girls or wives were called λουτρίδες or πλυντρίδες, since λούω is used of washing a person and πλύνω of cleaning clothes, it is possible that the garment was washed and the image was bathed.[86] The purpose of the bath was not only that of the actual removal of dirt, but also connected with it was the idea that the beneficial power of the image would wane unless it was bathed.[87] Not only do the sources provide us with a date, but they also indicate that the washing and bathing respectively were associated with both the goddess's image and its garments. It was presumably part of this rite (or even of a rite to follow) that the image was dressed again. Related to this is the main activity during the festival of the Panathenaea, when Athena receives a new *peplos* woven by the *arrhephoroi*.

We also have evidence for ritual cleansing of an image in the cult of Aphrodite Πάνδημος at Athens. The epigraphical source is dated to 283/2 BC and is very probably related to the historical circumstances during which Aphrodite, in her political function as Πάνδημος, was invoked.[88] The instruction that the temple should be looked after κατὰ τὰ πάτρια (8ff.) cannot be taken as proof that the rites are older.[89] The *probouleuma* provides modes for the organisation of the *pompe* of the goddess: "Whenever the procession is held in honor of Aphrodite Πάνδημος, *astynomoi* in office at the time are to provide a pigeon for the purification of the sanctuary, whitewash the altar, apply pitch to the wooden [doors] of the temple, and have the statues washed. They are also to provide purple dye — " (20f.).

> τοὺς ἀστυνό- | μους τοὺς ἀεὶ λαχόντας, ὅταν ἦι | ἡ πομπὴ τῆι Ἀφροδίτηι τεῖ Πανδή- | μωι, παρασκευάζειν εἰς κάθαρσι[ν] | τοῦ ἱεροῦ περιστεράν, καὶ περιαλε[ῖ]- | [ψα]ι τοὺς βωμοὺς καὶ πιττῶσαι τὰς | [θύρας] καὶ λοῦσαι τὰ ἕδη· παρασκευ- | [άσαι δὲ κα]ὶ πορφύραν ὁλκήν | – | – – – | – – τὰ ἐπὶ τ – – .

The term ἕδος implies that the statues were seated. The purple was intended to be used as painting for the statue.[90] It seems very likely that this cleansing of statues was also meant to be an act of ritual purification as indicated by εἰς κάθαρσι[ν].[91]

It would seem that, within the mythical narrative, the Charites actually enact what worshippers perform as a cult practice in later sources. This is also the case when they anoint her with sweet oil (. . . χρῖσαν ἐλαίῳ / ἀμβρότῳ . . . / ἀμβροσίῳ ἐδανῷ 61f.). That deities smell good when they show themselves to human beings is a traditional topos in narrative epiphany.[92] Aphrodite's temple, *temenos* and altar at Paphos are fragrant (θυώδεα νηὸν 58; τέμενος βωμός τε θυώδης 59), but the Homeric poems do not mention incense. There is evidence that cult images were also surrounded by a pleasant fragrance. Sappho's poems are the first to mention frankincense offerings for Aphrodite and one would assume that it was normally burnt in the sanctuary.[93] Frankincense, balms and perfumes were also special offerings for Ishtar-Astarte.[94] It seems that these were not only presented as gifts to the deity, but were also used for her image. There is in fact good literary and epigraphical evidence that cult statues were also treated with a variety of perfumes and fragrances which belonged to the κόσμησις. Pausanias (9,41,7) says that "perfume, distilled from roses, if used to anoint statues made of wood, also prevents rotting". Perfume was used, at least in the Hellenistic period, for the statues of the Artemiseion, for the temple of Apollo, and also for that of Hera.[95] We have no evidence to attest that this treatment was already adopted in the Archaic period. I suggest that mythical anointment reflects actual cultic procedures, but it is not to be completely ruled out that this activity was inspired by literary features such as those conveyed in our *Homeric Hymn to Aphrodite*.

We may turn at this point to Aphrodite's epiphanies before Anchises which are at the core of the hymn. That deities can be recognized in particular by their beauty and their figure (καλοὶ καὶ μεγάλοι) is a topos in narrative descriptions of epiphanies.[96] It is essential for the successful seduction of the mortal man that the goddess's true identity, in spite of his suspicions, remains concealed. Certain characteristic elements of narrative epiphany are therefore modified in the third epiphany within the hymn. Though she has taken the appearance and stature of a virgin (παρθένῳ ἀδμήτῃ μέγεθος καὶ εἶδος ὁμοίη 82) in order not to frighten him (μή μιν ταρβήσειεν 83), and to avoid being recognized, Anchises reacts in the way humans usually react when they face a divine epiphany.[97] He admires her (. . . θαύμαινέν τε / εἶδός τε μέγεθος καὶ εἵματα σιγαλόεντα 84f.), and we can infer from line 82 that it is not her height, but her εἶδος, above all her shining brightness which makes him think of a goddess and leads him to offer her an altar.[98] That he immediately desires her (Ἀγχίσην δ' ἔρος εἷλεν 91), though suspecting that she might be a goddess, does not quite fit the pattern, however. But one would not go so far as to suppose that Anchises' address to his guest as a goddess is simply a ploy to flatter a mortal woman and hence ironic. Thus Anchises' role veers between that of a lover and a worshipper.

What appearance of Aphrodite does her description in the hymn imply? That divine epiphanies in cult are related to images of deities has been mentioned earlier. I suggest that the poet in describing those epiphanies in such a detailed and lavish manner was drawing on cult statues of Aphrodite and meant to recall them to the audience's mind. It is possible too, however, that it was these hymnic depictions of divine epiphanies which inspired the artistic creativity of the sculptors. Whatever the case may be, according to what ancient, although later, sources tell us about the looks of cult images, certain features of literary epiphanies have correspondences in them. In what follows,

I examine the evidence for cult images of Aphrodite and other deities with a special focus on their adornments. Our available sources are limited to either literary descriptions such as we find them in Pausanias, coins (see Plates 10-12), or archaising vase painting. If we want to examine authentic epigraphical material recording details about the *kosmos* of cult images, we have to consider appurtenances of other goddesses, mostly those appertaining to the Classical and Hellenistic periods.

The tradition of cult images of Aphrodite seems to be quite old, if we can believe Pausanias' testimony.[99] Archaic cult images were normally wooden and called *xoana*.[100] He mentions nine Archaic wooden *xoana* of Aphrodite alone (2,19,6 at Argos; 2,25,1 in the Argolid;[101] 3,13,8f. Sparta; 3,15,10f. Sparta; 3,17,5 Sparta; 3,23,1 Cythera; 5,13,7 Temnos; 8,37,12 Lykosoura; 9,16,3 Thebes; 9,40,3 Delos); one is made of ivory (1,43,6). Some of them were still extant in his life-time, and he remarks upon their considerable old age—which is clearly not a reference to an exact dating.

We do not have much information about what Archaic images of Aphrodite looked like, since there are just two examples of descriptions of sculptures. Pausanias (9,40,3) tells us that the mythical sculptor Daedalus is said to have created a *xoanon* of Aphrodite which he offered to Ariadne, who brought it to Delos. It is a square pillar type with a damaged right hand and no feet.[102] The only other Archaic cult image is Canachus' chryselephantine statue at Sicyon, which can be dated to the last quarter of the 6th century BC, since this was the period when the sculptor was active.[103] It was seated, wore a *peplos*, and held a poppy in the one hand and an apple in the other. A ritual during which bath water was carried to the statue by two women (Paus. 2,10,4) has been men-tioned earlier. There are, however, images (possibly archaising) of Aphrodite on vases which convey what they looked like:[104] she is wearing a *peplos* (or *chiton*) and a *polos* on most of them and looks like one of the *korai* as we know them from Archaic sculpture, at least from the 6th century BC onwards, on the Greek mainland and the islands.[105]

Xoana were dressed in clothes which were regarded as part of the statue.[106] The adorning of cult statues has generally been considered a ritual act, a form of temple service.[107] It has been suggested that the consecration is realized by the κόσμος (see κοσμηθεῖσα in *Hymn. Hom.* V,65), the clothing and also the decorating, by which a statue is transformed into an object of worship and in this way becomes a cult image.[108] It is interesting that in the *Homeric Hymn* an emphasis is also placed upon Aphrodite's clothing and jewellery (85-90). We have evidence that an object of worship can be created by the investiture of col-umns or posts, such as appear on vases showing scenes of the Lenaea, a festival in honor of Dionysus, who is depicted as a column with a mask, a piece of cloth adumbrating his body, while wreaths adorn his head. Women dance around him. The clothing of these images conveys the god's presence by marking ritual epiphany.[109] It would seem, then, that garments play a significant role in the making of a cult image. Their meaning is also underlined in certain festivals in which the washing of the deities' clothes plays an important part.

There is good evidence suggesting that the way Anchises is said to perceive Aphrodite in her epiphany shows several correspondences with what we know about the εἶδος καὶ μέγεθος of cult statues. When Aphrodite stands in front of Anchises, of all the narrative elements of epiphany, it is the brightness and splendor of her appearance that are particularly significant: her clothes, merely beautiful (εἵματα καλά 64) in the temple-scene, are now glittering (εἵματα σιγαλόεντα 85).[110] Her *peplos* especially is shining more brightly than a beam of fire (πέπλον . . . φαεινότερον πυρὸς αὐγῆς 86).[111] Her skin (χροΐ 64) is now, according to the context of the seduction scene, highlighted in the cleavage, but simultaneously enhanced and intensified by being held up in comparison with the shining moon (. . . ὡς δὲ σελήνη / στήθεσιν ἀμφ' ἁπαλοῖσι ἐλάμπετο, θαῦμα ἰδέσθαι 89f.). However, the additional ornament, her jewellery, is given particular emphasis and is the focus of radiance and brilliance. She wears curved armlets (ἐπιγναμπτὰς ἕλικας 87) and dazzling earrings shaped like flowercups (κάλυκας τε φαεινάς 87).[112] Particular attention is paid to the detailed description of her lavish and precious necklace (ὅρμοι 88), which is at the same time "very beautiful" (περικαλλέες 88), "lovely" (καλοί 89), "golden" (χρύσειοι 89) and "of rich and varied work" (παμποίκιλοι 89).[113] All these ornaments occur again when, after telling her pack of lies, Anchises undresses her. At this point he also has to remove the brooch (πόρπας 163) which pins her clothes together.

This detailed description of Aphrodite's *kosmesis* has parallels in that of cult images: κόσμος ("ornament") in epic means either jewellery collectively or as a single piece, but it also includes clothes.[114] In the *Homeric Hymn to Aphrodite* κοσμηθεῖσα at first sight seems only to refer to her dress, but the following scenes make it obvious that her jewellery must also be meant. That κόσμος later indicates the jewellery alone becomes evident when Anchises first has to remove pins and the like (κόσμον μέν οἱ πρῶτον ἀπὸ χροὸς εἷλε φαεινόν 162) so that he can undress Aphrodite. A similar terminology (κόσμος, κόσμησις) is applied to the adornment of real images, . This is suggested by inscriptions recording the costs of material and labor for cult statues from the Archaic period onwards.[115]

According to an Archaic inscription on the temple of Athena at Lindos in Rhodes, the Lindians offered a tithe from the booty from Crete in the form of a golden crown (στεφάνη), necklaces (ὅρμοι) and most of the other pieces of adornment (κόσμος) which the statue used to have.[116] There is also evidence that κόσμος refers to jewellery and clothes. In the law of the Delphic Amphiktyones (380/79 BC) it is said that the image of Athena Pronaia was washed and provided with new κόσμος, consisting of a mantle with gold brooches, a gold diadem, a shield, helmet and spear.[117] From an inscription at Delos (246 BC) we learn that the craftsman Ophelion was given 125 drachmae for painting three statues (whose identity remains obscure) in the Pythion, scraping the parts that needed it, gilding them, and putting all the rest of the adornment (κόσμος) as it was in the originals.[118] He was also given an additional amount of 450 drachmae for applying 1000 or 1500 pieces of gold leaf. The gold could be used either for jewellery (see 239: Lysimachus received 5 drachmae for making gold pins and diadems) or for the golden colouring of the statues. The latter may be recalled in the *Homeric Hymn to Aphrodite*: ἑσσαμένη δ' εὖ πάντα περὶ χροΐ εἵματα καλὰ / χρυσῷ κοσμηθεῖσα φιλομμειδὴς Ἀφροδίτη (64f.).[119]

In mostly later epigraphical evidence, as well as on coins (see Plates 10–12), we find a set of jewellery similar to that worn by Aphrodite in the hymn. I do not claim that this evidence can simply be projected back to an earlier period or transferred to other deities; nevertheless, it is worth mentioning them as later parallels to cultic activity in Archaic literary depictions. There is some evidence that jewellery was put on cult statues as part of the κόσμος in the Archaic period. We have already seen that necklaces and neckbands are documented regarding the Archaic statue of Athena at Lindos. The image of Athena Polias at Athens was adorned with all kinds of jewellery; she even wore five ὅρμοι.[120] Earrings seem to have been popular offerings, as for example in the case of Stesileos' cult image of Aphrodite (late 4th century BC). There are contemporary earring offerings to the statue in Attic inventories: "In the Aphrodision: . . . gold earrings (ἐνοίδια) which the goddess is wearing, the weight of which is two drachmae, a dedication of Demetria."[121] "In the Aphrodision: ἐνοίδια which the goddess is wearing, the weight of which is two drachmae, a dedication of Demetria—these the priestess has outside [the sanctuary]—the other earrings which the goddess is wearing, of gilded silver, the previous priestess, Pleistarche dedicated."[122] Demeter and Kore are also adorned with earrings.[123] Rings also seem to have been used as offerings to various deities: at Delos inscriptions of the 3rd century BC mention that gold rings portraying Nike were offered to Apollo and Artemis.[124]

Descriptions of the radiance and brilliance with which deities are usually surrounded when they reveal themselves to human beings occur frequently in literary accounts.[125] The epithets χρύσεος and χρυσοστέφανος ("gold-crowned"), when used of deities like Aphrodite, are very probably a reflection of this.[126] For cult statues also golden head dresses (στέφανοι ("crowns"); στέφαναι ("tiaras")) are recorded; a bright and colourful coat of paint, sometimes even gilding, seems to be characteristic of statues, but it is not normally described in literary epiphanies. Expenses for gold are frequently mentioned in inscriptions. The statue of Aphrodite dedicated by Stesileos was repainted: "We gave 47 drachmae and two oboloi to Ophelion who contracted to paint in encaustic and to superadorn (ἐπικοσμῆσαι) the statue of Aphrodite" (money spent on gold leaves (πέταλα) is also noted).[127] Golden στέφανοι are attested for nearly all deities quoted in inscriptions: for Asclepius at Athens,[128] Apollo and the Charites at Delos,[129] Artemis Hecate at Delos,[130] and also for Athena

Lindia as we have seen earlier. This evidence suggests that the literary epithets χρύσεος, ἐϋστέφανος (ἐϋστεφάνου Κυθερείης 175) καλλιστέφανος (see the inscription on "Nestor's cup") and χρυσοστέφανος[131] are connected with the appearance of deities in epiphany and presumably also with statues.

In the undressing scene of the hymn, Anchises removes everything that had previously made him suspect Aphrodite of being of divine origin: her complete κόσμος, jewellery and clothes (162f.). It is at this point, I think, that he deprives her not only of her divine attributes, but also of her divinity. Here, Aphrodite is closest to being a mortal woman, while Anchises, being at most a man, is superior, though knowing nothing (οὐ σάφα εἰδώς 167). The concept which we have discerned earlier of Aphrodite appearing partly as a goddess, partly as a human virgin is continued. The narrative is at its most erotic when he is "loosening her belt". This is what gods usually do in erotic encounters with mortal women.[132] Here, however, the tables are turned: it is a mortal who loosens a goddess's girdle.

This is the *peripeteia* of the love story leading directly to the last stage of Aphrodite's metamorphosis, her fourth epiphany, in which it becomes evident that she is a real goddess. When she puts her clothes and jewellery on again,[133] she also regains at the same time her divine identity with εἵματα καλά (171) by reference back to the dressing-scene in the temple (64) and her divine height. It is not her jewellery which will make her unmistakably identifiable for Anchises. It is, apart from her superhuman height ("she stood up in the hut and her head touched the well-wrought roof-beam" (ἔστη ἄρα κλισίῃ, εὐποιήτοιο μελάθρου / κῦρε κάρη . . . 173f.)),[134] exclusively her beauty: this is not only reflected in her clothes (171), but even more so in her body: i. e. immortal beauty, a beauty which only Cythereia has, is glowing from her cheeks (κάλλος δὲ παρειάων ἀπέλαμπεν / ἄμβροτον, οἷόν τ᾽ ἐστὶν ἐϋστεφάνου Κυθερείης 174f.). When Anchises realizes the beauty of her skin and eyes (181f.), he reacts as any other mortal would at the sight of what is obviously a goddess. He starts trembling[135] and hides his face, which only here is said to be handsome. It is a peculiarity of this hymn that the actual epiphany, i.e. when the goddess Aphrodite finally reveals her divine identity to the mortal Anchises, is postponed within the mythical narrative in order to make the love story happen.[136]

3.5   CONCLUSION

The love story, which lies at the very centre of the hymn, shows Aphrodite losing her game and being defeated by her own weapons. Although she is not encomiastically complimented in a praiseworthy manner as one would expect in a hymn, her defeat, paradoxically, shows the power of love—the province she actually represents. Furthermore, it emerges that the narrative epiphanies are an almost voyeuristic display and praise of Aphrodite's irresistible beauty, which for the Greeks was inseparable from her divinity. The narrative, however, being part of a hymn, is not simply a love story, but also part of a religious mythology intended to demonstrate the goddess's power and her specific province on a more general level. Therefore it is not surprising that certain elements point to a religious sphere: the adornment scene, a conventional epic motif, is more than the preparation for an act of seduction. Taking place in her shrine, it shows Aphrodite assuming her unique power: anointment, dresses, jewellery are to be seen as symbolising the physical representation of Aphrodite's realm. Furthermore, Aphrodite's appearance in the shrine can also be related to a cultic background, since it can be interpreted as reminiscent of a ritual epiphany. The dressing, bathing and anointing of Aphrodite in the hymnic depiction is paralleled by rituals attested for the Archaic and later periods. The way Aphrodite is described in her epiphanies before Anchises, may reflect how she was visualized in cult images, as epigraphical evidence from the Archaic period onwards suggests.

Chapter Four
Erotic Personifications

4.1   INTRODUCTION

In many literary, cultic, and political contexts, Aphrodite does not appear or act alone, but is accompanied or even supported by an entourage of other deities who do not actually belong to the world of Olympian gods. These include, for example, the Charites, Eros, Himeros, Hebe, the Horae, Peitho and Pothos, all of whom I will consider under the category 'erotic personifications'. These figures are often sweepingly considered and simply treated separately as personifications of "abstract concepts" either under a poetic, philosophical, iconographical, or cultic aspect.[1] In the following chapters, which will focus on the Charites, Peitho and Eros, I will argue that these erotic personifications are of a dissimilar nature and origin. Some are already rooted and shaped in popular belief and cult, whereas others owe their specific character mainly to poetic inspiration and fantasy.[2] Often, however, it is difficult to judge which aspect prevails in a personification. Several attempts have been made to classify literary personifications. They have proved to be useful at times, but are not always sufficient for understanding this phenomenon.[3]

I suggest that in some cases poetic invention, which starts with Hesiod and Homer, played a vital role in the intellectual process by which abstract concepts were turned into living mythical creatures thus increasing the number of Greek deities.[4] More often, however, poets seem to refer to mythic tradition, popular belief, cult, or ritual when they present deities, taking those non-literary contexts as a basis for original poetic fictions. Thus they modified and reshaped deities they were acquainted with or created original characters according to the respective literary context or genre.[5] However, it is often problematic to distinguish between traditional cultic and mythic elements and poetic invention. Thus a fixed chronological order, in which personifications first emerge in poetry, go on to inspire artists and finally receive cultic veneration, cannot be assumed, particularly where erotic personifications are concerned.[6] In the case of the Charites and Peitho, literature rather seems to presuppose cultic worship.[7] An important indicator of the time and way in which poetic personifications were perceived and visualized is iconography. When they occur in poetic and cultic contexts, personifications can be more or less concrete, but sometimes their anthropomorphic shape and plasticity is not explicitly described. The human shape, however, seems to be the only way abstract concepts are represented.[8]

The next sections will map out the concepts and contents of "personification" (4.2) with regard to the Olympian gods (4.3). Various aspects of Aphrodite's magical garment, the κεστὸς ἱμάς, and its function in defining the love-goddess's province are discussed in 4.4–4.6. In a final section (4.7) I offer a detailed discussion of Hypnos and Thanatos; documented as personified gods at a very early stage, they may have influenced the shaping of the Greek love-god, known as Eros.

4.2   PERSONIFICATION: CONCEPTS AND CONTENTS

In most general terms, "personification" has been defined as an abstract or impersonal concept which is endowed with characteristics normally attributed to human or divine beings, such as physical life and movement, mental and emotional activities (feeling and thinking) and male or female physical appearance.[9] It has been argued that, as soon as a figure has been represented in the visual arts, he or she can be recognized as a personification.[10] But painters are perhaps more likely to have depicted personifications after poets had already described them as such.

The scope of what is imagined as personified by the Greeks in the Archaic period is significantly wide. As far as the gender of personifications is concerned, it seems remarkable that the majority of personified figures is female and, moreover, associated with predominantly positive, often political or civic connotations (Dike, Eirene, Eunomia, Harmonia and Homonoia &c.).[11] This striking phenomenon has usually been explained linguistically through the feminine gender of the abstract qualities which tend to be personified. This is certainly a relevant point. More recent scholarship, however, has drawn attention to the dynamics of a male-dominated society in which extremes of good and evil tend to be represented in a female shape. Perhaps the great number of female personifications occurring in cult and iconography are a reflection of positive male attitudes towards females. At least, personifications are depicted as beautiful young women of marriageable age, potential objects of desire, as for example, the Charites.[12] Possibly it is to be seen within the same context that among the few male personified abstracts we find erotic personifications, Eros, Himeros and Pothos, who appear as handsome youths in a smaller scale in iconography, particularly in the Classical period.[13] The male personifications most often depicted in epic and visual arts are, however, the brothers Hypnos and Thanatos.[14] Both appear in Homeric and Hesiodic epic, and Thanatos is featured even as a *dramatis persona* in Euripides' *Alkestis*. I will argue later in which ways these two deities influenced the creation of the male love-god. Personifications of neuter nouns such as κράτος or γῆρας also appear rarely in iconography. When they do, they are personified as males. A good case in example is probably Kratos in *Prometheus Bound*.[15]

Some other attempts at classification have been made. It is important that erotic personifications, according to their diverse nature and origins, belong to divergent categories. Personifications encompass natural phenomena including the Earth, Heaven, the Ocean, the Winds, the Sun and so on. They coexist as persons and phenomena. It is Hesiod and later the Presocratic philosophers who attribute a personal flavor not only to these natural manifestations, but also to invisible concepts which are considered as primeval and elemental (such as Eros).[16] Some of them may even have a civic implication, such as Eris, Neikos, Philia or Themis, Peitho and Harmonia as we have seen earlier. Also these personifications are usually imagined as lasting and persisting. Another group describes the reality of individual human experience and includes those which affect human beings physically, as e.g. Hypnos and Thanatos, or mentally and psychologically (Deimos, Phobos, Peitho, Eros, Himeros, Pothos, Ate &c.).[17] They were not considered as persistent, but temporally bound to the situation when they become effective. The Charites may be considered as being of a different nature since they too were established very early as cult goddesses in Greece. As their name suggests, they personify the idea of beauty and charm. Considering the implications (and the gender) of the term χάρις, it is not surprising that they were imagined as beautiful young women at a very early stage. A different category arises from the tendency to personify functions, gifts, or effects which can be imagined as caused or engendered by established Olympian deities. The personified gods are then related to them as children or attendants, thus Dike is Zeus' daughter, Deimos and Phobos are Ares' sons, Eros and Himeros are Aphrodite's companions.

Often it cannot be decided to what degree these personifications are in fact imagined as personally individualized and as concrete human beings or deities. Attempts to classify personifications according to their degree of individuality are not really satisfactory. T. Webster, for example, distinguishes in descending order between "deification", "strong personification", "weak personification" and "technical terms". "Deification", for example, marks the highest degree of personification. The Charites are a good example of this since they were venerated as goddesses in the Archaic period. Hypnos and Thanatos, as presented in the *Iliad*, fit his definition of a "strong personification" (when the "human qualities are clearly seen"). One type of what he calls a "weak personification" is interesting: emotions imagined as victors, captors, holders, or destroyers are counted among them. T. Webster suggests that this use was originally personal and that this sort of metaphor probably died out by the 5th century BC.[18] In the particular case of Eros, however, there is abundant evidence that this very metaphor was further developed by the poets and contributed to the love-god's personality.[19]

4.3 PERSONIFIED AND OLYMPIAN DEITIES

T. Webster's classification omits the category of divine personifications who are subordinated to the Olympian deities. The worship of deities whose names also denote abstract concepts can be traced back to the Archaic period, a stage at which they did not necessarily have any connection with the Olympian gods.[20] This, however, seems to have become the rule later on. Olympian deities are usually assigned a certain sphere in which they perform different functions and thus influence human life. Personified deities affect the human world in a different way. W. Burkert defines the particular characteristic of personified deities as follows: "the Archaic Greek personifications come to assume their distinctive character in that they mediate between the individual gods and the spheres of reality; they receive mythical and personal elements from the gods and in turn give the gods part in the conceptual order of things."[21] In Hesiods *Works&Days* (256f.), Dike exemplifies this concept very well when she comes to Zeus complaining that men have violated justice, i.e. the quality she represents as his daughter. Personified deities can operate on gods in the same way as on human beings and are therefore sometimes stronger than (or at least exercise influence over) the Olympians; thus, for example, when even Zeus is overcome by Hypnos, or Aphrodite is seized by ἵμερος which Zeus has put into her (*Hymn. Hom.* V,45).[22]

It would seem, then, that personified deities are conceived of simultaneously as divine anthropomorphic personalities and abstract concepts which belong to their individual realms. Examples illustrating the unity of a personal god and an abstract concept are commonly found in epic (Ares, Aphrodite, Themis, Oceanus &c.).[23] Another category of personifications—that of powers and qualities which affect either the human body or the mind and emotions—is exemplified particularly by erotic personifications like Eros, Himeros and Peitho. In the *Iliad* for example, Hypnos best represents the juxtaposition of god and abstract phenomenon as we will see later. Before W. Pötscher, H. Usener classified in a similar way a spontaneous and strong feeling or emotion, one whose overwhelming impact is conceived of as something divine, as an "Augenblicksgott" or δαίμων.[24] A sudden unexpected event or an overwhelming desire is explained by the interference of a δαίμων in the *Iliad*, for instance. The δαίμων can, but need not necessarily be identified with an Olympian god. In *Il.* 3,420 Helen is forced by the love-goddess to obey and is led to Paris' bedchamber not by Aphrodite herself but by the δαίμων (ἦρχε δὲ δαίμων). Δαίμων marks the effect of a power whose origin is either unclear or related to the gods, without being identical with them.[25] It is possible that Helen is led by an independent divine force which originally belongs to and is finally triggered by Aphrodite, without being identical with herself. It is probably the same power which operates on the goddess herself in the *Homeric Hymn* (45) and to which she finally has to succumb. This would be similar to the later Platonic conception of ἔρως as a δαίμων, a mediator between the human and divine world.[26] The Platonic idea may explain why originally unpersonified erotic phenomena such as Eros, Himeros and Pothos, which belong to Aphrodite's province, could be perceived as divine, since they too mediate between Aphrodite and human beings.

Personifications tend to be subordinated as a train or as individual companions, daughters, sons or attendants to Olympian gods to whose specific realm they can be related. It has been proposed by K. Reinhardt that the Olympian gods and their spheres of influence receive a more clearly defined image by their correlation to respective personifications.[27] Hesiod's *Theogony* is an attempt to systematize the interdependence of deities and personifications. This is exemplified in *Theog.* 934, where Phobos and Deimos are depicted as sons of Ares by Aphrodite. His paternity can be explained by the fact that "panic" and "fear" belong to "war". Aphrodite's association with them is due to her traditional relationship with Ares which is reflected in early common cults. Homer describes them as Ares' charioteers (*Il.* 15,119f.), Phobos is called Ares' son in *Il.* 13,298f. Sometimes personifications can relate the Olympians' activity to social norms (Dike is Zeus' daughter in *Works&Days* 256), or represent a function or an effect belonging to the sphere of influence of a particular deity. (Aphrodite's companions are Eros and Himeros in *Theog.* 201, see Plate 6). In some cases a function or hypostasis of an Olympian deity, as soon as it is separated, can operate on him or her as an independent personified deity. Sometimes this correlation between deities and their provinces is reflected in cult associations, as for example in the cult of Aphrodite Πάνδημος and Peitho.[28]

4.4 THE ORIGINS OF EROTIC PERSONIFICATIONS: MAGICAL LOVE SPELLS AND CHARMS OF APHRODITE

Hesiod and Homer not only defined Aphrodite's particular sphere of influence, but also significantly shaped her entourage. In comparison with the goddess's other companions, Eros is not individualized to a significant degree, nor does his role surpass theirs in literature, iconography and cult before the end of the 6th/beginning of the 5th century BC. This is surprising considering Eros' prominent role in the *Theogony* as a primeval entity whose attributes suggest a personified concept (120f.). Other extant Archaic hexametric poetry, including the Homeric poems, Hesiod's *Works&Days*, the *Homeric Hymns* and the surviving fragments of the *Epic Cycle*, represents the Charites and Peitho as personified deities, but not Eros who remains without any mythical story. I will argue in a subsequent chapter that his absence from these works may be explained through the special role Hesiod gave him in the *Theogony*; in spite of his "Olympian attributes" he is first of all a cosmogonic entity. In the *Theogony* (201), Eros is briefly mentioned together with Himeros as following Aphrodite, but Himeros makes an earlier appearance as neighbor of the Muses together with the Charites on Mount Olympus (64) and could therefore be expected to take a personal shape. Eros on the other hand, at the beginning of things, is primarily a complement to the non-personified cosmic entities Chaos and Earth (116f.).

Among the erotic personifications are the components of Aphrodite's magical garment, the κεστὸς ἱμάς, which the poet very probably intends us to imagine as visual representations in one of the most famous episodes of the *Iliad*, the *Dios Apate*.[29] Furthermore, this passage illustrates nicely the relationship and interaction between an Olympian deity and personifications. The κεστὸς ἱμάς has been discussed under various aspects, for example its shape, the design of possible embroidered components, its association with magical cult practices, and its illustrations in art. In what follows, I will discuss what the personifications could have looked like and what they could have been modelled on. Furthermore I suggest that Aphrodite's κεστὸς ἱμάς played a particular role in the *Iliad* as a means of defining Aphrodite's particular province. This concept of personification (i.e. defining a deity's realm), helps to explain the idea of a train of clearly personified companions as embodiments of different aspects of love (desire, longing &c.) and thus of Aphrodite.

The first surviving Greek epigraphical document to mention Aphrodite in an hexametrical verse is the inscription on "Nestor's cup", a Rhodian kotyle which has been securely dated to the late 8th century (735-720 BC).[30] It has been interpreted as a magical love spell[31] and can thus throw light on the nature and workings of Aphrodite's magical device, the κεστὸς ἱμάς as featured in the *Dios Apate*. The inscription appears to be our first evidence for one of Aphrodite's traditional mythical roles: "I am Nestor's wine-cup, good to drink from. Whoever drinks from this wine-cup, beautifully crowned Aphrodite's desire will seize him immediately."

Νέστορός : ε[ἰμ]ι[32] : εὔποτ[ον] : ποτέριον. |
hὸς δ' ἂν τόδε πίεσι : ποτερί[ο] : αὐτίκα κ̂ενον |
hίμερος hαιρέσει : καλλιστε[φά]νο : Ἀφροδίτες.

That the owner of the vessel is named "Nestor" has led scholars to assume that the inscription is an allusion to an episode in the *Iliad* (11,632-7), which tells of the old hero Nestor and his cup, a huge precious goblet, which only he can lift when it is full. Thus the vessel has also been a prominent topic in recent discussions about the dating of the *Iliad*. [33]

However, there is a second—linguistic—allusion to epic which has not been recognized so far: the hexametrical love spell which indicates that whoever may drink from the cup should be "seized by beautifully crowned Aphrodite's desire instantly" has affinities in language and motif with epic, the *Dios Apate* in particular.[34] The phrase hίμερος hαιρέσει (line 3) is a current formulaic feature in the Homeric repertoire too. The immediate activitiy of erotic desire is most clearly indicated in the formulaic expression ὥς σεο νῦν ἔραμαι καί με γλυκὺς ἵμερος αἱρεῖ, which is used when Zeus is immediately seized by desire for his consort (*Il.* 14,328).[35] Most importantly, as in the inscription, Aphrodite appears as the agent of desire. Therefore I prefer the translation "beautifully crowned Aphrodite's desire" over C. Faraone's "desire for beautifully crowned Aphrodite (i.e. sex)" in which, by metonymy, he equates the goddess's name with sexual intercourse.[36] Of course, this is the final target of the spell, but this translation seems perhaps too abstract here. In view of the *Iliad*, the notion of a myth about the goddess Aphrodite giving ἵμερος is suggested in the inscription.

An observation made by C. Faraone may suggest that the epic formula hίμερος haιρέσει originally belongs to a magical incantation. He points out that the stress on the immediate effect of erotic seizure indicated by αὐτίκα in the inscription on "Nestor's cup" has parallels in many instances of Greek magical spells and is thus a "subtle indication of its serious magical intent".[37] It is interesting that ἵμερος αἱρεῖν is also combined with adverbs denoting swiftness in the *Iliad* passage quoted above (νῦν). In general, we are of course not in a position to decide with certainty whether spells cite or adapt language which first occurs in narrative hexametric genres such as epic. For both epic and magical spells may borrow from an even earlier oral tradition of hexametric incantations. I would not exclude the possibility that incantatory language could have been adapted by narrative hexametrical genres. In any case the inscription on "Nestor's cup" need not be modelled on formulae occurring in our *Iliad*.[38]

What does the inscription on "Nestor's cup", the first epigraphical document to mention Aphrodite, tell us about how she could have been perceived in the 8th century BC? It seems that it presupposes a myth in which she functions as a goddess who causes ἵμερος. Such a mythical motif can easily be reflected in a spell or curse in which Aphrodite (which other goddess would be more naturally invoked?) is imagined to overcome somebody with ἵμερος. In any case the lines show that the association between Aphrodite and ἵμερος, which is considered as an aspect of her divine nature, is at least as old as the 8th century BC.

In the *Dios Apate* too Aphrodite is represented as the donor of ἵμερος. To prevent Zeus from noticing Poseidon's intervention in the war in favor of the Greeks, Hera plans how she could deceive his mind and decides to make him desire to sleep with her, and, after that, to pour sleep on his eyes and wits (159-65):

μερμήριξε δ' ἔπειτα βοῶπις πότνια Ἥρη,
ὅππως ἐξαπάφοιτο Διὸς νόον αἰγιόχοιο.
ἥδε δέ οἱ κατὰ θυμὸν ἀρίστη φαίνετο βουλή,
ἐλθεῖν εἰς Ἴδην εὖ ἐντύνασαν ἓ 'αὐτήν
εἴ πως ἱμείραιτο παραδραθέειν φιλότητι
ἧι χροιῆι, τῶι δ' ὕπνον ἀπήμονά τε λιαρόν τε
χεύηι ἐπὶ βλεφάροισιν ἰδὲ φρεσὶ πευκαλίμηισιν.

Concerned that her lavish beauty treatment (169-86) might still not be sufficient to increase Zeus' lust, Hera also asks Aphrodite for help.[39] On the pretext of reconciling her estranged parents Oceanus and Tethys, she asks the love-goddess: "Give me now love and desire, with which you subdue all immortals and mortal men" (*Il.* 14,198f.):

"δός νύν μοι φιλότητα καὶ ἵμερον, ὧι τε σὺ πάντας
δάμναι ἀθανάτους ἠδὲ θνητοὺς ἀνθρώπους."

The context suggests that φιλότης means "sexual love" here rather than "affection" or "friendship".[40] As lines 163f. above indicate, Hera's goal is clearly sexual. She wants to appear more physically attractive and hopes that ἵμερος, Zeus' "desire" for her, will increase.[41]

It is actually quite hard to imagine how this could happen. As the relative clause suggests, φιλότης and ἵμερος have to be interpreted as a device or power by which Aphrodite can overcome gods and men. Although she seems to be the original owner of φιλότης and ἵμερος, the ἱμάς makes them transferable. Thus she can donate it to other deities who can use it for their own purpose. A similar concept seems to underlie the love spell on "Nestor's cup" where Aphrodite appears as the mistress of ἵμερος: the drinker of the cup will be overcome by "Aphrodite's desire." The goddess's powers are contained in a personal accessory, the κεστὸς ἱμάς, which she normally wears on her chest. It can easily be transferred and its contents are at its current owner's disposal and guarantee the use of the bewitching powers (θελκτήρια) it includes: "She spoke, and loosened the embroidered garment from her bosom, the many-coloured one, in which all enchantments are wrought for her. In it is love, desire, alluring love talk, wheedling words which steal the senses even of the wise. This she put in her hands, and spoke the word and addressed her: "Take this garment now and put it in your bosom, the many-coloured one, in which everything is wrought. I say that you will not return without success, whatever you strive for in your mind". (*Il.* 14,214-21):

ἦ, καὶ ἀπὸ στήθεσφιν ἐλύσατο κεστὸν ἱμάντα
ποικίλον· ἔνθα δέ οἱ θελκτήρια πάντα τέτυκτο.
ἔνθ' ἔνι μὲν φιλότης, ἐν δ' ἵμερος, ἐν δ' ὀαριστύς
πάρφασις, ἥ τ' ἔκλεψε νόον πύκα περ φρονεόντων.
τόν ῥά οἱ ἔμβαλε χερσίν, ἔπος τ' ἔφατ' ἔκ τ' ὀνόμαζεν·
"τῆ νυν, τοῦτον ἱμάντα τεῶι ἐγκάτθεο κόλπωι,
ποικίλον, ὧι ἔνι πάντα τετεύχαται· οὐδέ σέ φημι
ἄπρηκτόν γε νέεσθαι, ὅ τι φρεσὶ σῆισι μενοινᾶις."

When referring to concrete objects θελκτήριον means simply "enchantment". Here, however, the θελκτήρια are the bewitching powers of seduction which are imagined as being present in the device and become effective through it. The contexts of the verb θέλγειν show the enchanting power of words.[42] Therefore it is not surprising that, in addition to φιλότης and ἵμερος, ὀαριστύς ("alluring love talk") and πάρφασις ("wheedling words which steal away shrewd senses") are among the θελκτήρια.[43] The contents of Aphrodite's ἱμάς clearly resemble those elements and concerns which define her province (τιμή/μοῖρα) as presented in Hesiod. "This sphere of influence (lit.: "honor and share") has been allotted to her from the very beginning among men and immortal gods: the whispering of girls, smiles, deceptions, sweet joy and gentle love" (*Theog.* 203-6):

ταύτην δ' ἐξ ἀρχῆς τιμὴν ἔχει ἠδὲ λέλογχε
μοῖραν ἐν ἀνθρώποισι καὶ ἀθανάτοισι θεοῖσι,
παρθενίους τ' ὀάρους μειδήματά τ' ἐξαπάτας τε
τέρψιν τε γλυκερὴν φιλότητά τε μειλιχίην τε.

These τιμαί encompass means of seduction as well as the actual goal, φιλότης, the consummation of love. Presumably they were traditional elements in myths about Aphrodite in oral poetry. It is, however, only in the *Iliad* that these aspects become more concrete and manifest because they are associated with the goddess's personal garment. The passage within the *Dios Apate* is very probably intended by the poet to define Aphrodite's sphere, functions and gifts, described earlier as ἔργα γάμοιο (*Il.* 5,428f.). The way in which the Homeric poet represents them as part of a garment, perhaps one he knew from iconography, is original and, as far as we can tell from extant literature of this period, his own poetic fiction.

Regarding the nature of the κεστὸς ἱμάς and its intended effect, C. Faraone has drawn parallels to *philia* spells which may be traced back to Mesopotamia.[44] There is abundant Near Eastern and later Greek evidence for magical devices such as knotted or beaded cords, tablets or rings with prayers and spells. They are intended either to restore affection and benevolence or to increase personal charm and attractiveness in the eye of a social or political superior. They need not be erotic at all, but there are several examples in which incantations are meant to settle an argument between spouses.[45]

C. Faraone refers to a tablet from Ashur (around 1000 BC), which contains a Neo-Assyrian magical spell by which a wife can win back her husband's love. The recipe includes instructions on how to make a cord which is to be worn around the waist. This incantation is recognizably addressed to Ishtar, as is a prayer in which a wife calls upon the goddess to make the sulking husband talk to her again.[46] Another source of parallels may be mentioned for the sake of comparison: the recipes for amulets in the much later Greek magical papyri which have much in common with the Near Eastern examples.[47] These invocations usually ask for some benefit for the wearer who also wants to influence the way other persons perceive him or her, for example when a public speaker wants the sympathy of the audience.[48] Other spells, written on tablets or even on the hooves of a race horse, are intended to increase attractiveness and charm,[49] or success and victory.[50] Some also provide *remedia amoris*.[51]

Magical elements and traditional invocation are certainly reflected in so far as the poet of the *Iliad* speaks of the content as θελκτήρια; also, the beginning of Hera's request (δός) follows the pattern of invocations which ask that a favor or benefit be conferred.[52] Her attempt to make Zeus better disposed towards her is paralleled in several spells in which somebody strives for the benevolence of a superior. That the κεστὸς ἱμάς can be also used to heal a non-functioning relationship is indicated in Hera's feigned concern for her quarrelling parents Oceanus and Tethys. Hence Aphrodite's garment has a function similar to that of *philia* spells which are meant to restore affection and to cure marriages. This suggests that the scene in the *Iliad* does not only show traces of Near Eastern magical *philia* spells, but also refers to Near Eastern myth, namely the quarrel between Apsu and Tiamat who are featured as parents of the gods in the epic *Enûma Elish*.[53]

As it turns out, Aphrodite's κεστὸς ἱμάς, as featured in the *Iliad*, is nonetheless unique both in its function and in the way it is used. As it is meant to enhance Hera's attractiveness and make her desirable to Zeus, the function is similar to that of an amulet. The important difference, however, is that Hera does not intend to win back his love, neither does she need a *remedium amoris*. She uses the spell in order to pursue a purely sexual goal, and this is unparalleled in the Near Eastern sources. Since its contents belong to Aphrodite, whose sphere of influence they are intended to define, the κεστὸς ἱμάς, unlike amulets or for instance, "Nestor's cup", does not contain invocations or prayers. The contents may even be embroidered on that which it mainly is: an ornament which originally belongs to the love-goddess herself. The poet could have been inspired by Eastern iconography, since the Eastern goddess of love is sometimes depicted with an ornament consisting of bands which she wears around her chest.

However, the κεστὸς ἱμάς occurs nowhere else in an erotic context of extant literature; it is not mentioned in the adornment scenes of the *Odyssey*, the *Homeric Hymns*, or the *Cypria*. Thus the poet seems to have used this concrete accessory in an unparalleled way as a means to define Aphrodite as a love-goddess, whose power is imagined to be somehow stored within the object. Moreover, the garment can even replace Aphrodite's presence.[54] Of course, Hera uses it as she would use an amulet or the like, but the context seems to confirm that it is primarily a unique poetic invention, designed and, as we will see later, modelled on other deities' weapons in order to define Aphrodite's province of ἔργα γάμοιο. As components of her power they are separable from her and representable on a piece of art. Once separated, they can operate independently, even on herself.[55]

It would seem, then, that "Nestor's cup" and Aphrodite's κεστὸς ἱμάς represent a sort of magical device supposed to cause the same effect—erotic seizure. The formulaic expression ἵμερος αἱρεῖν occurs in the inscription on the cup and is used as a formula in several contexts of the *Iliad*. The style and contents of the inscription are of an incantatory nature and applied in order either to make the wine an effective aphrodisiac or to emphasize innate qualities of this kind. Aphrodite's garment also has magical power and is imagined as containing ἵμερος. After Hera's successful application of the κεστὸς ἱμάς, Zeus is seized by "desire" and he too experiences what is meant to happen to the individual drinking from the cup. Compare Zeus' words in *Il.* 14,315-28 ("Never yet has desire for any goddess or mortal woman so been poured over and overcome the heart within my breast, . . . as now I desire you and sweet longing seizes me"):

οὐ γάρ πώ ποτέ μ' ὧδε θεᾶς ἔρος οὐδὲ γυναικός
θυμὸν ἐνὶ στήθεσσι περιπροχυθεὶς ἐδάμασσεν,
οὐδ' ὁπότ' ἠρασάμην Ἰξιονίης ἀλόχοιο
(here follows the catalogue of Zeus' previous beloveds)
ὥς σεο νῦν ἔραμαι καί με γλυκὺς ἵμερος αἱρεῖ.

with the inscription:

hὸς δ' ἂν τõδε πίεσι : ποτερί[ο] : αὐτίκα κ͂ενον |
hίμερος hαιρέσει : καλλιστε[φά]νο : Ἀφροδίτες.

At 14,198 Hera explicitly asks Aphrodite to provide her with ἵμερος and in 216 we learn that ἵμερος is a component of this curious garment.

One easy conclusion emerges from this survey. In the *Dios Apate*, ἵμερος is considered a magical power peculiar to Aphrodite. The consequences that result from drinking wine from a cup inscribed with a magical spell, and from wearing a garment in which magical powers seem to be stored are more or less the same. ἵμερος is imagined as inherent either in the divine garment (in the *Iliad*), or in the charmed wine (of "Nestor's cup"). In both instances ἵμερος represents an aspect of Aphrodite and can be triggered by the use of the respective magical objects. There is one point in which drinking vessel and κεστὸς ἱμάς diverge in their effect. Whereas the wine in the cup immediately affects the "user" of the cup, the κεστὸς ἱμάς provides adornment which gives magically effective physical beauty. Whoever wears the garment, can act upon the individual whose erotic desire they intend to arouse.

The similarities in wording and workings of garment and cup, however, do not suggest a dependency of the inscription on the *Iliad*. Thus, instead of understanding an allusion to the *Iliad*, one may rather argue that the Homeric poet, when referring to the motif and verbal phrasing which also occurs on "Nestor's cup", is working back to an earlier magical tradition. This can be explained by his unceasing endeavor to archaize.[56] Since hexameters are very likely to have been produced by the same oral techniques for a variety of different genres (hymns, incantations, epic narratives), the poet may rather have borrowed certain linguistic features and ideas from magical or ritual incantations and formulae. It seems then, that in the *Dios Apate*, the context of a magical incantation scene is used for a narrative purpose. It is transposed to the divine sphere and set in narrative epic scenery. It shows that Aphrodite is the ultimate mistress of love spells, which she conceals in a garment.

4.5 THE VISUALIZATION OF THE PERSONIFICATIONS ON APHRODITE'S κεστὸς ἱμάς

Aphrodite unties the ἱμάς from her bosom and then advises Hera to put it on hers (*Il.* 14,214 and 219). The material and appearance of the ἱμάς itself have caused much speculation. It has been suggested that it was inspired by an ornament, the "saltire" worn by the Eastern love-goddess on the waist or about the breasts, as shown by early iconographical documents.[57] Of more interest than the actual shape and material, however, is its design and possible illustrations of the θελκτήρια. It is, truly, not easy to imagine what they could have looked like since they are not explicitly described in the text. The verbal adjective κεστός, a *hapax legomenon*, has usually been explained as "stitched" or "embroidered".[58] It is impossible to infer from κεστός whether the ornament was decorated by lines of stitches, perhaps quilted, or whether it was embroidered with non figurative representations such as geometrical patterns, or even figures.[59] H. Shapiro suggests that Aphrodite's erotic spells (φιλότης, ἵμερος, ὀαριστύς) were in fact meant to be imagined as embroidered figures (ποικίλος) on the accessory which is stitched κεστός by seam work.[60] His argument is based upon the A-scholium.[61] However, the term ποικίλος alone normally indicates only color or pattern or both, and therefore would not necessarily suggest concrete figurative illustrations.[62]

More concrete and individualized are those personifications wrought on pieces of armor with whom the κεστὸς ἱμάς has often been compared.[63] We see the personifications in the war scene on the shield of Achilles (*Il.* 18,535-40) with Eris, Kydoimos and Ker intervening in the fight, handling the dead and the wounded soldiers. Their activity is explicitly compared to that of human beings—Ker is even wearing clothing: "And among them Eris and Kydoimos joined, and destructive Ker, seizing one man alive, with a fresh wound, another without a wound, and another man she dragged dead by the feet through the battle; and the clothing she had about her shoulders was red with the blood of men. Just like living mortals they joined and fought, each of them dragging away the bodies of the men killed by the others"(*Il.* 18,535-40):[64]

> {ἐν δ' Ἔρις ἐν δὲ Κυδοιμὸς ὁμίλεον, ἐν δ' ὀλοὴ Κήρ,
> ἄλλον ζωὸν ἔχουσα νεούτατον, ἄλλον ἄουτον,
> ἄλλον τεθνηῶτα κατὰ μόθον εἷλκε ποδοῖιν·
> εἷμα δ' ἔχ' ἀμφ' ὤμοισι δαφοινεὸν αἵματι φωτῶν.}[65]
> ὡμίλεον δ' ὥς τε ζωοὶ βροτοὶ ἠδ' ἐμάχοντο,
> νεκρούς τ' ἀλλήλων ἔρυον κατατεθνηῶτας.

On the shield of Agamemnon (*Il.* 11,32f.), Deimos and Phobos are depicted, but there is no indication what they look like. As they are active elsewhere in the *Iliad*, they are likely to bear traces of personified creatures here as well.[66]

The wording of the description of the κεστὸς ἱμάς also echoes other epic passages in which concrete objects are definitely featured on a piece of adornment. The θελκτήρια are "wrought" on the ἱμάς (215 τέτυκτο and 220 τετεύχαται), as are the illustrations on Achilles' shield and, even earlier, the evil monsters, nurtured by land and sea, which are presented on the first woman's στεφάνη (Hes. *Theog.* 581f.):[67]

τῇ δ᾽ ἐνὶ δαίδαλα πολλὰ τετεύχατο, θαῦμα ἰδέσθαι,
κνώδαλ᾽ ὅσ᾽ ἤπειρος δεινὰ τρέφει ἠδὲ θάλασσα·

One might assume that the depiction of images on the shields was inspired by real artworks of oriental origin, or influenced by oriental art in technique as well as motifs. K. Fittschen shows that the pictorial figures of Eris, Kydoimos and Ker are modelled on numerous mythical figures such as the Sphinx, Sirens, Harpies and Griffins which the early Greeks took over and identified with creatures of their own myths.[68] Phobos is in fact depicted with a lionhead on the *Chest of Cypselus* (on which see below). Thus it seems likely that not only the κεστὸς ἱμάς as an ornament is inherited from Eastern art, but also its illustrations, if, as we assume, the erotic personifications were similar to those on the shields.

The earliest concrete artwork representing personifications in Greece known to us is the *Chest of Cypselus*, of which Pausanias gives a detailed account (5,17-9). It dates from the early years of the 6th century BC.[69] Pausanias' account conveys that only some personifications, but not well-known mythological characters, were explained by inscriptions on the chest. His comment that they are not necessary for all personifications, as everybody would easily recognize Hypnos, Thanatos and Nyx, probably indicates that 6th-century Greeks are supposed to have been familiar with some representations of them as well.[70] Nonetheless, Pausanias describes them more precisely than the Olympian gods: Dike is a beautiful woman punishing an ugly one, Adikia (5,18,2). Eris too is repulsive (5,19,2). Both image and inscription of Phobos clearly are inspired by the depiction on Agamemnon's shield (*Il.* 11,32f.) That Phobos has a lionhead (5,19,4) is a refinement in detail in comparison to the Homeric model, but it is evident that the artist of the *Chest of Cypselus*, in the selection of personified motifs, does not go beyond the war personifications already featured in the *Iliad*. It seems quite significant that in the love stories featured on the chest Aphrodite appears and acts alone, without companions. One section shows Medea sitting on a throne with Jason on her right and Aphrodite on her left and bears the following inscription: Μήδειαν Ἰάσων γαμέει, κέλεται δ᾽ Ἀφροδίτα (5,18,3).[71]

I think that the Homeric poet wanted the audience to imagine that the erotic personifications were in fact visualized on Aphrodite's garment, looking similar to the war personifications Eris and Phobos, who operated as models in their function as content and decoration on an Olympian deity's attribute. However, judging from later iconography, Philotes, Oaristus and Parphasis were never represented, nor do later literary sources state that they are among Aphrodite's attendants.[72] Possibly ὀαριστύς and πάρφασις are functions which are later embodied by Peitho. Yet in the *Theogony* (224) Philotes is a child of Nyx, as are Hypnos and Thanatos, and is therefore already personified, in part at least. Himeros is more individualized elsewhere. He dwells near the Muses and Charites and is around Aphrodite as her companion from the time of Hesiod (*Theog.* 64; 201); in iconography he is attested from the 2nd quarter of the 6th century BC onwards.[73] We will see later that it is nevertheless Eros who becomes the male love-god and counterpart of Aphrodite, and find out why.

4.6   THE WORKINGS OF APHRODITE'S MAGICAL ACCESSORY

For our purposes, it is interesting that Aphrodite's κεστὸς ἱμάς shows parallels in particular with Athena's αἰγίς in three respects: (i) the style of its depiction (ἐν δέ), (ii) the nature of the objects (personifications), and (iii) in its function. After having agreed with Hera to stop Ares, Athena prepares to intervene in the war (*Il.* 5,733ff.). She takes off her "colorfully embroidered" (ποικίλος 735) *peplos*, gets dressed in the costume appropriate to her task, Zeus' warrior outfit, the "tunic" (χίτων 736), and takes the weapons and her specific instrument of defense, the αἰγίς (738). Like Aphrodite's κεστὸς ἱμάς, Athena's αἰγίς is decorated with personifications of abstracts which characterize her and her particular sphere of influence and activity, the "works of war" (πολεμήϊα ἔργα) given to her and Ares by Zeus (*Il.* 5,428-30). Before narrating the very first fight in the *Iliad*, Homer names the deities involved in it (*Il.* 4,439-45). The battle, instigated by Ares and Athena, Deimos, Phobos and Eris who is Ares' companion and sister, is imagined as filling the space between Earth and Heaven. Phobos is called Ares' son elsewhere (*Il.* 13,299), explicitly embodying a facet of his father's character and acting in his realm. Thus the αἰγίς displays Phobos ("Panic"), who frames the whole shield, Eris ("Strife"), Alke ("Strength"), the "chilling" Ioke ("Pursuit"), and the head of Gorgo, the only non-personification. That she is depicted suggests that the other personifications were illustrated too (*Il.* 5,738-42):

> ἀμφὶ δ᾽ ἄρ᾽ ὤμοισιν βάλετ᾽ αἰγίδα θυσανόεσσαν
> δεινήν, ἣν πέρι μὲν πάντηι Φόβος ἐστεφάνωται,
> ἐν δ᾽ Ἔρις, ἐν δ᾽ Ἀλκή, ἐν δὲ κρυόεσσα Ἰωκή,
> ἐν δέ τε Γοργείη κεφαλὴ δεινοῖο πελώρου,
> δεινή τε σμερδνή τε, Διὸς τέρας αἰγιόχοιο.

The contexts suggest that both the αἰγίς and the κεστὸς ἱμάς are normally worn by the goddess to whom they belong, since they seem to be necessary when they become active in their sphere. Here the difference is that Athena herself makes use of her αἰγίς, while Aphrodite lends it to Hera who, after her adornment, uses it as her special weapon to overcome her husband.

Whereas the αἰγίς covers different aspects of war, causes as well as powers and forces necessary to frighten and defeat an enemy, the κεστὸς ἱμάς embodies different aspects of love: its goal of consummation as well as its various means to this end, such as seduction and, subsequently, desire. As such, Aphrodite's accessory functions as a concrete means to enhance a goddess's sex-appeal, and is a vital supplement to Hera's beauty treatment, which concentrated on her visual attraction. In addition, Hera needs a medium which includes Aphrodite's specific energies and through which they can become effective. Thus the function of the garment is to replace Aphrodite's physical presence and at the same time her power. At the end of *Iliad*, book 3 she appears and accompanies Helen on her way to Paris' bedchamber, who is overcome by ἔρως, as is Zeus after having seen Hera armed with the ἱμάς.[74]

To sum up so far: as far as we can tell, Aphrodite's κεστὸς ἱμάς itself is an inheritance of her Eastern ancestors, one which the Greeks had already become acquainted with through artistic representations. Its magical contents may have been inspired by erotic spells on amulets used in magical practices. Nevertheless, Aphrodite's κεστὸς ἱμάς, as featured in the *Dios Apate*, is unique in Greek literature and art in its functions as a "love weapon" and as a medium of Aphrodite's specific powers. Moreover, Homer uses the ornament to define and illustrate Aphrodite's specific sphere of influence and to make it her individual attribute. It might also be considered as a poetic fiction which has been invented and created by Homer as an analogy to the depiction of Athena's αἰγίς. Whether the erotic powers really appeared as figures on concrete ornaments known to Homer's audience cannot be decided with certainty. One would, however, assume that the poet of the *Iliad* considered them susceptible to artistic depiction and wanted to inspire the audience to imagine them visually. The representations were probably influenced by images such as those of Eris or Phobos.

It is interesting that, in the inscription on "Nestor's cup" as well as in our epic sources apart from the *Theogony*, it is predominantly the non-personified ἵμερος that is related to Aphrodite. Being a component of her κεστὸς ἱμάς suggests that, in its abstract form, it is one of the effects imagined to be caused by her.[75] Once it becomes detached from Aphrodite however, its influencing forces may be turned around to have an effect upon her. In addition, other deities are in a position to avail themselves of its power for their own benefit.[76]

4.7   LOVE AND SLEEP

The reason why Hypnos and the corresponding abstract quality deserves attention is that his function and effect are strikingly similar to Eros' attributes in Hesiod's *Theogony* and to the components of Aphrodite's κεστὸς ἱμάς. I suggest that the personality of both Himeros and Eros is influenced by that of Hypnos (and probably also Thanatos), whose mythical identity was, as literary and iconographical evidence suggests, fully developed earlier.[77]

As lovemaking does not seem to be sufficient to wear out Zeus physically and mentally (such a god is not so easily wearied), Hera also has to plan how to "pour kind and sweet sleep on his eyelids and his shrewd senses" after their encounter (…) τῶι δ' ὕπνον ἀπήμονά τε λιαρόν τε / χεύηι ἐπὶ βλεφάροισιν ἰδὲ φρεσὶ πευκαλίμηισιν 164f.) so that her arrangements remain concealed. Unlike the previous means of seduction, sleep is not normally transmitted by any other medium or deity, but only by Hypnos' presence.[78] That Hypnos' help is necessary to create ὕπνος is one of the first examples in literature exemplifying the specific idea of a personification, i.e. that a phenomenon is perceived as a deity which coexists and interacts with an abstract quality. Moreover, when Hypnos himself says that he made Zeus' wits fall asleep by being poured around them (ἤτοι ἐγὼ μὲν ἔλεξα Διὸς νόον αἰγιόχοιο / νήδυμος ἀμφιχυθείς 14,252f.), this suggests that the abstract concept manifests itself both personally (he talks) and as a substance or fluid.[79]

It has been debated whether Hypnos' individualized representation in the *Iliad* is a poetic fiction, or whether his existence and individuality were already fully formed in mythical tradition and popular belief. There are good reasons for assuming that Hypnos and Thanatos, who is in many respects similar to him, symbolize two factors directing human life and are, therefore, traditional mythological figures with a cult established in early times.[80] The main argument for their old age is that, in contrast to Eros or Himeros, they had an established genealogy since Homer and Hesiod, and that they bear clear traces of personification in the works of both poets. They are both sons of Nyx in the *Theogony* (211f.; 758), mighty gods (759) of divergent character.[81] While Hypnos is calm and friendly (762f.) towards mankind, Thanatos is the opposite: having a heart of iron, he is without mercy and therefore hateful towards human beings (764f.). It is striking that their character is described in human terms. In the *Iliad* Nyx is personified too. She has children and functions. When she is said to have rescued Hypnos, who had been expelled from Heaven by Zeus, this implies that she is his mother (*Il.* 14,259). Hypnos is the twin brother of Thanatos in *Il.* 16,672.[82]

Nevertheless, this does not mean that the Homeric poet draws on known epic models in his mythical depiction. Thus one need not agree with Kullmann that Hypnos' initial refusal to assist Hera in her plan presupposes a Heracles epic in which Hypnos actively participated in the murder of Alcyoneus.[83]

Homer could simply be making this episode up in the *Iliad*. Whether Hypnos was actually featured in this epic is more than uncertain; we do not even know whether he is an original part of the Heracles myth itself.[84]

Hypnos' and Thanatos' roles as escorts of bodies have also been taken as a possible argument that their image had already been prefigured before it appeared in the *Iliad* and is paralleled in another mythical context (presumably displayed in the *Aithiopis*). Their specific mythical role as guards, escorts and transporters of the dead is also reflected in iconography.[85] M.L. West's conclusion that the figure of Hypnos in the *Iliad* is actually modelled on that of Hephaestus seems to presuppose an early personified image.[86] The frequent occurrence of Hypnos in Archaic iconography, as for example on the *Chest of Cypselus*, corroborates the assumption that he was conceived of as a developed personification at an early stage. According to Pausanias' description (5,18,1), a woman, Night, carries two boys with twisted feet, a white one (probably Hypnos) and a black one (presumably Thanatos), in her arms.[87] The earliest preserved vases featuring Hypnos and Thanatos show them together with a corpse (Sarpedon or Memnon). This seems to be the most common motif. *LIMC* lists at least 27 examples, of which 11 show them with the body of Sarpedon.[88] It is remarkable that on the earliest vases too, both Hypnos and Thanatos are normally winged in these scenes, as on Euphronius' *cylix*, where they are identified by inscription.[89] It has been suggested that they have wings because they make the transport of the bodies easier.[90] However, it seems also possible that the wings suggest the transport and thereby the transition from life to death. That the state of sleeping is similar to that of being dead is also reflected in the relationship of Hypnos and Thanatos as brothers.[91]

The depiction of Hypnos in iconography resembles the representations of Eros and Himeros, with whom he often appears. All three of them are youths, endowed with wings. The wings, however, have to be interpreted in a different way in the case of the love-gods. Eros' and Himeros' wings seem rather to make them able to move swiftly and easily between the divine world of the Olympians and that of mortals, suggesting that they even mediate between gods and men, making Aphrodite's power efficient. This mediating function, however, applies equally to all four. Among the earliest images of Eros and Himeros is the one on an Archaic pinax (dated to 560-550 BC) from the Acropolis, on which Aphrodite holds them in her arms (see Plate 6). This motif clearly recalls Pausanias' description of an earlier artwork which displays Nyx holding Hypnos and Thanatos—a genealogy which is attested already in Hesiod's *Theogony*.[92]

In the context of the *Dios Apate*, Hypnos is a fully elaborate personality whose abstract quality is also present throughout. He has a voice and talks to Hera, whom he is at first reluctant to obey and support for fear of being punished by Zeus. This shows a strong personal will on the one hand, but, in spite of his superhuman qualities, a clear subordination to the Olympians on the other. When Hera wants to persuade him, she can even make use of the fact that he is, as he says himself, already in love with one of the Graces, Pasithea (Πασιθέην, ἧς τ' αὐτὸς ἐέλδομαι ἤματα πάντα 14,276). She is the gift that finally makes Hypnos give in. He is able to fly onto fir trees as his presence near Mount Ida is necessary for making Zeus finally fall asleep (ὕπνωι καὶ φιλότητι δαμείς 14,353).[93] That his appearance on the tree is said to resemble that of a bird (ὄρνιθι λιγυρῆι ἐναλίγκιος 14,290) draws him close to the identity of a god. Presumably he is imagined as a winged male god here, as in later iconography.[94]

The way Hypnos is embedded in the context of the *Dios Apate* shows that Homer intended to assign an important role to him and therefore elaborated the personified image with which he may have already been familiar from the tradition.[95] The role of Hypnos as messenger very probably originates with the Homeric poet. It is he who informs Poseidon that Zeus is asleep, whereas elsewhere, this task usually belongs to Iris or Hermes. Hypnos is an early example demonstrating how a clear-cut mythological character can be developed and created out of a less sharply defined traditional figure.

In what follows, I offer a brief survey of terms describing desire and sleep. The correspondences in the descriptive terminology are probably due to the idea that desire, sleep and death are perceived as natural powers which human beings cannot escape or resist voluntarily.[96] Many of those terms are adapted later by the lyric poets when they describe the effects of desire and thus help to shape the male love-god along the lines of the earlier mythological figures Hypnos and Thanatos.[97]

Probably in order to contrast ὕπνος with θάνατος in *Il.* 14,164, the former is said to be "doing no harm" (ἀπήμων) and to be "gentle" (λιαρός); elsewhere, ὕπνος is "sweet to the mind" (μελίφρων *Il.* 2,34), "sweet" (ἡδύς *Il.* 4,131; γλυκύς *Il.* 1,610) and "delightful" (νήδυμος *Il.* 14,242. When Zeus sees Hera he is caught by "sweet longing" (γλυκὺς ἵμερος *Il.* 14,328). The phenomenon ἔρως does not seem to have a descriptive adjective in Archaic epic. Later, Sappho calls Eros a "bitter-sweet, irresistible creature" (fr. 130 V.).

The way these phenomena "seize", "subdue" or "overcome" men and deities alike is expressed in similar terms. Zeus is "seized by sweet longing" for Hera (γλυκὺς ἵμερος αἱρεῖ *Il.* 14,328). In *Il.* 24,4f. Achilles cannot fall asleep for grief over Patroclus, since "sleep the all-subduer did not seize him" (οὐδέ μιν ὕπνος / ἥιρει πανδαμάτωρ). Thanatos "holds fast the man he has seized" (ἔχει δ' ὃν πρῶτα λάβῃσιν / ἀνθρώπων *Theog.* 765). ἵμερος and φιλότης are the means by which Aphrodite "subdues" all human beings and gods (δάμναι *Il.* 14,199). The cosmogonic Eros in *Theog.* 122 "overcomes the mind and will of gods and men" (δάμναται).[98] A similar notion is given when Hera addresses Hypnos as ἄναξ πάντων τε θεῶν πάντων τ' ἀνθρώπων (*Il.* 14,233).

Sleep and desire (ἵμερος as well as ἔρως) also share the trait that they affect the mind and the senses.[99] They become effective upon the eyelids and are imagined as a substance being poured onto them or onto the mind.[100] In the *Theogony* ἔρος is said to emanate from the Charites' lovely eyes (910).[101] Hera thinks of how to pour sleep on Zeus' eyelids and his shrewd senses (τῶι δ' ὕπνον ἀπήμονά τε λιαρόν τε / χεύηι ἐπὶ βλεφάροισιν ἰδὲ φρεσὶ πευκαλίμηισι *Il.* 14,164f.).[102] Hypnos says that he himself was poured around Zeus mind and thus sent him to sleep (ἤτοι ἐγὼ μὲν ἔλεξα Διὸς νόον αἰγιόχοιο / νήδυμος ἀμφιχυθείς *Il.* 14,252f.).[103] In the same way, Zeus' senses are overcome by ἔρως which is poured around them (ἔρος . . . / θυμὸν ἐνὶ στήθεσσι περιπροχυθεὶς ἐδάμασσεν *Il.* 14,315f.).[104]

Moreover, the expressions chosen to describe the psychological and physical effects are the same: in Hes. *Theog.* 121 the cosmogonic Eros is "loosening the limbs" (λυσιμελής); ὕπνος "loosens the heart's sorrows" (λύων μελεδήματα θυμοῦ *Il.* 23,62) and the limbs (for λυσιμελής, see *Od.* 20,57; 23,343). In *Od.* 18,212f. it is the phenomenon ἔρως which, just like the contents of the κεστὸς ἱμάς, "bewitches" the suitors' senses so that their knees turn to jelly as they all desire to lie down with Penelope: τῶν δ' αὐτοῦ λύτο γούνατ', ἔρῳ δ' ἄρα θυμὸν ἔθελχθεν, / πάντες δ' ἠρήσαντο παραὶ λεχέεσσι κλιθῆναι. It is clear that the phenomenon of desire here is described in terms very similar to the attributes of Hesiod's cosmogonic Eros, as we will see later.

4.8   CONCLUSION

The episode of the *Dios Apate* is revealing for the development of erotic personifications. That φιλότης, ἵμερος, ὀαριστύς, and πάρφασις are represented on Aphrodite's accessory indicates that they are aspects belonging to her sphere which the poet invites us to imagine as personified. Already the inscription on "Nestor's cup" speaks of Aphrodite's ἵμερος as something caused by her.

The *Dios Apate* also shows the complementary roles of love, desire and sleep on the basis of the narrative itself, as well as the way in which these phenomena are imagined to affect gods and men. The crucial point in which they differ from each other also emerges: whereas ἵμερος (and indirectly also ἔρως) are a means and medium by which Aphrodite's power becomes manifest and effective, ὕπνος exists and operates through the god's own presence on the tree. Considering the refined personality and presence of Hypnos in the *Iliad*, his consistently traditional genealogy, together with the possibility that he was also active in other mythical contexts, it seems likely that Hypnos was a personification with an early established mythology. Hesiod presents his cosmogonic Eros fairly personified by applying to him attributes that are apt to describe the phenomenon itself or even sleep. But in comparison with Hypnos and Thanatos who have an almost human character, Eros remains a quite vague creature. As we shall see later, he has no cults, no fixed parents or mythical stories. As a predominantly cosmogonic deity he did not belong to the Olympian world. I suggest that this may be one of the reasons why

Homer suppresses the existence of a male love-god. Furthermore, the poet of the *Iliad* had already introduced an established Olympian deity with a cultic background to whom the poet makes Zeus attribute the ἔργα γάμοιο. It seems that the poet wanted to depict Aphrodite as the definitive authority in matters of love.

Plate 1. Archaic bronze mirror with a goddess, perhaps Aphrodite, standing on a lion. The figure shows orientalizing traits. Hermione (540-30 BC), Staatliche Antikensammlungen Munich 3482.

Plate 2.   Eros is holding a crown before a boy, also present is a male fig-
ure, supported by a stick. Attic red-figure cup (460-50 BC). Martin von Wagner
Museum L 487.

Plate 3.   Eros holds out an object (fruit?) to a boy in the presence of a male figure raising his arm. Attic red-figure cup (460-50 BC). Martin von Wagner Museum L 487.

Plate 4.   Winged Eros in pursuit of a young boy, brandishing a razor. The god
will shave the first beard of the boy who will no longer be an ἐρώμενος. On the
ground, a spinning top and a whip. Another youth flees, holding a hoop. Attic
red-figure cup by Douris (490-80 BC). Antikensammlung, Staatliche Museen zu
Berlin-Preussischer Kulturbesitz- V.I. 3168.

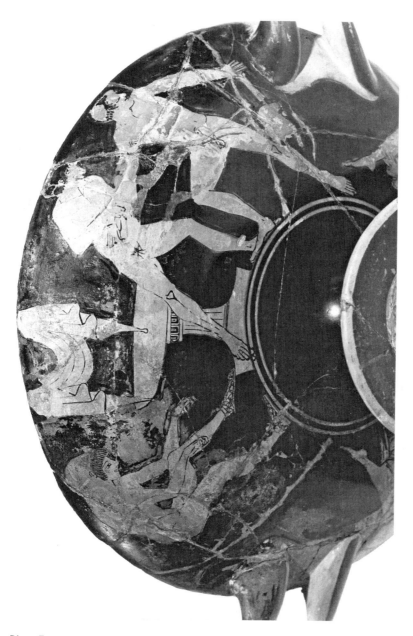

Plate 5. Athletes: The scenery of Eros' pursuit is the *palaestra*. Attic red-figure cup by Douris (490-80 BC). Antikensammlung, Staatliche Museen zu Berlin-Preussischer Kulturbesitz- V.I. 3168.

Plate 6.   Aphrodite carries HIMEROS and EROS (inscriptions), who are de-
picted as her children or as aspects of her sphere of influence, as the small scale
seems to indicate. Attic black-figure pinax (560-50 BC), National Archaeological
Museum of Athens 15131. After E. Simon (1998).

Plate 7.   Aphrodite and Hermes as cult associates at a Thymiaterion. On the goddess's forearm: a winged Eros holding a lyre. He may represent an aspect of the love-goddess. Terracotta Relief from Locri (ca. 460 BC). Staatliche Antikensammlungen Munich 5042.

Plate 8.   Aphrodite on her way to Paris' judgement, fluttered around by winged male gods, Erotes. Attic red-figure cup by Macron (490-80 BC). Antikensammlung, Staatliche Museen zu Berlin-Preussischer Kulturbesitz- F 2291. After Erika Simon (1998).

Plate 9.   Birth of Aphrodite from the sea, attended by two female figures, possibly Charites or Horae. Altar piece of the Ludovisi Throne (ca. 470-60 BC). Museo Nazionale Romano. After E. Simon (1998).

Plate 10. Aphrodite wearing a bonnet, held together by double bands. Aeginetan silver drachma (520-495 BC). After Franke-Hirmer (1972).

Plate 11.   Aphrodite wearing earrings and a necklace, her hair in an ornamented sphendone. Silver stater. Mallos (385-33 BC). After Franke-Hirmer (1972).

Plate 12.   Aphrodite with pinned up hair, held by beaded head bands and floral ornaments. Silver stater. Lycia (460-360 BC). Franke-Hirmer (1972).

Plate 13. Sappho and Alcaeus, both holding plectron and lyre. Both figures are inscribed with their names. Attic red-figure kalathos-psykter by the Brygos Painter (480-70 BC). Staatliche Antikensammlungen Munich 2416.

Plate 14. Eros crowns a young singer in the presence of a sitting musician, presumably in a symposiastic setting. Attic red-figure cup by the Telephos Painter (470-60 BC). Staatliche Antikensammlungen Munich 2669.

Plate 15.   Eros withdraws from a seated bearded man. Attic red-figure cup by the Telephos Painter (470-60 BC). Staatliche Antikensammlungen Munich 2669.

Plate 16.   Eros pursues a boy, who is spreading his arms. Attic red-figure lekythos by Douris (ca. 480 BC). National Archaeological Museum of Athens 15375.

Plate 17. Eros pursues a boy while holding a whip. Attic red-figure lekythos by Douris (ca. 480 BC). National Archaeological Museum of Athens 15375.

Chapter Five
Goddesses of Grace and Beauty: the Charites

5.1   INTRODUCTION

In its primary and most general sense, χάρις denotes the grace or loveliness of a person, a god, or a thing, but connected with this outward quality is always something which makes this loveliness erotic and attractive. With this meaning coexists a more subjective one, "grace" or "favor" in a general sense. On the part of the doer, χάρις is the "kindness", "goodwill" towards one; on the part of the receiver it means "thankfulness" or "gratitude" for a favour. χάρις also signifies in a concrete sense a "favor done or returned", a "boon".

In epic and later literature, χάρις is usually linked with female attractiveness, and it is without a doubt also for this reason that the Charites were imagined as lovely young women personifying grace and beauty.[1] Pindar asks them to bestow their "grace" and "loveliness" on his poetry, which is sometimes also called χάριτες.[2] In the homoerotic poems of Archaic lyric, χάρις is applied to a boy or youth—the ἐρώμενος.[3] In this erotic context another meaning emerges: χάρις is the "favor granted" by the boy in complying with the wishes of his lover.[4]

In the 5th century BC Thucydides, in Pericles' speech, emphasizes χάρις strikingly as a quality in which the Athenians particularly excel. Athens as a whole is the institution of education in Greece and "every man by himself, as it seems to me, presents himself in a highly competent way, as an autonomous and individual personality for most things and with grace."[5]

The Charites, being the embodiments of χάρις, are a special type of personification. As in the case of Eros, Himeros or Peitho, their name conveys an abstract meaning, but in contrast to the Charites are imagined as anthropomorphic at a very early stage. Although without an independent mythology, they are already assigned a genealogy and individual names in Hesiod and, while their number varies, the trinity Aglaea, Euphrosyne and Thalie, daughters of Zeus and Eurynome (*Theog.* 907-9), is by far the most widely accepted version.[6] Another significant criterion is that, unlike Eros for example, the Charites have an established existence in cult. They have a close affinity to divinities such as the Nymphs who are traditionally imagined as personified. This suggests that an elaborately developed personality of personifications, as we find in the early epics of Hesiod and Homer, is not necessarily a poetic invention, but can be rooted in traditional ideas also reflected in actual religious practices.[7] However, considering the antiquity of the Charites' cults, it seems peculiar that the Charites do not appear in literature by themselves, but only as Aphrodite's attendants. In what follows, I will examine first the Charites' role in epic and determine how it is reflected in cult. It will be further demonstrated that the Charites, originally independent nature deities with a specific realm and cult, were at some point subordinated to Aphrodite, particular aspects of whom they were considered to embody in different contexts.

5.2   THE CHARITES IN EPIC

In contrast to Peitho, for example, the Charites already appear strikingly anthropomorphic and individualized in epic.[8] Since they are a paradigm for beauty, it is not surprising that they appear in erotic contexts. Therefore it is a distinction for human beings to be compared with them as Nausicaa's handmaidens are: Χαρίτων ἄπο κάλλος ἔχουσαι.[9] This expression can be read in two ways. It implies that the girls' χάρις is equal to that of the Charites, and, in addition, that the Χάριτες can also bestow the χάρις in which they excel on mortals. Even a man's curls can be compared to those of the Charites, as are those of Euphorbus (αἵματί οἱ δεύοντο κόμαι Χαρίτεσσιν ὁμοῖαι).[10] To enhance the attractiveness of Hypnos' future wife, Hera explicitly describes the Charites as "young": ἀλλ' ἴθ', ἐγὼ δέ κέ τοι Χαρίτων μίαν ὁπλοτεράων / δώσω. Thus they appear to have been perceived as young women.[11]

The correspondence between the roles and the tasks the Charites fulfil in epic suggests that they were already firmly established in myth by the time of Homer and Hesiod. In Hesiod's *Works&Days*, Aphrodite offers χάρις to Pandora on Zeus' behalf while the Charites adorn her with golden chains in order to enhance her erotic attractiveness.[12] However, this kind of intervention is unique: it is only here that they become involved with a mortal in a myth. Traditionally, the Charites are in charge of Aphrodite's beauty and outfit, and so they are said to weave her *peplos* or dye it.[13] They bathe, dress, and anoint their mistress at her sanctuary at Paphos—both after the disastrous encounter with Ares and before she seduces Anchises.[14]

The Charites' presence is necessary to adorn Pandora and Aphrodite with χάρις, loveliness and attractiveness, as is Hypnos' in order to make Zeus fall asleep. It is characteristic of Greek personifications that they appear as a phenomenon and at the same time as a deity. The abstract χάρις evidently belongs, together with πόθος and μελεδῶναι, to Aphrodite's sphere. As suggested in Hesiod (*Op.* 65f.), these can be donated as a gift, since it is originally to Aphrodite that Zeus attributes the task of adorning Pandora. At the same time, the role of the Charites already appears to be institutionalized and specified in epic, where they number amongst the inhabitants of the Olympian world.

One reason engendering such a concrete personification of female deities is undoubtedly given by the gender and the meanings of the word χάρις, which denotes "beauty" and "grace" in a more material sense. χάρις is imagined as a sort of liquid which can be spread over the face or hair, and it is therefore not surprising that, in epic, female Charites anoint Aphrodite in order to beautify her.[15] I suggest that this highly personified image of the Charites at such an early stage must certainly have something to do with the fact that they were among the oldest cult deities in Greece.

5.3   THE CHARITES AS CULT GODDESSES

There are various documents which confirm that the Charites, unlike other personified deities such as Eros or Himeros, were worshipped individually in the Archaic period in many parts of the Greek mainland and the islands.[16] Herodotus (2,50,1ff.) says that almost all Greek names of the gods are foreign and that most of them have come to Greece from Egypt.[17] He counts the Charites among those few deities whose names his alleged Egyptian informants do not know and concludes that the Greeks had originally taken over their name from Pelasgian ancestors. Thus he considers the Charites' name not an inheritance of the Egyptians, but of Pelasgian origin, as is the case for the following gods: the Dioskouroi, Hera, Hestia, Themis and the Nereids. References to the Pelasgians begin with Homer and are frequent in subsequent writings, but much of this tradition is "worthless from the strictly historical point of view".[18] Perhaps we should see the traditional association of the Charites with the mysterious Pelasgians as an attempt to establish the antiquity of the goddesses as reflected in cults in Greece.

A. Lloyd and A. Fraschetti attribute some historicity to these assumptions, arguing that the Charites were "senza dubbio greche" and conceding that their very primitive cults may suggest a pre-Greek origin.[19] The Pelasgians, however, although considered pre-Doric and non-Greek in Greek tradition, were a fictitious people that never existed, an ingenious product of Greek historical speculation about their early days.[20] A. Lloyd suggests two reasons why Herodotus may have regarded the Charites as of Pelasgian origin: the antiquity of their cult at Orchomenus (on which see below), and the fluidity of their genealogy.[21] Pausanias mentions various cult places of the Charites in Greece, but only the one at Orchomenus (9,38,1) will be of interest since, firstly, it is the most important one and, secondly, it stems from the Archaic period.[22] However, the goddesses' particular function in cult as well as their identity are quite unclear.

It is therefore difficult to say whether they were related to beauty in cult as they were in myth and whether their mythical relationship with Aphrodite is reflected in religious contexts. The fact that the Charites' number varies in the same way as their names has led some scholars to assume that the variety of names results from a historical process during which long established cult-deities were interpreted as Charites.[23] They certainly show some affinity in looks and function with, for example, the Nymphs who were old goddesses of nature and reproduction. According to E. Harrison, the Nymphs sometimes take the place of the Charites. As it turns out, this phenomenon is reflected in cultic evidence and literature.[24]

The earliest known iconographical representation of the Charites was found in a sanctuary of Apollo in Thermon (Aetolia): terracotta metopes, which have been dated to the 7th-6th century BC, show two female figures facing each other (in dance?). They wear belted chitons and are identified as Χάριτες in an Aeolic script.[25] The earliest centres of traditional documented worship of the Charites include the Cycladic islands, as one of the earliest pieces of epigraphical evidence stems from Thera (6th century BC). The inscription, found at the end of the 19th century on a rock near the shrine of Apollo, mentions Κάριτες.[26] Like the find in Thermon, a relief from Paros which has been dated to 540-30 BC shows two female figures dancing; this activity, together with their provenance would seem to suggest that they represent Charites.[27] If this is correct, the cult which is mentioned by Callimachus and Apollodorus probably goes back to the Archaic period.[28] This dating is confirmed by two early 5th-century reliefs which were found in Paros' colony, Thasos. There the deities can be identified by means of the inscribed sacrificial regulations accompanying the reliefs. One relief shows Apollo with his cithara and Artemis crowning him. There are three other female figures which the inscription identifies as Nymphs. The relief on the opposite side of the wall displays the Charites together with Hermes and another female figure, Aphrodite or Peitho.[29] Perhaps the fact that Apollo is depicted with the Nymphs on the relief from Thasos, while the earliest iconography of the Charites was found in a sanctuary, also of Apollo, in Thera and Thermon, can account for the Charites' and Nymphs' interchangeability. The inscription accompanying the Charites-relief records a sacrificial regulation which is paralleled in the cult of Peitho at Thasos.[30] This correspondence, together with a dedication to both goddesses at Paros, suggest that cults and rites were already being brought from Paros to Thasos during the period of colonisation in the early 7th century BC.[31] There is good evidence that colonies tend to remain associated with the traditions of the mother city mainly by worshipping the same deities, their cults being transferred to the new locations.[32] We do not know exactly in which function they were worshipped on these islands. The absence of wreaths and flutes in ceremonies mentioned in Apollodorus (*Bibl.* 3,5,8) has been interpreted as a sign that they were chthonic deities, perhaps related to fertility. But this was certainly not their only significance, at least not in later times, when they were related to civic matters, usually in association with Aphrodite.[33]

The most frequently documented and for our purposes most interesting cult of the Charites is that at Orchomenus in Boeotia.[34] According to a scholium on Pindar, Hesiod had already mentioned the tradition which dates the cult to the mythical time of Eteocles, who was the first to worship them.[35] Pausanias too (9,38,1) records this tradition, but adds that stones are said to have fallen from the sky which were then worshipped in a sanctuary as the Charites. However, he refers to the cult images he had seen himself as τὰ δὲ ἀγάλματα <τὰ> σὺν κόσμωι πεποιημένα, which suggests adorned female figures. But, as in the case of the stone image of Eros in adjacent Thespiae, the mention of Charites' previous aniconic images in a late literary source would not necessarily prove that the cult is an ancient one. We do not know when this cult was actually founded, but the mythical tradition seems to presuppose a belief in their great age as cult deities.[36] This is supported by their frequent representation not only in early epic, but also in Pindar. Pindar's 14th *Olympian*, a victory ode for the young athlete Asopichus from Orchomenus, invokes and praises the Charites in hymnic style (κλῦτ᾽, ἐπεὶ εὔχομαι 5). The ode might have been sung during a procession towards the sanctuary and reveals interesting aspects of the Charites' realm and function in cult:[37] "You, who have obtained the waters of Cephisus and who dwell in a land of beautiful horses, Charites, queens of shining Orchomenus, famous in song, guardians of the ancient Minyans, hear me when I pray. For with your help all pleasant and sweet things are accomplished for mortals, whether a man be wise, handsome or famous":

> Καφισίων ὑδάτων
> λαχοῖσαι αἵτε ναίετε καλλίπωλον ἕδ᾽ραν,
> ὦ λιπαρᾶς ἀοίδιμοι βασίλειαι
> Χάριτες Ἐρχομενοῦ, παλαιγόνων Μινυᾶν ἐπίσκοποι,
> κλῦτ᾽, ἐπεὶ εὔχομαι· σὺν γὰρ ὑμῖν τά <τε> τερπνὰ καί
> τὰ γ᾽λυκέ᾽ ἄνεται πάντα βροτοῖς,
> εἰ σοφός, εἰ καλός, εἴ τις ἀγ᾽λαὸς ἀνήρ.   *Ol.* 14,1-7

Being associated with the "waters of Cephisus" and "the land of beautiful horses", and considered "guardians of the ancient Minyans", the Charites are referred to as goddesses traditionally linked with the vegetation and abundance of the area which is already mentioned by Homer. Thus it may be determined by their realm that they were established as personified goddesses in the Archaic period.[38] Female deities associated with rivers and springs are traditionally conceived of as Nymphs or water nymphs. The Nymphs' antiquity as divinities and their association with growth is already reflected in the *Hymn to Aphrodite* (V,256-90), where Aphrodite, in her prophecy, says that the Nymphs will bring up the child she has just conceived. The Nymphs are depicted as nature deities who are worshipped in woods.[39] This kind of worship in natural sanctuaries such as caves may also account for the Nymphs' worship in the Archaic age.[40] It is in fact not surprising that the Nymphs are imagined as female nature deities in human shape, since the term νύμφη means "young woman". The association of a young woman and a female nature deity has led one scholar to interpret the Nymphs as the "apotheosis of marriageable girls at the peak of beauty and desirability".[41] The Nymphs' closeness to the Charites is also suggested when, for example, Anchises, at the sight of Aphrodite's beauty, starts speculating about her true identity. First he guesses that she may be one of the Charites and then one of the Nymphs.[42] W. Burkert sees the latter as nature deities, not only in the context of myth: he also assigns to them a cultic function. He infers from a passage in the *Iliad* where not only the Olympian gods, but also Nymphs and Rivers are said to come to Olympus, that rivers were imagined as gods and springs as Nymphs before they were represented in poetry. In his view this actually corresponds to an earlier stage of ritual. Thus communities worship rivers and springs in personified shape.[43] I would suggest that the surprisingly early personified identity of the Charites can be explained by their affinity with the earliest goddesses, such as the Nymphs, with whom they share not only their looks, but also realm and function. Both seem to be related to springs and water and to growth. In Pindar, however, the Charites' proximity to delightful and sweet things (5-7) clearly refers to the grace and delight they bestow on victors and singers.[44]

The function which the Charites perform among the Olympians is significant: "For not even the gods arrange choruses or feasts without the revered Charites; but as stewards of all works in heaven they put their thrones beside Pythian Apollo with the golden bow and worship the ever flowing honor of the Olympian father":

> οὐδὲ γὰρ θεοὶ σεμνᾶν Χαρίτων ἄτερ
> κοιρανέοντι χοροὺς
>   οὔτε δαῖτας· ἀλλὰ πάντων ταμίαι
> ἔργων ἐν οὐρανῷ, χρυσότοξον θέμεναι πάρα
> Πύθιον Ἀπόλλωνα θ'ρόνους,
> αἰέναον σέβοντι πατ'ρὸς Ὀλυμπίοιο τιμάν.   *Ol.* 14,8-12

As in epic, the Charites are also goddesses in *Olympian* 14, with their own specific task amongst the Olympians, to whom they are somehow subordinated. They arrange feasts and dances for them. It seems to be an established concept which is current in epic and then continued in Pindar and the Archaic lyric poets, that personified deities, even when they have previously had an independent existence in cult, are subordinated to the Olympian gods as attendants. Here, however, they are not said to serve one specific deity, but all the Olympians. They are not addressed by their individual names, but by their collective term, probably in order to enhance the effects which are implied by Χάριτες and which they are able to produce by their presence.

Dancing (χόρους 9), apart from adorning and beautifying human beings and deities, is the other mythical occasion in which the Charites usually participate. Since this activity is often referred to, not only in Pindar's *Olympian* 14, but also elsewhere, it deserves some attention. Central too is their relationship with Apollo and Aphrodite, in whose honor these dances seem to have been performed. I suggest that this activity, as well as the link with the other deities, is not only reflected in mythical scenes, but also refers to cult practices. In the *Homeric Hymn to Apollo* (194-6) the Charites sing and dance together with the Horae, Harmonia, Hebe and Aphrodite, and they all reach out their hands for fruits.[45] This gesture clearly implies their common association with abundance, which they also seem to have shared with the Nymphs, who, in cult, were particularly associated with nature and growth: αὐτὰρ ἐϋπλόκαμοι Χάριτες καὶ ἐΰφρονες Ὧραι / Ἁρμονίη θ' Ἥβη τε Διὸς θυγάτηρ τ' Ἀφροδίτη / ὀρχεῦντ' ἀλλήλων ἐπὶ καρπῷ χεῖρας ἔχουσαι. It is the Charites who receive Aphrodite into their dance (*Od.* 18,194), and Artemis instructs the Muses' and Charites' dances at Apollo's temple (*Hymn. Hom.* XXVII, 13-5). In *Pyth.* 12,27, however, it is not the Charites who are described as χορευταί, but the worshippers themselves, performing their dance near the city of Orchomenus; the best reeds are said to grow there and are used for the *aulos*, the instrument which accompanies choral dance. For this reason, they are called πιστοὶ χορευτᾶν μάρτυρες.[46] Thus it seems that a mythical activity is related to real cultic dances or celebrations; maybe the worshippers imitate the Charites' dance (or the mythical feature reflects a cultic activity).

There is good evidence that the musical and dramatic festival of the Charitesia later included athletic competitions in honor of the Charites at Orchomenus, their most important cult place. Dancing was also a regular part of the festival.[47] How closely the Charites are related with dancing is confirmed by Pollux (*Onom.* 4,95). In the section on stage antiquities he mentions on ὄρχησις ("dancing") that Orchomenus received its name παρὰ τὴν τῶν Χαρίτων ὄρχησιν. He refers to Euphorion's saying that the Charites danced, possibly naked, at Orchomenus ('Ορχομενὸν Χαρίτεσσιν ἀφαρέσιν ὀρχηθέντα).[48] Here folk etymology may give some indication of how closely the Charites and the location of their cult were associated with dance. Moreover, the examples discussed suggest a link between the Charites' mythical dance and the real dance of the worshippers participating in festivals or ceremonies held in honor of the goddesses. Mythic motif and cult reality seem to correspond and interfere with each other in such a way that young women dancers are similar to the goddesses they worship and the other way round.

This idea of interference between the human and divine sphere finds its expression in Plato's *Leges* (815c2-4). Plato, in his discussion of dances, says that human beings, when performing Bacchic dance, actually imitate the divine Nymphs, Panes, Sileni and Satyrs.[49] This idea was discussed and further developed by W. Burkert. He asserts that those deities who usually appear in plurality ("societies of gods"), reflect real cult associations, *thiasoi*, which honor their god.[50] Mythical worshippers share with real worshippers subordination to an Olympian deity, Dionysus or Artemis for example, as their leader. Dance and music are performed amongst the human as well as amongst the divine entourage. W. Burkert takes up an idea which is already outlined in Plato, but he goes beyond Plato's statement that human worshippers imitate the mythical train and equates the two groups by tracing the real institutions back to "mythical times", suggesting that they were once a unity.[51] W. Burkert's examples include images of worshippers disguised as their mythical ancestors: men who are masked as Centaurs and women who gather as Eileithyai, but are actually midwives. His conclusion—that many mythical groups have corresponding features in real cult—may also be true for the Charites, who could be considered comparable with the Maenads.[52] It would seem, then, that their dance in mythical contexts is paralleled in the cultic dance of their worshippers.

It is, therefore, not surprising that the Charites, although personifications, are imagined and depicted as clearly anthropomorphic and like the Olympian gods. Their personal character is influenced and shaped by the very ancient mythical figures such as Nymphs, with whom they share their dwelling places, waters and springs, and from whom they sometimes cannot be distinguished in iconography.[53] We have already seen that the mythical events in which they usually appear are scenes of adornment, when they bathe, anoint and dress Aphrodite. This fact not only conveys the Charites' subordination to the Olympian goddess, on a mythical level, but may also reflect a cult activity. When the Charites attire Aphrodite or weave her *peplos* in myth, they can be compared with the women who were in charge of the dress for the cult image.[54]

The Charites' mythical association with Apollo as displayed in *Hymn. Hom.* XXVII,13f. is also reflected in their early cults in Thera and Thermon, possibly in Thasos too, as we saw above. Charites are also mentioned in a badly preserved Pindaric *paean*. It is very likely that they appear in association with Apollo here, but his name can only be restored.[55] In Apollo's cult place at Delos, they were also associated with him. Pausanias describes a statue of Apollo, who is holding the three Charites in his hands. This description fits an Archaic statue which has been dated to between 650 and 550 BC.[56] However, the association of the Charites with Apollo in cult in Archaic times seems to have been the exception rather than the rule. According to our epigraphical evidence the Charites' joint worship with other Olympian deities seems to be the norm in the Classical period.[57] It would seem, then, that some personifications were perceived as independent in ancient times, but subordinated to Olympians when they came to characterize a particular aspect of them.

Considering the close relationship and the frequency with which the Charites and Aphrodite appear together in myth, it is surprising that there seem to be only a few occasions on which they are linked in cult, and these all date from the Classical and Hellenistic periods. Furthermore, in contrast to mythic contexts, in these cults they do not seem to be explicitly related to sexuality and reproduction. These are, however, implied in the cult association of Aphrodite and the Charites at Athens. An inscription on a stele mentions an oath of Athenian ephebes from the 4th century BC. They have to swear by the Charites Thallo, Auxo and Hegemone.[58] Their individual names would suggest that the Charites are associated with the growing up and thriving of youth; Hegemone may be considered as conducive to prosperity. According to Pausanias, the cult of the Charites Auxo and Hegemone dates from the Archaic period (τιμῶσι γὰρ ἐκ παλαιοῦ καὶ Ἀθηναῖοι Χάριτας Αὐξώ καὶ Ἡγεμόνην).[59] It is apparently related that a late 3rd-century inscription from a *temenos* at Athens which the Charites shared with Demos,[60] testifies to the dedication of an altar Ἀφροδίτει ἡγεμόνει τοῦ δήμου καὶ Χάρισιν.[61] Here the Charites seem to have lost their individuality, since the name of one of the Charites has become the epithet of the Olympian goddess Aphrodite, used, as the context of the dedication suggests, to describe her political function.[62] Since this cult of Aphrodite is new and is attested elsewhere only in Rhamnus, it may reflect a development by which the ancient cult of the Charites was subordinated to a major deity, in this case Aphrodite.[63] During a period of cultic syncretism, she assumed a role which formerly belonged to one of the Charites, Hegemone, in a modified context: the epithet ἡγεμόνη τοῦ δήμου clearly has a civic meaning.[64] The other names of the Charites—Thallo and Auxo—may be interpreted in political terms too, since they could also be related to the growth and welfare of the *polis*. That the Charites were originally related to the thriving and prosperity of youth, without a specific public purpose, may be indicated by the earlier cult association of Demos with the Nymphs which is testified by a 5th century BC inscription. This epigraphical evidence may also account for the affinity between Nymphs and Charites.[65]

The cult associations show that a syncretism probably took place by which Aphrodite assumed the place of one of the Charites in a reinterpreted, now political function. Thus the Charites became her subordinates. Syncretism may also be indicated when we consider that the Charites' origins in Greece go further back than those of Aphrodite, since they may have already been worshipped in the Bronze age. There may be evidence for this in the form of a golden Mycenean seal ring found at Athens and dating to the 14th century BC. It displays two female figures with neck garlands and waist bands. They do not have heavy breasts and keep their hands on their hips, apparently dancing. They are accompanied by a male god who has been interpreted as Hermes or Dionysus. The identification with the Charites (or Nymphs) is not only suggested by their looks, but also by the fact that dance appears as a traditional element in the worship of vegetation divinities in the Minoan-Mycenean world.[66] Other archaeological evidence from the Cycladic islands can be taken as proof that Κάριτες as they are named in the Archaic inscription cited above, existed there a long time before the 6th century BC. A great number of slim elegant female figures dated between 2400-2200 BC have survived from there and E. Simon interprets them as Charites, goddesses embodying χάρις.[67] Perhaps these slim and delicate figures may at least be considered as the latters' forerunners. E. Simon goes one step further and argues that these Charites have influenced the image of the Greek Aphrodite.[68] Aphrodite certainly has some affinity with these figures, pre-maternal beauty and χάρις having become her prevailing characteristic in literary and particularly iconographic depictions.[69]

Early epic also suggests a close relationship, maybe even an interchange between Aphrodite and the Charites: Hephaestus' wife is called Charis in the *Iliad*, but Aphrodite in the *Odyssey* (see Appendix, Fig. 1a).[70] Similarly, in the *Works&Days* Aphrodite equips Pandora with χάρις, irresistible charm, and the Charites adorn her with golden necklaces.[71] Here Aphrodite seems to have assumed a function that would actually better suit the Charites. This mythical interchange of Aphrodite and the Charites may reflect a historical process within cult reality during which Aphrodite gradually assumed characteristics and functions of the earlier Greek goddesses and somehow replaced them so that the latter then became her attendants.

5.4   CONCLUSION

It was the aim of this chapter to illuminate the divine character of the personified Charites and their relationship and interchange with Aphrodite, the goddess with whom they have much in common. In contrast to other personifications in Aphrodite's train, such as Peitho or Eros, they are represented as clearly visualized young women with a specific task as Aphrodite's beauty attendants.

We have seen that this early definition of their personality is due to the fact that, in popular belief, the Charites were traced back to the same origins as the Nymphs. Their affinity with these nature deities becomes palpable when one considers that they share, apart from their looks, dwelling places, springs and an association with nature and growth. Springs and rivers have been traditionally conceived of as Nymphs and water gods. The similarity with ancient nature gods is not the only reason for the Charites' clearly defined personality in the Archaic period. There seems to be a close connection between divine beings who usually appear in the plural (Maenads for example) and their real worshippers in cult. This could be so in the case of the Charites too, since in myth they share their dance with their worshippers. Dancing seems to be the most characteristic cult activity not only in the famous cult place at Orchomenus, where dance competitions are attested in both literary and epigraphical texts. Reliefs from the Cycladic islands also display dancing Charites.

Their close affinity with Aphrodite and their ultimate subordination to her can be explained by the deities' history on the Greek mainland and the islands. That the Charites were ancient Greek goddesses is not only endorsed by the assumed similarity with the Nymphs in myth and cult, but also by direct epigraphical evidence. The inscription Κάριτες, which was discovered on the island of Thera, undoubtedly represents an Archaic document. In contrast to the Charites, Aphrodite's origins are non-Greek. She probably came to Greece from the East during a period of lively trade with Phoenicia. Being the goddess of love, beauty and also reproduction, she probably assumed the role of the originally Greek Charites because they were similar to her. It is likely that their subordination to Aphrodite and occasional interchange reflects this historical development.

Chapter Six
Peitho: the Power of Persuasion

6.1   INTRODUCTION

In addition to Eros and the Charites, another major figure in Aphrodite's en-
tourage is Peitho.[1] Although there is evidence suggesting that Peitho, like the
Charites, received cultic veneration at least as early as the 5th century BC, her
personality remains undefined. This is all the more surprising, when one con-
siders the importance that the phenomenon of persuasion itself has in erotic
poetry as well as in other areas of Greek culture (i.e. persuasion in its differ-
ent rhetorical, philosophical and also political coinages). In these contexts,
Peitho has the status of a concept rather than a goddess.[2] In this chapter I fo-
cus on literary contexts involving amatory subjects and consider whether she
has in these a role which gives her independence from Aphrodite. Surprisingly,
Peitho's genealogies and the stories related to those cults in which she seems
to have been worshipped as an independent goddess do not associate her with
eroticism.[3] This fact is also reflected by her role in early hexameter poetry. In
the *Theogony*, she is the daughter of Oceanus and Tethys and as such is one of
the Nymphs of groves and springs; their only specifically mentioned task is
to take care of the young, but Peitho remains without a particular function.[4]
This, however, does not necessarily mean that her involvement in love mat-
ters is a more recent development which then occasioned an association with
Aphrodite.[5] The following section will briefly outline non-erotic connotations
of Peitho (ch. 6.2), then her implications in erotic contexts will be considered
in more detail (chs. 6.3-6.6).

6.2   NON-EROTIC CONNOTATIONS OF PEITHO

Pausanias mentions the cult of Peitho at Sicyon, one of the few cults in which
she was worshipped as an independent deity.[6] The foundation myth is particu-
larly interesting since—if related to an early cult—it may be able to provide an
explanation for the goddess's original associations and functions. However, we

cannot be sure about the age of the cult, since we have no epigraphical docu-
ments to confirm it.[7] The myth does not present Peitho as a personified, active
deity. Instead, Peitho embodies "persuasion" in the actual sense of the word,
without reference to any specific cultic or social context. Pausanias tells us that
Peitho is regarded there as a phenomenon so mighty that it can even persuade
gods, and describes a ceremony which was still performed in his time. At a fes-
tival of Apollo, seven boys and girls go to the river Sythas and, after bringing the
statues of Apollo and Artemis to the sanctuary of Peitho in the agora of Sicyon,
take them back to the temple of Apollo. The aetiology of the rite is described
as follows: Apollo and Artemis had left Sicyon because the people there did
not purify them after the Python had been slain. When the town was struck
by plague, seven boys and girls were sent out to the river to offer supplication.
Persuaded by the children, Apollo and Artemis came back to the city; the tem-
ple of Peitho marks the place where they first arrived. According to Pausanias,
there was no cult image. This may imply that it was actually the abstract power
of "persuasion" itself which was considered as divine and hence worshipped.
On the other hand, the absence of an image at the time of Pausanias does not
necessarily mean that there had never been one.[8] One can infer from the cult
itself that Peitho, embodying the concrete and very general meaning of her ap-
pellation, was certainly conceived of as a significant divinity since, according to
the story, Peitho could even persuade the more powerful Olympians. This may
be the reason why she was given a cult instead of Apollo and Artemis.[9]

The meaning of Peitho becomes more specific in political or forensic
contexts.[10] Peitho's meaning in forensic persuasion is also reflected in a myth.
Pausanias (2,21,2) links her with the plot of Aeschylus' *Danaid trilogy* in order
to explain Artemis' epithet in the cult of Artemis Peitho at Argos: Hypermnestra
spared her husband and persuaded the court of the justice of her deed and so
founded the cult.[11] Here, however, Peitho is not an independent goddess, but
instead specifies the kind of support she lent to Artemis. It is she who is thought
of as having given Hypermnestra persuasive powers at court. The reason why
Artemis is called Peitho here may point to a syncretism with a real Peitho cult,
since the fact that Peitho enjoyed a particular position as local goddess and
progenitress of the royal family at Argos is confirmed by later sources.[12]

Besides, in the 5th century BC, the political dimension of Peitho was
prominent and at Athens she had even become a political concept. Pausanias
(1,22,3) follows the tradition tracing the cult of Aphrodite Πάνδημος and
Peitho at Athens back to the mythical times of Theseus. This may give some
idea of the antiquity of their cult association. As Aphrodite's epithet Πάνδημος
("of the whole people") implies, the association has a clear civic and politi-
cal significance. Our other source for the foundation of the cult of Aphrodite
Πάνδημος, the grammarian Apollodorus, does not mention Peitho in this con-
text, but he explains Aphrodite's epithet with its proximity to the ancient agora
where the *demos* held their assemblies.[13] I would therefore suggest that Peitho,

who is only mentioned by Pausanias, is an accretion to the cult of Aphrodite Πάνδημος, introduced in order to enhance the political significance of persuasion in the context of civic debate on the one hand, and Aphrodite's political functions on the other. The increasing importance of persuasion as a political tool in 5th-century Athens is reflected in later cults of Peitho. Amongst 4th-century literary sources, Demosthenes and Isocrates mention an annual sacrifice which was given to Peitho with other *polis*-deities.[14] This suggests that she had been interpreted in the 4th century BC as an independent goddess equal to the Olympians.[15] Among the many dedications to Aphrodite found in her precinct at Daphni, there is also one (dating from the 4th century BC) addressed to Peitho alone.[16]

As far as we can see in extant literature, the political aspect of Peitho first occurred in a fragment of Alcman (fr. 64 *PMGF*). He calls Tyche "sister of Eunomia and Peitho, daughter of Prometheia" and thus relates her to the political or public sphere.[17] What looks at first sight like a mythical genealogy of personifications, is actually an ideal abstract political order ("reflexion d' ordre politique").[18] Prometheia indicates the "foresight" of a ruler;[19] Eunomia signifies respect for laws and hospitality from the *Odyssey* onwards and becomes particularly important in Tyrtaeus (fr. 1-4 W.) and Solon (fr. 4 W.).[20] Tyche means the "good fortune" of a city. The role taken by Peitho here is that of persuasion and understanding, probably as a contrast to compulsion. The welfare of a city is based on the foresight of the ruler(s) who enforce(s) the good laws not by violence but by persuading the people of their correctitude by words.[21]

This is the plan of the Argive king in *Supplices*. As the citizens are to decide whether the supplicants will be given asylum or not, the king attempts to make the assembly well disposed before Danaus argues his daughters' case. He hopes that his attempt will be made by means of persuasion on which success may follow (πειθὼ δ' ἔποιτο καὶ τύχη πρακτήριος).[22]

The same strategy of describing a political order in terms of a mythical genealogy of personified concepts is also found in Pindar at the beginning of *Olympian* 13. The praise of Corinth is based on the fact that Eunomia and her sisters, Dike and Eirene, all three daughters of Themis, dwell there.[23] Thus we have a mythologizing of political concepts in which personifications are conceived of as divinities. Their relationship towards each other, which is expressed in terms of genealogy, is used to describe a political entity: the state. These personifications also have a mediating function, embodying a divine concept of political order in the human world.

Peitho, as a mode of political activity, embodying the concept of persuasive speech in contrast to violence and compulsion, is also reflected in a passage in Herodotus (8,111,2): when the Andrians refused his demand for money, Themistocles, by referring to the Athenians' powerful gods, Πειθώ and Ἀναγκαία, stated that they could not avoid paying. This clearly suggests polarized concepts of political behaviour. If the Athenians could not get their payment by persuasion, they would apply violence. Since this is related to Athenian matters, Themistocles may be referring to the cult of Aphrodite Πάνδημος in which the political Peitho, originally perhaps only an aspect of Aphrodite, has gained at least some independence.[24] In their response, the Andrians argued that being a small island with little land, they had two utterly worthless (as opposed to the Athenians' powerful) gods: Πενίη and Ἀμηχανίη, who would never enable their incapacity to pay to be transformed into an ability to pay. Of all of these, only Peitho received real cult. The others are mythologized abstract concepts invented for the discourse of the debate. We seem to see abstract divinities in the process of being born in Herodotus' tale.

Peitho's personality remains very vague in the myths which are related to her cults at Argos and Sicyon. The myths present Peitho more as a phenomenon than as a deity with individual personal traits. Unlike, for example, the Charites, she is without a specific mythical role. This may explain why she is often worshipped conjointly with other deities, Aphrodite in particular. The association of Aphrodite Πάνδημος and Peitho at Athens suggests that Peitho is not an independent goddess, but occupies part of Aphrodite's sphere. We will see later that this sort of relationship is also reflected in erotic literary contexts in which Peitho performs the role as Aphrodite's θεράπαινα in love matters. A real syncretism is not likely since Apollodorus does not mention Peitho in the context of the foundation of the cult, but one may suspect that this association reflects a syncretism which was aetiological, i.e. invented in order to enhance Aphrodite's political function. This seems even more probable when we consider the examples in which the phenomenon of persuasion has a political implication.

6.3   PEITHO IN EPIC EROTIC CONTEXTS

Peitho, in her first appearance in an erotic context, is not given the particular function one would expect considering her appellation. In the narration of the first mortal woman's adornment in Hesiod's *Works&Days*, Zeus charges Aphrodite with quite abstract tasks: (he told) "golden Aphrodite to pour charm about her head and painful yearning and limb-devouring sorrows; he ordered Hermes, the messenger god, the killer of Argos, to put into her the mind of a bitch and a thievish nature. (. . .) Athene the brighteyed goddess dressed and decked her; the divine Charites and lady Peitho put golden necklaces about her body, the beautiful-haired Horae garlanded her with spring flowers. (. . .) In her breast the messenger god, the killer of Argos, fashioned lies and wheedling words and a thievish nature according to the plan of the deep-thundering Zeus":

> (ἐκέλευσε Ζεύς)
> καὶ χάριν ἀμφιχέαι κεφαλῇ χρυσέην Ἀφροδίτην
> καὶ πόθον ἀργαλέον καὶ γυιοβόρους μελεδώνας·

ἐν δὲ θέμεν κύνεόν τε νόον καὶ ἐπίκλοπον ἦθος
Ἑρμείην ἤνωγε, διάκτορον Ἀργεϊφόντην.   65-8

ζῶσε δὲ καὶ κόσμησε θεὰ γλαυκῶπις Ἀθήνη·
ἀμφὶ δέ οἱ Χάριτές τε θεαὶ καὶ πότνια Πειθὼ
ὅρμους χρυσείους ἔθεσαν χροΐ· ἀμφὶ δὲ τήν γε
Ὧραι καλλίκομοι στέφον ἄνθεσι εἰαρινοῖσιν·   72-5

ἐν δ' ἄρα οἱ στήθεσσι διάκτορος Ἀργεϊφόντης
ψεύδεά θ' αἱμυλίους τε λόγους καὶ ἐπίκλοπον ἦθος
τεῦξε Διὸς βουλῆσι βαρυκτύπου·   77-9

To enhance Pandora's power of attractiveness, Aphrodite is to pour grace (χάριν) on the woman's head, which is to create emotional effects of desire (πόθου) and limb-eating sorrows (γυιοβόρους μελεδώνας) in the man who shall be thereby attracted to her.[25] After Athena's work, it is the Charites and Peitho who fulfil the task on behalf of Aphrodite with concrete objects.[26] By equipping her with golden necklaces (the Horae add spring flower wreaths), they create the desired effect of making Pandora irresistible. Two incidents are remarkable: firstly, this task is most suited to the Charites' capacities, but seems rather unusual for Peitho, whom one would expect instead to donate the gift of αἱμυλίους λόγους. Surprisingly, this is done by Hermes. Secondly, those "seductive words" are closely associated with a female character who is supposed to be shameless and deceitful from the very beginning.[27]

What is Peitho's role and how is it reflected in her description? That πείθειν is not only associated with the idea of persuading by words is shown by another Hesiodic example: just as gods can be persuaded or bribed by gifts, Peitho helps to "persuade", i.e. to seduce, the man by putting lovely necklaces on Pandora which make her appear even more attractive.[28] The gift of words is not, as one would expect, included in Peitho's sphere of influence, but belongs to the task which Hermes is subsequently to accomplish. The image of the woman, which has been positive so far, now turns into its opposite. Hesiod's negative portrayal of Pandora runs parallel to the mythical pattern of Hermes as a cunning liar and thief. For this reason he is the appropriate provider for a thievish character (ἐπίκλοπον ἦθος) and "mendacious and wheedling words" (ψεύδεά θ' αἱμυλίους τε λόγους), being called "of winning wiles" (αἱμυλομήτης) himself.[29] Here it is obvious that words as a means of seduction have a negative connotation in so far as they are considered to be deceptive. In the same way as Hermes deceives Apollo in the story narrated in the *Hymn to Hermes*, seductive words contribute to the ἀπάτη of the man who is going to fall for Pandora, who represents woman as a species.[30] Hesiod's preference for Hermes instead of Peitho as bestower of persuasive speech in an amatory context may be due to his intention to equip the woman with the god's specific characteristics, since he is associated with trickery and deception.[31]

In contrast to Hesiod's *Works&Days*, neither the *Iliad,* the *Odyssey,* nor the *Homeric Hymns* feature Peitho as a personified deity. Although she is never mentioned, the power of persuasive words as a means of seduction is not irrelevant in the erotic mythological contexts. In *Il.* 6,160-2, Glaucus describes Anteia's failure to seduce Bellerophon with the expression that she could "not persuade" or "win him over" "The wife of Proetus, divine Anteia, madly desired to lie in secret love with him; but she could not persuade the wise Bellerophon, since he was of an upright mind":[32]

> τῶι δὲ γυνὴ Προίτου ἐπεμήνατο, δῖ' Ἄντεια,
> κρυπταδίηι φιλότητι μιγήμεναι· ἀλλὰ τὸν οὔ τι
> πεῖθ' ἀγαθὰ φρονέοντα, δαΐφρονα Βελλεροφόντην.

Here the meaning of πείθειν is clearly suggested by the mythical story and thus marks the activity of a woman trying to win over a man with seductive words; ἀγαθὰ φρονέοντα stresses Bellerophon's insensitivity towards these words and thus towards the effects of desire, which normally disturbs the senses. In the *Hymn to Aphrodite*, it is the goddess herself who cannot persuade and "deceive" the three goddesses Athena, Artemis and Hestia to give in to love in general, i.e. to Aphrodite's province of the ἔργα γάμοιο, to which seductive and persuasive words normally belong.[33] As we have seen earlier, these are among the erotic spells kept in her κεστὸς ἱμάς (*Il.* 14,216f.):

> ἔνθ' ἔνι μὲν φιλότης, ἐν δ' ἵμερος, ἐν δ' ὀαριστύς
> πάρφασις, ἥ τ' ἔκλεψε νόον πύκα περ φρονεόντων.

ὀαριστύς and πάρφασις are slightly different in meaning, both denoting a means of seduction, a preliminary step towards φιλότης. ὀαριστύς has been translated as "alluring love-talk" or "whispered endearment".[34] As a derivative of ὄαρ ("wife"), it suggests a familiar love conversation between partners who have known each other for a long time. Whereas the verb ὀαρίζειν is normally used for conversation between husband and wife, the use of the more frequent term ὄαρος suggests that ὀαριστύς may not be limited to just marital relationships.[35] παρθενίους ὀάρους ("of unmarried girls") are among Aphrodite's τιμαί in Hesiod (*Theog.* 205f.) and, together with μειδήματα ("smiles") and ἐξαπάτας ("deceiving"), they form the arsenal of devices employed by women when seducing a man. That those ὄαροι are closely associated with Aphrodite as something caused by her is also implied in the *Homeric Hymn* when she complains that now, after her affair with a mortal, she will lose all respect of the gods who once were frightened of her "seductive love-talks and plans" (ὀάρους καὶ μήτιας *Hymn. Hom.* V,249).[36]

The unusual asyndetic link of ὀαριστύς and πάρφασις could either be an intended hendiadys or the result of a gloss.[37] If the combination of terms is original, πάρφασις adds a persuasive note to ὀαριστύς.[38] It may go one step further, suggesting the idea that the seducer actually persuades somebody to have a sexual adventure. Therefore the expressions are less likely to signify a later stage of an erotic encounter, a "love-whispering" accompanying the consummation of love itself.[39] Theocritus' *Idyll* 27 which is entitled ΩΑΡΙΣΤΥΣ ends with a seduction scene. It is a dialogue of sorts in which the cowherd Daphnis successfully persuades a shepherdess to grant him her favours.[40]

The terms discussed above may be regarded as synonyms of πειθώ. The concept that "persuasion" or "seductive words" are regarded as something which leads to the fulfilment of love is reflected in Pindaric imagery where Peitho is personified, holding the "secret keys to holy love" (Pind. *Pyth.* 9,39f.):

> . . .   κρυπταὶ κλαῖδες ἐντὶ σοφᾶς
> Πειθοῦς ἱερᾶν φιλοτάτων.

Thus we may conclude that Peitho is not featured as an erotic personification in early hexameter poetry; consequently, there are no specific myths which associate her with eroticism. As a cult goddess she is venerated already in the Archaic period, but there is no evidence that she performed a specific function in amatory persuasion in cult. Familiar conversation and persuasive words are originally part of Aphrodite's province, as a preparation for sexual fulfilment; this is true from *Works&Days* and the *Iliad* onwards, as has been demonstrated above. Aphrodite was regarded as persuasive through these means, and it would seem, then, that Peitho becomes their subsequent stylisation. Peitho's role as the embodiment of erotic persuasion is a more recent motif, and according to our literary evidence, not fully formed before Sappho, in whose poems Peitho appears as Aphrodite's daughter or attendant.[41]

6.4   PEITHO IN SAPPHO'S POEMS

According to our literary sources, it is Sappho who first puts Peitho in an amatory context and gives her a close relationship to Aphrodite. Yet she appears as a fairly independent deity.[42] The evidence we have suggests that Sappho achieved this by introducing genealogies rather than by actually assigning to her the functions of the love-goddess.[43] We have seen earlier that a common type of personification is to portray a concept as being related to an Olympian deity as a child or attendant (ch. 4.3). Unlike Hypnos' and Thanatos' pedigree, which is unanimously attested in early sources, that of Peitho seems to vary within the work of even a single poetess. One example shows how uncertain and unformed Peitho's nature was at the time of the Archaic poets. Three fragments of Sappho each attest a different origin for Peitho, each time bringing her into a relationship with Aphrodite. In a scholium on Hes. *Op.* 73 we find that Sappho made Peitho the daughter of Aphrodite (39 Pertusi =fr. 200 V.):

> Σαπφὼ δέ φησι τὴν Πειθὼ Ἀφροδίτης θυγατέρα.

This is confirmed by a commentary dating from the 2nd century AD found on a papyrus (P. Oxy. 2293 = Sappho fr. 90a V.):

fr. 1 (a) col. ii 5ss.

εν.[   ]Κυθερήας τρό –
φος[θ]ρέπτη ἐν ἄλλοις
δὲ θυγ[ατέρα (τῆς) Ἀφρο]δίτης εἴρηκε τὴ[ν
Πειθώ·

This comment is interesting in two respects, firstly, as it suggests that there were various genealogies of Peitho, secondly, as it indicates that in more than one she is called Aphrodite's daughter (θυγ[ατέρα). ἐν ἄλλοις is to be interpreted as "elsewhere in her poetry".[44] The idea of Peitho as Aphrodite's nurse (τρόφος) is not common.[45]

It seems, however, very probable that there was another Sapphic version in which Peitho's relationship with Aphrodite was defined. The relevant passage is transmitted in Philodemus' *De pietate* (p. 42 Gomperz) and appears within an account of the different functions in which different poets subordinated minor deities to the Olympians.[46] However, proof that Sappho made Peitho Aphrodite's attendant in one of her poems depends on whether Philodemus' badly preserved text allows (i) the acceptance of attribution to Sappho, which also requires partial restoration of Sappho's name; (ii) the acceptance of the restoration of Peitho's name. I will argue that both are possible.

Σαπ]φὼ{ι} δὲ τὴ[ν Πειθὼ
"χρυσοφάη‹ν›[47] θερ[άπαι–
ν]αν Ἀφροδίτ[ας".

1 Σαπ]– suppl. Gomperz, L.-P. (fort. recte) Σαπ]φὼ{ι} Nauck, Campbell: Σαπ]φῶι Gomperz, Bergk³
–[ν Πειθὼ suppl. Bergk³ : –[ν αὐτὴν Gomperz : –[ν θεὸν Edmonds, Campbell : –[ν Ἥβην Musso (ZPE 22 (1976), 37f.)

The attribution to Sappho, whose name was first supplemented by Th. Gomperz (accepted also by Nauck, Bergk³, Campbell), seems certain because there are no other possibilities, given the transmitted text.[48]

The restoration of Peitho's name, first suggested by Th. Bergk, is more problematic.[49] The main objection against the supplement Πειθώ has been raised by U. v. Wilamowitz, who argued that five letters would exceed the available space ("spatium excedit").[50] The same is true for Th. Gomperz' supplement τὴ[ν αυτὴν].[51] Several editors have therefore supplemented τὴ[ν θεὸν] (Edmonds, Campbell), which would also refer back to the previous lines, in which Hecate is discussed. Hecate's personality and function are well-defined from Hesiod onwards, but, quite apart from the fact that she has no relationship with Aphrodite, she seems particularly inappropriate in the role of her servant.

One may ask whether Iris, who is χρυσόπτερος in the *Iliad* (8,398 = 11,185), would not be a suitable supplement. However, she is not attested as Aphrodite's companion, nor does she appear in the extant fragments of Sappho. O. Musso's suggestion Ἥβην is tempting in view of the textual transmission, since "Hebe" does fit nicely into the space.[52] Yet Hebe does not seem suited to the role as an attendant of Aphrodite. In the *Hymn to Apollo* (*Hymn. Hom.* III,194f.) Aphrodite is said to dance with the Charites, the Horae, Harmonia and Hebe, but these deities are not explicitly called her attendants. Only the Charites occur in other extant poems of Sappho, but in the plural alone, which does not fit here.[53] Hebe does not appear as a companion of Aphrodite in any of the Sapphic fragments, whereas Peitho appears frequently in association with Aphrodite. Apart from the two testimonies quoted above, she is also attested together with Aphrodite in the following papyrus fragment (*P.Berol.* 9722 fol.5=96,26f. V.): "Aphrodite . . . poured nectar from a golden . . . (far from the boundaries?) . . . with her hands Peitho".

καὶ δ[.]μ[	]ος Ἀφροδίτα
καμ[	] νέκταρ ἔχευ' ἀπὺ
χρυσίας [	]ναν
. . . (.)]απουρ[	]χέρσι Πείθω.

Antipater of Sidon posits an association of Peitho with Aphrodite (and Eros) in his epitaph on Sappho in which Peitho is said to have woven the undying wreath of song with the poetess. This epitaph may also be taken as a testimony that Peitho was not only among the deities who most frequently appear in Sappho's poetry, but even had a particular role in making her songs immortal.[54]

moreover, her name fits as neatly as Hebe's into the available space if spelt with the iotacism Πιθώ (ι for ει) common in this papyrus.[55] Given Sappho's poetic mythologization of concepts into the love deities, Aphrodite and her attendants, preference may therefore be given to Peitho, who elsewhere fulfils the role of an attendant in representing one aspect of Aphrodite.

The supplement θερ[άπαιν]αν,[56] which has been accepted by all editors, appears to be the only one possible, although θεράπαινα is attested only in prose.[57] It is the term θεράπνη which occurs as early as the *Hymn to Apollo* (*Hymn. Hom.* III,157) and could therefore more reasonably be expected to appear in the Sapphic text. In the hymn, θεράπνη refers, however, to Apollo's human "handmaids": the girls of Delos who worship the god (κοῦραι Δηλιάδες, Ἑκατηβελέταο θεράπναι).[58] But the context in which Philodemus cites the text excludes the possibility of a human attendant and the epithet χρυσοφάης suggests instead the name of a divinity.

Therefore it seems very likely that in Sappho, θεράπαινα characterizes the relationship of a personification with an Olympian deity. This is, aside from genealogies, another mode of qualifying and expressing the relationship between Aphrodite and her train.

There are two instances which corroborate the assumption that a divine θεράπαινα is meant in the fragment and that it was Peitho to whom Sappho gave the role of Aphrodite's attendant. Another, albeit male, erotic personification functions as Aphrodite's servant (θεράπων): Eros—according to the testimony of Maximus of Tyre (18.9 (232 Hobein) = fr. 159 V.):

λέγει που καὶ Σαπφοῖ ἡ Ἀφροδίτη ἐν ᾄσματι·

σύ τε κἄμος θεράπων Ἔρος.

The preference for Peitho as a θεράπαινα of Aphrodite in fr. inc. 23 V. is also recommended by the preserved adjective χρυσοφάης ("gold-shining"). E.-M. Voigt notes only one similar passage in which χρυσοφάης occurs, and there it is an epithet of Eros (Eur. *Hipp.* 1274f.).[59] The attribution of χρυσοφάης to a personification seems to be justifiable, since in this form it is never applied to Olympian deities, although other compounds with χρυσ– are frequent, particularly as epithets of Aphrodite.[60] They normally signalize that a concrete part of the body or a particular garment or ornament is golden, whereas χρυσοφάης ("gold-shining") is more general. Poets frequently use compounds of "golden" to describe Aphrodite in her epiphanies. Golden cult-statues may be a reflection of this or vice-versa. The "gold-shining attendant" may be a subsequent poetic stylisation of the idea that other (personified) deities in the entourage of golden Aphrodite appear in her radiance and thus shine themselves. In Euripides' *Hippolytus*, Eros too is depicted in Aphrodite's company: "you carry along the unyielding hearts of gods and men, Cypris, and with you is the bright-winged one, encompassing them with swift wing. He flies over the earth and the resounding salt sea. Winged and gold-shining, Eros bewitches those on whose frenzied heart he darts" (1268-75):

σὺ τὰν θεῶν ἄκαμπτον φρένα καί βροτῶν
    ἄγεις, Κύπρι, σὺν δ'
ὁ ποικιλόπτερος ἀμφιβαλὼν
    ὠκυτάτωι πτερῶι·
ποτᾶται δὲ γαῖαν εὐάχητόν θ'
    ἁλμυρὸν ἐπὶ πόντον.
θέλγει δ' Ἔρως, ᾧ μαινομένᾳ κραδίᾳ
    πτανὸς ἐφορμάσῃ χρυσοφαής.

Both Peitho and Eros share the same function in Sappho, being θεράπαινα or θεράπων of Aphrodite; moreover, the epithet χρυσοφάης is common to both in poetry: if we accept that Peitho is the right supplement in fr. inc. 23 V., then she is χρυσοφάης in Sappho, as is Eros in *Hippolytus*.

However, Eros' association with golden color is attested as early as Anacreon, in a poem where Eros is imagined flying past the poet with "gold-shining wings" (χρυσοφαέννων πτερύγων).[61] Perhaps it is Eros' wings in particular with which the golden color is associated, since in Aristophanes (*Av.* 1738) Eros is likewise χρυσόπτερος ("with golden wings"). The image of the winged Eros may also be indicated in Sappho fr. 54 V. when Eros, in a purple cloak, is coming down from Heaven: (Ἔρωτα) ἔλθοντ᾽ ἐξ ὀράνω πορφυρίαν περθέμενον χλάμυν.[62] Thus it does seem possible after all that χρυσοφάης refers to the golden color of wings. One may argue that it was originally an epithet of Eros and that it was transferred to Peitho as soon as she was imagined as sharing with him the function of an attendant.[63] If this is the case, then Hecate would be an even less likely restoration in fr. inc. 23 V., since golden wings are never associated with her. Iris is already χρυσόπτερος in the *Iliad*, and her name would fit into the space, but her accustomed mythical image as Zeus' messenger-goddess does not quite fit with the role of attendant to the love-goddess.[64]

Thus we can infer from Sappho's extant fragments that Peitho as a personified deity is featured in the environment of Aphrodite: either as her daughter or her attendant.[65]

6.5   PEITHO IN PINDAR'S 4TH *PYTHIAN ODE*

We have seen earlier that in Pindar's 9th *Pythian Ode* (39f.), Peitho embodies persuasion as a preliminary stage to the consummation of love. Elsewhere, Pindar presents Peitho in a role which is characterized by violence and compulsion. In the 4th *Pythian Ode* (213-9), she is linked with Aphrodite, but in contrast to her appearances in epic, she is not presented in association with "seducing words", ὀαριστύς, πάρφασις and αἱμύλιοι λόγοι, i.e. with means by which female charm wins over a man.

Peitho's specific significance and function in this ode is due to the particular role of Aphrodite. The goddess's function as a matchmaker is a traditional element in the story.[66] It is, however, unique in literature that she is presented as the inventor of erotic magical practices: she is the πρῶτος εὑρετής of the *iynx*, a device for producing erotic charms, and of "prayers and incantations", which Jason is the first to learn from her in order to win Medea's love. I suggest in what follows that Peitho's function in *Pythian* 4 is due to the personality and skills of the particular woman who in this case has to be won (i.e. Medea). Simple seductive words uttered by a man are not enough to conquer a prophetess who is a "wise woman" herself, particularly specialized in words and acquainted with magical charms. Pindar calls her a παμφάρμακος ξείνα (233), a foreign woman who is experienced in φάρμακα and the like, but she is not primarily depicted as a magician or witch, a φαρμακευτρία like Simaetha in Theocritus (*Id.* 2).[67] It seems that it is her superhuman nature which attracts Jason to her, since his life is dependant on her particular skills. But the point is that his rhetorical skills are probably not sufficient to win her over. A special type of persuasion (i.e. magical spells) is necessary for Medea, the prophetess, to be overpowered by her own weapons.

It is for this reason that Aphrodite endows Jason with equal skills in magic. The device which she provides, the *iynx*, is comparable to her own accessory, the κεστὸς ἱμάς, through which her power becomes effective and replaces her presence in the *Dios Apate*. Peitho is not exactly linked as closely with the effective device itself as are ὀαριστύς and πάρφασις with Aphrodite's κεστὸς ἱμάς, but she is given a special meaning in this context as she embodies the divine magical spells taught to Jason by Aphrodite. "The Cyprus-born mistress of the sharpest arrows brought from Olympus for the first time to men the many-coloured wryneck, bound to the inescapable four-spoked wheel, that bird of madness; and she taught the clever son of Aison prayers and charms, so that he might take away Medea's respect for her parents and so that the longed for Hellas might drive her who was already burning in her heart with the whip of Peitho":

> πότ'νια δ' ὀξυτάτων βελέων
> ποικίλαν ἴϋγγα τετ'ράκ'ναμον Οὐλυμπόθεν
> ἐν ἀλύτῳ ζεύξαισα κύκ'λῳ
> μαινάδ' ὄρνιν Κυπ'ρογένεια φέρεν
> πρῶτον ἀνθρώποισι, λιτάς τ' ἐπαοιδὰς
> ἐκδιδάσκησεν σοφὸν Αἰσονίδαν·
> ὄφ'ρα Μηδείας τοκέων ἀφέλοιτ' αἰ-
> δῶ, ποθεινὰ δ' Ἑλλὰς αὐτάν
> ἐν φρασί καιομέναν δονέοι μάστιγι Πειθοῦς.   (*Pyth.* 4,213-9)

The meaning and function of the device and its desired effect on Medea, as well as the prayers and incantations in the Pindaric myth show features of erotic magical practices. As we have seen in the previous chapters (see especially ch. 4), love spells are attested in epigraphy as early as the inscription on "Nestor's cup". In literature, they occur first in the *Iliad* where they are related to Aphrodite's sphere of influence. It is later in Alcman fr. 1,73 *PMGF* that the woman called Ainesimbrota is represented as a mistress of love-magic.[68] Given the conservative nature of magical practices in general, it may well be that Pindar, when introducing the *iynx* into literature, refers to current practice.[69] C. Faraone argues that Pindar's description of the *iynx* spell reflects the use of *agoge* spells in Classical Greece, which "drive" the woman from the house of her father right into the arms of the man performing the spell. Although the preserved later spells transmitted in the Greek magical papyri may go back to an Eastern tradition earlier than Pindar, the following examples are mentioned here only for the sake of comparison.[70]

The *iynx* spell existed as a form of curse in which a sacrificial bird is bound to a wheel. The bird normally used for this magical practice has been identified as a wryneck since it is, as in Pindar, associated with madness (μαινάδ' ὄρνιν) and sex drive and therefore considered appropriate for erotic magic. The bird is imagined to evoke its own characteristics in the victims, and this is the aim of the spell: the victim is to be "vexed", i.e. the person desired is to be made "mad with love".[71] There are clear indications of torture and physical violence in Pindar's mythical account, mirroring the purpose of the erotic spells described. This is indicated by the imagery of Medea "burning" (καιομέναν 219) and "agitated by the whip of Peitho" (δονέοι μάστιγι Πειθοῦς 219). Therefore the effect of the *iynx* is likely to be related to the brutal physical torments of love, an effect paralleled in the torment of the bird vexed on the wheel.[72] A different interpretation has been suggested by S. Johnston. She considers the *iynx* a device primarily associated with sound and voice. Her source is Philostratus (*Vita Apollonii* 1,25), who mentions four ἴυγγες in a temple which are said to have been referred to as tongues of gods and "could be interpreted as divine voices." Thus her next step is to connect the *iynx* with Peitho, arguing that the orders uttered by the "divine voices" produced by the *iynges* are hard to resist for human beings.[73]

Considering the element of torture which is indicated by Medea's sufferings and, as C. Faraone has shown, seems to be primarily related to the magical device, the additional association with Peitho is problematic. I would suggest that Peitho is not to be related to the device, the *iynx* itself, but instead to the "prayers and incantations" which Aphrodite taught Jason and which cause Medea's torments as symbolized by the *iynx*, the suffering bird knotted on the wheel. The earliest evidence to confirm that Aphrodite is considered the authority in love-magic is the spell on "Nestor's cup" which is meant to induce erotic seizure; it is her ἵμερος which is supposed to overcome the user of the vessel. The notion of a sort of violence is indicated, since the drinker will be conquered by "desire" even against his will. In the mythical context of *Pythian* 4, Aphrodite is, in a sense, in charge of erotic magical spells, words which are represented by Peitho; therefore they are of a divine nature here. Being very different from αἱμύλιοι λόγοι, ὀαριστύς and πάρφασις, the seductive words which feature in Hesiod and Homer, Peitho represents here a particularly compulsive and violent aspect of Aphrodite's power which is symbolized by her whip. Violence in the workings of the goddess of love also may be felt in, for instance, the way she forces Helen to go to Paris in *Iliad* 3.

It is, however, not only for the sake of rounding off the erotic imagery that Pindar equips Peitho with a whip: whips also appear in erotic spells.[74] But to take μάστιξ in the concrete sense as a proper whip also seems justified by the image of Hellas "driving" (δονέοι) Medea "about" with it (towards Hellas): δονεῖν has this concrete meaning also in *Od.* 22,300 where it is the gadfly driving the cattle mad. Of course, the image also has an erotic connotation, as in Sappho fr. 130 V., where it is Eros who "drives about" his victim.[75] However, considering that Medea is said to be already "burning" (219), it means instead that the goal of the incantations is not to arouse Medea's desire, but that she should be "driven" towards Hellas, the home of her future husband.[76]

What is the meaning of Peitho in this context? I suggest that in the mythic imagery Peitho is perceived as quite individual and personified, since she is holding a whip which, being a means of beating and castigating, associates her with principles of force which characterize violent "persuasion".[77] This seems to exclude the possibility that Jason is to win Medea over merely with seductive, persuasive words. Thus Peitho stands for those "prayers and incantations" which Aphrodite taught Jason. It is in this way that the association of the goddess of love and Peitho becomes manifest; but they are by no means identical.[78] I would not, then, see the *iynx* as a tool of Peitho, but instead an accessory of Aphrodite functioning as a medium through which, or through whose movement, the contents of the incantations become effective.[79] This effect is depicted in the image of Peitho castigating Medea with the whip. The λιταὶ καὶ ἐπαοιδαί associated with Peitho are magical spells which force the victim to comply with another person's wishes.[80] The most famous literary depiction to illustrate the effect of erotic spells is Theocritus' 2nd idyll, in which Simaetha performs rituals and spells to win her lover back. Similarly, in *Pythian* 4, the loving Jason does not address Medea herself and ask her for her love, but instead he performs the magical incantations, probably by turning Aphrodite's device, the *iynx*, which functions as a medium between him and his beloved, as does perhaps the κεστὸς ἱμάς between Hera and Zeus. Being related to words of a magical nature, Peitho has a specific realm.

It is indeed remarkable that Jason and Medea never seem to speak to each other although they are both presented as skilled orators throughout the ode: Jason delivers two long speeches, first a reply to Pelias' questions directed towards the citizens (101-19), and secondly one addressed to Pelias (138-55). Another speech (to uncles and cousins) is referred to as λόγοι μειλίχιοι (128), which shows that he can also command a softer mode of speech. He ought, therefore, also to have been able to find a tone appropriate for seducing Medea: ὀαριστύς, πάρφασις, λόγοι μειλίχιοι, and the like. Jason's rhetorical skills are also referred to when he is called σοφός.[81] At the same time it is implied that this is not enough to seduce Medea, otherwise Aphrodite would not have to teach him. Medea is also distinguished in skills which are related to words, but they are different from Jason's. At the beginning of the ode, she is introduced not as a witch or magician delivering magical speeches, but as a prophetess. The prophecy (13-56) which the inspired daughter of Aietes is breathing out from her immortal mouth is going to be fulfilled; her words are referred to as coming from an immortal mouth: the term ἀπέπνευσε even associates her with the Muses. "And the word spoken by Medea . . . which the mighty daughter of Aietes had once breathed forth from her immortal mouth, the queen of the Kolchians" (9-12):[82]

καὶ τὸ Μηδείας ἔπος (…)
(…)
          Αἰήτα τό ποτε ζαμενής

παῖς ἀπέπ'νευσ' ἀθανάτου στόματος, δέσ-
ποινα Κόλχων.   (9-12)

It seems that Medea's wisdom and rhetorical skills are given more emphasis than her knowledge of magic, which is referred to in terms that could also imply medicine.[83] I would suggest, then, that the introduction of the *iynx* and incantations by Aphrodite is not due to the fact that Medea is a witch or magician herself—this aspect of Medea's skills is not particularly emphasized in Pindar.[84] I think that the emphasis on λιταί and ἐπαοιδαί, which is also confirmed by their association with Peitho, the goddess of persuasion, implies that Medea cannot simply be won over by Jason's word, although his rhetorical excellence is pointed out many times. As a wise and eloquent prophetess she is superior to him, and divine instructions and "words" are needed to persuade her. It is true that the magical means by which she is finally conquered are somehow related to the skills which make her a physician rather than a magician. Pindar did not want to present Medea as a witch who had to be won by magical spells. He presented her as a clever, eloquent prophetess who could not simply be taken in by a man's words—without the help of incantations which Jason learnt from Aphrodite, and of the goddess who represents this aspect of Aphrodite, Peitho.

The desired result that Medea will lose her reverence for her parents and leave them (ὄφ'ρα Μηδείας τοκέων ἀφέλοιτ' αἰ- / δῶ) corresponds to the goal of *agoge* spells. They are represented in an erotic incantation in which the performer wishes that the desired woman will abandon her husband and child and come and stay with him, as a sign that his love is going to be fulfilled.[85] We find this motif also in mythical contexts. Sappho fr. 16 V. describes Helen's situation after giving in to her love for Paris in a similar way: she left her husband, child and parents.[86] It was Aphrodite who caused all of this. In *Od.* 4,261-64 Helen accuses Aphrodite of having affected her with ἄτη, which had the same effect.

In Pindar, Medea loses reverence for her parents in two ways. The idea that Greece, the country she is longing to go to (ποθεινὰ δ' Ἑλλάς), is agitating her implies that she is going to abandon her parents physically by following Jason to Hellas. In the case of Medea, however, there is another implication, as the aim is to make her not just leave, but actually betray her parents by helping Jason with drugs she specializes in herself so that he can overcome his tasks. It is also the purpose of the spell, symbolized by the μάστιξ Πειθοῦς, not just to arouse Medea's desire, but to remove with violence this last obstacle, the reverence for her parents. Lines 218ff. imply that Medea is already in love with Jason. Greece is already the object of her desire (ποθεινά), and the present form of the participle καιομέναν suggests that she is "already burning in her heart".[87] If it were the main purpose of Peitho to set her on fire, one would expect instead a future participle.

It seems, then, that in *Pythian* 4 it is the man who tries to win over the woman not with seductive words, but through the medium of a violent love spell, whose origins go back to the love-goddess. In the epic passages discussed above, however, it was the woman who used words as a means of seduction. This clearly shows that there is no fixed pattern for Peitho as the embodiment of persuasion whereby man persuades woman or the other way round. As in the *Dios Apate*, where Aphrodite's power becomes effective through the medium of the κεστὸς ἱμάς which she gives to Hera, it is activated through the *iynx* and incantations which she gives to Jason in Pindar's *Pythian* 4. Both Hera and Jason are now able to win over their beloved. In both cases love is not the real aim, but just a means by which the actual purpose is achieved: it is Hera's aim to deceive Zeus, and Jason wants Medea's help in order to fulfil his tasks and save his own life.

6.6   PEITHO'S SERVANTS IN PINDAR FR. 122

An interesting aspect of the relationship between Aphrodite and Peitho occurs in one of Pindar's fragments: Xenophon of Corinth, on the occasion of his victory at the Olympics in 464 BC, commissioned from Pindar not only an epinikion, but also a drinking-song, a *skolion*.[88] Together with the context in which it was performed, it is given in Athenaeus (13,573E-574B). Xenophon had "led" or "brought" a hundred-limbed herd of women to the precinct of Aphrodite in gladness at the fulfillment of his prayers for victory:[89]

> ὦ Κύπρου δέσποινα, τεὸν δεῦτ᾽ ἐς ἄλσος
> φορβάδων κορᾶν ἀγέλαν ἑκατόγγυι–
>   ον Ξενοφῶν τελέαις
> ἐπάγαγ᾽ εὐχωλαῖς ἰανθείς.   17-20

Athenaeus' account, in conjunction with earlier evidence, has been taken as proof that ritual temple prostitution existed at the Corinthian sanctuary of Aphrodite to whom Xenophon allegedly promised the women as sacred prostitutes. But Athenaeus only speaks in his account about invited *hetairai*, and there is no indication of an institutionalized dedication of the women to Aphrodite.[90] The only literary source to refer to the *hetairai* as *hierodouloi* in this context and thus to imply sacred prostitution is Strabo, but this is not confirmed by any other source, e.g. epigraphical evidence.[91] Considering the peculiarity of the alleged phenomenon of cultic prostitution, it is indeed surprising that neither Athenaeus nor Herodotus, when mentioning sacred prostitution in the Orient, refer to this phenomenon at Corinth. While some scholars take Pindar's *skolion* together with the passage in Strabo as proof that sacred prostitution was practiced in Corinth,[92] others deny that the type of institutionalized sacred prostitution which existed in the Near East ever existed in Greece.[93] Those in defence of sacred prostitution base their argument mainly on Meineke's emendation ἀπάγειν (20), "lead", which is then interpreted as a "ritual term" that can indicate a dedication.[94] Pindar's text as it is transmitted by the mss. does not give any indication at all whether the women are *hetairai*, sacred or non-sacred prostitutes, since he uses completely neutral terms such as ἀμφίπολοι Πειθοῦς, νεάνιδες, παῖδες, γυναῖκες, κόραι, but never πορναί, ἱεροδοῦλοι or ἑταίραι. "Young women, visited by many guests, servants of Peitho in rich Corinth, you who burn the golden tears of the pale frankincense tree, often fluttering in your thoughts to Aphrodite, the heavenly mother of desires, to you, o children, she has brought about to pluck without blame the fruit of soft youth in lovely beds. Under compulsion, everything is fair":

> Πολύξεναι νεάνιδες, ἀμφίπολοι
> Πειθοῦς ἐν ἀφνειῷ Κορίνθῳ,
> αἵ τε τᾶς χλωρᾶς λιβάνου ξανθὰ δάκρη
> θυμιᾶτε, πολλάκι ματέρ' ἐρώτων
>   οὐρανίαν πτάμεναι
> νοήματι πρὸς Ἀφροδίταν,   5
> ὑμῖν ἄνευθ' ἐπαγορίας ἔπορεν,
> ὦ παῖδες, ἐρατειναῖς <ἐν> εὐναῖς
> μαλθακᾶς ὥρας ἀπὸ καρπὸν δρέπεσθαι.
> σὺν δ' ἀνάγκᾳ πᾶν καλόν . . .

The context in which Athenaeus cites the fragment suggests that the celebrations of the victory consisted of two phases: firstly, there were ritual sacrifices in honor of Aphrodite in her sanctuary, in which the *hetairai* participated together with Xenophon.[95] *Olympian* 13 may have been performed during this part of the ceremony. The last stanza cited earlier includes an address to Aphrodite and must refer back to this ceremony. When Xenophon led them to Aphrodite's precinct this does not mean that he in some sense "dedicated" them to the goddess: *hetairai* were a specific group of worshippers of Aphrodite with a particular role, and therefore the sort of sacrifice performed by Xenophon made their presence and participation necessary.[96]

According to the context described by Athenaeus, the *skolion* itself was sung not during the cultic celebrations in the sanctuary of Aphrodite, but afterwards, most likely in the second phase of the celebrations, a feast or dinner party. This is indicated by the genre of the fragment which describes itself as a *skolion*, a drinking song of the kind that was usually performed after dinner.[97] Presumably it was sung during offerings that were made by the same *hetairai* who had performed sacrifices together with Xenophon earlier and are addressed in lines 3-4: "you women who burn the golden tears of the pale frankincense tree".[98]

Apart from the implications of the literary genre there is another indication which corroborates the assumption that the *skolion* was performed during a dinner party: no commentator has pointed out and discussed the odd nature of the first lines of the *skolion*, which address the women, whom Athenaeus refers to as *hetairai*, with the words: πολύξεναι νεάνιδες, ἀμφίπολοι Πειθοῦς ἐν ἀφνείῳ Κορίνθῳ. Why are they called "servants of Peitho, visited by many guests" and not "servants of Aphrodite", although she is the goddess in whose service the young women had, according to the *skolion*, made the sacrifices in the temple?

The switch of deities could indicate that the *skolion* was performed in a different context and thus marks the transition from the cultic to the symposiastic sphere. Peitho cannot simply substitute for Aphrodite in a cultic context, but is a goddess who is at home at dinner parties and symposia. The introduction of one of Aphrodite's attendants, Peitho, can be related to the role which the *hetairai* play at the symposium. Thus the address to Peitho need not be based on a cultic background, but may be a poetic stylisation of the activity of the *hetairai* at the symposium. This is supported by lines 1-9: while they are performing the offering, they often flutter in thought to the 'heavenly mother of desires', Aphrodite, who here embodies sexual fulfilment, as lines 7-8 suggest. It is the job of the *hetairai* at the symposium to provide this for the guests and πολύξεναι "visited by many" can be read in the sense of professional secular prostitution and need not be related to sacred prostitution. When the women are called "servants of Peitho", this could well refer to their activity during a symposium where they seduce men by words, and, as line 6 suggests, they are successful at doing that: Aphrodite herself has granted sexual pleasure to them without the possibility of blame (ὑμῖν ἄνευθ᾽ ἐπαγορίας ἔπορεν). Here Peitho is not linked with magical spells but simply embodies seductive words of the type we find in Aphrodite's κεστὸς ἱμάς.

In this context it is interesting that much later epigraphical evidence from Olynthus in Chalkidike establishes an indirect relationship between *hetairai* and Peitho in cult. From an inscription which has been dated between the 2nd-1st century BC we discover that Peitho was offered a votive statue from the committee of the *agoranomoi* at Olynthus.[99] According to *Suda* I 528 (2,54,4 Adler), they were responsible for fixing the price of how much a *hetaira* "is allowed to take".[100] It seems that the function of the *agoranomoi* was similar to that of the *astynomoi* at Athens and Piraeus, which has been discussed earlier (see ch. 2). Perhaps the *agoranomoi* received a share of the *hetairais'* earnings which they used for the dedication.[101] Of course, this inscription cannot provide evidence of cultic veneration of Peitho in Corinth.

It cannot be mere coincidence when Peitho, as an embodiment of erotic persuasion, becomes important in certain literary genres and in the places where they are usually performed. The personified Peitho hardly appears in early hexameter poetry, but suddenly arises in the poems of Sappho, which may well have been performed at festivals and symposia, occasions which lend themselves to flirtation and seduction.[102] The *skolia* too were performed at such venues. Maybe one can also see here that the occasion or event for which a poem is written influences the poets' creativity in the inventing and styling of personified deities. The *hetairai* are called ἀμφίπολοι Πειθοῦς in Pindar fr. 122 M. since they are meant to persuade their male customers. Thus Peitho is associated here with the power of seduction, which is supposed to lead to sexual intercourse. But Peitho, as shown by the example of *Pythian* 4,213f., can also be linked with persuasion, the attempt made by the lover to remove obstacles which hinder the satisfaction of his or her desire.[103]

6.7   CONCLUSION

The comparison of cultic and literary evidence has shown that the goddess Peitho also has her own history. Although a relatively old cult goddess, she seems, by comparison with the Charites, to have had little individualized, anthropomorphic personality. Some of her early genealogies suggest that she originally had nothing to do with erotic persuasion, a fact which is also confirmed by Hesiod and Homer, who do not call the means of erotic persuasion "Peitho", but use other terms to express this particular aspect of Aphrodite. In *Works&Days*, expertise in seductive words is instead the task of another god, Hermes. It was Sappho, who by making Peitho the daughter and attendant of Aphrodite, explicitly associated her with erotic persuasion. This clearly signals a subordination to the Olympian goddess of love, and one would not consider Peitho simply a "divinity whose province was the alluring power of sexual love."[104] As a part of Aphrodite, she serves to bring lovers together, i.e. towards the love-goddess's actual domain, the consummation of love. Thus in her relationship with Aphrodite, Peitho certainly experiences a restriction of her power, a fact reflected in cult associations where she represents a particular aspect of Aphrodite. It is no coincidence that Peitho emerges as the deity of seductive words and persuasion in the context of symposiastic poetry, which the examples in Sappho and Pindar show. The poets seem to have created and stylized the love-goddess Peitho according to the occasion of performance. Seduction and flirting belong to drinking parties and symposiastic encounters.

Chapter Seven
The Origins of Eros

7.1   INTRODUCTION

Among Aphrodite's companions, Eros is the only personification who is finally credited with the role of a fully individualized god by the poets. This tendency is recognizable in our literary evidence in individual attempts to mythologize a male love-god, yet it will not be completely developed before Apollonius Rhodius. Although subordinated to Aphrodite as attendant or, later, as son, he is the only one to compete with her over what is traditionally her sphere of interest. This is surprising since apart from the *Theogony*, to our knowledge, none of the early literary works (*Iliad, Works&Days, Odyssey,* the *Homeric Hymns* or the fragments preserved from the *Epic Cycle*) features a personified god of love, whereas other erotic and also non-erotic personifications (the Charites, Peitho, Hypnos, Thanatos, Dike &c.) appear in these epics and hymns from the Archaic period.

    Bearing this in mind, I will argue that Eros' appearance in the *Theogony* was determined by the cosmogonic genre—at least as far as we can tell from extant literature. This may be the reason why he is different from the other personifications associated with Aphrodite and why he is after all, as a proper mythological figure, a latecomer among the deities concerned with love. We have seen in earlier chapters that the mythical role not only of the Olympian Aphrodite, but also that of the Charites or Peitho is related to its meaning and function in cult. It seems that the earlier and more securely cultic veneration of a personified deity is attested, the more clearly defined he or she appears to be in early hexamter poetry. Is the main difference between Eros and his companions and Aphrodite the fact that he is not originally a cult god? And, is this also the reason why the formation of his full personality is a later phenomenon? The present chapter sets out the origins and components that contributed to and shaped the figure of Eros. The complexity of Eros' identity is reflected in the variety of genealogies which provide a basis for examining the various versions of his origins.[1]

It has often been considered remarkable that Eros appears as a personification performing a prominent role among the primeval entities in the context of a cosmogonic poem—the *Theogony*—but is not endowed with any attribute which could imply the image of a personified god elsewhere in extant epics or the *Homeric Hymns*: ἔρως is just the impulse of desire. I argue that the absence of Eros here is due to the fact that, originally, he was neither an established figure with his own myth nor did he have any cults at that stage in Greece. Pausanias' frequently cited testimony (9,27,1) cannot, as will be shown, prove that the god's cult at Thespiae in Boeotia was an ancient one. Therefore Hesiod need not have drawn on cultic experience and myths related to it when representing the god, but may instead have been influenced by the tradition of another kind of mythic source: that which is concerned with cosmological speculation. Several cosmic concepts, as for example a Phoenician cosmogony or the so-called Orphic poems, set "desire" (ἔρως, πόθος) among the very first standard primeval entities.[2]

In what follows I will argue that Hesiod, aware of cosmogonic traditions, attributed to Eros his prominent role in the cosmic context of his *Theogony*, and in so doing outlined the decisive characteristics of the image of Eros in Greek culture in general. In comparison with the other primeval entities, the amorphous Chaos and Earth, Eros is considerably more clearly defined by his "Olympian looks" and functions, which actually do not seem to fit his position as they are related to the love affair of human beings and anthropomorphic gods. This characterization, together with his second appearance as Aphrodite's companion, has provoked the question in scholarship as to whether Hesiod could have combined two different, already existing traditions of Eros: that of the cosmic deity and that of the love-god. We will see that Eros as presented in the *Theogony*, seems to be—as far as we can tell from extant literature—Hesiod's own creation as inspired by the exigencies of the cosmogonic genre. In spite of this context, however, some of the god's particular features and activities (e.g. his beauty and the way he exerts power over gods and men) do not diverge from the ideas displayed later in lyric and drama. Apart from Hesiod's scheme, there is additionally another significant source which gradually influenced the image of the Greek love-god. Certain features of Eros (alias Phanes or Protogonos) as presented in some versions of the Orphic cosmogonies are reminiscent of images in which poets and artists depict Eros equipped with wings and shining with gold.

I suggest in the final chapter that the Hesiodic epithet κάλλιστος (*Theog.* 120) may allude to another characteristic of Eros, one that is due to the symposiastic context in which lyric poetry was performed. There is clear evidence that the poets praise beautiful youths present at the banquet, the ἐρώμενοι, with whom Eros is identified. However, we cannot tell whether this practice was already taking place in Hesiod's time. It seems that it does not emerge before Anacreon and Ibycus.

7.2 EVIDENCE FOR EROS AS A CULT FIGURE IN THE ARCHAIC AND CLASSICAL PERIOD

Modern scholars have found evidence for cults of Eros throughout Greece, the most famous being that at Thespiae in Boeotia.[3] Although it has been conceded that official worship was rare, Eros is generally thought to have been established as a cult deity in very early times. The main source for the scholars' argument, Pausanias' *Description of Greece* (9,27,1), however, is comparatively late (2nd century AD) and inconsistent with the only two ancient literary testimonies which make reference to cults of Eros. In the hymn to Eros in Euripides' *Hippolytus* (538-40), the chorus complains that the deity whose power and ubiquity they have just praised is not worshipped anywhere. "Eros, however, the tyrant of men, the keyholder of Aphrodite's dearest chambers, we do not worship":

> Ἔρωτα δέ, τὸν τύραννον ἀνδρῶν,
> τὸν τᾶς Ἀφροδίτας
> φιλτάτων θαλάμων κλῃδοῦχον, οὐ σεβίζομεν.

A similar statement is made in Plato's *Symposium* (189c4-8) by Aristophanes, whose motivation for praising Eros in speech is that the god's power has been neglected by mankind, who do not honor him with sanctuaries, altars or sacrifices. "I think that people have wholly failed to realize the power of desire; if they had realized it, they would have built the greatest sanctuaries and altars for him and have made the greatest sacrifices, whereas none of these is done for him now, although he would deserve it most of all":

> ἐμοὶ γὰρ δοκοῦσιν ἄνθρωποι παντάπασι τὴν τοῦ ἔρωτος δύναμιν οὐκ
> ᾐσθῆσθαι, ἐπεὶ αἰσθανόμενοί γε μέγιστ᾽ ἂν αὐτοῦ ἱερὰ κατασκευάσαι
> καὶ βωμούς, καὶ θυσίας ἂν ποιεῖν μεγίστας, οὐχ ὥσπερ νῦν τούτων
> οὐδὲν γίγνεται περὶ αὐτόν, δέον πάντων μάλιστα γίγνεσθαι.

It is in accordance with this lack of cultic veneration that Eros, in contrast to other gods, and in spite of his age and importance, never had any hymns, *paeans* or *encomia* written for him by the poets. "Is it not terrible, Eryximachus, he says, that hymns and *paeans* have been composed to other gods by the poets, but that for Eros, although he is such an ancient and important god, not one of so many poets has ever composed an *encomium*" (177a5-b1):

> οὐ δεινόν, φησίν, ὦ Ἐρυξίμαχε, ἄλλοις μέν τισι θεῶν ὕμνους
> καὶ παίωνας εἶναι ὑπὸ τῶν ποιητῶν πεποιημένους, τῷ δὲ Ἔρωτι,
> τηλικούτῳ ὄντι καὶ τοσούτῳ θεῷ, μηδὲ ἕνα πώποτε τοσούτων
> γεγονότων ποιητῶν πεποιηκέναι μηδὲν ἐγκώμιον;

This statement ignores the hymns addressed to Eros in 5th-century BC tragedy (Sophocles' *Antigone* and Euripides' *Hippolytus*); perhaps they were not thought to be based on tradition and cult, but poetic inventions.[4] The same may be true of the fragment by Alcaeus which has been interpreted as a hymn to Eros.[5]

These testimonies do not seem to have been taken into account by scholars who claim that Eros was an established figure in cult. On the other hand, no commentator of the *Symposium* has ever considered this passage worth discussing under the aspect of cultic evidence. W. Barrett, in his commentary on Euripides' *Hippolytus*, points to the lack of consistency with archaeological evidence at Thespiae and at Athens, where in 1931 O. Broneer discovered a rock-cut shrine of Eros and Aphrodite on the North slope of the Acropolis.[6] Two inscriptions show that Eros and Aphrodite were worshipped there from the mid-5th century BC onwards, with a festival of Eros taking place on the 4th day of the month Mounychion (*IG* I³.1382a and b).[7]

τõι Ἔροτι hε εορτὲ   Ἀφροδ[ί]τ[ες] (b)
τ]ετράδι hισταμέν[ο
Μονιχιõν[ο]ς μεν[ός. (a)

However, it is striking that neither Euripides nor Plato nor any other literary source mention the association of Eros and Aphrodite in this cult or a role for Eros in this festival.[8] Barrett suggests that the passage in Euripides can be explained by the fact that Eros had only fertility cults and that these were considered primitive in comparison with the lavish worship of the Olympian gods. However, I doubt that this can be the reason here, since he is associated with a major Olympian deity, Aphrodite. The silence of the literary sources regarding this Eros cult on the one hand, and on the other the testimony in *Symposium* and *Hippolytus* that there was no Eros cult suggest that this *temenos* was still mainly considered a sanctuary of Aphrodite in the 5th and at the beginning of the 4th century BC and cannot count as an example of independent worship of Eros. It would seem, then, that his role must have been entirely secondary.[9]

How can the inconsistency between epigraphical and literary evidence as documented in Euripides and Plato be explained? The festival of Eros mentioned in *IG* I³.1382 a was celebrated in spring-time (April/March) and marked Aphrodite's birthday. Scholars inferred from the season that Eros must have been worshipped there as donor of vegetation and reproduction.[10] Although the inscription suggests that it was a festival only in honor of Eros and therefore confirms some independence from Aphrodite, it seems likely that Eros did not function as an autonomous deity of reproduction.[11] One might in this case assume that in the cultic sphere he represents an aspect of the Olympian goddess Aphrodite, whose link with fecundity and growth is already documented in the *Theogony* and the *Homeric Hymn*. She shares this characteristic with her Phoenician predecessor. Fasce's view, however, that Eros is a long-established deity of reproduction and fecundity with cultic worship all over Greece has to be reconsidered, since Pausanias is in most cases the earliest, and often only source. His statements on this point are not confirmed by archaeological evidence or earlier writers, and it is therefore doubtful whether they can be really taken as probative of the Archaic period.[12]

It is significant that Eros is related to reproduction and fertility at Athens but does not appear to have been worshipped as a love-god whom lovers invoked in order that he might fulfil their desires. He may of course be already on his way, however, to assuming such a role in literature, as the hymns to Eros in *Antigone* and *Hippolytus* suggest. The function of Eros as a love-god is reflected in cult later, at least in the 4th century, as a lamp from the nearby Kerameikos, bearing a 4th-century BC dedication to Eros, suggests.[13] However, it is surprising that the Hellenistic dedicatory epigrams in the *Greek Anthology* do not provide any evidence that Eros was invoked as a god of love matters in a cultic environment. Images of him are usually gifts for Aphrodite.[14] The statuettes of Eros and Aphrodite which O. Broneer found in the shrine at Athens date from the 3rd century BC.[15] This date also suggests that Eros had only gradually become a personified cult god. One might in this case assume that cultic developments are strongly influenced by the poetic features of Eros as a god involved in private human love matters, as depicted in literature as early as the end of the 6th century BC.

S. Fasce suggested that the official veneration of the god at Athens began with the cult founded by the Pisistratids.[16] Pausanias and Athenaeus both claim that Eros' first altar at Athens was the one founded by an intimate of the Pisistratids in the Academy, but it is questionable whether one can speak of an actual cult. According to Pausanias, there was an altar of Eros at the entrance of the Academy, dedicated by an intimate of the Pisistratids, Charmos, who was, according to the inscription, the first Athenian to dedicate an altar to Eros.[17] The text of the dedication, an elegiac couplet, has been preserved by Athenaeus, who also gives additional information about Charmos (*Anth. Pal. App.* 1,31). He had been the lover of the Pisistratid Hippias as a young man (later tyrant) and for the very first time had an altar for Eros erected near the Academy: "Eros, full of various devices, for you Charmos set up this altar by the shady boundaries of the gymnasium."[18]

ποικιλομήχαν' Ἔρως, σοὶ τόνδ' ἰδρύσατο βωμὸν
Χάρμος ἐπὶ σκιεροῖς τέρμασι γυμνασίου.

Apart from the personal elegiac couplet, we have no surviving epigraphical evidence to confirm that a public, civic cult of Eros could have been set up there. Moreover, the epigrammatic inscription on the altar recalls the style of sympotic poetry: it describes the dedication of the altar as though it were a statue of Eros, i.e. the Eros of the symposium and lyric poetry, not of cult.[19] It is implausible that a public cult of Eros should have been founded on the grounds of a private love affair, whether in the Archaic period or later. Clearly the occasion for the dedication of the altar was a homoerotic one. This is indicated by the foundation stories romanticising the homoerotic love affairs notorious in the family of the Pisistratids.[20]

The second cult place which is mentioned by Barrett in order to confirm that Eros did have cult places in Greece is more interesting: Thespiae in Boeotia. Once again it is Pausanias who refers to it (9,27,1). He says that "the Thespians from the very beginning onwards worshipped Eros above all the gods, and their very ancient cult image was an unworked stone".

θεῶν δὲ οἱ Θεσπιεῖς τιμῶσιν Ἔρωτα μάλιστα ἐξ ἀρχῆς, καί σφισιν ἄγαλμα παλαιότατόν ἐστιν ἀργὸς λίθος.

Although Pausanias concedes that many people consider Eros as the youngest among the gods, the validity of his statement concerning the antiquity of this cult has been widely accepted.[21] Some scholars explained the prominent place of Eros in the *Theogony* with reference to the position which the god held in a local cult during the author's life-time.[22] A. Schachter, however, rejects the possibility of an early dating of the cult and argues that the stone image of Eros might not even have been in existence when Hesiod wrote the *Theogony*.[23] He agrees that the unworked stone seen by Pausanias could have been a cult image, but it need not necessarily have been old. There is in fact good evidence that the creation and veneration of aniconic images is by no means restricted to the Archaic period. Apollo's worship seems to have always been particularly linked with stones, we also know of stone images of Hermes and Dionysos. Passages in Xenophon and Theophrastus suggest that the veneration of stones was performed during their life, but was perceived as a very unusual or even superstitious practice. Perhaps this may account for a revival of primitive cults in later times when they were contrasted with "proper" religious worship of cult images. The introduction of a new cult in 468/7 BC in which a fallen meteorite was worshipped as a cult object is recorded in the *Marmor Parium*.[24] Even if we assume the antiquity of the stone image, the question still remains whether it had always been related to Eros. Pausanias' only source were local informants who claimed that it was. However, we have to bear in mind another possibility: the fact that the image was aniconic may refer to a stage when Eros was not already personified, and thus the assignment of the stone to Eros could be early.

Judging from the lack of sources, both literary (except Pausanias) and epigraphical, A. Schachter even considers the possibility that this cult may not have existed at all. His speculation is supported by the fact that this cult at Thespiae does not appear in hymns: Alcaeus does not mention it in the fragment, which has been interpreted as a hymn to Eros, nor is it referred to in the hymns of *Antigone* or *Hippolytus*. In the latter the chorus even complains about the lack of general cultic veneration, as does Aristophanes in his speech in the *Symposium*. Had Thespiae been one of the cult places of Eros, it would seem astonishing that the literary sources do not hint at it. Furthermore, Eros is absent from the Thespian reliefs which record the deities who were worshipped there in the Archaic and Classical periods:[25] Demeter and Heracles;[26] five figures on a relief (4th century BC) have been interpreted as Dionysos, Heracles, and three Nymphs.[27] We might also have expected an old local cult god, albeit aniconic, to have appeared somehow or other—at least as an epithet of one of the Olympians. It would seem, then, that Eros' absence there is consistent with the lack of earlier literary evidence for his cult at Thespiae.

A. Schachter's idea as to how Thespiae could later have become known as the cult place of Eros is tempting. If we are to believe the anecdotes which come from sources centuries later, it is the personal achievement of the well-known *hetaira* Phryne, who, in the 4th century BC, set up the famous statue of Eros by Praxiteles in her home town Thespiae.[28] Phryne's close association with the Eros cult at Boeotia emerges when we consider that not only the famous statue of Eros, but also a statue of Aphrodite and herself (all by Praxiteles) had been placed in the temple.[29] The close relationship between Thespiae and Praxiteles' Eros is also indicated in the statements of Cicero (*in Verrem* 4,2,4; 4,60,135) and Strabo (9,2,25 [410]), who declare that the only reason visitors came to Thespiae was to see the famous statue by Praxiteles, which was, moreover, praised in numerous Hellenistic epigrams.[30] The erecting of a statue of Eros at Thespiae does not presuppose an established cult of Eros there, since Phryne, being a *hetaira*, will have considered Eros and Aphrodite as the deities to whom she felt most related and to whom she therefore wanted to make a dedication.[31]

But in which context should this cult image of Eros be interpreted? The Praxitelean Eros has, in fact, nothing in common with an ancient god of fecundity. The epigrammatists describe him as a beautiful young man, in the manner of the Archaic poets who praise young men at the symposium. At Thespiae Eros is the companion (rather than son) of Aphrodite, and both share a place with the statue of a mortal who was, according to later anecdotal evidence, the most famous *hetaira* (πολὺ ἐπιφανεστάτη τῶν ἑταιρῶν) of the 4th century BC, renowned for her beauty and her humour.[32] Galen, for example, says that her beauty did not require any make-up.[33] Some of her witty remarks (in symposiastic contexts) are collected in Athenaeus' *Deipnosophistai*.[34] The anecdotes about her life are transmitted in the biographical tradition of her lovers. She was well known for her relationships with artists, Praxiteles in particular, who is said to have chosen her as a model for his Knidian Aphrodite.[35] The lawyer Hyperides, who is also said to have been her lover, defended her when she was accused of *asebeia*.[36] However, it was not because of his speech alone that she was finally acquitted. Apparently, when Hyperides' defence was likely to be unsuccessful, he brought her to court and convinced the judges by uncovering her breasts.[37] The renown of Phryne's beauty forms an essential part of the tradition according to which she let "her body speak" and gave a sight so stunning that the judges were overwhelmed and decided in her favour.[38]

Phryne's particular role as a *hetaira* in the symposiastic culture allows us to identify her dedication, Praxiteles' Eros, with the love-god of banquets and symposia, i.e. who represents the ideal of the handsome young man. If Eros' origins at Thespiae are associated with Phryne's dedication, then it seems justified to assume that Eros ascended from the symposiastic to the sacred sphere there. Formerly, according to our epigraphical evidence, Thespiae had been limited to the Olympian gods.

It is interesting that Pausanias, although emphasizing the antiquity of the cult, says somewhat apologetically that he is unable to give a cult *aition* which could tell us about the origins of the veneration of Eros at this place (9,27,1):

> ὅστις δὲ ὁ καταστησάμενος Θεσπιεῦσιν Ἔρωτα θεῶν σέβεσθαι μάλιστα, οὐκ οἶδα.

This remark suggests that he may have expected the Thespians and their guides to know of one, but apparently they did not. Elsewhere, Pausanias usually records foundation myths of cults discussed.[39]

The absence of a myth narrating the foundation of the cult to which Pausanias himself draws attention, together with the lack of epigraphical evidence, also may suggest Eros' late arrival at Thespiae. Of course, these are only arguments from silence against the assumption that Eros had a long tradition as a cult god there. It would seem, then, that the antiquity of the cult which was claimed by Pausanias' informants probably refers more to the age of the literary source in which Eros played a prominent role for the first time, Hesiod's *Theogony*. An inscription from Thespiae referring to the "Muses of Hesiod" confirms how much Hesiod's name was linked to this place:

> ὅρος τᾶς γᾶς τᾶς [ἰα]ρᾶς τῶν σ[υν]θυτάων τᾶμ Μωσά[ων τῶ]ν Εἰσιοδείων.[40]

7.3 THE MEANINGS OF THE PHENOMENON ἔρως IN EPIC AND EARLY LYRIC POETRY

When modern scholars speak of "Eros", they often refer neither to the love-god nor to the non-personified meanings of the term ἔρως, but to the phenomenon of "Greek love" more generally.[41] Whereas aspects of cult have been frequently discussed in recent scholarship, the examination of the original, literal meanings of ἔρως has been a matter of less interest.[42]

Certain ideas and expressions denoting the effects of desire occur in the Homeric and Hesiodic poems and are common in the *Homeric Hymns* as well.[43] One particular expression referring, however, to the workings of ἵμερος, is documented already in our earliest datable literary medium, the inscription on "Nestor's cup" cited earlier. Variations of this expression and the idea involved occur also e.g. in the *Iliad* and the *Homeric Hymn to Aphrodite*. This suggests that these formulae, together with the concepts they describe, are older than all our extant works and very probably rooted in oral tradition.[44]

I begin with a discussion of the poetic features and formulaic expressions denoting the physical and psychological connotations of the non-personified ἔρως which are commonly used in Homeric and Hesiodic epic and the *Homeric Hymns*. These contexts show how poetic illustrations of ἔρως and their developments became significant in lyric poetry and made a major contribution to the identity of the male love-god who first appears personified in the cosmogonic context of Hesiod's *Theogony*. As it will turn out, Eros' representation there is very peculiar, and as it seems, unique.

Although the non-personified ἔρως is not mentioned among Aphrodite's erotic spells, either in the inscription on "Nestor's cup" or as an element on the goddess's κεστὸς ἱμάς, the term is not entirely absent and appears in various contexts, including the famous love scenes in book 3 and 14 of the *Iliad* and the suitors' scene in book 18 of the *Odyssey*. It is here that we can observe the implications and workings of desire in a mythical context: ἔρως in its erotic sense is a natural physical need which, like hunger or thirst, seeks satisfaction. It has no moral component, but is neutral. I have suggested earlier that the expressions in which the activity and effects of ἔρως are displayed in the *Iliad* can be compared with those of sleep.

Whereas erotic desire occurs only twice (*Il.* 3,441ff. and 14,294) in the *Iliad*, the ἔρως "for food and drink" occurs twenty times, exclusively in the following formulaic verse which is also twice attested in Hesiod (fr. 266a,8 (=266c,1) M.-W.). "But when they had put from them the desire for drink and food":[45]

αὐτὰρ ἐπεὶ πόσιος καὶ ἐδητύος ἐξ ἔρον ἕντο.

Here ἔρως denotes a natural and neutral physical need for food and drink which is "sent out" when it is satisfied ("but when they had rid themselves of their desire for food and drink"). Homer also refers to an ἔρως γόου, a "desire for weeping" or "mourning" (e.g. *Il.* 24,227f.), which is also seen under the aspect of satisfaction of a desire or impulse.[46]

In the erotic sense, however, ἔρως is not exclusively seen under the aspect of having already been satisfied. Instead, the actions which ἔρως performs suggest the immediate influence of sexual desire on the body and mind of Paris and Zeus: no sooner have they spotted the beloved, than they want to have sex with them. In both cases the subject points out that his desire has never been as strong as it is now. In *Iliad* 3, Aphrodite has forced Helen to join Paris in his bedchamber. The presence of the beloved makes Paris encourage her to lie down with him. "But come now. Let us lie down together and enjoy love. For never yet has desire so enfolded my senses—not even when I first snatched you from lovely Lacedaemon and sailed with you on my sea-faring ships, and when we on the island of Cranae were joined in love, sharing the same bed—as I now love you and sweet desire seizes me":

ἀλλ' ἄγε δὴ φιλότητι τραπείομεν εὐνηθέντε·
οὐ γάρ πώ ποτέ μ' ὧδέ γ' ἔρως φρένας ἀμφεκάλυψεν,
οὐδ' ὅτε σε πρῶτον Λακεδαίμονος ἐξ ἐρατεινῆς

ἔπλεον ἁρπάξας ἐν ποντοπόροισι νέεσσιν,
νήσωι δ' ἐν Κραναῆι ἐμίγην φιλότητι καὶ εὐνῆι,
ὥς σεο νῦν ἔραμαι καί με γλυκὺς ἵμερος αἱρεῖ.   *Il.* 3,441-6

In the *Dios Apate*, Hera's plan to seduce Zeus is successful, since, as soon as he beholds Hera, Zeus' feelings and utterances are similar to those of Paris. "And when he saw her, then desire enfolded his shrewd mind, just as when, concealed from their dear parents, rushing off to bed, they had for the very first time joined in love":

ὡς δ' ἴδεν, ὥς μιν ἔρος πυκινὰς φρένας ἀμφεκάλυψεν,
οἷον ὅτε πρώτιστον ἐμισγέσθην φιλότητι
εἰς εὐνὴν φοιτῶντε, φίλους λήθοντε τοκῆας.   *Il.* 14,294-6

Next he compliments her by saying: "For never yet has desire for any other goddess or mortal woman so been poured over and overcome the heart within my breast—not even when I was seized with desire for Ixion's wife . . . as now I desire you and sweet longing seizes me":

οὐ γάρ πώ ποτέ μ' ὧδε θεᾶς ἔρος οὐδὲ γυναικός
θυμὸν ἐνὶ στήθεσσι περιπροχυθεὶς ἐδάμασσεν,
οὐδ' ὁπότ' ἠρασάμην Ἰξιονίης ἀλόχοιο
(here follows the catalogue of Zeus' previous beloveds)
ὥς σεο νῦν ἔραμαι καί με γλυκὺς ἵμερος αἱρεῖ.   *Il.* 14,315-28

The way in which Aphrodite arouses Anchises' desire is described in similar terms in the *Homeric Hymn*. "Like the moon it shone about her tender breasts, a marvel to behold. Anchises was seized by desire":

ὡς δὲ σελήνη
στήθεσιν ἀμφ' ἁπαλοῖσιν ἐλάμπετο, θαῦμα ἰδέσθαι.
Ἀγχίσην δ' ἔρος εἷλεν.   *Hymn. Hom.* V, 89-91

However, not only Aphrodite's physical beauty, but also her words can arouse Anchises' sexual feelings. "When she had thus spoken, the goddess cast sweet longing into his heart. Anchises was seized by desire":

Ὣς εἰποῦσα θεὰ γλυκὺν ἵμερον ἔμβαλε θυμῷ.
Ἀγχίσην δ' ἔρος εἷλεν.   *Hymn. Hom.* V,143f.

The common feature in these situations is that Paris', Zeus' and Anchises' ἔρως is triggered by an external impulse, the sight (or words) of the beloved, so explicitly in *Il.* 14,294 (ὡς δ' ἴδεν) and implicitly in *Hymn. Hom.* V, 90f. with the formulaic θαῦμα ἰδέσθαι. Helen's presence is indicated in *Il.* 3,441f. as Paris talks to her. The effects of desire are described in the *Iliad* in the following images, which display interesting parallels: ἔρως "enfolds" (ἀμφεκάλυψεν *Il.* 3,442;

14,294), is "poured over" (περιπροχυθείς *Il.* 14,316), "overcomes" (ἐδάμασσεν *Il.* 14,316); besides, it "bewitches" (ἔθελχθεν *Od.* 18,212). We have seen earlier that the effects of ἔρως on the lover is described with the same verbs as that of sleep and death, which appear personified not only in the *Theogony*, but also in the *Iliad*. In the same way in which desire "enfolds" (ἀμφικαλύπτειν 3,442; 14,294) the mind (φρένες), which entails a restriction of perception or a sort of mental disturbance, or even that "the senses are overcome", sleep not only affects the eyes and disturbs visual perception, but is also a state of complete sensory deprivation or unconsciousness.[47]

The expression ἔρως (sc. θεᾶς / γυναικός) θυμὸν ἐνὶ στήθεσσι περιπροχυθεὶς ἐδάμασσεν (also applied to the personified Eros in *Theog.* 122) is further paralleled by descriptions of states like sleep and death, which are said to overcome gods and men.[48] ἔρως affects gods and men in a particular area: the "heart" (θυμὸς ἐνὶ στήθεσσι) or the "mind" (φρένες); these zones indicate that ἔρως causes a mental disturbance and a restriction of perception similar to sleep's effect on sight.[49]

In the *Iliad* two aspects of ἔρως are significant: firstly, on a poetic level, the images representing the effects of desire are identical to those of sleep. Secondly, ἔρως tends to influence the mind, whereas sleep tends to affect the body, especially the eyes. But both phenomena have in common that they restrict the means of human perception. What, however, makes the concept of ἔρως in the *Iliad* unique in Greek literature is that its effect is not perceived as a physical or psychological pain or distress by Paris or Zeus.[50] Anchises is not worried about his desire as such, but rather about the consequences involved in an erotic encounter with a goddess.

An erotic context in which ἔρως is perceived as a psychological but primarily physical pain can be found in book 18 of the *Odyssey* (18,212-3). When the suitors see Penelope after Athena's beauty treatment, ἔρως bewitches their minds and makes them go weak at the knees, "for they all desired to lie down with her":

τῶν δ' αὐτοῦ λύτο γούνατ', ἔρῳ δ' ἄρα θυμὸν ἔθελχθεν,
πάντες δ' ἠρήσαντο παραὶ λεχέεσσι κλιθῆναι.

Here the mere perception of beauty affects first the mind, and then has physical repercussions. This does not necessarily mean pain, but rather that they can hardly bear their strong sexual desire for Penelope. As in the passages of the *Iliad*, desire affects the θυμός; the verb θέλγειν brings ἔρως close to the components of Aphrodite's κεστὸς ἱμάς, the θελκτήρια.

The expression τῶν δ' αὐτοῦ λύτο γούνατ' is revealing as regards the origins and development of the terminology of the effects of ἔρως. It could explain Eros' earliest epithet λυσιμελής, which first appears, according to our sources, in Hesiod's *Theogony* 121.[51] The meaning of the adjective is hard to grasp from this passage, since in this context, characterizing one of the primeval entities, it appears quite isolated. However, although the adjective λυσιμελής itself is not actually used in the *Iliad*, its original meaning can be inferred from a similar phrase (λῦσε δὲ γυῖα) which appears there. To "loosen someone's limbs" is nothing but a euphemism for wounding and killing somebody.[52] Agenor, a Trojan soldier, kills Elphenor with a bronze-tipped spear thrust into his unprotected ribs. Thus λυσιμελής reflects an early association between ἔρως and θάνατος.

> οὔτησε ξυστῶι χαλκήρεϊ, λῦσε δὲ γυῖα.[53]   *Il.* 4,469

Later in the *Odyssey* (20,57) λυσιμελής functions for the first time as an epithet of sleep, implying here a positive but overwhelming and irresistible weakening; sleep brings relaxation and a release from cares:[54]

> εὖτε τὸν ὕπνος ἔμαρπτε, λύων μελεδήματα θυμοῦ
> λυσιμελής.   *Od.* 20,56f.

The fact that desire and sleep share the same epithet confirms the analogies observed so far.[55]

The concept of ἔρως in the *Odyssey* is distinguished from that in the *Iliad*: we see that ἔρως can affect the human body in a negative way. The motif, which becomes so frequent in Greek literature, that love is little short of dying, is indicated by the image of ἔρως "loosening the limbs", which originally seems to have belonged to the sphere of battle and war. These images are next found in the fragments of Archilochus, who describes his own unrequited desire in similar terms, using, however, the term πόθος.[56] The first reference to the physical pain of love being like a wound caused by a weapon is found in the works of this poet. The lover is depicted as being seriously wounded, like a soldier on the verge of death (ἄψυχος), prostrate and pierced to the bone by desire (fr. 193 W.):[57]

> δύστηνος ἔγκειμαι πόθωι
> ἄψυχος, χαλεπῆισι θεῶν ὀδύνηισιν ἕκητι
> πεπαρμένος δι᾿ ὀστέων.

These examples, again, show that the images and terms which describe the activity and effects of ἔρως have parallels with other phenomena. Thus λυσιμελής is an epithet of both desire and sleep. In expressing the painful physical experience of unfulfilled desire, the poet of the *Odyssey* and Archilochus use a terminology which is applied in contexts of wounding and death in warfare.

It may seem surprising that neither in the *Iliad* nor in the *Odyssey* is there at first sight a direct affinity between the aspects of Aphrodite's province and ἔρως; Eros is not personified there and cannot be a divine attendant and, in contrast to ἵμερος, ἔρως is not a component of Aphrodite's κεστὸς ἱμάς either. The two erotic contexts in the *Iliad*, however, show that, after Aphrodite's personal intervention in book 3, ἔρως enfolds Paris' senses as soon as the latter has seen Helen. It is only by Aphrodite's magical ἱμάς, that Hera can seduce Zeus and achieve the same effect. Although the goddess and the effect, ἔρως, are never presented as directly interconnected, the imagery used by Zeus in describing the effect of ἔρως as "overcoming" his senses (θυμὸν ἐνὶ στήθεσσι περιπροχυθεὶς ἐδάμασσεν) is not only applied to the personified Hypnos, but also to Aphrodite in the *Iliad* (14,198f.):

> δός νύν μοι φιλότητα καὶ ἵμερον, ὧι τε σὺ πάντας
> δάμναι ἀθανάτους ἠδὲ θνητοὺς ἀνθρώπους.

and the *Homeric Hymn* to Aphrodite (V,3):

> καί τ' ἐδαμάσσατο φῦλα καταθνητῶν ἀνθρώπων.

It becomes evident that the terminology which describes the effects of ἔρως in the *Iliad* is the same as that applied to the activity of two other gods: Aphrodite and Hypnos. There is another interesting similarity: the contents of Aphrodite's κεστὸς ἱμάς are called θελκτήρια, and the effect of ἔρως on the suitors is expressed with θέλγειν as we have seen in the passage cited above.

Thus it seems that a proper independent love terminology describing the effects of desire does not yet exist. Therefore the expressions in which ἔρως is described in the *Iliad*, *Odyssey* and the *Theogony* are paralleled by other phenomena of the non-erotic sphere or other already personified deities. The mythological contexts convey that the non-personified ἔρως and ἵμερος are closely linked with the presence and workings of Aphrodite; they represent an aspect of her province.

The frequency and importance of ἵμερος in epic and in the *Iliad* in particular makes it necessary to delimit it from ἔρως. It seems that in Homeric epic they represent different aspects of desire. The terms do not seem to be etymologically connected.[58] We have seen that ἵμερος belongs to Aphrodite according to the inscription on "Nestor's cup". In the *Dios Apate* only ἵμερος is part of Aphrodite's magic κεστὸς ἱμάς, and it is also ἵμερος that Hera asks for, not ἔρως. Both Paris and Zeus refer to their ἵμερος at the end of their respective confessions: ὡς σέο νῦν ἔραμαι καί με γλυκὺς ἵμερος αἱρεῖ (*Il.* 3,446 = 14,328). ἵμερος appears to be used often with verbs indicating the "beginning" of desire (ὀρνύναι and αἱρεῖν).[59] It is remarkable that these verbs are often also linked with abstract terms conveying negative feelings and discomfort, such as δέος, χόλος or φόβος. In a similar way ἵμερος (though sweet) is used in an almost erotic context: Iris puts ἵμερος "for her former husband, her home town, and her parents" in Helen's mind (*Il.* 3,139f.).[60] There is some evidence that ἵμερος is emotional and psychological rather than physical and that it is connected with the memory of erotic pleasures experienced in the past.[61] This is true not only in the case of Helen; Paris and Zeus also think of earlier encounters they have had with the women they now desire.[62] However, although Anchises and Aphrodite have not met before, Anchises feels ἵμερος too when it is "thrown"

into Anchises' mind by Aphrodite (*Hymn. Hom.* V,143). The inscription on
"Nestor's cup", where the expression ἵμερος αἱρεῖ first occurs, undoubtedly does
not indicate the owner's desire for a familiar beloved. These contexts suggest
that we should perhaps not differentiate too sharply between the two terms.
ἔρως appears to be an imminent condition, a neutral, physical and instinctive,
but not necessarily painful desire, that can be aroused from time to time and
has to be appeased by action. ἵμερος, by contrast, seems to affect emotions too,
sometimes even in a painful way; as opposed to ἔρως, it is not only sexual, but
implies an affection that can be linked to the memory of a former experience.

7.4   THE PECULIARITY OF HESIOD'S CONCEPTION OF EROS

Hesiod is the first to present Eros as a god with personified traits, albeit only
in the *Theogony*. In the *Works&Days*, Eros is not found among the atten-
dants (Charites, Horae, Peitho) of Aphrodite who come to array Pandora.
Considering that a personified Eros does not appear in any other preserved
hexametric works of this period, we may conclude that Eros' prominent role
in the *Theogony* is unique in the Greek tradition at this date and due to its
cosmogonic genre. Some scholars have tried to explain this phenomenon by
associating it with a local Eros cult at Thespiae to which Hesiod allegedly
referred. The problematic connection of this cult with Eros in the Archaic
period has already been discussed. Moreover, we can see from the examples
of Zeus and Hecate in the *Theogony* how Hesiod presented detailed myths of
deities who had an established cult.[63] If one compares Eros' depiction with
theirs, he remains, in spite of his outstanding position among the three pri-
meval entities, relatively weak despite his individuality and particular activ-
ity.[64] It is obvious that Hesiod's knowledge of Eros cannot be drawn from
cultic experience or from myths which featured the god in a specific story,
such as we find in hymns to other deities.[65] For there seems to have been
no mythical tradition about Eros similar, for example, to the one in which
Aphrodite is featured with Anchises, as presented in the *Homeric Hymn*; nor
is there a story of the birth of Eros comparable to that of Apollo and Artemis
at Delos, which is certainly earlier than its literary narration in the *Hymn to
Apollo*. And, in contrast to the Charites or the Horae, he does not even ap-
pear in a minor role in hymns to the Olympian gods. In his description of
Eros in the *Theogony*, Hesiod uses elements which are current features in
the praise of Olympian deities and as such also found in the *Iliad*, *Odyssey*
and the *Homeric Hymns*. Eros' features have therefore been occasionally in-
terpreted as "Homeric" and regarded as being incompatible with the vague
and shapeless representation of Chaos and Gaia.[66] So far we have failed to
determine more precisely how Hesiod modified and combined expressions
probably already available in the oral tradition, in order to create a god who

had no ancient cults. I suggest that the very first literary representation of Eros as a personified god and his importance are due to the specific context and the tradition to which the *Theogony* belongs, and that he owes his prominent role to its cosmogonic genre. Eros' external equipment and characterization of his outward appearance and functions are expressed in the same poetic features as those of the phenomenon ἔρως which occurs in the Homeric and Hesiodic poems. The presentation of these attributes recalls the hymnic style in which Olympian gods are praised.[67]

In the *Theogony*, Eros is introduced as one of the first primeval entities, after Chaos (116) and Gaia (117): "Eros, the most beautiful among the immortal gods, the limb-loosener, who overcomes the mind and thoughtful will of gods and men in their hearts" (120-3):

ἠδ' Ἔρος, ὃς κάλλιστος ἐν ἀθανάτοισι θεοῖσι,
λυσιμελής, πάντων τε θεῶν πάντων τ' ἀνθρώπων
δάμναται ἐν στήθεσσι νόον καὶ ἐπίφρονα βουλήν.

The image of Eros which is described here is that of a personified god who is at the same time endowed with characteristics of the non-personified ἔρως. These, however, are further developed. Three aspects are particularly interesting; firstly, the god is visually discernible by his beauty; secondly, by characterizing Eros with attributes (relative clause and the epithet), Hesiod seems also to have integrated him formally into the sphere of the Olympian gods; thirdly, the authority of the personified deity is, compared with the effects of the non-personified ἔρως, clearly extended.

Beauty seems to be a characteristic common to many divinities. And it is actually the adjective κάλλιστος alone that suggests the idea of an anthropomorphic deity. That mortals can recognize gods and goddesses alike primarily by their beauty is a common feature of divine epiphanies where they are described as καλοὶ καὶ μεγάλοι. Aphrodite for example, with her epiphany-like birth from the sea, is called καλὴ θεός (*Theog.* 194). Besides, the motif occurs frequently in the *Homeric Hymns*: Demeter, when talking to Metaneira, is surrounded by beauty and Aphrodite's cheeks are shining with beauty when she stands before Anchises.[68] Whereas in the hymns the deity's beauty is normally emphasized in particular parts (cheeks, breast or clothes), Eros in Hesiod excels them all by being the "most beautiful".[69] The stress on Eros' beauty is an element, the inclusion of which in Hesiod's introduction of the god as a cosmic entity, may have been inspired by the hymnic tradition. That the poet was acquainted with hymnic features is obvious, given his praises of the Muses, Hecate or Zeus.

We also find another element of hymn when a typical effect or action of Eros among men is described with an epithet or a relative clause.[70] The epithet λυσιμελής implies the effect of the emotion ἔρως as described in *Theog.* 910, where it is said to emanate from the Charites' eyes, and besides in *Od.* 18,212f., when the suitors go weak at the knees; the epithet itself is also that of sleep (εὖτε τὸν ὕπνος ἔμαρπτε, λύων μελεδήματα θυμοῦ, / λυσιμελής *Od.* 20,56f.).[71] Hesiod applies this adjective to Eros in order to define the sphere of the personified god. It could be seen as an analogy to features such as Zeus' description as ὑψιβρεμέτης (*Op.* 8), but since Eros is a personification, his epithet is closely linked to the effects of the non-personified ἔρως. In fact, λυσιμελής is never applied to any other deity in epic.[72] The god's activity is displayed in a relative clause which is a familiar feature in hymns to cult gods and may therefore imply that Eros is treated as a god of cult.[73] But it will become clear that this is a literary product in which implications of a non-personified feeling and an activity of a deity have been modified and combined.

As we have seen, Eros conquers the mind and will of all men and gods. The contents of the relative clause first of all recall the workings of ἵμερος as described on "Nestor's cup". It is said to "seize" or "capture"—a comparable image. In addition, the effects of the non-personified ἔρως are the same as those described in the *Iliad* (14,316) when Zeus sighted his beloved, with the same impact on mind (θυμὸν ἐνὶ στήθεσσι . . . ἐδάμασσεν). In the *Theogony*, it is even extended to the influence of the lovers' will (indicated by βουλή). Maybe these are variations of the same formula, one current in oral tradition. What we can observe with certainty is that, according to our evidence, Hesiod applies the formula to a personified Eros, whereas elsewhere the expression describes the workings of a phenomenon. It is significant that Hesiod emphasizes the more mental or psychological aspect and that he omits the physical impact of ἔρως as displayed later in the *Odyssey* or, even more elaborately, in the fragments of Archilochus.[74]

The gods' power over all human beings seems to be a common topos in hymns in Hesiod's time, as the hymn to Zeus (*Op.* 3f.) suggests. Besides, as has already been pointed out, the action of δαμάζειν is among Aphrodite's ἔργα displayed at the beginning of the *Homeric Hymn*. "Muse, speak to me of the works of golden Aphrodite, the Cyprian goddess, who sends sweet longing to the gods, and overcomes the races of mortal men, and the birds that fly in heaven, and all the many creatures that are nurtured by land and sea"(V,1-5):

> Μοῦσά μοι ἔννεπε ἔργα πολυχρύσου Ἀφροδίτης
> Κύπριδος, ἥ τε θεοῖσιν ἐπὶ γλυκὺν ἵμερον ὦρσε
> καί τ᾽ ἐδαμάσσατο φῦλα καταθνητῶν ἀνθρώπων,
> οἰωνούς τε διιπετέας καὶ θηρία πάντα,
> ἠμὲν ὅσ᾽ ἤπειρος πολλὰ τρέφει ἠδ᾽ ὅσα πόντος·

But there is a difference between Aphrodite's authority and Eros'. Whereas she arouses the gods' desire, but explicitly "overcomes" mortals and animals, Eros' power in the hymnic introduction of the *Theogony* is extended without exception to the immortal gods (πάντων τε θεῶν πάντων τ᾽ ἀνθρώπων / δάμναται ἐν στήθεσσι νόον καὶ ἐπίφρονα βουλήν 121f.). This is an expansion also in comparison with Zeus' power in *Works&Days* (3). In order to define

Eros' authority, Hesiod deliberately makes use of a formulaic expression which recalls the ἔργα of Olympian deities whose sphere of influence Eros even seems to surpass.

As it turns out, Eros as a personified deity appears first in Hesiod's *Theogony*. Hesiod achieved this by attributing to him, on a poetic level, characteristics either of other personified (but mythically already established) gods or of Olympian deities. His characteristics, formulated in hymnic style, cannot be separated from the effects of the non-personified ἔρως, featured in the *Iliad* or the *Odyssey* as an erotic personification belonging to Aphrodite. But Homeric epic focuses on an aspect different from that of the *Theogony*: ἔρως is a phenomenon which becomes effective among human beings and anthropomorphic gods without procreative functions. At the beginning of the cosmic context of the *Theogony*, when neither gods nor men yet existed, Eros, by his placement, is perceived as the element responsible for reproduction, a function not necessarily implied by his Homeric attributes.

7.5   HESIOD AND THE COSMOLOGICAL TRADITION

As presented in the *Theogony*, Eros' activity is closely related to the sphere of mortals and anthropomorphic gods, but his role and function are those of a primeval element among two other, non-anthropomorphic principles: Chaos and Gaia. In order to resolve this ambiguity, which is also reflected in the god's second appearance as Aphrodite's companion (*Theog.* 201f.), scholars suggested that there were originally two different traditions of the god which Hesiod has combined: Eros the cosmic principle and Eros the love-god.[75] More recent scholarship has denied the idea of two parallel traditions, suggesting that the role of the "cosmic Eros" is not different from the "divinized desire . . . defined by the poets."[76] I will argue that one cannot distinguish between two types of Eros, but that different genres focus on different aspects of one and the same phenomenon. Whereas cosmogonic sources (including Orphic literature) display the reproductive aspect of desire, lyric and tragedy display the negative, destructive side of it, since it is often unfulfilled. We find this last aspect indicated in *Od.* 18,212f., whereas the above-mentioned passages in the *Iliad* do not suggest that "desire" does any harm. But here too "desire" is not associated with reproduction.

I begin with the evidence for a phenomenon comparable to Eros in other cosmogonic sources and will then examine Eros' function in the context of the *Theogony*. A survey of cosmogonic or theogonic literature shows that Hesiod's work is not the only one of its kind, but representative of a traditional and widespread type.[77] Although it is the earliest extant Greek example, the *Theogony* belongs to an already traditional poetic genre.[78] Cosmogonic and theogonic myths which describe the origin of the world and the gods are found everywhere, but Hesiod's *Theogony* seems to be particularly influenced by the

Near East, as similar motifs in Egyptian, Babylonian or Hebrew literature suggest. For the cosmic sections in Hesiod, parallels may be found especially in Phoenician myths.[79]

Similarities between the *Theogony* and older Near-Eastern myths recounting the succession of rulers, including the motif of the castration of the sky god and the swallowing of descendants, have been recognized as regards their narrative structure.[80] The parallels of the genealogical sections and the succession myths in Hesiod in particular with the Hittite *Song of Kumarbi* are evident: Anu, the God of Heaven (Uranus), is castrated by his son Kumarbi (Cronus), whose reign is threatened by his son Teshub (the equivalent of Zeus as the weather god). When Kumarbi wants to devour him, he receives a stone instead, as does Cronus in the *Theogony*. Thus they have the following points in common: the sequence of the gods Anu, Kumarbi and Teshub is paralleled by Uranus, Cronus and Zeus. Anu has his genitals cut off as does Uranus.[81] An Akkadian text from Babylon, the cosmogonic epic *Enûma Elish*, also shows correspondences with the *Theogony*, but these are not as close as those of the *Theogony* with the Hittite epic. Both epics commence with a pair of primeval parents: Apsu and Tiamat, Uranus and Gaia. Each pair has children who cannot be born because their father hates them and so they are trapped inside their mother until a couragous and wise brother liberates them.[82]

However, close as these similarities in the narrative structure are, neither of the two epics provides a parallel for the first things that came into being in the context of the *Theogony*: Chaos, Tartarus and Eros. The Near-Eastern epics discussed so far do not seem to have had a primeval force, a generative principle like Eros in the *Theogony*. The *Song of Kumarbi* starts, after an invocation of diverse gods, with the reign of Alalu, omitting, as does *Enûma Elish*, a genealogical part.[83] In what follows I will discuss Near-Eastern cosmogonic and theogonic myths which have an element that is analogous to Eros among their primeval entities and whose main motifs are paralleled in Hesiod.[84]

It has been acknowledged that a primeval element equivalent to Eros is a traditional feature in the cosmogonic genre, a power without which creation could not happen.[85] It seems therefore very unlikely that Hesiod himself could have invented such a motif. There is in particular one cosmologic tradition in which a phenomenon similar to Eros, and also Chaos, is among the first elements: the Phoenician tradition.[86] But from what source could Hesiod have become acquainted with cosmogonic ideas? It need not have been a written source, as he could easily have received this information through oral tradition. Considering the lively exchange which took place between Greece and Phoenicia during the period of the "orientalizing revolution", Hesiod could easily have heard various foreign myths and stories from Phoenician merchants.[87]

Besides, underlying the Greek cosmogonic accounts starting from Hesiod, Pherecydes of Syrus, the Orphic theogonies, and the philosophical concepts of the Presocratics there seems to have been an originally Phoenician core, or even an earlier "Near-Eastern" archetype consisting of elements that occur regularly.[88] In the following I will distinguish between three different sources recounting a Phoenician tradition. These sources are most likely to promote an old tradition, but this cannot be proved with certainty. Firstly, there are late, mainly Neoplatonic accounts recording a Phoenician cosmogony (1st category): i) Eudemus' "Sidonian" version, paraphrased by the Neoplatonist Damascius,[89] ii) Mochos' version, which differs slightly from Eudemus concerning its primeval entities,[90] iii) Philo of Byblos who in his *Phoenician History* claims to give a translation of an authentic Phoenician source, the work of Sanchuniathon of Beirut.[91] Orphic literature (2nd category) does not explicitly refer to Phoenician models, but is certainly influenced by them.[92] An additional group encompasses manifestations of Greek cosmogonies which also draw on Eastern material (3rd category). Among them, Hesiod's cosmogony is the earliest Greek source to show such traces. Next to Hesiod, it is in Pherecydes of Syrus' oeuvre that the Near-Eastern myth of the oriental god of Unaging Time, Chronos, first appears (before the mid-6th century BC). The cosmic egg is first documented in the earliest theogonies attributed to Orpheus which have been dated to the late 6th or early 5th century. From this egg either Heaven and Earth emerge, or—a constant motif in subsequent Orphic literature—Eros, alias Protogonos or Phanes. The Orphic theogonies in particular seem to draw on Eastern motifs, as the early example of a parody in Aristophanes' *Birds* conveys. According to M.L. West, its motifs may be traced back to a 7th-century Phoenician cosmogony.[93]

Hesiod's setting of Eros among the first elements together with Chaos (*Theog.* 116) and its descendants Erebos and Nyx (123) is paralleled in the Phoenician tradition. This is suggested by the frequency and consistency with which they occur in all three categories defined above. M.L. West gives an overview of those motifs which are common in Greek versions and those which seem to reflect a Phoenician tradition. They perhaps go back to a more widespread Near-Eastern archetype. At least three out of nine motifs appear in the cosmic section of the *Theogony*.[94] There is a "primeval watery abyss" in the theogony attributed to Orpheus and in Philo's translation of Sanchuniathon's work; the term used for the phenomenon by "Orpheus" is "Chasma", Philo refers to "Chaos", which we also have in Hesiod.[95] The "primeval darkness" which occurs in Orpheus, Epimenides, Aristophanes and Sanchuniathon seems to be the same as Erebos in the *Theogony*. Whereas the roles of the wind, the god Time, and the cosmic egg cannot be paralleled in the *Theogony*, one might conjecture that Hesiod's Eros has his predecessor in the personified Desire of the Phoenician tradition, which is reflected in the works of Eudemus and Sachuniathon. Therefore, assuming that Desire was an established element in those accounts, it is very unlikely that Eudemus' or Philo's accounts, or the texts reflecting Orphic ideas (such as the parody in Aristophanes' *Birds*) would have simply drawn on the *Theogony* when featuring Eros (or his equivalents Phanes or Protogonos).[96]

The authenticity of Eudemus' "Sidonian" cosmogony has been disputed because it was quoted by Damascius, a Neoplatonist, and is therefore suspected of having been influenced and amplified by him. The discussion of the quality of Philo's translation of Sanchuniathon's work also has a long history in classical scholarship, with assessments ranging from "authentic" to "Hellenistic pastiche".[97] It seems, however, quite likely that the personified Desire is an authentic element within cosmogonic myths, given its well-founded position within various cosmic contexts and its interaction with the other elements which cannot have been inspired by Hesiod. In the following section which focuses on the depiction of Desire in the Phoenician accounts I will discuss in what aspects the Hesiodic Eros is deficient, and in which ways it differs, when compared with Phoenician Desire. Perhaps the question of why Eudemus and Philo may have chosen the appellation "Πόθος" instead of Eros is interconnected. I suggest they did it in order to contrast him with the Hesiodic Eros.[98]

The "Sidonian" version of the Peripatetic Eudemus of Rhodes (fr. 150 Wehrli) is paraphrased in Damascius:[99]

"The Sidonians set Time (Χρόνον) before anything else and Pothos (Πόθον) and Darkness ('Ομίχλην); from the union of Pothos and Darkness Aer (Ἀήρ) and Aura (Αὖρα) come into being, and again from those two an egg."

Thus the first three primordial entities are Time, Desire and Darkness, but only the latter two become active in the creation of the cosmos. Desire is imagined as an active element operating on a static one, Darkness. Their union is described in sexual terms (μιγέντων), and the result is the egg from which other phenomena emerge. This cosmogonic myth shares with Hesiod's *Theogony* two primeval elements, Desire and Darkness, but it is at the same time different, as Desire becomes explicitly productive and participates in the act of creation by creating itself. In comparison, Eros' activity in the cosmic process of the *Theogony* hardly comes to the fore. It is not easy to see why Hesiod did not integrate the god and his activity properly into the cosmogonic system. One might assume that he was more interested in the theogonies of anthropomorphic gods.[100]

The other cosmogonic source of Phoenician origin relevant for its parallels with Hesiod's primordial principles is the work which has been attributed to Sanchuniathon of Beirut, a Phoenician whose lifetime is set before the Trojan war; he is said to have collected diverse histories and traditions in various cities. We possess parts of the *Phoenician History* of Philo of Byblos (64-140 AD) which claims to give a Greek translation of this text.[101] That there are genuine Phoenician ideas behind Philo's testimony has been generally accepted, on their date, however, scholars disagree.[102] Most recently, A. Baumgarten has argued that Philo's own age (he lived in the Hadrianic period) and environment significantly shaped the *Phoenician History*. Hesiod's direct influence has also been taken into account by him.[103]

However, it seems unlikely that Philo should have had Hesiod in mind when introducing Chaos or Pothos in his cosmogony. As it turns out, their definition and function are far more developed and complex there than in the Hesiodic version. In the Phoenician cosmogony, Philo "posits at the origin of all things the murky, boundless air [or a blast of dark-colored air] and the muddy and gloomy chaos. These elements were infinite and remained without boundaries for a long time. But, he says, when the wind fell in love with its own beginnings and a commixture came into being, this synthesis was called Pothos."[104]

> τὴν τῶν ὅλων ἀρχὴν ὑποτίθεται ἀέρα ζοφώδη καὶ πνευματώδη [ἢ πνοὴν ἀέρος ζοφώδους][105] καὶ χάος θολερὸν ἐρεβῶδες· ταῦτα δὲ εἶναι ἄπειρα καὶ διὰ πολὺν αἰῶνα μὴ ἔχειν πέρας. «ὅτε δέ» φησίν «ἠράσθη τὸ πνεῦμα τῶν ἰδίων ἀρχῶν, καὶ ἐγένετο σύγκρασις, ἡ πλοκὴ ἐκείνη ἐκλήθη Πόθος.»

The reason why Philo refers to Pothos, not—as one might have expected from ἐρᾶσθαι—Eros, may be that he wanted to distinguish the merely cosmic Desire from Eros, who in Hesiod, as his attributes suggest, was not exclusively cosmic. This aspect of Eros seems to become less and less important from the late Archaic period onwards. On the other hand ἐρᾶσθαι may have been given preference over ποθεῖν because of its stronger sexual implication.[106]

We find a cosmic element similar to the wind not in the *Theogony*, but in two other accounts of Phoenician cosmogonies where the role of the air is likewise distinctly defined: in that of Eudemus who, however, posits it in the second stage of the cosmogonic process (see above), and that of Mochos.[107] Moreover, here too the wind itself participates in procreation. In Philo, the wind generates Pothos by self-eroticism (which may even imply a demiurgic function), whereas in Mochos, wind together with Αἰθήρ creates Οὐλωμός, the Phoenician equivalent of Time.[108] Thus Philo's text undeniably contains elements that suggest a genuine Phoenician origin.

This is also true for Χάος, as it too is found in the old Orphic theogony (Orph. fr. 66a/b Kern), where, however, it is called Χάσμα. Moreover, Χάος is paralleled in Hesiod, where it remains similarly undefined as regards its activity and functions.[109] As we have seen, this also holds true for Eros, who in his origin and function as a cosmic principle is not very clear-cut in Hesiod either. In this respect he is very different from his equivalent Pothos in the Phoenician source. Pothos' evidently more intricate involvement in the process of cosmic creation, specifically his role as an actively creating principle is not only different, but even, as I hope to demonstrate, the very opposite of Eros' in the *Theogony*. In Eudemus, together with Χρόνος and Ὁμίχλη, Pothos is one of the three primordial entities which are not created. In this respect, Pothos is similar to Hesiod's Eros. However, whereas Pothos, by mixing with Ὀμίχλη, becomes explicitly active himself in the process of reproduction (their progeny are Ἀήρ and Αὔρα), Eros' activity is never developed or made explicit by Hesiod; it is only provided by his position. On the other hand, the motif of Eros' giving birth to himself occurs as a common feature not only in the Orphic theogonies, as Aristophanes' parody suggests (see below), but even earlier in Pherecydes, when Zeus transforms himself into Eros in order to create the universe.[110] In those examples Eros is evidently credited with a positive, demiurgic function. In Philo, similarly, Pothos stands at the beginning of everything (ἡ πλοκὴ ἐκείνη ἐκλήθη Πόθος. αὕτη δὲ ἀρχὴ κτίσεως ἁπάντων); however, unlike Hesiod's Eros, he is not primeval, but created as a result of the wind's self-fructification.[111]

This complex motif certainly cannot be Philo's own fancy, since it occurs in several other cosmogonic accounts; although these are not Phoenician, they also originate in the Near East. U. Hölscher has compared the poetic style of Philo's account with the beginning of *Genesis*, and a parallel has also been seen in the primeval elements, Darkness and Chaos, and in the way in which the winds become active there.[112] For it says (1:2): "and darkness was above the abyss and the wind (of god) flapped against the waters".[113] The association of Pothos and the wind's self-eroticism can also be discovered in the Ugaritic myth of Baal. L. Clapham has argued on linguistic and narrative grounds that a phenomenon similar to the Pothos in Philo's account of Sanchuniathon is found there as well.[114] In text 62:50 we learn that Baal of Ugarit who is, like the winds, a cosmogonic creator, assaults the waters, as a result of which *ars* (identified with *arsu*, which is the equivalent to Greek πόθος) comes into being and from then on lives in the waters.[115] The association of Pothos and the winds (which, like Pothos' role of a creative agent, is very probably authentic) is not elaborated at all in Hesiod, but Orphic literature seems to be particularly influenced by these ideas, as numerous examples show: Pothos (alias Phanes, Protogonos or Eros) is also endowed with a demiurgic function.[116]

This can be seen even more clearly in Aristophanes' parody in *Birds* of a cosmogony which has been classified as the "ancient version" of an Orphic theogony.[117] It also shows similarities with the version transmitted by Philo. Considering the different genres, however, it seems very unlikely that he would have borrowed from the parody of a comic poet. One might in this case rather assume that Aristophanes and Philo both refer to motifs of a tradition indebted to earlier Phoenician concepts which were then adopted by the Orphic tradition. The relevance of the contextual similarities with Philo and Orphic texts has not been accepted by the most recent commentator on *Birds*, N. Dunbar, who considers the birds' theogony to be mainly influenced by Greek literary sources. Thus she sees the main model here in the theogony composed by Hesiod.[118]

In the *Birds*, Peisetaerus persuades the birds to seize control of the air and thus become the new gods for human beings and the Olympians alike by building a city in the air. A wall, built around this city, should cut the Olympians off from the food they receive from men's sacrifices. The *parabasis*, performed by the chorus of birds, is entirely integrated into the plot of the action. The birds, by tracing their origins directly back to Eros, who is represented as one of the first entities creating the universe, legitimize their claim to be the divine rulers.

According to *Birds* (693-700) the world began with Chaos, Night, the dark Erebos and the broad Tartarus (693):[119]

Χάος ἦν καὶ Νὺξ Ἔρεβός τε μέλαν πρῶτον καὶ Τάρταρος εὐρύς·

This type of primeval stage is paralleled, as we have seen above, in the Phoenician versions, since Χάος is also found in Philo, and Ἔρεβος occurs in Philo and Eudemus (here called Ὀμίχλη). They are also represented in various later sources collected as the so-called Orphic theogonies, in which Νύξ, as a first generation god, played a particular part—in Hesiod Νύξ is born as child of Chaos and Erebos and therefore belongs to the next-generation of elements.[120] Thus Chaos and Tartarus correspond only with Hesiod's primordial entities. I would therefore argue that the combination and succession in *Birds* and the Orphic texts suggest that Hesiod was not Aristophanes' main source, particularly as Hesiod numbers Gaia amongst the first entities, whereas in *Birds* the non-existence of Gaia, Aer and Uranus is pointedly asserted (694a):

γῆ δ᾽ οὐδ᾽ ἀὴρ οὐδ᾽ οὐρανὸς ἦν·

Moreover, the fact that Gaia and Uranus are absent at the beginning of things is paralleled in Near-Eastern and Orphic cosmogony.[121]

The second stage of the cosmic creation in *Birds* also diverges considerably from that of the *Theogony*. The process of creation begins with Νύξ. "She gives birth to the first of all beings in the boundless recesses of Erebos: an egg (having wind underneath) from which, when the seasons came round, Eros, who inspires longing, leapt out, sparkling with golden wings on his back, very much like wind-swift whirlings" (694b-697):[122]

Ἐρέβους δ᾽ ἐν ἀπείροσι
    κόλποις
τίκτει πρώτιστον ὑπηνέμιον Νὺξ ἡ μελανόπτερος ᾠόν,
ἐξ οὗ περιτελλομέναις ὥραις ἔβλαστεν Ἔρως ὁ ποθεινός,
στίλβων νῶτον πτερύγοιν χρυσαῖν, εἰκὼς ἀνεμώκεσι
    δίναις.

Here, Eros does not belong to the first non-created generation of gods, but emerges as a child of Νύξ from the cosmic wind-egg and is described in considerable detail which is paralleled in Phoenician sources. Eros' association with the egg and the golden wings fits the context of the *Birds* superbly since it is the aim of the animals to trace back their origin to a worthy ancestor. However, those motifs are not Aristophanes' invention, but taken from cosmogonic myth. That Eros is not primeval is paralleled in the tradition recorded in Philo. There Pothos is also the result of fructification. In Eudemus, Pothos is primeval, but he actively participates in the process of reproduction, as does Aristophanes' Eros when we hear in the following that he mates with the winged Chaos and "produced as chicks" the birds' race (698-9):

οὗτος δὲ Χάει πτερόεντι μιγεὶς νυχίῳ κατὰ Τάρταρον εὐρὺν
ἐνεόττευσεν γένος ἡμέτερον, καὶ πρῶτον ἀνήγαγεν ἐς
φῶς.

Moreover, the race of the immortal gods only then came into being when Eros blended all the things together (700):

πρότερον δ' οὐκ ἦν γένος ἀθανάτων, πρὶν Ἔρως ξυν-
έμειξεν ἅπαντα·

It would seem, then, that there are at least five characteristics which Eros in Aristophanes shares with Phoenician or Orphic concepts of Desire and which are entirely absent from Hesiod's depiction of Eros. The first thing we learn in *Birds* concerning Eros is that he sprang out of an egg. An egg is mentioned in Eudemus' "Sidonian" cosmogony, where it is the progeny of Aer and Aura. In Philo the creation is said to be shaped like an egg (καὶ ἀνεπλάσθη ὁμοίως [. . .] ὠιοῦ σχήματι), and the third Phoenician account, Mochos, also refers to an egg, which is here the result of Oulomos' self-fructification. The cosmic egg is also a common feature in Orphic literature, as for example in the theogony attributed to Orpheus where Chronos fashions a shining egg (ἔπειτα δ' ἔτευξε μέγας Χρόνος Αἰθέρι δίωι ὠεὸν ἀργύφεον fr. 70 Kern); elsewhere it says that Phanes (equivalent of Protogonos/Eros) developed inside the egg, enclosed in a bright cloak (fr. 60 Kern).

Eros' association with the wind is documented twice in *Birds*: the egg from which he emerges is called an ὑπηνέμιον ὠόν, an egg "having wind underneath" and Eros himself resembles the whirling wind (εἰκὼς ἀνεμώκεσι δίναις). The role played by the wind in the process of creation is confirmed not only in all three Phoenician accounts, but also in Hebrew cosmogonic tradition, which knew the wind as a creative power as we have seen above. The link between Eros and the winds seems to have become an Orphic motif too: a scholium on *Argonautica* 3,26 mentions a cosmogony in which Chronos gave birth to Eros and all the winds.[123]

Eros' demiurgic function, which is made explicit in Aristophanes' parody, is also paralleled in Phoenician and Orphic accounts; we find it again in some Greek philosophers' writings, e.g. in Pherecydes, Parmenides and Empedocles. This aspect is not developed at all in Hesiod, but is merely implied by the position the poet ascribes to Eros; we learn nothing about the way he operates, and, paradoxically, his epithet λυσιμελής suggests that he is destructive and therefore the opposite of a creative power.

The only physical and visual details referred to by Aristophanes are Eros' wings: his back is "shining with golden wings" (στίλβων νῶτον πτερύγοιν χρυσαῖν 697). They are referred to again later (ὁ δ᾽ ἀμφιθαλὴς Ἔρως / χρυσόπτερος 1737f.) and may have been inspired by those of other mythical figures such as Iris, who, as we have seen, is golden-winged in epic, or Hypnos and Thanatos, who are usually depicted as winged in the literature and iconography discussed earlier. However, the motif of the wings also occurs subsequently in Orphic writings, since at least two Orphic fragments provide evidence that Phanes, Eros' equivalent, has a golden skin (fr. 86,4 Kern) or, as in Aristophanes, golden wings on which he flies to and fro (fr. 78 Kern). Even though the sources which transmit the text are later than Aristophanes, this does not necessarily mean that the motifs are later as well.[124] Therefore the assumption that "Aristophanes' language may itself have influenced later cosmogonic literature rather than vice versa" has to be considered with care.[125] The motif of the wings in its slightly altered versions is far too frequent in different Orphic fragments for one to assume that they are all Hellenistic variations of an Aristophanic invention.

It seems likely that this element is, if not originally embedded, at least foreshadowed in Near-Eastern thought: the motif of the wings is not separable from that of the wind. This combination is also clearly echoed in *Birds* (697). Perhaps the originally Near-Eastern idea of the association between desire and wind—as suggested in the Phoenician accounts as well as in *Genesis*—has been developed further by later Orphic poets and envisaged as an Eros or Phanes endowed with wings. That Aristophanes of all poets provided the source and motif for Orphic cosmogonic literature in *Birds* (produced at the City Dionysia in 414 BC) is in fact unlikely. There were other poets earlier than he who depicted Eros with golden shining wings: Anacreon and, fourteen years before *Birds*, Euripides in *Hippolytus*.[126] One would in this case assume that it is more likely that the Orphic writers combined the early poetic, non-cosmogonic image of Eros' wings, which is foreshadowed already in epic, with that of the Near-Eastern cosmogonic motif of desire's relationship with the wind.

This synthesis allows us to draw some conclusions. As it turns out, Hesiod is not likely to be the source for Philo's, Eudemus' or Aristophanes' cosmogonic accounts. In fact, it would seem that they are all influenced by original Near-Eastern concepts, as was Hesiod. Those Greek accounts purporting Phoenician cosmogonic ideas use the term "Pothos", which may be the equivalent of Hebrew *rûah*, the unpersonified cosmic desire clearly associated with the wind.[127] The peculiarity of Hesiod's Eros in *Theogony*, however, is that though he holds the position of Pothos, he does not seem to develop a cosmic activity, which is at most implied by his position. He does not mix primeval elements, nor is he himself involved in any process of creating or reproducing. His characterization, as conveyed by the epithet and the relative clause, corresponds completely with his second appearance as Aphrodite's companion (*Theog.* 201ff.). Here he is conceived of as an erotic personification representing an aspect of an Olympian deity, Aphrodite, in much the same way as, for example, Deimos and Phobos are related to Ares. His attribute λυσιμελής actually describes the effect of the emotion "desire" in the way it is perceived by the Greeks; his activity of "conquering all gods and men alike" (*Theog.* 122f.) corresponds to that of other Olympian deities (Zeus or Aphrodite). As a result, this Eros appears to be a conglomerate, a poetic fiction combining the function of a cosmic primordial entity with the looks and activities of an Olympian deity. As such Hesiod's Eros is, according to our literary evidence, unique. Two details are noteworthy: The relative clause does not convey a cosmic demiurgic function, but relates to Eros' activity among anthropomorphic gods and men. Paradoxically, the creative function even seems to be negated by the fact that he is λυσιμελής, which connotes closeness to death, as argued above. This more negative aspect of Eros, which becomes characteristic in lyric poetry and tragedy, is prefigured, although not elaborated, in Hesiod.

In Aristophanes, however, Eros' role as a cosmic god is emphasized by his participation in the act of creation and recalls the idea of "desire" as an unpersonified power of reproduction. The visualisation of Eros is strongly influenced by epic and also Orphic motifs—a process, however, which already seems to have started before Aristophanes, as the motif of the wings suggests.

M.L. West argued that Orphic motifs have in general not been taken up in the poetic tradition, since they remained limited to the mystery cults and doctrines of the Orphic sphere.[128] On the other hand, it seems that in this case the trajectory was from the poetic tradition to the Orphic sphere. The motifs and imagery which the lyric poets used when they mythologized Eros as the Greek love-god also occur in the later Orphic writings, which, however, are not earlier than the late 6th century BC.[129] Eros' gold-shining wings are a constant motif in the Orphic writings, but are, as has been shown, certainly attested earlier and inspired by epic features. Thus lyric and no doubt other forms of poetry seem to have provided material for the imagery for the Orphic tradition. The description of Eros "who had come from heaven dressed in a purple mantle" (ἔλθοντ' ἐξ ὀράνω πορφυρίαν περθέμενον χλάμυν) in Sappho (fr. 54 V.) could be linked with a fragment (fr. 60 Kern), where Phanes, inside an egg, is enclosed in a bright tunic or cloud: τὸ κύον ὠὸν τὸν θεόν, ἢ τὸν ἀργῆτα χιτῶνα, ἢ τὴν νεφέλην, ὅτι ἐκ τούτων ἐκθρώσκει ὁ Φάνης. The Phoenician tradition may have been a common source for both the lyric poems and the Orphic writings.

Those early lyric images which relate Eros' activity directly to the wind are obvious parallels for the cosmogonic association of wind and desire.[130]

Eros thus has many facets and is a mixture of different elements. Where cosmic functions are concerned, Eros is influenced by the implications of the Near-Eastern unpersonified desire. The demiurgic function (which was unfolded in detail not in Hesiod, but in Aristophanes or in the philosophical concept of Pherecydes) also bears traces of the Orphic Phanes or Protogonos. But the connotation of ἔρως as a human (or divine) emotion and its epic descriptions have also contributed to the image of the male love-god: related to the actual meaning of ἔρως, he is characterized as an erotic personification, representing an aspect of Aphrodite's province; this aspect comes clearly to the fore when he is called λυσιμελής or assumes Aphrodite's activity of subduing gods and men. Eros' visual characteristics, the wings, go back to the lyric poets, who already visualized the god with golden wings or wearing a purple cloak—motifs which the Orphic poets adopted to depict the cosmic Eros.

7.6   THE GOD OF LOVE AND THE COSMIC PRINCIPLE: TWO DIFFERENT TRADITIONS?

While the figure of Eros can be traced back to various constituents, one cannot simply assume that there existed two or more parallel mythical and cultic traditions of Eros as a deity in the time of Hesiod and referred to by him in the *Theogony*. A theory along these lines, which seems to be rooted in Eros' two different appearances there—as cosmic entity and as Aphrodite's attendant—has, however, been advanced by F. Lasserre.[131] Similarly, S. Fasce states that it was only natural for Hesiod to give the cosmic principle Eros his identity by assimilating him to a better known figure, such as the deity at Thespiae, or by making him the attendant of Aphrodite.[132] It becomes evident that she, like F. Lasserre, distinguishes between an established tradition of Eros the love-god and Eros the cult god. By emphasizing the generative function of the latter, she argues that he provided Hesiod with an appropriate model for a cosmic deity which is concerned with reproduction. This assumption, however, is easy to refute. Firstly, there is no proof to be deduced from Homeric epic, the *Homeric Hymns*, the fragments of the *Epic Cycle* and the fragments of Archilochus that Eros' function as Aphrodite's accustomed divine attendant was traditional at the time these works were composed. Secondly, there is no contemporary literary or epigraphical evidence for cults of Eros in the Archaic period.

It is therefore unlikely that Hesiod, inspired by a popular local cult god, synthesized two traditions (or three, if we include the cosmic version). I would argue instead that Hesiod is the only one we know of who presented a love-god characterized by his role as a cosmic entity as dictated by the genre of the *Theogony* on the one hand, and by the imagery for personifications provided in the oral (epic) tradition on the other. The inconsistency between cosmic role and divine attributes conveyed by the hymnic epithet and relative clause (ἠδ'

Ἔρος, ὅς κάλλιστος ἐν ἀθάνατοισι θεοῖσι, / λυσιμελής, πάντων τε θεῶν πάντων
τ' ἀνθρώπων / δάμναται ἐν στήθεσσι νόον καὶ ἐπίφρονα βουλήν 120f.) must
therefore be explained not by presupposing two traditions, but by conceding
that these represent two different aspects of one and the same phenomenon.
Eros can be reproductive if fulfilled, but if unrequited turns out to be a painful
experience: the latter aspect is indicated by λυσιμελής. In Greek culture the first
aspect of Eros remains restricted to cosmic and philosophical concepts;[133] lyric
and tragedy draw exclusively on the second, rather negative facet.[134]

It is in Hesiod that we first see Eros mythologized as all of these compo-
nents of different origins brought together. The god's poetic characteristics are
very much indebted to the functions of the phenomenon, and a personified
Eros is not attested in the Homeric poems and the *Homeric Hymns*. For all we
know, this Eros originated in Hesiod. At any rate, before Hesiod one cannot as-
sume that Eros was already Aphrodite's established divine companion. Typical
features of Eros, such as his overwhelming effect on gods and men, combined
with his role as Aphrodite's companion, appear, so far as we can tell, only in
Hesiod. One of the earliest depictions of this relationship is that on an Attic
red-figure cup by Macron (see Plate 8, cf. also Plates 6 and 7). In fact it makes
good sense that such a representation of the love-god was actually inspired by
the predominant role which Desire plays in the cosmogonic genre. The tradi-
tional Near-Eastern forerunners, however, do not seem to have known a per-
sonified version of the primordial desire. I suspect that it was Hesiod who made
the cosmic divine element a proper deity by relating Eros to the sphere of the
Olympians, and that he illustrated him using poetic means, creating an (erotic)
personification by applying the formulaic patterns provided perhaps already in
the oral tradition.

7.7   EROS-GENEALOGIES AS A PROOF FOR A COMPLEX (AND NON-CULTIC) ORIGIN

The great number of different parentages invented for Eros by the lyric poets
also have to be interpreted as attempts to mythologize Eros and integrate him
into the sphere of the Olympian deities (see Appendix, Fig. 2).[135] I suggest that
the diverse genealogies are poetic responses to the various influences and con-
stituents which shaped the image of Eros. The different genealogies also reflect
the idea of Eros' participation in the cosmogonic process on the one hand, and
his identity as a personification representing an aspect of Aphrodite's sphere on
the other. As such he came closer to the Olympian divinities and was thus re-
lated to the goddess of love (see Plates 6, 7 and 8).[136] The contexts in which Eros'
various pedigrees are transmitted show that in the Greek world poets and prose
writers traditionally invent ad-hoc parentages of a god according to different
contexts and genres.[137] The variety of genealogies of Eros can be categorized as
"no parentage", "cosmic parents" or "Olympian parents", according to the pre-
vailing aspect and role of the god.

Although Aristophanes' statement in Plato's *Symposium* that there were no cults of Eros in Greece (189c4-8) is confirmed by epigraphical and iconographical evidence, Phaedrus' claim (178b2-11) that no prose writer or poet ever referred to any parents of Eros can easily be disputed if we consider literary sources other than Hesiod, Acusilaus and Parmenides, the authorities cited by Phaedrus.[138] The reason why Phaedrus refers to them is that all three in fact place Eros among the first non-generated principles in their concepts. These writers, then, give no parents and can thus support Phaedrus' own arguments in his speech that Eros is among the oldest of deities and responsible for the greatest blessings to mankind.[139]

This, however, seems to conflict with the plethora of parentages given by other authors to Eros, who even point out the difficulty of fixing Eros' genealogy, since there are so many of them. These sources imply that this variety already existed in the Archaic period, and none of them finds anything remarkable in this. Pausanias (9,27,3), after referring to three different parentages, shows that one and the same poet can provide different genealogies of Eros: Sappho (in her poems) sang "many things not in agreement with each other concerning Eros" (Σαπφὼ δὲ ἡ Λεσβία πολλά τε καὶ οὐχ ὁμολογοῦντα ἀλλήλοις ἐς Ἔρωτα ᾖσε).[140] Besides, in the Hellenistic period Theocritus utters doubts at the beginning of *Idyll* 13 about Eros' parents: addressing Nikias he says that not for them alone "did (the god), whichever one it was who had this son, beget Eros" (οὐχ ἁμῖν τὸν Ἔρωτα μόνοις ἔτεχ᾿, ὡς ἐδοκεῦμες, / Νικία, ᾧτινι τοῦτο θεῶν ποκα τέκνον ἔγεντο).[141] This motif, implying multiple claims for parentage, is playfully reinterpreted by the poet of a Hellenistic epigram, Meleager (*Anth. Pal.* 5,177): since Eros is such an exhausting child, nobody wants to be his father.

Sappho's different genealogies of Eros may be reconstructed from the scholium on *Argonautica* 3,26b (216 Wendel); it refers to a variety of parents of Eros and says that Sappho traces Eros' pedigree back to Gaia and Uranus.[142] The scholium on Theocritus *Id.* 13,1/2 c (258 Wendel), however, claims that the poetess made him the son of Aphrodite and Uranus.[143] Two things are remarkable: Sappho seems to have been the first we know of to call Eros explicitly "son of Aphrodite" and thus to relate him genetically to the younger Olympian sphere. On the other hand, the place of Eros in the primordial cosmogonic tradition is echoed by the parenthood of Heaven in both versions and that of Earth in one. Eros' descent from Gaia and Uranus has been linked with the Orphic idea that Eros comes out of the cosmic egg (which is imagined to have been then divided into Heaven and Earth).[144] One could, however, also interpret it as a poetic attempt to place Eros among the first concrete and visible primordial entities, without assuming that Sappho had a particular cosmogonic version in mind. But one could not exclude the possibility that this genealogy could also be an ad-hoc invention inspired by the idea of Heaven making love to Earth, as depicted in the *Theogony*.

When, elsewhere, Sappho makes Eros the child of Aphrodite and Uranus, she may also be inspired by Hesiod's *Theogony*, although this was perhaps not her only source. Hesiod's Eros, when he makes his second appearance, is subordinated to Aphrodite as her attendant, not as her son. The ideas which may have led to this poetic concept are hard to disentangle, but it is this complexity which again reflects that the figure of Eros is embedded and rooted in different contexts. The combination of Uranus, Aphrodite and Eros is significant, since they have in common an ambiguity which is based on different mythic accounts and traditions. With reference to the *Theogony*, Eros is given a cosmic, non-anthropomorphic father and a mother who is of ambiguous origin. On the one hand, she is conceived of as being a beautiful young woman; after her birth, she approaches the sphere of the Olympian gods (*Theogony* 191f.). There Aphrodite is depicted as in the *Iliad*: the daughter of Zeus, anthropomorphic goddess of love. The *timai* attributed to her later (*Theogony* 201f.) define her province among the Olympians. But another version of her myth, which is suggested by her birth from the foam of Uranus' testicles in the Hesiodic version—itself probably a reflection of her cult-epithet Οὐρανία—links her to her Phoenician predecessor Ishtar-Astarte, the Queen of Heaven and spouse of the King of Heaven. Thus the parentage of Uranus and Aphrodite can be interpreted as the Greek version of the Phoenician couple of Heaven. Being personified and related to each other as a pair, they are suited to functioning as parents of a personified Eros. On the other hand, Uranus shares with Eros his ambiguous identity: in cosmogonic accounts they have a traditional place and function as amorphic primordial entities. However, in cosmic accounts other than the *Theogony*, Eros is also older than Uranus, who usually is of the same generation as Oceanus and/or Gaia.[145]

The association of Aphrodite and Eros as portrayed by Hesiod can also be interpreted as a reflection of the poetic tendency to subordinate aspects of Olympians as their attendants or children. This last step, however, is carried out by Sappho, who is the first to bring Eros and Aphrodite into a genealogical relationship and makes him at least a half-Olympian. When Eros appears twice in the *Theogony* at two different chronological stages, this may reflect Hesiod's attempt to combine two diverging facets of Eros.

When mythologizing Eros, Alcaeus too invented a poetic genealogy suggestive of a Near-Eastern idea. The fact that Eros, as a cosmic element, is associated with the winds seems to be reflected in the father. The mother given to Eros here confirms, however, the assumption that poetic fancy has a tendency to relate pre-personified concepts to an already existing, fully developed mythological figure with similar functions and attributes. Alcaeus (fr. 327 V.), in a hymn, makes Eros the son of Iris and Zephyrus:[146]

δεινότατον θέων,
<τὸν> γέννατ' εὐπέδιλος Ἶρις
χρυσοκόμαι Ζεφύρωι μίγεισα.

This parentage is striking: Homer in the *Iliad* clearly distinguishes between ἶρις the "rainbow" and Ἶρις the messenger-goddess by means of different epithets for each: ἶρις, the "rainbow", is simply "dark red", πορφυρέη.[147] The attributes of Ἶρις refer either to the swiftness of her movements, when the poet calls her "swiftfooted" (ποδήνεμος) and "stormfooted" (ἀελλόπος),[148] or they are related not to the swiftness, but the color of her other means of movement, the wings: she is Ἶρις χρυσόπτερος, the "golden-winged" Iris.[149]

Although Iris' wings are not mentioned in the fragment by Alcaeus—for she is εὐπέδιλος, "well-sandalled"—I would assume that it is this attribute of the golden wings which occurs in epic, that makes the genealogical link between Iris and Eros. The winged image of Iris seems to be a traditional mythical motif because her first documented appearance in iconography is as early as the late 7th century BC. A metope found at Thermos and dated circa 620 BC shows Iris with traces of wings on her shoulders.[150] The depiction of Iris as a winged female deity is by far the most conventional. When Eros, too, has golden wings, it could be due to his association with Iris in a similar function, as suggested by the *Iliad*. Interpreted as an erotic personification, his function and activity can be also seen to be that of a messenger, flying (on golden wings) and thus mediating between the world of the Olympians and the world of men. In this case the golden wings of Eros would be a poetic inheritance from other mythological figures with whom he shares distinctive characteristics: apart from Iris also Hypnos and Thanatos, as we have seen earlier. Another possibility, however, is that Eros was associated with Iris as a consequence of having golden wings. However, we have no evidence for this before Anacreon.[151]

So, if it is the common attribute of the golden wings which inspired Alcaeus to bring Iris and Eros into genealogical relationship, what could relate Eros to Zephyrus and Zephyrus to Iris? It has been argued above that the Near-Eastern idea of cosmic desire being associated with the winds had repercussions on the Greek image of Eros. One of the winds is therefore predestined to become the mythical father of Eros. Like Iris, Zephyrus (and the other winds Notus and Boreas) is already personified in the *Iliad* and the *Theogony*, as he has parents and offspring.[152] In the *Theogony* (378f.) he is the son of Astraios and Eos and brother of Notus and Boreas; in the *Iliad* (16,149ff.) Zephyrus together with the Harpy Podagre engenders Achilleus' horses Xanthus and Balius. In *Hymn. Hom.* VI,1-4. Zephyrus is related to the love-deity Aphrodite. He is imagined as having brought Aphrodite in her soft foam to Cyprus. It is probably by virtue of his being a warm and humid wind that he is related to deities of reproduction.[153] In addition Zephyrus' association with light might have led Alcaeus to see him as an ideal father and husband of golden winged creatures.[154]

It becomes clear that Alcaeus also tries to make Iris and Zephyrus appear as mythological figures and as concrete and personified as possible by emphasizing physical details: Iris is wearing beautiful sandals and Zephyrus is "golden-haired". When Zephyrus is called χρυσοκόμης in the Alcaeus fragment, he is close to being an anthropomorphic Olympian. χρυσοκόμης is a common epithet for male gods in erotic contexts.[155] Dionysus is χρυσοκόμης when he makes Ariadne his wife (see Hes. *Theog.* 947), and in Pindar it is a frequent epithet of Apollo.[156] In Alcaeus, "golden-haired" is an appropriate epithet for Zephyrus too, because the West wind is associated with light and he is the lover or husband of a goddess whose brightness is indicated by her golden wings. However, since χρυσοκόμης is such a common epithet for male gods, Anacreon need not have had Alcaeus' genealogy in mind when he made Eros χρυσοκόμης too (358 *PMG*), depicting him as a ball-playing youth:[157]

> σφαίρηι δηὖτέ με πορφυρῆι
> βάλλων χρυσοκόμης Ἔρως.

A. Broger rightly states that the association of Iris and Zephyrus is a poetic invention, a "Dichtereinfall". However, considering the developments which created this poetic genealogy, it seems unlikely that Alcaeus was simply inspired by a "Wettererlebnis" during which the rain appeared golden in the sunshine—the combination which creates ἶρις, the rainbow.[158] It has been shown that the background is far more complex than this facile meteorological allegory. Moreover, although it explains the match between Iris and Zephyrus, it is not at all clear why the personifications of two weather phenomena should have become parents of Eros. To make this comprehensible, one has to see Iris first of all as a winged messenger goddess.

Simonides, a hundred years later, makes Eros the son of Ares and Aphrodite (575 *PMG*).[159] He is then the "wicked child" of "wily Aphrodite and Ares", who is "contriving wiles":

> σχέτλιε παῖ δολομήδεος Ἀφροδίτας,
> τὸν Ἄρηι †δολομηχάνωι τέκεν.

> 1 δολομήδεος Rickmann (Diss. Rostoch. 1884 p. 36) : δολόμηδες cod. L.
> 2 δολομηχάνωι codd. : κακομαχάνωι Bergk : θρασυμαχάνωι Wilamowitz : δολομήχανον Davies

The two lines have been considered corrupt for several reasons.[160] There can be, however, no doubt that this is a poetic genealogy different in type from the one created by Alcaeus. Whereas he makes Eros' parents reminiscent of the latter's origins as a cosmic element and relates him to a goddess similar in looks and functions, Simonides simply makes him the result of a well-known mythical love story of which the *Odyssey* (8,266-366.) gives a humorous account: the affair between Ares and Aphrodite, who is unfaithful to her husband Hephaestus.[161] When Eros is the son of Aphrodite and Ares, he is somehow a romantic result, a poetic instalment of a traditional mythical love story. By relating Eros genetically to Aphrodite and Ares, Simonides at the same time makes him (although illegitimate by birth) a legitimate member of the Olympian family. The possibility cannot be excluded that a similar poetic attempt had been made earlier by Ibycus. The scholium on *Argonautica* 3,26b (216 Wendel) seems also to have mentioned a genealogy by Ibycus (fr. 324 *PMGF*). As the text is unfortunately badly preserved, we do not learn who the parents were there.[162] It is suggested by other fragments (286 and 287 *PMGF*) that Ibycus probably made Aphrodite Eros' mother. However, whether U. v. Wilamowitz' widely accepted conjecture in which he makes Hephaestus Eros' father (Ἴβυκος ‹δὲ Ἀφροδίτης καὶ Ἡφαίστου›) is correct or not, cannot be proved. In Archaic lyric poetry there is definitely already an overt tendency to mythologize Eros as an Olympian god by relating him to Aphrodite (see Plate 7).

7.8   CONCLUSION

It was the purpose of this chapter to examine Eros from different perspectives. In view of the literary and epigraphical evidence it would seem, then, that Eros, in contrast to Aphrodite and other companions, did not enjoy cultic veneration. This may also be the reason why he does not have any mythical stories. In Hesiod's *Theogony* he is related to two different concepts. One is that of the cosmic desire, which is rooted in the tradition of Eastern cosmic mythology; the other makes him a specific aspect of Olympian Aphrodite. Eros' role as the love-goddess's companion is indicated in the *Theogony*, but not attested in Homeric epic, the *Homeric Hymns* or the fragments preserved from the *Epic Cycle*. The varying genealogies are suited to prove Eros' ambivalent origins and show, moreover, that the creation of his personality is a poetic innovation. The next chapter will demonstrate that an important social phenomenon in Greek culture provided another decisive component for the creation of a male love-god.

Chapter Eight
The Creation and Birth of Eros at the Symposium

8.1   INTRODUCTION

"For at the time when Aphrodite was born, the gods feasted, and among them was the son of Metis, Poros. When the banquet was finished, Penia arrived in order to beg, as one would expect on a festive occasion, and stood by the door. Poros, drunken with nectar—there was no wine yet at that time—entered Zeus' garden and, overcome by drunkenness, fell asleep. Penia, by reason of her own poverty, secretly planned to conceive a child from Poros; she lay down next to him and became pregnant with Eros."

Plato, *Symposium* 203b2-c1

The only detailed narrative account of Eros' procreation is Plato's myth in the *Symposium*: his parents Poros and Penia meet at the feast where the gods celebrate Aphrodite's birth. In this symposiastic environment Penia seduces the drunken Poros in Zeus' garden. Here the context of Eros' mythological engendering is telling for his origin in Greek social history.

So far ways have been explored in which the poets' creativity, by inventing genealogies or borrowing attributes from other deities, mythologized certain features into a male love-god Eros as an aspect of Aphrodite. If these were the only modes of poetic stylization, Eros' birth would just be a fabrication based on imitation of births of other Olympian divinities. But Eros' nature is not as simple as that, since he is not merely Aphrodite's mythologized companion or her son. In the poets' attempts to mythologize a male counterpart to Aphrodite, Eros becomes more than simply a personified aspect of the goddess. This is corroborated by a social, non-literary phenomenon, namely the context in which poetry was performed.

We have seen that there is evidence that Aphrodite's figuration in mythical narrative, however complex, is often related to cult realities and that therefore many of her characteristics are a mythologization of cultic features. This cannot be true of Eros since it is unlikely that he was venerated in cult. Instead, Eros is closely connected with the background in which the poetry that represents him as most individualized and personified was performed (see Plates 14 and 15).

Scholars agree that most Archaic monodic poetry, particularly when concerned with erotic themes, was performed at the symposium.[1] Since the symposium became the place where the male aristocracy could indulge in and express their passion for younger men and boys, it may be argued that the homoerotic ideal of the symposiasts was gradually projected onto, or even divinized by the god Eros. This idea enriched the mythological features of Eros and accomplished his final shape. In what follows I offer a detailed analysis of this phenomenon from two sides: first, from a cultural and poetic point of view, addressing the context, themes and performance of choral and monodic lyric; second, from a more historical perspective. I will try to elucidate the strategic, political and social changes in late Archaic society which made the symposium the place where members of the aristocracy could indulge in the beauty of young men and boys.

8.2   THE "PERSONAL ELEMENT" IN LYRIC POETRY

The Greek lyric poetry we have was not the creation of the first lyric poets known to us, in the sense that they invented this genre. The tradition of composing songs accompanied by the lyre is without doubt older.[2] It would therefore be wrong to infer from our earliest preserved works—the Homeric and Hesiodic poems—that the hexameter is the oldest metre and that epic poetry is the earliest of all genres. Nor would it be right to conclude that monodic and choral lyric poetry is chronologically subsequent to Homeric and Hesiodic poems. Thus, if a persona for the poet is a more obvious component in lyric poems, this cannot be seen as the result of a development during which the focus shifts to the individual and individual concerns, e.g. love: it seems instead to be due to differences demanded by different genres.

One of our earliest pieces of literature is a fragment written by the choral lyric poet Eumelus which has been dated to the first half of the 7th century BC.[3] The next poet of whom a substantial number of fragments of choral lyric has survived, is Alcman.[4] The preserved fragments will be examined under the following aspects: the relative importance of mythical content and references to the performing chorus and the poet. Mythical features often provide the linguistic background for such dramatization of real people. I will argue later that this phenomenon is determined by the context and occasion of performance.

Poetic creation of the 7th/6th centuries BC is not limited to the sphere of public occasions and religious festivals. The symposium was also a place where poetry was performed. Its late Archaic stage in particular was to play a crucial role not only in the transmission of poetry, but also in determining its contents.

However, it was not only the aristocratic gatherings, but in particular the symposia held at the courts of tyrants, the Pisistratids at Athens and Polycrates in Samos, which had a great impact on the artistic, and especially literary culture of the age.[5] We know that among the artists they employed were two of the most influential lyric poets, Ibycus (at the court of Polycrates) and Anacreon (at both courts: Samos and Athens).

Choral and monodic lyric have one thing in common which reflects the general trends of their times: however different the context of performance is, the tendency to speak about individual personalities and integrate them into the poetic context can be found in both genres. As a result, myth is always present as well, but it is not narrated for its own sake, since familiar mythological features are now being used to describe individuals or to communicate between poet and audience. How these developments also led to the establishment of the male love-god remains to be examined.

8.3 CONTEXT AND PERFORMERS OF CHORAL LYRIC

Choral lyric has a civic dimension that is, relatively speaking, stronger than that of monodic lyric: it was performed at festivals, public or private, and thus before a larger audience. Even festivals which took place at more private occasions, such as weddings, funerals and the like, have a social significance.[6] In choruses of men and women, the participation especially of adolescents was substantial. An early testimony confirming the participation of young men and women in choral performance is the *Homeric Hymn to Apollo* (156-61). It refers to girls from Delos who praise Apollo in hymns and commemorate men and women of the past (probably mythical themes).[7] Alcman too wrote both for young women and young men at Sparta, and his *partheneia* were composed for young women or even girls to perform at religious festivals.[8] A 2nd-century BC testimony confirms that young people had participated in choral performances from earliest times.[9]

From the 7th century BC onwards we have reliable evidence that choruses not only performed hymns, but also other types of poems, or rather songs, at occasions which were not necessarily religious. Two composers of choral lyric are Alcman (end of 7th century BC) and Pindar (first half of 5th century BC). There are of course many more, but I shall focus on Alcman's *partheneia*, since they are the earliest extant literary sources providing original evidence for the actual performance of choral lyric, and are also significant for their dramatizing of individuals within the poetic performance.[10] They are of further significance in so far as they are composed and adapted for a particular group.[11]

In the *partheneion* partly preserved in the Louvre Papyrus (fr. 1 *PMGF*) and in another fragmentary song, probably also a *partheneion* (fr. 3 *PMGF*), there is a clear emphasis on the performers' personae and erotic concerns, and in fr. 38 and fr. 39 *PMGF* even on the poet's own personality. This is achieved by dramatization in the text of participating individuals, who are praised and at times described in detail.[12] The emphasis which is put on the individualization of the singers (as opposed e.g. to gods in hymns) suggests that the *partheneia* were performed at an event which was not celebrated exclusively in honor of gods, since it refers to the personal situation of the girls themselves.[13] This may be the reason why divine and heroic myths play an almost subordinated role, as far as we can tell from the extant fragments: what seem to be originally mythical features (e.g. encomiastic epithets) are here applied to persons involved in the performance. It therefore seems justified to claim that in these songs the participants, above all the chorus leader, replace the gods and are themselves the protagonists of the "story". One might in this case assume that this aspect and the fact that the poet too emerges from his anonymity underlines the interest in the individual personality. This phenomenon is absent from heroic epic, but finds its expression especially in lyric poetry for which the representation of contemporary human beings in choral song may have been crucial.

The *partheneion* (fr. 1 *PMGF*), following the traditional choral pattern, begins with a mythical narration accompanied by reflexions about human life (13-21 and 34-39).[14] It then switches to the performance. From line 39 onwards it is the girls themselves who become the actual protagonists of the "story". The Delian girls' identity had remained fairly anonymous in the hymns they were said to sing for the god.[15] The performers of this *partheneion*, by contrast, become the subject of their own song, and the focus is placed on the ten singing dancers, who are all named in the course of the performance; the 11th, Ainesimbrota, does not seem to be a member of the chorus, but appears rather as the seller of magical charms.[16] The two main figures are Agido and Hagesichora who is, as suggested by her name, the chorus leader. They seem to function as a pair, and their beauty surpasses that of the other chorus members of whom, however, we also get an impression. Lines 64-68 give more details about the singers' splendid ornaments.

When they start singing about themselves and address each other they almost seem to introduce themselves to the audience. Though inferior to Hagesichora and Agido, some of them are vividly represented, and the most distinguished details of their beauty are also encomiastically emphasized, although they cannot compete with their leaders (39-77):[17] "But I sing Agido's radiance, I see her like the sun . . . but my cousin's hair, Hagesichora's, blooms like purest gold, . . . for neither is the abundance of the purple of our dresses enough for our protection, nor snake-bangles of solid gold, nor the Lydian headscarf, the pride of soft-eyed girls, not even Nanno's tresses will suffice, nor Areta the goddess-like girl, nor Thylakis nor Kleesisera. Nor would you go to Ainesimbrota and say: Let Astaphis be mine, let Philylla look my way, or Damareta, or lovely Vianthemis—it is Hagesichora who wears me out with longing. For is not Hagesichora, the one with the lovely ankles, here beside us?":

... ἐγὼν δ' ἀείδω	39-41
Ἀγιδῶς τὸ φῶς· ὁρῶ	
ϝ' ὥτ' ἄλιον ...	
... ἁ δὲ χαίτα	51-54
τᾶς ἐμᾶς ἀνεψιᾶς	
Ἀγησιχόρας ἐπανθεῖ	
χρυσὸς [ὡ]ς ἀκήρατος·	
...	
οὔτε γάρ τι πορφύρας	64-79
τόσσος κόρος ὥστ' ἀμύναι,	
οὔτε ποικίλος δράκων	
παγχρύσιος, οὐδὲ μίτ'ρα	
Λυδία, νεανίδων	
ἰανογ[λ]εφάρων ἄγαλμα,	
οὐδὲ ταὶ Ναννῶς κόμαι,	
ἀλλ' οὐ[δ'] Ἀρέτα σιειδής,	
οὐδὲ Σύλακίς τε καὶ Κλεησισήρα,	
οὐδ' ἐς Αἰνησιμβρ[ό]τας ἐνθοῖσα φασεῖς·	
Ἀσταφίς [τ]έ μοι γένοιτο	
καὶ ποτιγλέποι Φίλυλλα	
Δαμαρ[έ]τα τ' ἐρατά τε ϝιανθεμίς·	
ἀλλ' Ἀγησιχόρα με τείρει.	
οὐ γὰρ ἁ κ[α]λλίσφυρος	
Ἀγησιχ[ό]ρ[α] πάρ' αὐτεῖ.	

These examples show that poetic devices such as encomiastic epithets (see καλλίσφυρος 78), which are normally used to describe gods and goddesses in epic, can also be adopted to describe the contemporary young women in the poem.[18] There seem to be two types of such poetic devices. One kind is taken from the poetic tradition, praising beauty in particular; for example, the image in which Agido's attraction is described and compared to the sun and light recalls descriptions of divine epiphanies.[19] Another kind is shaped by Alcman and adapted to the uniqueness of the chorus for which he composed. Here some of the devices are directly related to the situation of either the rehearsals or even the actual performance, and in both cases the composer comes into the dialogue with his singers. In fr. 33 *PMGF* girls performing their dance correctly are called ὁμόστοιχοι ("in the same line together"); a girl who likes to stand at the edge of the chorus is φιλόψιλος (fr. 32 *PMGF*).[20]

It is, however, not only the chorus members, but also the poet himself who is presented in his songs. In fr. 38 *PMGF* Alcman calls himself κιθαριστής and elsewhere (fr. 39 *PMGF*) even mentions his name and reveals himself as composer and producer: "these words, this song Alcman discovered." The mythical narration appears to be relatively subordinated. Instead, the protagonists of the poems are actually now the chorus and, in other songs, also the poet. In contrast to hymns, the chorus praise themselves instead of gods, and they do so in a similar idiom. Thus the focus of interest is upon the girls themselves. Their relationship and familarity with each other or the poet also come to the fore. The degree of intimacy with which the chorus members express their admiration and longing for Hagesichora is erotic and rather reminiscent of monodic lyric, e.g. Sappho's poems. The relationship of Hagesichora and Agido, who appear as a pair and are elevated by their beauty above the other members of the chorus, may refer to the background of the song.[21]

However, what is significant for our argument is that here, for the first time, we get a detailed description of the performing individuals, and the tone in which they address one another is surprisingly familiar. The girls not only describe each other's feminine qualities and beauty, but express admiration and affection for the chorus leader with a degree of intimacy which makes their words sound like personal confessions of affection or love. Perhaps they refer to homoerotic relationships which were institutionalized before marriage within this group, but this is not necessary to explain the chorus' utterances of affection and desire for Hagesichora.[22] Elsewhere, this kind of familiar tone can only be found in the poetry performed in a more private environment, such as symposiastic gatherings. These personal elements occur not only in choral lyric; we find a similar set in the motifs and style of symposiastic monodic lyric. It seems that lyricists sometimes were even directly inspired by certain images which they adapted to their specific intention and to the context of performance. I will illustrate this later with an example taken from a *partheneion* (fr. 3 *PMGF*) by Alcman, which Ibycus (fr. 287 *PMGF*) developed in his own particular way. He applies the imagery used by the girls to describe their chorus leader's irresistible glance to express the impression a beloved boy's look has on him.

8.4   CONTEXT AND PERFORMANCE OF MONODIC LYRIC

Monodic lyric encompasses all those shorter poems which were originally written for performance by the poets themselves to the accompaniment of a stringed instrument, usually the lyre. The literary tradition mentions as the main representatives Sappho, Alcaeus and Anacreon, whom vase paintings frequently depict as playing the lyre (see Plate 13), and also Ibycus, but there were also many more.[23]

The solo presentation allowed stronger self-involvement and therefore an even more individual and intimate choice of voice, themes and topics than in choral song. Poets like Sappho, Alcaeus and Anacreon even developed their idiosyncratic metres and expressed their personal concerns in their own dialect. This is also reflected in the occasion of performance. Unlike choral lyric, these poems were not composed for a broader public audience, but for more private gatherings. Most of monodic lyric was performed at symposia.[24] It was the small and intimate atmosphere of the symposium which provided the ideal scenery and background for a more individually oriented poetry. It not only allowed poets to express their personal world, but also encouraged the guests to participate actively and address other symposiasts in their poems.[25] Many themes of this type of monodic poetry are taken from the immediate environment and are concerned with wine and song, but mostly with love. Sometimes the beloved praised in song (not necessarily a guest, sometimes also the wine pourer) was present and therefore directly addressed at the moment of performance.[26]

But what were these symposia like? Classical scholars have only recently shown an interest in historical and anthropological studies.[27] They are a phenomenon of the 2nd half of the 6th century BC which cannot be fully understood without taking into consideration the historical changes and developments that shaped the age and which lasted throughout antiquity. Viewed from this perspective, it is clear that the poetry of Ibycus and Anacreon has also to be interpreted within the context that is responsible for the transformation of the symposium. I suggest that diverse strategic, political, and finally social developments led to creating the type of symposium which fostered a literary culture that promoted the emergence and accomplishment of the male god of love.

Monodic poetry is in scope and theme essentially a product of the aristocratic symposium. In what follows I examine to what extent these developments affected the link between the symposiastic context and the erotic relationships of men and boys. Several convincing attempts have been made to relate the sudden, yet limited, popularity of homoerotic motifs on vase paintings (ca. 560-475 BC) to these changes and developments.[28] But no scholar has yet considered whether the equally sudden emergence of identifiable winged male love-gods—Erotes—in art (from 520 BC onwards) can be explained within the same historical and literary context. It also remains to ask whether the poetry that emerged in this symposiastic environment has not only inspired art, but also cult.[29]

8.5   RELEVANT ASPECTS OF SYMPOTIC HISTORY

Starting from the early form of the symposium as we found, for instance, in Homeric epic, I will now chart the changes and developments in its civic implications, in its function as a place of performance of poetry, and then, finally, consider the role of youths and boys there.[30]

The "Homeric" feast or banquet, not called συμπόσιον, but rather δαίς, had a strong public, political and social meaning as an "organ of social control".[31] It was chiefly a means by which an aristocratic family established and reaffirmed their power within the Archaic society. Thus the generosity which manifested itself in the feasting as well as in the entertainment was intended to secure the support of fellow male aristocrats in military affairs.[32] The symposium at that time was an institution of the warrior élite; being a structural element within Archaic society, it occupied a central political position in the city.[33] Feasting and entertainment were private activities, but in wartime when the support of the community was required, they received a public meaning. Thus at the meals of Homeric aristocracy, the heroic epics were not performed for their own sake, but were always also meant to reinforce the values of the aristocratic society. The narrations refer to the mythical past and to the lives of the heroes (see the personal stories of Nestor, Phoenix and Odysseus in Homer) and thus they are normally not related to the present context of performance.[34]

Whereas O. Murray looks at the public and social significance of the early Archaic symposium from a chiefly political angle, other scholars also take into account its role in the education of boys and young men.[35] There is in fact good literary and archaeological evidence that these were always present at banquets with their fathers, often in the role of wine pourers, which seems to have been a traditional function. In the *Iliad* it was the κοῦροι who poured the wine at the meals of the aristocrats, and the fact that Menelaus' son fulfilled the same task at a banquet arranged by his father suggests that the wine pouring was more than a simple service, since it would otherwise have been the task of a slave.[36] The scholia and commentaries on the *Iliad* confirm that the wine pouring was a duty of young nobles, and we often see young beardless and naked men in banquet scenes in Archaic and also Classical art.[37]

These sources do not inform us about the further implications of this duty, but evidence concerning similar practices in other parts of Greece does. In Crete, young boys served the wine at their fathers' meals at the ἀνδρεῖον. They also had to bring food to their fathers and to themselves, but they had to eat sitting on the ground. The boys shared one drinking cup and were allowed to have their own only after they had been initiated into the adults' world. It is significant for the educational function of this custom that after the meal the boys were summoned to listen to their fathers' discussions and learned how to be brave.[38] Similar customs are known in Sparta. While the adults were reclining and discussing the latest political issues and other citizens' achievements in society, the young boys present had to listen and serve wine to their elders. They were even encouraged to pose questions which, according to Lycurgus, was considered a means of instruction and education for the future citizens.[39]

Boys were sent to symposia in Classical Athens for educational purposes. They had to glorify the exploits of their role models, the mythical heroes. It is hard to imagine that the participation of young males in symposia had no homoerotic implications. It has been generally agreed that pederasty was institutionalized in many parts of Greece and had educational and initiatory functions, the purpose of which was to prepare the young for their future role as citizens. In Crete and Sparta pederasty was part of coming-of-age rituals, and at Thebes the male lover offered his beloved a garment once he had entered the community of adults.[40]

We have traces of the educational functions of the young boys' presence at symposia in early didactic poems from the 7th century BC onwards. They are of a popular philosophical content and addressed to young boys, and these admonitions should be seen as an initiation to real life: Semonides addresses a boy (ὦ παῖ) in a poem where he complains that men do not realize their ephemeral nature and therefore become slaves to hope and expectation. Alcaeus does this too when he speaks about wine and truth (οἶνος, ὦ φίλε παῖ, καὶ ἀλάθεα). Theognis' verses addressed to Cyrnus or Solon's elegies also encompass rules for proper behavior as well as political considerations. These addresses imply a certain familiarity and intimacy.[41]

There is, then, sufficient evidence that there had always been a more pleasurable and passionate side to the boys' presence at symposia beyond the mere educational or initiatory function. Even in the poems of didactic content the poets warmly and kindly address their παῖδες. This sort of poetry, however, is of course not merely didactic, and the homoerotic component which in the above examples is merely implied, is not fictitious but had probably always been a reality at the banquets. The first poet to describe overtly the sexual passion for a beloved boy in an elegiac couplet, perhaps within a symposiastic context, is, according to our evidence, Solon:[42] "while one loves a boy in the lovely bloom of youth, desiring his thighs and his sweet mouth" (fr. 25 W.).

> ἔσθ' ἥβης ἐρατοῖσιν ἐπ' ἄνθεσι παιδοφιλήσηι,
> μηρῶν ἱμείρων καὶ γλυκεροῦ στόματος.

This shows how well established and accepted the relationships between ἐραστής and ἐρώμενος were at the time of Solon (and very probably much earlier, but no literary evidence has survived). The fragment also conveys an erotic and emotional element, which goes beyond the institutionalized initiatory and educational functions of pederasty.[43] This type of homoerotic relationship, however, seems to have been limited to the aristocratic stratum of society for whom it was a fashionable pastime. The physical and aesthetic aspects of these relationships also come to the fore in the places where lovers met. It had always been in the gymnasium and the *palaestra* where men could watch their beloveds exercising, normally naked. Just as the agora was the political centre for Archaic aristocrats, the gymnasium and *palaestra* were the centres of physical and intellectual life and the focal points for the education of the young (see Plate 5).[44] But apart from these venues it was certainly also the symposium where the aristocratic élite could more or less openly gratify their passions and admiration for younger men or boys.

The political events of the later Archaic age, i.e. at the beginning of the 6th century BC, entailed major changes in the lifestyle of the aristocracy. The shift of military power from the warrior élite to the hoplite army of the *polis* deprived the aristocracy's symposiastic gatherings of their political significance, and the gatherings became more and more private, that of an "aristocracy of leisure".[45] Thus the symposium became a refuge from the real world, an escape into entertainment and luxury for its own sake.[46]

The symposium of the more or less privatized aristocracy was now the appropriate place for an even more personally oriented poetry, a kind in which personal opinions and issues were expressed among like-minded participants sitting and drinking together. It has been argued that the change in lifestyle, and the fact that people now needed to express their personal world created both new literary forms and new social gatherings. This led to a novel and somehow more private symposium.[47] Numerous vase paintings convey what the atmosphere was like there; one can well imagine that it was the guests who participated in the poetic presentation and that they referred to each other in their performances. The myths which symbolically transmit the values of the aristocracy seem to have become less important.[48]

How are these changes in strategic, political and social structures reflected in the sympotic culture? J. Bremmer explains the increasing number of homoerotic courtship scenes (from 560 BC onwards) on Attic vase painting within the context of the disintegration of the aristocratic society and establishes a direct relationship between pederasty and the symposium.[49] He argues that sports and pederasty become a surrogate for the competitive and agonistic aspirations of the former warrior élite, now deprived of their strategic and thus political meaning. In fact, the *Pythian* games were founded in 582 BC, the *Isthmian* in 581 BC, and the *Nemean* in 573 BC. [50] The disintegration of the old aristocracy and its ideals and institutions also entailed a depoliticization of the symposium, formerly the place where, via love relationships between men and boys, the education of future citizens took place. While the symposium lost its former shape together with its political meaning and educational function, new figures, athletes and *hetairai*, appear on the scene whereas solid food disappears.[51]

That these circumstances affected the spirit of the symposium is understandable, but the increasing popularity of pederasty (as reflected in art) is not necessarily a consequence of depoliticization. As it turns out, it was particularly those who had monopolized political power at that time, the tyrants, who in an extraordinary way lived and cultivated the male erotic relationship. This finds expression in the arts that they patronized, particularly in literature, but also in the sudden emergence of courting scenes on vases of the mid-6th century BC. H. Shapiro considers them also in their socio-historical context and interprets them as a reflexion of the taste which was fostered not by the now idle aristocrats, but by those who were in power, the tyrants. He draws a link between the Pisistratids at Athens and the court of Polycrates of Samos in Ionian Greece, both of whom patronized the poet Anacreon, and he argues that the cultural environment at the tyrants' courts was responsible for the cultural *ambience* in which the homoerotic relationship could flourish.[52]

Both approaches, J. Bremmer's, which is more politically and socio-historically oriented, and H. Shapiro's, which is based more on the evidence in art and literature, are illuminating and useful. However, neither of them has pointed out that, during all these changes, male love relationships became more romanticized—a fact which is particularly well documented in poetry and which has certainly favoured their popularity in art. In what follows, I will combine J. Bremmer's and H. Shapiro's results and attempt to develop them further. I suggest that the general changes probably meant that the wine pourers at the symposium were not necessarily the sons of the participants. For our purposes it is significant that this, together with the advanced privatization of the symposiastic sphere, gave way to a new romanticization of the homoerotic love relationship as we find it expressed in the poetry of Ibycus and Anacreon. It will then remain to ask whether the sudden emergence of Erotes in Attic vase painting and the alleged cult of Eros in the Academy at Athens can also be related to the courts of the tyrants in Samos and Athens where this poetry was composed.

It has been documented above that at the early Archaic symposia it was the duty of aristocratic κοῦροι, youths, to fulfil the task of pouring the wine. On vases we see them usually beardless, sometimes naked. J. Bremmer does not distinguish between the noble wine pourers referred to as κοῦροι and those addressed as ὦ παῖ; for the latter we have numerous examples in lyric poetry: Hipponax mentions a boy who has just broken a cup, and Anacreon asks boys to serve him with wine.[53] I suspect that aristocratic youths still seem to have been present at the symposium, even when it had lost its educational functions, but that they were joined in their function as wine pourers by younger boys, very much παῖδες whom poets immortalized in various contexts of lyric poetry.[54] The identity of these παῖδες has, as far as I can see, not yet been investigated. It seems that the wine pourers need not be aristocratic, but could now also come from a lower social class.[55] In an Archaic *skolion* (fr. 906 *PMG*), the wine pourer is addressed as διάκονε which means "servant" or "waiting man":[56]

ἔγχει καὶ Κήδωνι, διάκονε, μηδ' ἐπιλήθου,
εἰ χρὴ τοῖς ἀγαθοῖς ἀνδράσιν οἰνοχοεῖν.

A scholium on the *Iliad* which comments on a passage describing how boys pour wine into bowls also seems to indicate a change. It says that it is an "ancient custom" that boys perform the duty of wine pouring and mentions the son of Menelaus as an example.[57] The conclusion of the scholium, giving the reason why "nowadays" slaves are "still" called παῖδες, suggests that slaves at some point started performing the job that had been in the hands of noble boys, such as Menelaus' son "in ancient times". It seems clear that these alterations which allowed slaves to pour the wine, also affected the courtship scenery of the symposium.[58]

Usually it seems to have been the wine pouring youths or boys in particular who inspired the erotic and sexual fantasies of the older symposiasts. In myth it is told that Zeus fell in love with Ganymedes while the latter was serving him with wine, and that he finally abducted him.[59] This sensual element was certainly always present in symposiastic situations, but it was not prevailing in the iambic and elegiac symposiastic poetry of Callinus and Tyrtaeus where it was instead linked with or even subordinated to didactic purposes as we have seen.[60] This can be explained by the fact that at that time the symposium still had an educational function. Thus the quite discreet compliments paid to the παῖδες in earlier poetry seem to reflect the didactic character of the environment in which it was performed: the "former" symposium, a place of education and instruction for future citizens. It is within this context—the lower status of the wine pourers, and, of course, also their younger age, together with the privatization of the symposium and consequent loss of its educational function—that we can explain the more intense and passionate celebration of the beloved youths and the new romanticization of these love relationships as we find them depicted in the type of poetry to which we now turn.

8.6   THE COURT OF POLYCRATES OF SAMOS AND THE POETRY OF IBYCUS AND ANACREON

The cultural *ambience* of the court of the tyrant Polycrates in Samos was the ideal context for the celebration of homoeroticism, which had always been linked to the wealthy upper classes of society who had enough leisure and could afford to indulge their passions.[61] At the lavish court of the tyrant, the symposium seems to have been exclusively the place of pleasure, distraction—and of sophisticated literary entertainment, as the fragments of the two most important court poets, Ibycus and Anacreon, indicate. The hypothesis that both poets went to Samos during the rule of Polycrates' father, Aeaces, possibly at his invitation, seems open to no objection.[62] This is corroborated by two independent ancient testimonies. According to the Suda entry, Ibycus came to Samos when the father of Polycrates the tyrant was in power.[63] Himerius tells the story of a father who invited Anacreon to teach his son Polycrates music, who at that time was still an ephebe.[64] If Ibycus' *encomium* (on which see below) was really composed for the young Polycrates (fr. S 151 *PMGF*), it could have been written for him when he was either not yet tyrant or shortly after his and his brothers' coup in 538 BC.[65] The political structure previously in place remains unclear. It is possible that members of the family of Polycrates wielded some power in the early 6th century BC.[66] If Aeaces had been deposed then or earlier, as has been suggested, one would assume that he was either a tyrant himself or another type of ruler who, in order to enrich the cultural life at his court, invited the two poets, who left Samos after Polycrates' death in 522 BC.[67]

During Polycrates' reign, after the annexation of other Greek cities by the Persians, Samos emerged as the commercial and intellectual centre of Ionia.[68] The tyrant was already famous in antiquity for his patronage of the arts and his expensive and luxurious lifestyle. He attracted the famous physician Democedes from Croton to his court after offering him a salary of two talents, which was twelve times more than what the Pisistratids had paid him. Obviously the tyrant wanted not only the best poets, but also the best doctors and engineers. He employed the Megarian Eupalinus to build a tunnel.[69] The historian Alexis gives a vivid account of the tyrant's love for luxury goods and boys:[70]

"Samos was embellished with products of many cities by Polycrates, who imported Molossian and Laconian hounds, goats from Scyros and Naxos and sheep from Miletus and Attica. He also summoned artisans (to his court), paying very high wages. Before he became tyrant, he had extravagant beds and cups produced, and allowed them to be used by those celebrating a marriage or the larger sort of receptions. What is striking in all of this is that the tyrant is nowhere recorded as having sent for women or boys, although he was so passionately excited by the company of males (καίτοι περὶ τὰς τῶν ἀρρένων ὁμιλίας ἐπτοημένος) that he even became a rival in love to Anacreon the poet: in his jealous rage he cut off the hair of his beloved boy (ὡς καὶ ἀντερᾶν Ἀνακρέοντι τῶι ποιητῆι, ὅτε καὶ δι' ὀργὴν ἀπέκειρε τὸν ἐρώμενον). Polycrates was the first to construct certain ships called 'Samainai', after the name of his country."

One can now better understand the environment of refined entertainment. The symposium obviously became the place for poetry in which the elegant and cultured, but also playful lifestyle of the tyrant's court, and especially its symposia were stylized. Wine, song and love were now the main themes of this symposiastic poetry. The high degree of intimacy which comes to the fore in the way the loved ones are addressed reflects how private these court gatherings were - a happening which favoured romanticizing the relationships. This is also suggested by the fact that, as W.A. Percy has pointed out, there is, in contrast to Crete and Sparta, no institutional and traditional pederasty attested for Ionia. That this kind of pederasty was of a different quality, being voluntary rather than compulsory, and intellectual as well as voluptuous, is well reflected in Ionic symposiastic poetry.[71] Considering Ionian culture in general and the personal preferences of the tyrant, in particular his luxurious life-style (his love for art, together with his desires for adolescents), it is easy to appreciate the background to Ibycus' and Anacreon's poetry.

It now seems to be the wine pourers who openly become objects of desire and subjects of poetry. Falling in love seems to have taken place during the wine pouring at the symposium. Therefore, it is certainly no coincidence that in this context Ibycus is the first to testify that the abduction of the mythical wine pourer par excellence, Ganymedes, is motivated by Zeus' sexual desire for him.[72] I would suggest that now—since this sort of poetry and more private environment allows more personal and intimate themes—the homoerotic component can be more overtly expressed. However, it is already strongly indicated in the *Iliad*, where Ganymedes' "beauty", κάλλος, is stressed twice.[73] The adjective καλός is precisely the term assigned to the loved ones in many vase paintings and recently discovered graffiti.[74] It can be interpreted as a direct response to this poetic development that in the late Archaic period Ganymedes and Zeus are featured in courtship scenes.[75] Since in this myth homoeroticism is embedded in the symposiastic context, it is no surprise that it enjoyed high popularity in such an environment. P.A. Bernardini is certainly right in pointing out that this myth, performed and narrated in this context, is used to illuminate "il potere dell' amore pederastico".[76]

Other myths involving male homoeroticism are also linked to the banquet. In Pindar (*Ol.* 1,42-5), Poseidon abducts Pelops, with whom he fell in love when he was born, to Olympus "where later also came Ganymedes"—to do the same service to Zeus. In both myths, boys perform the duty of wine pouring and the sexual connotation is obvious. Besides, the association between wine pouring and falling in love also becomes clear in Philostratus' description of a painting (*Imag.* 1,17) which displays Poseidon falling in love with Pelops while he is pouring the wine in his father's house.[77] How closely related these mythical motifs were to the symposiastic reality, is well illustrated in the anecdote transmitted by Athenaeus: while Pericles was fighting against the Samians, Sophocles was sent to Lesbos to gain support for Athens. On his way he was invited by a certain Hermesilaus of Chios to a banquet. There he fell in love with the boy wine pourer and told him that if he wanted him to drink with pleasure he should not be too rapid in handing him the cup and taking it away. When he finally managed to kiss him he commented on his success by pointing out that his strategies were not as bad as Pericles always claimed.[78]

Against this background I assume that many of Ibycus' and Anacreon's love-poems actually celebrated the young and handsome wine pourers, who are exclusively addressed as boys, as in Anacreon's ὦ παῖ παρθένιον βλέπων or φέρ' ὕδωρ, φέρ' οἶνον ὦ παῖ.[79] The impression arises that it is exclusively these boys whom Anacreon, either in his own voice or in that of his patron, wants to court with his poems.[80] In one case, it seems to have been reported that they both competed for the love of one and the same boy (fr. 414 *PMG*). It is indeed hard to imagine that such spontaneous and passionate lines as the following, clearly addressed to an ἐρώμενος, could ever have been publicly said to a noble boy at a public banquet. Perhaps they were even composed and performed on the spot. Whatever the case, the threefold repetition of the boy's name lend the poem and its content the wit and playfulness which are so characteristic of Anacreon's love poetry: "I desire Cleobulus, I'm mad about Cleobulus, I gaze at Cleobulus" (fr. 359 *PMG*).[81]

> Κλεοβούλου μὲν ἔγωγ' ἐρέω,
> Κλεοβούλωι δ' ἐπιμαίνομαι,
> Κλεόβουλον δὲ διοσκέω.

Since the desire and madness for the boy are caused by looking at him, this fragment gives a good impression of the symposiastic situation.[82] In fr. 357 *PMG*, a prayer to Dionysus, the poet, almost in a Sapphic manner, asks the god to make Cleobulus accept his love. This is certainly also a form of poetic courting. That the name "Cleobulus" occurs twice in the extant fragments suggests that he attended the banquets at least more than once. Possibly he was the wine pouring boyfriend of the poet, or more likely, of the tyrant.[83] Elsewhere, wine pouring is not only connected with falling in love, but even with making love: fragment 407 *PMG* is a quite direct encouragement to have sex, and the image clearly refers to the duty the beloved boy normally performs: the scholiast on Pindar explaining that προπίνειν, actually "to pledge", means to make a gift of the cup together with the mixed wine, quotes verses of Anacreon where πρόπινε is used instead of χαρίζου ("grant"): "come "pledge" me, beloved boy, your slender thighs":[84]

> ἀλλὰ πρόπινε
> ῥαδινοὺς ὦ φίλε μηρούς.

The wording here demonstrates that it was the young wine pourers, "ordinary παῖδες καλοί", who were the objects of song and sexual desire.[85] The verses find their correspondence in many scenes in Archaic vase painting displaying an older man rubbing his penis between the thighs of a boy.[86]

We know many of Anacreon's boys by name, and we also know of their specific physical qualities. These, however, are not described with the same amount of detail as is given in early choral lyric to the physical attributes of young girls. As we have seen earlier, in their cases epithets paralleling mythical and epic contexts are applied and adapted to reality by the poets.[87] According to the testimony of Maximus of Tyre, Bathyllus' youthful beauty, Cleobulus' eyes, the blond hair and refined disposition of Smerdies are recurrent themes in Anacreon's erotic poems.[88] Unfortunately, none of the extant fragments conveys what these praises of beauty were like, the only example is fr. 414 *PMG*, where the poet is chiding a boy for having "cut off the perfect flower of his soft hair".[89]

In the poems of Ibycus, Anacreon's fellow poet at the court of Polycrates, the playful and spontaneous element so characteristic of Anacreon is replaced by a strong emphasis on physical beauty on the one hand, and a more intense expression of emotion and passion on the other.[90] One can still understand why in antiquity he was considered "the most passionate in ephebic love".[91] For our purposes it is interesting that the far richer imagery of Ibycus' erotic *encomia*, which draw on mythical features, contributes to a more idealized image of the ἐρώμενος than anything we find in Anacreon's preserved poems.[92] This subtle praise of beauty could suggest a more romanticized love relationship. Athenaeus cites a poem in which the boy Euryalus is imagined to originate in the divine world, since the only explanation for his superhuman beauty can be that he was the nursling of Aphrodite and her mythical train, the specialists in beauty: the Charites, the Horae, Aphrodite herself and Peitho, who also adorned Pandora in Hesiod's *Works&Days*. "Euryalus, child of blue-eyed Charites, darling of beautiful-haired Horae, Cypris and mild-eyed Peitho raised you in beds of roses" (fr. 288 *PMGF*):

> Εὐρύαλε γλ'αυκέων Χαρίτων θάλος, <Ὡρᾶν>[93]
> καλλικόμων μελέδημα, σὲ μὲν Κύπρις
> ἅ τ' ἀγανοβλέφαρος Πει–
> θὼ ῥοδέοισιν ἐν ἄνθεσι θρέψαν.

The boy Euryalus is also the result of this divine cooperation and, like Pandora, he too is an object of seduction. It appears that Ibycus drew on this scene to create, as it were, a male counterpart to Pandora.[94] However, his relationship with the goddesses is even closer, since he is not only adorned, but even nurtured (suggested by θάλος and θρέψαν) by them. Each goddess seems to be a mother who has bestowed upon him her most characteristic feature of beauty: the Charites have given him their shining or even blue eyes,[95] the Horae their lovely hair, Peitho her soft eyes. That Aphrodite and Peitho raised him in beds of roses may refer to his skin.[96] Thus, nurtured by them, in his beauty he seems equal to these divine beings, or even superior since, due to his origin, he combines all of their qualities. Constructed out of divine attributes of beauty, he is a god of mythology himself—but real and visible at the banquet, perhaps even as a wine pourer, perhaps as a noble.[97]

Why is Eros not among the companions of Aphrodite who helped to produce the handsome boy? As we have seen earlier, Eros had been established since Hesiod as a cosmic entity and Aphrodite's companion; Alcaeus and Sappho had also mythologized him. One might ask whether here the boy could be Eros himself personified. This seems to be the case in another fragment where Ibycus developed these motifs further. It is Eros who "looks at me meltingly under dark eyelashes and attempts with every charm to make me fall into Cypris' endless hunting-net" (fr. 287 *PMGF*):

> Ἔρος αὐτέ με κυανέοισιν ὑπὸ
> β'λεφάροις τακέρ' ὄμμασι δερκόμενος
> κηλήμασι παντοδαποῖς ἐς ἄπει–
> ρα δίκτυα Κύπ'ριδος ἐσβάλλει·

I suggest that here Eros who seems so real that he can even look at the speaker, is identified with the divinized ἐρώμενος.[98] We find a similar set of imagery and wording in Alcman's *partheneion* (fr. 3 *PMGF*). There it was clearly the look of the beautiful chorus leader, Astymeloisa, which had a similar effect on the person who was being looked at.[99] "She was also looking with a glance more melting than sleep and death and not in vain—she is sweet. But Astymeloisa answers me nothing, holding her garland, like a star shooting through the shining sky, like a golden leafspray, or the delicate wing of . . . on slender feet she has passed through":

λυσιμελεῖ τε πόσωι, τακερώτερα
δ' ὕπνω καὶ σανάτω ποτιδέρκεται·
οὐδέ τι μαψιδίως γλυκ .. ήνα·
Ἀ[σ]τυμέλοισα δέ μ' οὐδὲν ἀμείβεται
ἀλλὰ τὸ]ν πυλεῶν' ἔχοισα
[ὤ] τις αἰγλά[ε]ντος ἀστήρ
ὠρανῶ διαιπετής
ἢ χρύσιον ἔρνος ἢ ἀπαλὸ[ν ψίλ]ον
     ..]ν
     ] . διέβα ταναοῖς πο[σί·]   61-70

Both fragments refer to the present situation of performance which is being dramatized in the song or poem. In Alcman's *partheneion*, the girls address each other within the context of the song. It seems to be a fixed pattern that the chorus leader (here Astymeloisa) sends the magic looks to her fellow companions which make them fall in love with her; but this love seems to remain unrequited, as the following lines suggest. This parallel in choral lyric, which certainly served as a model, helps us to understand that Eros is not just a mythologized divinity in Ibycus fr. 287 *PMGF*. He is in fact identified with the real boy present at the banquet, whose beauty is considered divine and who is looking at the poet from under his dark eyelashes.

The concurrence of divine and human identity is also supported by the fact that Ibycus in both fragments related either the eyes (fr. 288 *PMGF*), or the gaze from under the dark eyelashes (fr. 287 *PMGF*) to a divine origin: the adjective κυάνεος is traditionally used to describe Zeus' divine eye-brows in epic, and the eyes themselves are described in the *encomium* for Euryalus as a divine gift made by the Charites.[100] Furthermore, I would assume that the inescapable power which is associated with the gaze of the beloved upon the lover is considered as something divine and therefore may have contributed to causing the former to be seen as a god. It is Eros who by the power of his glance ensnares his prey, the poet, into the "nets" of Aphrodite. This image is not merely a mythological imitation but a new metaphor for Eros who is hunting on behalf of his mistress Aphrodite. The motif of the hunter Eros can easily be understood when we remember that already in the *Iliad* the non-personified ἔρως captures or conquers.[101]

The two fragments have shown that the beloved boy, endowed with conventional features which are first only a means of praising his beauty (fr. 288 *PMGF*), is not only compared to gods, but seems finally to become an independent god himself: Eros (fr. 287 *PMGF*). It emerges how much the banquet as the occasion of performance, together with the poetic tendency to dramatize the present reality, has contributed to this development. It is tempting to think that the romanticizing of the love for boys, for which the intimate symposiastic *ambience* provided a fitting occasion, finally culminates in the divinization of the beloved boys, and this may also explain the plurality of Erotes.

It has been suggested that Ibycus' eulogy for the young tyrant Polycrates (fr. S 151 *PMGF*) was sung at a banquet too.[102] However, whether it included a praise which makes him equal to the mythical heroes in their beauty cannot be decided upon with certainty. The sense of the last three lines (46-48) of this poorly preserved fragment depends on the punctuation of line 46:

> τοῖς μὲν πέδα κάλλεος αἰὲν
> καὶ σύ, Πολύκ'ρατες, κλέος ἄφθιτον ἑξεῖς
> ὡς κατ' ἀοιδὰν καὶ ἐμὸν κλέος.

This is the text given in *PMGF* and *PMG*. The meaning of the text would be: "among them (i.e. Cyanippus, Zeuxippus and Troilus) for evermore, Polycrates you too shall have fame for beauty everlasting" (Page).[103] It has been pointed out by J. Barron that the papyrus shows a stop at the end of line 46. If we keep it, it makes a difference to the sense: "their beauty is for ever; and you too shall have fame undying, Polycrates" (M.L. West).[104] The reading in *PMGF* and *PMG* seems preferable. If we exclude this link, which compares Polycrates with heroes in beauty, the transition from the mythical section to Polycrates seems quite abrupt. Also, this version produces a nice parallel between "by virtue of song" and "by virtue of beauty", referring to the κλέος of Polycrates and that of the poet which is expressed in 48.[105] The reference to Polycrates' beauty invites us to imagine the poet enamoured with the boy, perhaps at a symposium. Presumably he had not gained his beard yet.[106] The lines resemble other fragments in which boys are praised as objects of desire. Athenaeus (13,564F) cites the poem for the beautiful boy Euryalus (fr. 288 *PMGF*) as an example of a poem of praise (*epainos*) and presumably the poem for Polycrates fits this category as well—if he really was compared in beauty to the mythical heroes.[107] The possibility cannot be excluded that in a cheerful symposiastic context wine pourers were praised in the same way.

Anacreon's poetry does not emphasize the encomiastic elements which give Ibycus' erotic poetry a certain serious flavour, but it is still more playful and bantering. This playfulness manifests itself in the erotic themes, their poetic representation and, finally, in the image of Eros himself. Ibycus and Anacreon more than any other poets have been remembered as influential with regard to the representation of Eros. It is certainly no coincidence that they were both colleagues and therefore inspired by the same artistic environment. Although they both refer to the homoerotic ideal which they found in the symposiastic *ambience*, they diverge in their depiction of Eros. This is probably a reflection of their differing attitudes towards love itself. At the same time, we discern how close Eros remains to the characteristics of the pre-personified ἔρως, as an aspect of Aphrodite's sphere. Ibycus emphasizes the dark, violent and inescapable sides of love, as does Archilochus; thus, Eros is looking at him under dark eyelashes: temptingly beautiful, but also scary and frightening. Anacreon's favourite terms are παίζειν or συμπαίζειν (fr. 358,4; fr. 417,10; fr. 357,4 *PMG*), and thus his divinized Eros is also engaged in play: with knuckle-bones (fr. 398 *PMG*), with a ball (fr. 358 *PMG*). Even when he is taken out of the symposiastic context and placed among "serious" and conventional divinities such as Aphrodite, the Nymphs and Dionysus (fr. 357 *PMG*), he is still at play. According to our literary evidence, the earliest extant example of Eros at play is to be found in Alcman (fr. 58 *PMGF*); it will be discussed later, since Eros is brought into a mythical relationship with Aphrodite there and cannot be directly related to handsome boys present at a symposium.

As in Ibycus, Eros can hardly be separated in Anacreon from the handsome boys who were present at the symposium. There is certainly an indication of this in the anecdote relating that the poet, when asked why he composed poems for boys and not hymns to the gods, replied: "because it is they who are my gods!"[108] I would suggest that the divinized loved ones are actually the Erotes. This could explain why Erotes can also appear in the plural and why in vase painting they are scarcely distinguishable from young mortals, unless they are winged (see Plates 14, 15, 16, 17). But apart from these encomiastic, bantering compliments for Bathyllus, Cleobulus or Smerdies, there are also poems featuring Eros. Although being one of the few fragments dealing with heterosexual love, fr. 358 *PMG* is a good example of how the playful character of the games of love is reflected in the image of Eros at play, an image which is usually combined with the homoerotic ideal of the beloved boys. In Anacreon we are also left with the impression that Eros is, as regards his looks, the divinized ideal of the ἐρώμενος, inspired by the context of the symposium, whereas his character is moody and capricious, as is love itself. In fr. 358 *PMG*, Eros summons the poet to play ball games with a girl (1–4):

> σφαίρηι δηὖτέ με πορφυρῆι
> βάλλων χρυσοκόμης Ἔρως
> νήνι ποικιλοσαμβάλωι
> συμπαίζειν προκαλεῖται·

This image bears clear traces of a momentary situation in a symposiastic context, since not only the famous *kottabos*-play, but all kinds of games, especially ball-games were performed there.[109] The ball, together with lyres or hares, is also among the usual presents offered to the boy by the lover. The donation of such gifts is also a common feature in courtship scenes in art.[110]

It is not hard to explain why Eros has "golden" hair, since this is a feature characterizing male deities. The first god to be called "golden-haired" is, according to our extant literature, Dionysus when he makes Ariadne his wife (Hes. *Theog.* 947f.). Alcaeus calls Zephyrus the "golden-haired" lover of Iris (fr. 327 V.). The male deity, however, for whom χρυσοκόμης has become a stock

epithet in literature, is Apollo.[111] As a symbol of male virility and apt descrip-
tion for a master of seduction, golden hair occurs in erotic contexts.[112] However,
the epithet is not only found in literary depictions, but also seems to have been
associated with Apollo in cult, as a 6th-century BC inscription (*SEG* x 327)
suggests. Thus it is not surprising that it is often stressed in the characterization
of beloved boys as well. The reason why male gods, particularly renowned for
their beauty, seem to have been imagined as "golden-haired" may be that blond
hair has always been a rarity in Southern countries: it was considered to be spe-
cial and could therefore understandably have become an ideal of female, divine
and homoerotic beauty. In this context it is significant that, in 1980, French
archaeologists discovered amorous graffiti (dating from the second quarter of
the 4th century BC) on a wall in Kalami on Thasos, all of a pederastic type.[113]
The names of the beloved boys to whom these graffiti are dedicated are accom-
panied by several qualifying adjectives, which include χρυσός.[114]

It is, then, not surprising that Eros in Anacreon is "golden-haired" as well.
Although he seems to join the game, he is actually on the outside. The ball-
game appears to be a metaphor for the game of love which Eros is playing with
the poet's feelings, and the 2nd stanza conveys that his love for the girl remains
unrequited. Similar imagery is depicted in fr. 398 *PMG*, where Eros is playing
knucklebones (a pastime also at home in the symposium):

> ἀστραγάλαι δ' Ἔρωτός εἰσιν
> μανίαι τε καὶ κυδοιμοί.

But here too the god is playing with boyish delight with the "tumults and
madness" he causes for those who are in love; a similar idea finds expression in
fr. 428 *PMG*:

> ἐρέω τε δηὖτε κοὐκ ἐρέω
> καὶ μαίνομαι κοὐ μαίνομαι.

Although Eros appears as an independent entity who seems to intervene in
the symposiastic scene from outside, it is still obvious that in him the beloved
is always also present, since the power which the beloved has over the lover can
be of a divine quality. Perhaps the metaphor is not simply a playful "I love him,
I love him not" experience.[115] Since the frenzies and quarrels of human beings
are just a game of knucklebones in the god's hands, this could also mark the
terrifying aspects of desire.

Alcman (fr. 58 *PMGF*), at first sight, may at least have anticipated Eros'
association with the symposiastic environment which is, however, not fully de-
veloped before the homoerotic poems composed by Ibycus and Anacreon: "For
it is not Aphrodite, but the wild Eros who like a boy plays his boyish games,
alighting on the petals—please don't touch!—of my galingale garland."[116]

> Ἀφ'ροδίτα μὲν οὐκ ἔστι, μάργος δ' Ἔρως οἷα <παῖς>[117] παίσδει,

ἄ'κρ' ἐπ' ἄνθη καβαίνων, ἃ μή μοι θίγῃς, τῷ κυπαιρίσκω.

Alcman sets Eros in opposition to Aphrodite as a sort of mythical coun-
terpart. Thus the association with a beloved boy at the symposium which is
so obvious in the poetry of Ibycus and Anacreon is not apparent here at all.[118]
I find P. Easterling's suggestion is attractive: she interprets Eros as a phenom-
enon, a "dangerous kind of emotion", playing with human emotions as if it were
a game.[119] She does not draw a parallel to boys. Represented in this manner,
Eros could equally well embody a specific aspect of the love-goddess. Thus we
cannot infer that the personified image of Eros in Alcman has been inspired by
real παῖδες.

It has been suggested that the "galingale" represents an allusion to garlands
which belong to the familiar symposium. This interpretation makes good sense:
Alcman is warning an addressee to be on his or her guard against a dangerous
kind of emotion called Eros, "an irresponsible boy playing with human affec-
tions as if it were all a delightful game." In comparing Eros to a playing παῖς,
Alcman describes a specific aspect of the lover's emotion.[120] I would interpret
the "lust" or "madness", here attributed to Eros as a qualifying epithet (μάργος),
as actually the effect which the presence of an object of desire has on the lover.
It is tempting to interpret Eros here as an erotic personification of Aphrodite's
province, from whom he is separated and virtually independent. Eros' role is
perhaps comparable to Alcman (fr. 59a *PMGF*), where, as it seems, Eros is act-
ing on behalf of his mistress Aphrodite: "Eros once again at Cypris' command
pours sweetly down and warms my heart".

Ἔρως με δηὖτε Κύπ' ριδος ϝέκατι
γλυκὺς κατείβων καρδίαν ἰαίνει.

In this case, we need not associate the image of Eros with that of any hu-
man being present at the symposium, but instead consider the symposiastic
background as the place where amorous encounters are most likely to hap-
pen. Perhaps this aspect is represented by the presence of Aphrodite and Eros,
embodying the "raging mad" or "lustful" aspect (μάργος) of the love-goddess's
province, i.e. what P. Easterling calls "the arbitrariness of this impulse as the
whimsical mischief of a boy at play." Furthermore, she provides an interesting
explanation for the distinction drawn between Aphrodite and Eros, suggesting
that the early poets did not believe in the reality of Eros as a divine being and
could therefore use him in order to be rude about love without offending the
Olympian goddess Aphrodite. Thus Alcman's fragment may explain why po-
ets felt the need to create an additional love-deity. However, this interpretation
cannot explain why the other love-deity is male or why he looked the way he
did; the homoerotic element cannot be inferred from Alcman's poetry, where
Eros has a mythical relationship with the Aphrodite of whom he represents a
personified aspect. He has no independent role, but only works on her behalf.

What we can say is that the fragment, if the interpretation of "galingale" is correct, may reflect the symposiastic environment. However, it does not have the implications which we find in Ibycus and Anacreon: that Eros is related to the institution of the symposium, the historical development of which has emerged to provide the background for a poetic stylization of Eros who is identified with the ἐρώμενος.

8.7   CONCLUSION

It was the aim of this chapter to chart the emergence of the Greek love-god within certain contexts: the dramatic and thematic peculiarities in poetry and its tendency to dramatize reality and to refer directly to the context of performance; the historical changes that made the symposium the appropriate place for the creation of Eros. The contribution of Ibycus and Anacreon, who made Eros an independent god and no longer simply an aspect of Aphrodite, serves to explain three phenomena in art, cult and literature.

We have seen that a great number of homoerotic courting scenes emerged between 550 and 500 BC. It is particularly interesting that Eros himself does not yet appear in these black-figure and early red-figure vases. A. Greifenhagen has demonstrated that the first examples of Erotes unaccompanied by Aphrodite appear on Attic vases after 520 BC, and that the number of such vases increases greatly around 500 BC and shortly afterwards.[121] The innovation is that the Erotes are now independent and depicted on a larger scale (see Plates 2, 3, 14, 15, 16, 17). What confirms the close relationship or even identification between Eros and the ἐρώμενος attested in poetry, especially in Ibycus fr. 287 and fr. 288 *PMGF*, is that the two look very similar and are, indeed, distinguishable only by Eros' wings. In some depictions a winged Eros carries a love gift, whereas it is normally the ἐρώμενος who holds such gifts. Thus we see Eros with a bird and a ring, which may also refer to the games of the symposiastic context,[122] with a flute or lyre in numerous examples,[123] or even playing "tag" with other boys (see Plates 16 and 17).[124]

This phenomenon may explain why early Archaic Erotes, who normally flutter around Aphrodite in her most popular mythical context, the judgement of Paris, are depicted on a much smaller scale, as if they were intended to represent minor daimones or simply erotic personifications of Aphrodite's province (see Plate 8). This is how we must interpret the earliest evidence for Eros and Aphrodite shown together, the Attic pinax, dated to 570 BC, in which Aphrodite holds Eros (and Himeros) in her arms (see Plate 6). It is only now, in red-figure vase painting that Eros is depicted as an independent deity.[125]

There is, then, good evidence that the vase paintings are a direct response to poetic activity, since the appearance of Anacreon at the court of the Pisistratids in Athens is followed by numerous depictions of Eros on art works. In 522 BC, after the murder of Polycrates by the Persian satrap Oroetes, Anacreon accepted an invitation from Hipparchus, who functioned as a sort of *arbiter elegantiae* at the court of his brother, the tyrant Hippias. The latter reportedly sent a warship to Samos to fetch him.[126] It seems likely that he would take his own poetry and maybe also that of Ibycus with him from Samos and that this was then adapted for vase painting by Athenian artists, or at least influenced it. Anacreon himself even appears performing his poetry on several vase paintings of that period.[127] Also, the iconographical appearance of the male love-god cannot be separated from Ibycus' and Anacreon's contribution in the creation of Eros.

These developments shed new light on how both the "cult" of Eros in the Academy at Athens and the epigram which has been discussed earlier can be interpreted (ch. 7.2). Can there be a doubt that this inscription is inspired not by a sacred, but by the symposiastic and therefore homoerotic spirit which was so characteristic of the life-style of the tyrants and their court? The wording and form of address to Eros also conveys a feeling of the poetry which was performed there: adjectives with ποικιλο– also occur several times in Anacreon and later epigrammatists.[128] Even if it cannot be proved that Anacreon wrote the inscription, it has something of the spirit of his poetry. This "cult" of Eros at Athens probably never had any genuinely cultic or religious implications, but was established on private initiative. In this case one might assume that it is more a manifestation of the "cult" that was made of the idealized young beloved boy and which the Athenian aristocracy, above all the court of the Pisistratids, celebrated extensively.[129] This "cult" was supported by the poetic imports from luxurious Ionian Greece, the court of Polycrates in particular, with whom they always had close connections.

From this survey the following conclusion emerges: Eros is neither merely a personified aspect of Aphrodite nor a cosmogonic primeval entity. There is an additional component of the complex figure of Eros which was inspired by an attractive youth, with whom the god could even be identified. This may give an additional reason why he remains without a specific mythological story. Eros has a real dwelling place, since the environment which led to the development of the Eros-figure is the symposium.

This is confirmed when we look at the later Hellenistic representations of Eros in Apollonius Rhodius' *Argonautica*. Here he is integrated into a genuine myth, the story of Jason and Medea. According to Hellenistic tradition he is depicted as a naughty boy. The features in which his characteristics are illustrated, his looks, playful activities and character are now Hellenistic epic stylizations of the Archaic symposiastic Eros in which the homoerotic component is replaced, or perhaps enhanced, by turning him into a young child. This becomes all too evident when we see that in his literary expressions Apollonius is heavily indebted to Anacreon, whose favourite images of love as an act of play become manifest in Eros' boyish games. In the 3rd book of the *Argonautica* (114-40) we see Eros in fact playing knucklebones. Who could be surprised now that his playmate is none other than Ganymedes, the mythical wine pourer and darling of Zeus? The ball, Aphrodite's bribe and gift for Eros, clearly also has a parallel in Anacreontic imagery (358 *PMGF*).[130] It is also striking that, in the mythological contexts of their odes, Pindar and Bacchylides never mention a personified Eros. This coincides with the fact that Eros does not have any individual myth or story. A Pindaric *skolion* (fr. 123,1f. M.) indicates clearly that there were several personified Erotes, and here too there can be no doubt that there is a link with beloved boys: "one has to pluck" the ἔρωτες "at the right time, at the right age"; then he continues praising the beloved boy Theoxenus:

> Χρῆν μὲν κατὰ καιρὸν ἐρώ–
> των δρέπεσθαι, θυμέ, σὺν ἁλικίᾳ·

This may also explain the plurality of Erotes.[131] As we have learnt from the anecdote about Anacreon, which was cited earlier, every beloved boy could be seen as a god.[132]

It would seem, then, that Plato's σύνδειπνον, as featured in the *Symposium*, is a reprise of the Archaic scenery whereby philosophical speeches and discussions have replaced poetry and music, but not the intimacy of the atmosphere and the favourite themes: Eros and beloved boys. Here too the participants come from a privileged upper class which celebrates homoeroticism (sc. Pausanias, Agathon, Socrates and Alkibiades). Therefore, it can be no coincidence that Plato set his philosophical discourse about Eros in a symposiastic environment. Moreover, he has even mythologized this in the birth myth in the *Symposium* (203b2-c6) when he narrates how Eros' parents met: the gods had a feast when Aphrodite was born and Poros, drunken, went out into the garden, where he was seduced by Penia.[133] Thus Plato's myth may be interpreted as reflecting Eros' origin in Greek social history.

Chapter Nine
Some Final Conclusions

Examination of literary, epigraphical and iconographical material from primarily the Archaic period demonstrates that Greek erotic mythology is not a homogeneous conglomerate of deities and personifications with the same background and origin, or with the same type of myths or cults. A development can be charted in the relationship between Aphrodite and her companions, specifically Eros. With the exception of the latter, the other deities of love appear in mythical as well as in cultic contexts, which can be different from within the areas of love or marriage as they can also be related to the civic and political sphere. Aphrodite's companions, the Charites, Peitho and Eros are all personified aspects of her sphere of influence. However, whereas the Charites and Peitho are Aphrodite's attendants in early myth and her associates in cult, Eros is different, on account of his idiosyncrasy clarified above. It is probably due to the important phenomenon of Greek homosexuality that in Greek mythology the established goddess of love, Aphrodite, was joined by a male counterpart who came into being in the Archaic period and who seems to have been created in a process of invention by successive poets. Whereas Aphrodite, and also the Charites and Peitho could be approached in a more synchronic way by comparing their role and function in myth and cult and their relationship towards each other, the complex personality of Eros required a more diachronic method. In contrast to the other erotic deities, he seems not to have enjoyed cultic veneration, but was rooted traditionally in cosmogonic myth as a primeval entity. Moreover, like the other erotic personifications, he too embodies an aspect of Aphrodite's province, which explains how they finally came to be correlated with each other as mother and son. The reason why his personality is much more refined and individual than those of the other companions, and why he later even becomes independent from Aphrodite, can, as has been demonstrated, be found in his link to the phenomenon of Greek homosexuality, where he embodied the divinized ideal of the beloved youth. This may be the main reason for the creation of Eros as a second love-deity and male counterpart to Aphrodite.

Chapter One attempted to establish Aphrodite's Eastern origins. Several aspects in myth, cult and iconography which she has in common with her predecessor Ishtar-Astarte have been used to show that it is the Aphrodite Οὐρανία type whom the Greeks seem to have most closely associated with the Eastern Queen of Heaven. The subsequent Chapters Two and Three gave a portrait of Aphrodite by focusing on her Greek idiosyncrasy; this required a contrast to be drawn between myth, which features her adventurous sex-life, and cult, where she is concerned with more "serious" issues such as marriage and civic harmony. How far she is conceived as goddess of love and beauty in myth appears clearly in an episode of the *Iliad* (book 5) where she is dissociated from military and matrimonial concerns, and therefore also clearly differentiated from Athena and Hera. It was demonstrated that in the *Homeric Hymn*, the cult phenomenon of epiphany is taken as a means to promote her beauty and seductive skills when she meets Anchises. On the other hand, epigraphical evidence and her appearance in Attic myth could show Aphrodite as a source of harmony among the people; this seems to be the political understanding of the role she plays between lovers. The section dealing with "erotic personifications" (Chapter Four), examined the phenomenon of personified deities. As early as the *Theogony*, they represent aspects of the individual realms of the Olympian gods, to whom they can be related as attendants or children. Aphrodite's power is seen to become effective via her magic girdle, the κεστὸς ἱμάς, in which erotic personifications were imagined to be contained and probably visibly embroidered. Two other, apparently already well established personifications, Hypnos and Thanatos, seem to have provided some epic features for Eros who, however, does not appear in the *Iliad*. Chapters Five and Six on the Charites and Peitho demonstrated that some personified deities who appear as Aphrodite's attendants and executives of her province had an early independent role in cult as well. Not only in cult associations do they seem to represent a particular aspect of Aphrodite, but also in civic and political contexts.

The final two chapters were devoted to Eros. It was their aim to work out what makes him different from other erotic personifications and why he could finally become a mythological figure equal to Aphrodite. The characteristic he has in common with the other companions is that he too is part of Aphrodite's province. However, disregarding this, he also seems to be deeply rooted in Near-Eastern cosmogonic mythical tradition, as a non-personified primeval entity. It emerged that Eros' personality was developed in different stages: Hesiod was probably the first in a series of poets to mythologize a personified male love-god. That he could be perceived as a cosmic entity and aspect of Aphrodite becomes evident also in diverse genealogies of Eros invented by the lyric poets. Apart from attributes such as wings, which seem to have been inherited from established mythological figures, or arrows, which may have originally belonged to Apollo as bringer of disease or are perhaps metaphors for the pains love usually causes, Eros' fully developed personality seems to have been an achievement of the poets who were inspired by the environment in which their poetry was performed: the symposium. It seems to have been the young wine pourers in particular who became the objects of desire and were celebrated in symposiastic poetry. This is already indicated in Solon's poems, but it is only in the poetry composed by Ibycus and Anacreon at the court of Polycrates at Samos that the praise of the beloved boy becomes a praise of Eros himself. The symposium seems to be Eros' birthplace. In contrast to Aphrodite and her other companions, Eros did not have a place in public cult, but as early as the 6th century BC he was at least welcome at the best of parties.

Notes

Chapter 1

1. For oriental influence generally, not only on the Greek concepts of deities, but also on Greek craftsmanship, magic and medicine, see Burkert (1992) and id. (2003), esp. 28-54; M.L. West (1997) with a focus on poetry and myth.
2. This is the name applied to the deity by e.g. Burkert (1985), 152-156, esp. 152, and M.L. West (1997), 56 and 451: Ishtar and Astarte denote one and the same goddess. Ishtar is the Akkadian name and occurs e.g. in the Babylonian epic of *Gilgamesh*; Astarte is the West Semitic equivalent and was used by the Phoenicians (see Luc. *Syr. D.* 4); on Astarte see Bonnet (1996); on interactions between Astarte and Aphrodite see Bonnet, Pirenne-Delforge (1999), 249-73. S. Price (1999), 16 also includes Inanna, the love-goddess of the Sumerians (circa 3000-2100 BC) among the Eastern goddesses with whom Aphrodite has an affinity; on the goddess see also Seidl, Wilcke (1976-80), 74-89.
3. S. Price (1999), 17.
4. For a brief overview see Pirenne-Delforge (1994), 6-9. This is the most recent monograph on Aphrodite, and is mainly a description of cults of Aphrodite on the Greek mainland and the islands; the question of Aphrodite's origin is therefore not central.
5. Farnell (1896), vol. 2, 618-69, esp. 619f.; he was followed by v. Wilamowitz-Moellendorff (1932), vol. 2,150-6; Otto (1947), 92-104, Nilsson (1967), vol. 1, 519-26, id. (1906), 363; see also Flemberg (1991), 12-28, esp. 17f., Burkert (1992), (2003)) and West (e.g. (1997), (2000)) in recent publications.
6. See most recently: Boedeker (1974) who minimizes the transmitting role of Cyprus and argues that Aphrodite is originally Mycenean, going back to the Indian goddess of dawn; Friedrich (1978) in his structural approach sees in her a syncretic version of different love deities and infers that Aphrodite is a female symbol of love. He points out her affinities with the Indo-European sky goddess in particular.
7. See e.g. Enmann (1886), XIII; Dunbabin (1957), 51.
8. See S. Price (1999), 16.
9. See M.L. West (2000), 134-8. He argues that Aphrodite's name is genuinely Semitic, but refutes Hommel's theory that it is to be derived from the Semitic variant "Aštoreth" which he considers unsound (see Hommel (1882), 176 who is followed by Burkert (1992), 98 with n. 7); more cautious Nilsson (1906), 363.
10. So Burkert (1985), 152f., similarly also Simon (1998), 203f. But Parker (1996), 196 is more reluctant to believe in Aphrodite's oriental origin. He thinks that the correspondence of Aphrodite's epithet Οὐρανία with Astarte's title "Queen of Heaven" is coincidental. He agrees, however, that Aphrodite Οὐρανία was certainly the type of Aphrodite the Greeks themselves mostly related to comparable Eastern figures.
11. For incense offerings to Aphrodite see Sappho fr. 2 V.

12. On Aphrodite's mythical representations in war contexts and her cultic function as a warrior-goddess see ch. 2.3.
13. See (1985), 152f.; for more details see below, ch. 1.5. However, one has to concede that images of Aphrodite which are partly painted with gold may have also been inspired by the idea that deities appear shining and brilliant in epiphanies. On cult images of Aphrodite in the context of epiphany, see ch. 3.4. Aphrodite's companions, particularly Eros and Peitho are associated with gold as well, see chs. 6.4 and 7.7.
14. M.L. West (1997), 56, 361f. and 383f.
15. See Burkert (1992), 96-100; id. (2003), 46-9; M.L. West (1997), 360-362.
16. See ch. 2.3.
17. For an overview see Burkert (1992), 1-8; id. (2003).
18. See e.g. Pirenne-Delforge (1994), 309 with n. 1 for further bibliography; see also Burkert (1992), esp. 11ff. and 101-04 and M.L. West (1997), esp. 611ff. and 628.
19. For their mythical depiction within Hesiod's account of Aphrodite's birth, see below, ch. 1.4.
20. See e.g. Burkert (1992), 9f.; before him similarly Lloyd (1975), 10.
21. See Penglase (1994), 161; see also Albright (1975), 507-36, esp. 523 (on the basis of inscriptions): "The now certain date of the inscriptions in question proves that the beginning of Phoenician colonization in Cyprus and Sardinia cannot well be placed later than the tenth century." See also Harden (1962), 62ff.; on Homer's references to Phoenicians particularly in the *Odyssey* see S. West (1988), ad 4,618 (with bibliography); the mentioning of the Phoenician trader (*Od.* 14,488f.) has been interpreted as reflecting Phoenician maritime expansion (see Lloyd (1975), 11); see also Niemeyer (1984), 3-94.
22. On the problem see Burkert (1985), 153; on the excavations see Pirenne-Delforge (1994), 334-40, with n. 131 (with bibliography).
23. Argued by Penglase (1994), 161.
24. Wilson (1975), 446-55, esp. 450f. and Fauth (1966), 6.
25. See *IG* II².337; see Burkert (1992), 11 with n. 6 for evidence and further bibliography; Powell (1997), 3-32, esp. 20.
26. See Huxley (1972), 34ff.
27. See Fehling (1989), 1-11 (introduction) and *passim*.
28. Her. 1,105,2: ἐσύλησαν (sc. οἱ Σκύθαι) τῆς οὐρανίης Ἀφροδίτης τὸ ἱρόν. ἔστι δὲ τοῦτο τὸ ἱρόν, ὡς ἐγὼ πυνθανόμενος εὑρίσκω, πάντων ἀρχαιότατον ἱρῶν, ὅσα ταύτης τῆς θεοῦ· καὶ γὰρ τὸ ἐν Κύπρῳ ἱρὸν ἐνθεῦτεν ἐγένετο, ὡς αὐτοὶ Κύπριοι λέγουσι, καὶ τὸ ἐν Κυθήροισι Φοίνικές εἰσι οἱ ἱδρυσάμενοι ἐκ ταύτης τῆς Συρίης ἐόντες.
29. According to Fehling (1989), 59-65 and 142f. the role of the Phoenicians worshipping Aphrodite was so traditional and well known among his readers that Herodotus (2,112-20) could use it as a literary means to bolster the credibility of the (in Fehling's opinion fictitious) story of Proteus and Helen and the latter's *temenos* in Egypt, which was allegedly surrounded by the Phoenician community who, correspondingly, worshipped her as ξείνη Ἀφροδίτη. Fehling argues that the story which Herodotus put into the mouth of priests at Memphis can actually be easily deduced from Greek sources (e.g., the story of Helen in Egypt as presented in the *Odyssey*).
30. Paus. 1,14,7: πρώτοις δὲ ἀνθρώπων Ἀσσυρίοις κατέστη σέβεσθαι τὴν Οὐρανίαν, μετὰ δὲ Ἀσσυρίους Κυπρίων Παφίοις καὶ Φοινίκων τοῖς Ἀσκάλωνα ἔχουσιν ἐν τῆι Παλαιστίνηι, παρὰ δὲ Φοινίκων Κυθήριοι μαθόντες σέβουσιν.
31. Paus. 3,23,1: τὸ δὲ ἱερὸν τῆς Οὐρανίας ἁγιώτατον καὶ ἱερῶν ὁπόσα Ἀφροδίτης παρ' Ἕλλησίν ἐστιν ἀρχαιότατον· αὐτὴ δὲ ἡ θεὸς ξόανον ὡπλισμένον.
32. See n. 2 above.
33. An exception is Herodotus 2,112: the Phoenician sanctuary in Egypt is called that of ξείνη Ἀφροδίτη (see n. 29).

34. Jeremiah 7,18 and 44,17-9. For modern interpretations of the association of the Greek Aphrodite with Ishtar-Astarte, see Burkert (1985), 152f.; M.L. West (1997), 56; see also Asheri (1989), vol. 1, ad 1,105 and Pirenne-Delforge (1994), 217f. and 437f.

35. It is interesting that Herodotus (1,131,3) regularly applies "Aphrodite Οὐρανία" when referring to foreign love-goddesses such as the Assyrian Mylitta or the Arabian Alilat; he never uses the mere name "Aphrodite". On this, see Burkert (1990), 1-32, esp. 20f.

36. *IDélos*. 1719 and 2305; on this see Parker (1996), 196 with n. 158

37. *IG* II².4636: Ἀριστοκλέα Κιτιὰς Ἀφροδίτηι Οὐρανίαι εὐξαμένη ἀνέθηκεν.

38. For a collection of the evidence see Pirenne-Delforge (1994), 437 with n. 194: in Athens, Athmonia (Attica), Piraeus, Argos, Epidaurus, Cythera, Sparta, Megalopolis, Olympia, Elis, Thebes, Agai; also on the islands: e.g. Amorgos (*IG* XII.7.57) and Didyma. Oberhummer (1961), 931-42, esp. 941 mentions epigraphical evidence only of Hera Οὐρανία in Cos and of Nemesis Οὐρανία in Athens.

39. The meaning of Aphrodite Πάνδημος, her cults and worshippers will be discussed in chs. 2.4.-2.6.

40. It has, however, to be conceded that it is not always Aphrodite Οὐρανία who is linked with children and wedlock. In Sparta, it is Aphrodite Hera whom mothers make dedications to when their daughters are getting married (see Paus. 3,13,9); see ch. 2.3 with n. 51; on Aphrodite's links with marriage and children in general, see Pirenne-Delforge (1994), 419-28.

41. Paus. 1,14,7: Ἀθηναίοις δὲ κατεστήσατο Αἰγεύς, αὑτῶι τε οὐκ εἶναι παῖδας νομίζων—οὐ γάρ πω τότε ἦσαν—καὶ ταῖς ἀδελφαῖς γενέσθαι τὴν συμφορὰν ἐκ μηνίματος τῆς Οὐρανίας.

42. So Edwards (1984), 59-72, esp. 64. See also Pirenne-Delforge (1994), 21 with ns. 24 and 25 for further bibliography.

43. *SEG* xli 182:   θησαυρὸς ἀπαρχὲς ὁ
                     Ἀφροδίτει Οὐρανίαι
                     Προτέλεια γάμο.
   The editio princeps was published by Tsakos (1990-1), 17-28.

44. So Parker (1996), 196.

45. For a discussion of these facets of Aphrodite and their reflection in myth and cult, see ch. 2.3.

46. It is, however, implied in Pindar, fr. 122 M. Here Aphrodite is called ματέρ' ἐρώτων οὐρανίαν; for an interpretation of the *skolion*, see ch. 6.6.

47. Schwabl in his extensive overview of Greek and Eastern cosmogonies ((1962), 1433-1589) does not mention a direct mythical parallel. On the basis of archaeological evidence, one may associate the Hesiodic myth with a terracotta figurine of a bearded female figure (dated 675-650 BC, from Perachora). This figure emerges from what can be interpreted as male genitals (on the figure see M.L. West (1966), 213). Moreover, this figure recalls images of Ishtar-Astarte, who was frequently depicted as bearded (see Burkert (1985), 152f.). Even if the birth out of the genitals finds its parallel there, the transformation of an androgynous creature into a beautiful young woman is a remarkable difference and probably Hesiod's creation; see Delcourt (1958), 43-7 on the cult of a bearded Aphrodite on Cyprus.

48. Similarly Nilsson (1967), 522 and M.L. West (1966), 212.

49. The uniqueness of Aphrodite's birth story manifests itself by comparison with other hymns in the *Theogony*, see Walcot (1958), 5-14, esp. 9f.

50. See e.g. *Theog.* 979-81: κούρη δ' Ὠκεανοῦ, Χρυσάορι καρτεροθύμῳ / μιχθεῖσ' ἐν φιλότητι πολυχρύσου Ἀφροδίτης, / Καλλιρόη; on the expression φιλότητι μίσγεσθαι see Mader (1993), 225-9, esp. 228, 2 d. Rudhardt (1986), 10ff. contrasts this role of Aphrodite with Eros' cosmological function.

51. On the Hittite succession myth see ch. 7.5.

52. Indicated in line 197; on the etymology, see Friedrich (1978), 201ff. He associates ἀφρός with Indic *abhrá-* ("cloud"), cf. West (2000), 134. The etymological explanation of φιλομμηδής, "genital-loving" is probably a later re-interpretation of Aphrodite's frequent

literary epithet φιλομμειδής, "laughter-loving", see M.L. West (1966) ad loc. Perhaps Aphrodite's cultic link to the sea is also integrated into the myth. We have epigraphical evidence that in the 4th century BC she was worshipped by sailors as Aphrodite Euploia. We do not know whether such cults were established earlier; for the cult of Aphrodite Euploia in general, see Parker (1996), 238 and ch. 2.1 with n. 4.

53. So e.g. *Il.* 5,330; 422; 458; 760; 883; *Hymn. Hom.* V,1f.: ἔργα πολυχρύσου Ἀφροδίτης / Κύπριδος.

54. E.g. *Od.* 8,288 and 18,193.

55. But cf. M.L. West (1997), 56f., who argues on a linguistic basis that Κυθέρεια cannot be derived from Κύθηρα. He takes it as the female form of the Ugaritic god Kothar, who corresponds to Hephaestus.

56. Her temple in Cyprus is frequently mentioned and thus suggested to be her most common cult place in *Hymn. Hom.* V,58f.; see also 2; 6; 291 (also linked with Cythera).

57. Ares himself leaves for Thrace (8,361) which is actually his traditional cult place.

58. See *Hymn. Hom.* V, 58f.

59. See above, ch.1.3.

60. So Nilsson (1906), 364; see also Pirenne-Delforge (1994), 309f.

61. See *IG* II².337; on the cult, see S. Price (1999), 76f.; Parker (1996), 160. In Piraeus a Kitian woman makes a dedication to Aphrodite Οὐρανία (*IG* II².4636; for a quotation, see n. 37 above).

62. On the term *xoanon* see Donohue (1988).

63. The passage is cited above, n. 31; on the goddess in weapons see ch. 2.3. It has been argued by Graf (1984), 245-54, esp. 250 that the cult of the armed Aphrodite at Sparta came from the East, but he suspects via the island Cyprus.

64. Burkert (1992); id. (2003).

65. Burkert (1992), 20.

66. For other motifs which were imitated, see Burkert (1992), 23.

67. For examples see Riis (1949), 69-90.

68. For an imported clay relief plaque in Corinth (7th century BC), see Boardman (1980), 76f. (pl. 72); for more examples see also Kantor (1962), 93-117, esp. 109.

69. So e.g. the implications of epiphany, see ch. 3.4.

70. See Boardman (1980), 62; but cf. Simon (1998), 212 (pls. 228 and 229): she also refers to their Eastern origin, but points out that they look somehow modified. She sees something "Greek" in them and therefore she interprets them as Greek goddesses, as "Charites". On Aphrodite and the Charites, see ch. 5.3.

71. Boardman (1980), 56.

72. Compare, for example, the ivory girl from Athens (pl. 34) with the ivory girl from Nimrud (pl. 35) in Boardman (1980), 62.

73. On the other hand, Phoenicians may have seen in these fuller shapes of Ishtar-Astarte the ideal of female beauty.

74. So Nilsson (1967), 520; on an etymology relating Aphrodite's name with pigeons, see West (2000), 137f.

75. Nilsson (1967), 520 and Burkert (1985), 42 with n. 47. The earliest epigraphical evidence of Aphrodite appears in the inscription on "Nestor's cup", which has been dated to 735-720 BC. Her name was also found on a 7th century BC black figured amphora from Naxos (according to Delivorrias (1984), II.1., 124, see also II.2., no. 1285). It remains uncertain whether the iconographical material of earlier periods reflects Ishtar-Astarte or Aphrodite, since, as we have seen, they have typical features and gestures in common and can hardly be distinguished (see Delivorrias (1984), II.1., 46, where the Mycenean leaf figures and the ivory statuettes in question are treated in the "Aphrodite" section).

76. On this see Burkert (1985), 153 and Pirenne-Delforge (1996), 838-43, esp. 842. In Greek, doves are either περιστεραί (as in the Hellenistic decree in Athens which is discussed in ch.

3.4) or πέλειαι, but these terms do not seem to have cultic relevance (see Thompson (1936), 224-31 and 238-47).

77. See *LSAM* 86; for an interpretation see L. Robert (1971), 91-197.

78. See Welz (1959), 33-137.

79. *SEG* xxxi 317: τᾶς Ἀφρ[οδίτ]ας.

80. Daux (1968), 711-1135, esp. 1028.

81. Travlos (1988), 185 with pls. 233-434.

82. *FGrH* 244 F 114: ἡ περιστερὰ ἱερὰ Ἀφροδίτης διὰ τὸ λάγνον ("lecherousness") · παρὰ γὰρ τὸ περισσῶς ἐρᾶν λέγεται.

83. For the inscription see also chs. 2.5. and 3.4. Cornutus (*Theol. Gr. 24*) says that it is because of the purity and cleanliness of the dove, symbolized by their white colour, that they became Aphrodite's companions; for a discussion, see also Pirenne-Delforge (1994), 388ff.

84. Beschi (1967-68), 511-36.

85. See Nilsson (1967), 521 and Burkert (1985), 153.

86. See de Visser (1903), *passim*; followed by Nilsson (1967), 201f.; 278f. and Delivorrias (1984), II.1., 9. As aniconic representations occur in oriental Ishtar-Astarte cults, we might expect to find examples in Greece as well. However, the black conical figure in Paphos mentioned by Delivorrias seems to be an exception (ibid.).

87. Burkert (1985), 152f. also notes among the parallels that both can be androgynous and therefore be bearded.

88. See Asheri, Antelami (1989), vol. 1, ad 1,105: the cult image of Astarte in Ascalon is a fish with a female head.

89. Examples in Simon (1998), 210-3.

90. See Simon (1998), 207, who argues that the Greek Aphrodite actually has three predecessors: Ishtar-Astarte, the Charites and Dione; on Dione's Indo-European origin see Dunkel (1988/90), 1-26; for a discussion of this episode against the background of Aphrodite's provinces, see ch. 2.3.

91. Burkert (1992), 96-999; more recently id. (2003), 47-9; see also M.L. West (1997), 361-262; on similarities of the narrative structure, see ch. 2.3.

92. See 5,382 and 428: Dione and Zeus call Aphrodite τέκνον ἐμόν, which certainly has to be taken literally here.

93. See M.L. West (1997), 362 and Burkert (1992), 98, with n.8 for examples of how the Greek suffix –ώνη was used for the formation of other female derivatives.

94. See Burkert (1992), 98; on the Mycenean female derivative of Zeus, *di-u-jo*, see Ventris, Chadwick (1973), 125f. This form, interpreted as a nominative feminine singular of an adjective meaning "of Zeus", was also found on the tablets in Pylos, see 168.

95. On the archaeological evidence for this cult place see bibliography in Gartziou-Tatti (1990), 175-84, esp. 175 n. 1. Later Diane also had an altar on the Acropolis, built probably during a period when the Athenians tried to intensify their relationships with Dodona. An inscription (dated to 409-08 BC) is preserved in *IG* I².373.130, see Simon (1986b), 411-13, esp. 411. On the oracle at Dodona in general, see Parke (1967).

96. See *Il.* 16,233f.: Ζεῦ ἄνα, Δωδωναῖε, Πελασγικέ, τηλόθι ναίων, / Δωδώνης μεδέων δυσχειμέρου, ἀμφὶ δὲ Σελλοί / σοὶ ναίουσ' ὑποφῆται ἀνιπτόποδες χαμαιεῦναι. For the depiction of Dodona from Hesiod to Sophocles, see Parke (1967), 46ff.

97. A late 3rd-century BC inscription recording a dedication to Aphrodite was found at Dodona and it has been assumed that she had a sanctuary there (see Parke (1967), 119). However, we have no earlier evidence for that.

98. See Parke (1967), 68; for a collection of numerous inscriptions conveying oracles in connection with Ζεὺς Νάϊος, see Parke (1967), 259-73. On the questionable application of this epithet to Dione, see however Simon (1986b), 411. Maybe the address to Zeus as τηλόθι ναίων ("dwelling afar") in *Il.* 16, 233 which (only) sounds similar to Νάϊος, is a playful reference to the cult epithet.

99. Ζεὺς ἦν, Ζεὺς ἐστίν, Ζεὺς ἔσσεται, ὦ μεγάλε Ζεῦ, / Γᾶ καρποὺς ἀνιεῖ, διὸ κλήϊζετε Ματέρα
      Γαῖαν.
100. See Pind. *Paean* F 2 (Rutherford) (= schol. on Soph. *Trach.* 172 (290 Papageorgius)):
      Εὐριπίδης δὲ τρεῖς γεγονέναι φησὶν αὐτάς, οἱ δὲ δύο, καὶ τὴν μὲν εἰς Λιβύην ἀφικέσθαι
      Θήβηθεν εἰς τὸ τοῦ Ἄμμωνος χρηστήριον, τὴν <δὲ εἰς τὸ> περὶ τὴν Δωδώνην, ὡς καὶ
      Πίνδαρος Παιᾶσιν ("Euripides says that there were three of them, others say that there were
      just two; originating from Thebes, one was coming to Libya, to the sanctuary of Ammon,
      the other one near Dodona—so says Pindar too in his *paianes*"). That Pindar meant two
      doves (not priestesses) seems more likely in view of schol. D/A ad *Il.* 16,234d2 (Erbse), com-
      menting on the Σελλοί: It says that Pindar wrote Ἑλλοὶ without a σ because people say that
      it was Hellus the wood-cutter whom the dove introduced into the method of divination:
      ἀπὸ Ἑλλοῦ τοῦ δρυτόμου, ᾧ φασι τὴν περιστερὰν πρώτην καταδεῖξαι τὸ μαντεῖον. On this
      see Rutherford (2001), 352; for the discussion, with which Pindaric fragments F 2 could be
      grouped, see 354f.
101. The scholium on *Il.* 16,234 seems to specify this foundation myth: people say that it was Hellus
      the wood cutter whom the dove initiated into the method of divination (see n. 100 above).
102. ὡς τὴν παλαιὰν φηγὸν αὐδῆσαί ποτε / Δωδῶνι δισσῶν ἐκ πελειάδων ἔφη.
103. This is how most editors take the term here (see Easterling (1982) ad loc.). Pausanias
      (10,12,10) mentions the Πελειάδες together with other prophesying priestesses in other
      oracular places. For examples of cult personnel or worshippers bearing the name of animals,
      see Sourvinou-Inwood (1979), 231-51, esp. 240 with n. 49.
104. See Parke (1967), 63; followed by Easterling (1982), ad loc.
105. For the possibility that Pindar may have anticipated Herodotus, see Rutherford (2001), 352.
106. It has been argued by Fehling (1989), 65-70 that the way in which the two accounts dovetail
      and have such reasonable-looking sources cited for them is a clear indication of Herodotus'
      method of fictionalizing source-citations. He develops his argument in four points: the
      Egyptian version is based on two theories of Herodotus himself, namely that Greek religion
      originates in Egypt (as developed in preceding passages 2,50ff.) and the Egyptian god
      Ammon is identical with Zeus (point 1); without these premises, neither version could
      have been told (point 2); the Dodonean version can only be conceived as mythicisation
      of the Egyptian one (point 3); the versions told by different sources dovetail strikingly in
      Herodotus and thus must be inventions (point 4). However, the fact that Herodotus men-
      tions the names of his priestly informants at Dodona (2,55: Promeneia, Timarete, Nicandra)
      does not suggest an invented source since Dodona was not out of the world and the sources
      could have been verified easily.
107. See Fehling (1989), 68 with n. 6.
108. See Dakaris (1993), 9.
109. So Gartziou-Tatti (1990), 178, followed by Pirenne-Delforge (1994), 416f.
110. When Hesiod attributes the epithet καλὴ to Διώνη in *Theog.* 17 and makes her, the daughter
      of the Ocean and Tethys, the ἐρατὴ Διώνη in *Theog.* 353, it seems that she, in spite of her
      primeval parents, is a lovely woman, a beautiful nymph (see M.L. West, *Theog.* ad 353). In
      their female character and beauty also, Dione and Aphrodite are similar. Perhaps the motif
      of ἐρατὴ Διώνη was traditional in which case it may have been a source of inspiration for
      the Homeric poet as well.
111. Kirk (1990), ad 5,370.
112. See Boedeker (1974), 35ff.; on this see also v. Wilamowitz (1931), vol. 1, 95ff. and Friedrich
      (1978), 80.
113. Apart from Aphrodite also Ares, Apollo and Dionysus.
114. So Nilsson (1967), 522.
115. Hera and Zeus appear as a couple in Linear B, see Chadwick (1970), 124.

Chapter 2

1. So Burkert (1985), 152. These aspects have also been particularly emphasized e.g. by Henrichs (1990), 116-62, esp. 124f. and Bremmer (1996), 15.
2. So e.g. Farnell (1896), vol. 2, 664: "In the minds of the people, and most of Greek mythology, no doubt Aphrodite was little more than the power that personified beauty and human love; and this idea, which receives such glowing impression in poetry, is expressed also by a sufficient number of cult titles, which are neither moral nor immoral, but refer merely to the power of love in life."
3. So Sokolowski (1964), 1-8, esp. 1 ("The devotion of magistrates to the goddess of love, (…), displays such an astonishing singularity that a further approach and investigation seem to be expedient.") and 4.
4. The love-goddess's association with brides is perhaps more in keeping with stereotype. But that some magistrates are under Aphrodite's patronage may be explained by the fact that marriage is a legal status. It is important to note that not only magistrates worshipped Aphrodite. She is venerated, as is Hermes, as protectress of merchants shipping on the sea (see Sokolowski (1964), 4f.). Aphrodite's protection of sailors, which is reflected in epithets such as "Euploia", also has to be interpreted within this context (see Miranda (1989), 123-44), as well as within her mythical relationship with the sea, particularly with the myth of her birth. We have numerous, mainly Hellenistic epigrams on objects dedicated to the marine Aphrodite after a successful crossing of the sea, see e.g. Callimachus' remarkable epigram on a nautilus shell dedicated to Aphrodite-Arsinoe by the girl Selenaia (14 G.-P.=5 Pf.); for an interpretation see Gutzwiller (1992), 194-209.
5. See Simon (1970), 5-19, esp. 13 and 18: for the same dating of the cult of Aphrodite Πάνδημος, see also Shapiro (1995), 118-24, esp. 118; see also ch. 2.4 below.
6. The only exception is Attic myth: see below, ch. 2.4.
7. See Burkert (1985), 119; Henrichs (1990), 124; Bremmer (1996), 62f.
8. See e.g. Graf (1985), esp. 64-7, 260-4. He analyzes the various cults of four related Northern Ionian cities in Asia Minor. Pirenne-Delforge's extensive monograph (1994) examines the cults of Aphrodite on the mainland and the islands of Greece from literary, iconographical, and epigraphical evidence (see esp. 15-369).
9. See Buxton (1994), 145f. He maintains that one of the most important aspects of a divinity is that any activity of a human being (being born, fighting, getting married, committing adultery etc.) is "related to a structure mapped out at the divine level".
10. Henrichs (1990), 130.
11. Seaford (1990), 173f.
12. See e.g. most recently Bremmer (1996), 15f., see also Burkert (1985), 119f.
13. See the definition given in Burkert (1979), 23 with n. 5: "Myth is a traditional tale with secondary, partial reference to something of collective importance."
14. Similarly Buxton (1994), 146: "The most detailed picture (of the gods) appears in epic since it was a convention of the genre".
15. The Greek word is τέρπειν; see also below, ch. 2.3.
16. This is charted out in ch. 3.
17. The question to what degree the narrative content of myths (particularly those represented in the *Iliad*) corresponds to activities of ritual has been a matter of increasing interest over the past years, see Burkert (1985), 119; Henrichs (1990), 124f.; Graf (1997), 54f. and 98f., id. (1984), 252, and most recently id. (1991), 331-62; for a more general overview see Buxton (1994), 151-5.
18. See Burkert (1991), 81-91, esp. 81f.
19. For the most recent translation see George (1999).
20. On the frequency of this aspect of Aphrodite see Graf (1985), 177ff.; 262ff.; 311ff.
21. For the most extensive discussion see Burkert (1981), 81f., id. (1982), 35f., id. (1992), 96-9 and id. (2003), 47-9. He points out that especially the representation of gods in an anthropo-

morphic way is characteristic of Oriental narrative; most recently see also M.L. West (1997), 362ff., arguing that the episode is most extraordinary in terms of common Greek sentiment, since it would be inconceivable that mortals could ever overcome the gods.

22. See 256ff.; for the motif and later literary development of the scene, see M.L. West (1978) ad 259.

23. On this see particularly Burkert (1992), 97f.

24. Burkert (1991), 81 has denied any reference to cult and ritual within this kind of episode and says that the institution of ritual has its autonomy in the *Iliad*, so for example in book 6 when the women of Troy present the *peplos* to Athena. He argues that "to present gods in an unheroic, all-too-human vein is a traditional form of narrative (…) developed in Greece under the influence of Oriental models (…). Even in Homer the unquestionable seriousness of religion is not based on such tales, but on traditional ritual which is essentially non-anthropomorphic".

25. See Diomedes' mocking comment (*Il.* 5,348-51): "εἶκε, Διὸς θύγατερ, πολέμου καὶ δηϊοτῆτος. / ἦ οὐχ ἅλις, ὅττι γυναῖκας ἀνάλκιδας ἠπεροπεύεις; / εἰ δὲ σύ γ᾽ ἐς πόλεμον πωλήσεαι, ἦ τέ σ᾽ ὀΐω / ῥιγήσειν πόλεμόν γε, καὶ εἴ χ᾽ ἑτέρωθι πύθηαι"; a similar tone is recognizable in Hera's (*Il.* 21,418-21) and Athena's (*Il.* 5,421-5) statements; on this scene as a model for Sappho fr.1 V., see Winkler (1990), 167ff.

26. *Il.* 6,492; on this see Graf (1984), 245f.

27. That the warlike aspect of Aphrodite is an Oriental trait has recently been pointed out, e.g. by Flemberg (1991), 12ff., esp. 15. He also discusses other common characteristics of Aphrodite and Eastern love-goddesses there; see also Burkert (1985), 153 and Graf (1985), 178.

28. For evidence see Burkert (1960), 130-44, with n. 44.

29. Aphrodite's associations with warfare are also reflected in her cult epithet Στρατηγίς, which identifies her as the patroness of military chiefs (see ch. 2.6); for an inscription of Ἀφροδίτη Στρατεία in a calendar of festivals at Erythrae see Graf (1985), 177.

30. For descriptions of armed images of the Eastern goddess see also Flemberg (1991), 15f.

31. See Hsch. s.v. Ἔγχειος; see Chantraine (1970), vol. 2, 311; and Graf (1984), 245-54, esp. 250; Farnell (1896), vol. 2, 563. On the warlike nature of Aphrodite's forerunners, see also Friedrich (1978), esp. 14-9.

32. *FGrH* 640 F 1. This could have been an imitation of her cult image there. He does not describe the goddess, and so we do not know for certain whether she was armed or not.

33. So Graf (1984), 250f.

34. For a collection of testimonia see Flemberg (1991), 29-42; for other regions see Graf (1985), 177f., 262ff. and 311.

35. See also Plut. *Mor.* 239 A (= *Instituta Laconica*).

36. Pausanias also mentions a story (unconvincing to him) in which Tyndareus put Aphrodite in bonds to signify women's faithfulness in marriage, also to take revenge on her for causing his daughters' adulteries.

37. See Graf (1984), 248-51. The important ancient source for this festival is Plut. *Mor.* 245 C (= *Mulierum Virtutes*). He says that during the celebration of the Hybristica women dressed as men and men as women. The festival itself was held in order to commemorate the victory in which, again, armed women defended Argos against the Spartan enemies. However, he does not mention which deities in particular were involved in the Hybristica. It is noteworthy, that Argos was also a place where an armed Aphrodite and, moreover, a cult association with Ares is mentioned (Paus. 2,25,1). The Hybristica have been interpreted as a rite of passage with sexual role reversal (so first by Halliday (1909-10), 212-19, followed by Graf (1984), 249f. with n. 34; see also Pirenne-Delforge (1994), 168f.).

38. But cf. Burkert's interpretation of similar scenes (1991), 82: for him, the function of those divine burlesques is merely narrative and supposed to provide an entertainment which should make the audience smile.

39. So similarly Simon (1998), 203f.
40. See e.g. Antimachus (*Anth. Pal.* 9,321), Antipater (*Anth. Plan.* 176) and two epigrams by Leonidas of Tarentum: Aphrodite is armed in *Anth. Pal.* 16,171, but unarmed in *Anth. Pal.* 9,320 (=24 G.-P.). On the contrasting pair see Gutzwiller (1998), 317; see also Gow, Page (1965), vol. 2, 334f. The idea of an armed Aphrodite was such an unusual topic that it was considered suitable for Roman students of rhetoric practising their declamation skills. According to Quintilian (*Inst.* 2,4,26) the question "Cur armata apud Lacedaemonios Venus?" was a theme in declamations.
41. *Od.* 8,266-366.
42. Burkert (1985), 152 simply: "joyous consummation of sexuality"; Lesky (1976), 18: "Wer hier *liebliche Werke der Hochzeit* übersetzt, verkennt den Sinn der Stelle. Aphrodite ist keine Hochzeitsgöttin und γάμος ist ganz konkret von der geschlechtlichen Vereinigung zu verstehen, in der Aphrodite wirkt."; Kirk (1990) does not discuss this (see ad loc.). On Aphrodite's fertility aspect see the structural approach of Friedrichs (1978), 95-7.
43. So the distinction drawn by Rüter, Schmidt (1984), 119f.
44. See *Il.* 13, 382
45. So *LSJ*, s.v. γάμος.
46. See e.g. Sappho fr. 194 V. (= Himer. *Or.* 9,4 (p. 75f. Colonna)): Aphrodite is present in wedding songs.
47. So Richardson (1993), see ad loc.; *LSJ* translate "lust", "lewdness"; see also Mader (1993), 49.
48. See fr. 132 M.-W., on the daughters of Proitus; and *Op.* 586 etc. Paris is quite an effeminate type himself, good looking, after women, but not interested in warfare (*Il.* 3,39ff. and 11,385: παρθενοπίπης).
49. Lines 25-30 of *Il.* 24 were athetized by Aristarchus for reasons concerning content and language (schol. Ariston./A ad *Il.* 24, 25-30 (Erbse)), see Richardson (1993), ad 23-30, who argues that nearly all objections could be avoided by eliminating lines 29 and 30 only; M.L. West (2000) also considers these lines (29f.) as an interpolation and encloses them in square-brackets (see his *app. crit.* and *testimonia*). Although presupposed by the plot of the *Iliad*, "Paris' judgement" is not developed in the epic itself. Reinhardt (1938) has shown that the reason must be sought in the different character of the story: having close affinity to folktale elements, it does not quite fit the ethos and tone of the heroic world. The *Cypria* refer to it in more detail (see fr. 4 and 5 (Bernabé/Davies) for the contest, and p. 38f.,6-8 (Bernabé) and p. 31,7-11 (Davies) for Proclus' account of the *Cypria*).
50. See Davies (1981), 56-62, esp. 57f. For the development of the myth of Paris' judgement, see Stinton (1965), 2-77, esp. 51-64 . Normally Aphrodite punishes those who are not willing to succumb to her power by inflicting upon them immoderate desire which turns out to be promiscuous and immoral.
51. See Paus. 3,13,9 (apropos a *xoanon* of Aphrodite Hera at Sparta): ἐπὶ δὲ θυγατρὶ γαμουμένῃ νενομίκασι τὰς μητέρας τῇ θεῷ θύειν; on the rites see Calame (1977a), 350f., esp. 356; on a Spartan ritual marriage of Helen, see M.L. West (1975b).
52. On that see most recently Parker (1996), 196 with n. 159 and ch. 1.3.
53. Segre's collection of inscriptions from Cos is edited by Peppa-Delmousou, Rizza (1993); see also Habicht (1996), 83-94; *SEG* xliii 549. For a recent discussion of the epigraphical material see Dillon (1999), 63-80. An inscription indicating sales of priesthoods in the cults of "Aphrodite Pandamos and Pontia" has been recently published by Parker, Obbink (2000), 416-47. In the Coan dialect of the decree she is called Πάνδαμος. I will, however, use the conventional *koine* variant Πάνδημος.
54. *ED* 178a(A) in Segre's edition.
55. On the role of the *nothoi* and *nothai* (they are neither full citizens, nor outsiders), see Dillon (1999), 75.
56. Here I follow the editors of *SEG* xliii 549 (see p. 180), who suggest ἐξωμοσίας instead of the stone's ΕΙΣΩΜΟΣΙΑΣ. This has also been accepted by Dillon (1999), 66f.

57. Dillon (1999), 71f. has shown that in many places it was the goddess Artemis who was to receive pre-nuptial offerings from girls, such as locks, toys, girdles, which were dedicated as a sign of the girls' transition to womanhood.

58. The only other marriage offerings we know of that were required by the state appear in the Cyrene cathartic law. It requires that the bride "must go down to the bride-room to Artemis" before sacrificing to the goddess at the Artemisia. Otherwise the woman has to purify the shrine and in addition sacrifice a full grown animal (on this see also Dillon (1999), 67). For the text see Solmsen, Fraenkel (1966), 59 (no. 39B, 9-14).

59. For discussion, see Seaford (1987), 106-30, esp. 110-9.

60. The hymnic praise of Aphrodite also addresses her train of personifications (Pothos, Peitho, Harmonia) representing aspects of the goddess's sphere of influence, here in context of marriage (*Supp.* 1034-42). For a different view, i.e. that the song was performed by the Argive guards, see Taplin (1977), 230ff. where he discusses the possibility of a supplementary chorus; see also Friis Johansen, Whittle (1980), vol. 3, ad loc. (= p. 319ff.) and the edition of M.L. West (1990).

61. See Pirenne-Delforge (1994), 153; for Aphrodite's cultic function in marriage affairs in Argos see esp. 424.

62. See chs. 4.4-4.6.

63. *Od.* 22,444.

64. See ch. 3.4.

65. *Theog.* 203-6: ταύτην δ' ἐξ ἀρχῆς τιμὴν ἔχει ἠδὲ λέλογχε / μοῖραν ἐν ἀνθρώποισι καὶ ἀθανάτοισι θεοῖσι, / παρθενίους τ' ὀάρους μειδήματά τ' ἐξαπάτας τε / τέρψιν τε γλυκερὴν φιλότητά τε μειλιχίην τε. On these aspects see also chs. 4.4 (translation) and 4.6.

66. So *Il.* 9,186 of Achilles (τὸν δ' ηὗρον φρένα τερπόμενον φόρμιγγι λιγείηι) and 189f. (τῇ ὅ γε θυμὸν ἔτερπεν, ἄειδε δ' ἄρα κλέα ἀνδρῶν).

67. So *Od.* 8,368f. (for more examples see Latacz (1966), esp. 210-14).

68. For the adaptation of love and strife as philosophical principles, see e.g. Empedocles (31 F 26,5f. D.-K.): ἄλλοτε μὲν Φιλότητι συνερχόμεν' εἰς ἕνα κόσμον, ἄλλοτε δ' αὖ δίχ' ἕκαστα φορούμενα Νείκεος ἔχθει. In early poetry Stesichorus in his *Oresteia* (fr. 210 *PMGF*) summons the Muse to reject songs of battle and celebrate the weddings, banquets and feasts of gods and men: Μοῖσα σὺ μὲν πολέμους ἀπωσαμένα πεδ' ἐμεῦ κλείοισα θεῶν τε γάμους ἀνδρῶν τε δαῖτας καὶ θαλίας μακάρων. (...) In a similar way, Lucretius (1,27ff.) symbolizes the superiority of peace over war by Mars' indulging in his love for Venus.

69. Just how important it is for the understanding of Greek religion to take into account its different regional characters was pointed out by Henrichs (1990), 133: "im regionalen Charakter der griechischen Religion liegt der eigentliche Schlüssel zu ihrem Verständnis"; similarly Parker (1996), 212: "Most Greek states honoured most Greek gods; the difference between them are of emphasis and degree."

70. Parker (1986), 187-214, esp. 187f. On theories of political myth in general, see Tudor (1972).

71. Pointed out by Parker (1986), 187.

72. The Athenian hero Cephalus, after his involvement with the goddess Eos, marries a mortal, Procris. Their marriage is characterized by jealousy, entailing mutual tests of faithfulness in which they both fail. After reconciliation Procris follows her husband having learned that he used to call for a cloud (νεφέλη) on his hunting trip, suspecting that he was actually calling his mistress. While she was hiding in the bushes, Cephalus killed her, supposing that she was a beast. The main sources of the slightly varying story are Apollodorus (*Bibl.* 1,9,4; 2,4,7; 3,15,1); Hyginus (*Fab.* 189); Ovid (*Met.* 7,655). None of these sources mentions Aphrodite. She is only involved in so far as Hesiod (*Theog.* 986) says that Phaethon, the son of Cephalus and Eos, is the attendant of Aphrodite.

73. Aphrodite's intervention is not explicitly mentioned. The classical sources are Apollodorus, *Bibl.* 3,14,8 and Ovid, *Met.* 6,424ff. Sophocles treated the myth in his Tereus tragedy (see Radt, TrGF 4 (1977), fr. 580-95b and hypothesis p. 435ff.).

74. The personified wind god Boreas (see also *Il.* 20,223f.) seizes the Athenian princess Oreithuia, daughter of Erechtheus, from the banks of the Ilissos. This myth is frequently treated in literature: Simonides fr. 534 *PMG*; Acusilaus *FGrH* 2 F 30-31; Pherecydes *FGrH* 3 F 145; for Aeschylus see Radt, *TrGF* 3 (1985), fr. 281; for Sophocles see Radt, *TrGF* 4 (1977), fr. 768 and 956). The story frequently occurs in vase painting (see S. Kaempf-Dimitriadou (1986), 133-42). The myth is interpreted in Pl. *Phaedr.* 229c-d. Here an altar of Boreas is mentioned too.

75. On Theseus' meaning for the Athenians, see most recently Mills (1997), 43-86 who does not, however, discuss the relationship between Theseus and Aphrodite; similarly previously Herter (1939), 244-326; Oliver (1960), 47; see also Connor (1970), 143-74; Calame (1990), esp. 403-12; Garland (1992), esp. 82-98.

76. See Kearns (1996), 1508f.; Mills (1997), 6.

77. See the definition in Burkert (1979), 23 with n. 5: "Myth is a traditional tale with secondary, partial reference to something of collective importance"; according to Bremmer, myths are "traditional tales relevant to society" (both definitions are cited in Bremmer (1994), 56f.).

78. For evidence see Deubner (1932), 215f.; Simon (1983), 40f.; Pirenne-Delforge (1994), 393ff. Aphrodite seems to have had little or no significance in the main Athenian women's festivals such as Arrhephoria, Thesmophoria or Haloa. The latter were fertility festivals, and the deities celebrated there were Demeter and Kore and, at the Haloa only, Dionysus (see schol. on Lucian 275 (23 Rabe) (Thesmophoria) and 280. 16-17 Rabe (Haloa)); see also Parker (1983), 74-103). Burkert (1964), 1-25, esp. 15f. suggests that Aphrodite was involved in initiation rites of the Arrephoroi, actually a festival of Athena since the girls descend during the procession into an underground passage running through the precinct of Aphrodite in the Gardens. But there she certainly just had a subordinated role; on a rite in which the cult image of Aphrodite Πάνδημος was purified, see ch. 3.4; on the more or less private Aphrodisia celebrated by magistrates (*polemarchoi*), see ch. 2.6.

79. So Shapiro (1995), 118. On the most recent excavations and findings on the agora see Shear (1984), 24-32 and 38-40.

80. On the date of the cult see Simon (1970), 19: she identifies Aphrodite Πάνδημος on coins of the last decade of the 6th century. An altar found in Aphrodite's shrine in the agora during recent excavations suggests that the sanctuary of Aphrodite Πάνδημος there existed at least before 500 (see Shapiro (1995), 118-24, esp. 118 with n. 6 for bibliography.); Pirenne-Delforge (1994), 29.

81. Ἀφροδίτην δὲ τὴν Πάνδημον, ἐπείτε Ἀθηναίους Θησεὺς ἐς μίαν ἤγαγεν ἀπὸ τῶν δήμων πόλιν, αὐτήν τε σέβεσθαι καὶ Πειθὼ κατέστησε· (on Peitho's political meaning see ch. 2.7 and ch. 6.2). Theseus' exploit is also related to the festival of the Synoikia (on which see Graf (1997), 134).

82. For a survey of myths about Theseus and Aphrodite, see Brommer (1982), 129.

83. So Parker (1986), 187: The "extraordinary development that Theseus underwent in the 5th century is a glittering example of an invention of tradition which was also a forging of political myth." On this phenomenon see also Graf (1997), 117-37.

84. See Calame (1990), 403-12 and Pirenne-Delforge (1994), 449. It is doubtful that the 5th century BC can really be the "terminus ante quem" for Aphrodite's entry into the public and political scene. Oliver (1960), 106-17 argues that Aphrodite's revival as Πάνδημος or Ἡγεμόνη in the Hellenistic period, as documented by epigraphical evidence, can be interpreted as a reactualisation of earlier aspects of Aphrodite at the moment when Athens again found its independence. On the gradual emergence of Attic myth in literature see Ermatinger (1897), 1-36; see also Connor (1970), 143-74. On Theseus' special link with Athens see Graf (1997), 131.

85. For an extensive analysis see Brommer (1982).

86. On this see the discussion by Mills (1997), 19 with n. 70 for bibliography.

87. Sciron, who throws people from cliffs, Sinis, who tears apart travellers; Procrustes, who fits people to his bed, Cercyon, the wrestler who smashes his victims; see Graf (1997), 132.

88. On the establishing of the date see Barron (1980), 1-8, esp. 2. For a discussion of the literary reflexions of Theseus' deeds and their iconography, see e.g. Calame (1990), 403f.

89. Plut. *Thes.* 28,1 and the scholiast on Pind. *Ol.* 3,50b (119 Drachmann) refer to an "author of the *Theseid*'; the latter lists the author before Pisander and Pherecydes, which may suggest an early date as well as the author's anonymity (I follow Mills (1997), 19 with n. 74). Aristotle (*Poet.* 1451a20) mentions poets who have written epics about Heracles and Theseus, but does not give a date.

90. I follow Barron (1980), esp. 1ff.

91. *FGrH* 3 F 145-155.

92. See Huxley (1973), 137-45, esp. 141 and Calame (1990), 407; cf. Jacoby (1947), 13-94 who argues from fr. 146 that Pherecydes antedated the rise of Cimon.

93. So Barron (1980), 2 with n. 20.

94. Graf (1997), 135.

95. Parker (1996), 49 links also the festival of the Synoikia with this "political spirit".

96. Both elements are pointed out by Jacoby (1926), vol. 2 (commentary), 768.

97. *FGrH* 244 F 113.

98. Solon was ἄρχων in 594/593 BC. On Solon's activities to establish "public religion", see Parker (1996), 43-55, esp. 48f.

99. *FGrH* 244 F 113. According to *LSJ* στεγῖτις means "room" and "prostitute" (Poll. *Onom.* 7,201).

100. Kassel, Austin *PCG* 7 (1989), fr. 3 (p. 230f.): σὺ δ' εἰς ἅπαντας εὗρες ἀνθρώπους, Σόλων / σὲ γὰρ λέγουσιν τοῦτ' ἰδεῖν πρῶτον, μόνον / δημοτικόν, ὦ Ζεῦ, πρᾶγμα καὶ σωτήριον, / (…) / μεστὴν ὁρῶντα τὴν πόλιν νεωτέρων / τούτους τ' ἔχοντας τὴν ἀναγκαίαν φύσιν / ἁμαρτάνοντάς τ' εἰς ὃ μὴ προσῆκον ἦν, / στῆσαι πριάμενόν τοι γυναῖκας κατὰ τόπους / κοινὰς ἅπασι καὶ κατεσκευασμένας.

101. Cf. Pirenne-Delforge (1994), 29 ("la fondation solonienne en relation avec des mesures pour les jeunes gens peut également être interprété dans un cadre socio-politique"); Stafford (2000), 125f. considers "the state prostitution which Solon had established" as historical, but the interpretation of Πάνδημος as "vulgar" as a philosophical innovation.

102. See Jacoby (1944), 65-75, esp. 72: he sees in Pausanias' ἀπὸ τῶν δήμων πόλιν (1,22,3) a later mythologizing of Theseus' *synoicism* and considers that Apollodorus' explanation διὰ τὸ ἐνταῦθα πάντα τὸν δῆμον συνάγεσθαι conveys an authentic explanation.

103. See Farnell (1896), vol. 2, 758 for a collection of epigraphical and literary evidence; Graf (1985), 260f. with n. 3 and 4; Pirenne-Delforge (1994), 448f.

104. *IG* I³.832 (= *CEG* I no. 268); on the inscription see Stafford (2000), 123.

105. See Simon (1970), 5-19, esp. 19.

106. See Shapiro (1995), 120.

107. See Farnell (1896), 661: there is no evidence that the state religion of Greece ever recognized the sense of the epithet Πάνδημος as bad love. Also her cult in Cos, where she receives marriage offerings, has to be interpreted within the public and civic meaning of Aphrodite.

108. On that see Oliver (1960), 91-117, esp. 109.

109. So Graf (1985), 260.

110. *SEG* xxxvi 1039 (ed. pr. by Merkelbach (1986), 15-18); the inscription is dated to "ca. 400 BC".

111. See Merkelbach (1986), 15: the θεοπρόποι asked "wie man ὁμόνοια unter den Bürgern herstellen könne." His interpretation is accepted in the commentary in *SEG* xxxvi 1039 ("how homonoia could be restored among the citizens").

112. The role of Aphrodite as guardian of magistrates has received great attention. The evidence has been collected mainly by J. & L. Robert and Solokowski and Croissant, Salviat, see below, ch. 2.6. These dedications are not limited to Aphrodite Πάνδημος, although this cult title is certainly by far the most common one suggesting civic and public implications; similar to Πάνδημος are Ἀφροδίτη ἡγεμόνη τοῦ δήμου (*IG* II².2798); on this inscription see

below; and Ἀφροδίτη Ὁμόνοια (*IG* X.2.61); on identification of these with Πάνδημος see Graf (1985), 260.

113. πανδήμιος occurs only once in epic (*Od.* 18,1: "public beggar"). The number of occurrences (also of πάνδημος) significantly increases in the genres of the 5th century BC which are closely related to Athenian democracy: tragedy and historiography. Here, πάνδημος and the adverbs πανδημίᾳ, πανδημεί are related to matters which concern the whole *demos*, usually in political, civic and religious contexts, see Aesch. *Supp.* 607 (πανδημίᾳ, "the whole people", as a civic and political unit; similar meaning in Soph. *Ant.* 7). In Soph. *Aj.* 844, a military notion is added (in a curse *Ajax* summons the Furies not to spare the "army of the whole people", πανδήμου στρατοῦ). In Eur. *Alc.* 1026, a πάνδημος ἀγών indicates a "public contest held for all the people". In Thucydides *TLG* counts 35 entries of the adverb πανδημεί which is used in different contexts. The religious and political unity of the Athenian people is particularly emphasized in situations where the *polis* is in danger and all the citizens fight for her welfare. The people as a whole, a political unit including all citizens (Athenians, women, children) is meant e.g. in 1,90,3: Themistocles proposes sending himself as an ambassador to Sparta while the wall should be raised to such a height as necessary for the defence—and the whole Athenian population, men, women and children should take part in the wall-building. The unity of all the Athenians as a religious community is indicated in 1,126,6: at the festival of Zeus Meilichius "all the people" offer sacrifices (similarly 3,3,3). When the Athenians once heard during this festival that their city was in jeopardy, they came, "all the people", from the fields and went against the enemy and, sitting down before the Acropolis, laid siege to it (1,126,7). The unity of military forces is referred to in 1,73,4; 1,107; 2,94,2.

114. For a quotation of the decree see above, ch. 2.3.

115. See Sherwin-White (1978), 304.

116. See similarly Dillon (1999), 71.

117. τοὺς δὲ λοιποὺς χρὴ (…) μᾶλλον τὴν τῆς πόλεως δύναμιν καθ' ἡμέραν ἔργῳ θεωμένους καὶ ἐραστὰς γιγνομένους αὐτῆς.

118. See Mikalson (1998), 107f. On the historical events in the period see Mikalson (1998), 75ff.; see also Habicht (1997) and id. (1982).

119. So Mikalson (1998), 108; 290; see *IG* II².659 (= *LSCG* 39): in the regulations concerning the sanctuary of Aphrodite Πάνδημος, ἀστυνόμοι are charged to restore and purify her temple. On the inscription see also ch. 3.4.

120. See *IG* II².2798. See Welter (1939), 23-38; esp. 35-36 for the date (215-202 BC according to the inscription recording the dedication by the *archon* Dionysios) and description of the altar itself; see also Oliver (1960), 106 and Mikalson (1998), 168f.; see also ch. 5.3 with n. 61.

121. So first Oliver (1960), 109. His interpretation has also been accepted by Sokolowski (1964), 5; Pirenne-Delforge (1994), 403 and Parker (1996), 272.

122. On the events, see e.g. Habicht (1982), 13-20.

123. The role of the *demos* is mentioned in *IG* II².834.10-14 and also in a decree from Rhamnous. The sacrifices to Zeus Soter and Athena Soteira have also been related to the independence of Athens, see Garlan (1978), 97-108, esp. 103ff.: τῶι Διὶ τῶι Σωτῆ[ρι] καὶ [τῆι Σω]τείραι [καθ' ὃν καιρὸν ὁ δῆμ]ος ἐκομίσατο τὴν πάτρ[ιο]ν ἐλευθερί]αν; both inscriptions date most probably from 229 BC and are related to the liberation of Athens from Macedonian rule (on the latter see Garlan (1978), 105). The merits of the πολῖται are also emphasized in another decree from Rhamnous, see Pouilloux (1956), 57-75, esp. 57f. Pouilloux assumes a date of 229 BC. On the two brothers see Habicht (1982), 84-96 and (1997), 180f. with n. 25 and Parker (1996), 269 with n. 60 for evidence and bibliography.

124. Plut. *Thes.* 18: λέγεται δ' αὐτῷ τὸν μὲν ἐν Δελφοῖς ἀνελεῖν θεὸν Ἀφροδίτην καθηγεμόνα ποιεῖσθαι καὶ παρακαλεῖν συνέμπορον. An honorary decree (dated circa 220 BC) found on the fragment of a stele in Rhamnous also mentions a sanctuary of Aphrodite Ἡγεμόνη (see *SEG* xli 91). For substantial new evidence in regard to this cult from recent excavations, see Petrakos (1992), 1-7 and id. (1995), 13-20, esp. 18f.

125. For the epigraphical evidence, see mainly J. & L. Robert (1959), 219-39, no. 325; Sokolowski (1964), 1-8; see also Pirenne-Delforge (1994), 403-8 with n. 165 (bibliography); she also quotes some inscriptions. Evidence for the island of Thasos is documented in Croissant, Salviat (1966), 460-71, see esp. the diagram (468f.) which records the various types of magistrates; for Paros, Samos, Delos, see Sokolowski (1964), 2.
126. See IG XII.5.552: Θεοκύδης· Ἀρισταίχμου | Ἀφροδίτηι ἀνέθηκεν ἄρξας (for a brief discussion of the inscription see also J. & L. Robert (1962), 195-96, no. 264); on the date see Pirenne-Delforge (1994), 406.
127. See Graf (1985), 263 for examples (Hermes, Dioskouroi).
128. See Sokolowski (1964), 2ff.; Graf (1985), 264; Pirenne-Delforge (1994), 404f. Unfortunately, none of these scholars discusses the functions of the magistrates in order to explain why they make dedications to Aphrodite. For an overview of dedications of those colleges in different places in Greece see J. & L. Robert (1959). On the magistrates and their functions in general see Busolt (1920), 480-509. See also the diagram documenting offerings of *agoranomoi, epistates, gynaikonomoi, apologoi* and their respective secretaries to Aphrodite in Thasos in Croissant, Salviat (1966), 468f.
129. For an inscription (dated to the first half of 3rd century BC) and an interpretation see Daux (1928), 57f. and Martin (1944-45), 158-61, esp. 161 ("les agoranomes avaient sans doute dans leurs attributions la police des marchés thasiens").
130. For epigraphical evidence see Launey (1933), 410: on a small marble base (dated to the beginning of the 3rd century BC) there is an inscription conveying a dedication of six *epistatai* to Aphrodite: Ἐπιστάτ[αι] Ἀφροδ[ίτ]η[ι]; for a dedication (first half of 3rd century) of six *epistatai* and two *agoranomoi* to Aphrodite see Daux (1928), 57.
131. For dedications to other deities see Graf (1985), 263f.: e.g. *agoranomoi* also offer to Hermes; *strategoi* make dedications also to Ares, Heracles and Arete. On the function of *gynaiko-nomoi* see Busolt (1920), 493f. and Martin (1944-45), 159f. who calls them a "police de mœurs".
132. See Pouilloux (1954), 406-9, esp. 408f. no. 155 implies a regulation for colours: women should not wear purple.
133. See Pouilloux (1954), 371, no. 141; 407.
134. Arist. *Pol.* 4,1300a4-7: παιδονόμος δὲ καὶ γυναικονόμος καὶ εἴ τις ἄλλος ἄρχων κύριός ἐστι τοιαύτης ἐπιμελείας ἀριστοκρατικόν, δημοκρατικὸν δ᾽ οὔ (πῶς γὰρ οἷόν τε κωλύειν ἐξιέναι τὰς τῶν ἀπόρων;) οὐδ᾽ ὀλιγαρχικὸν (τρυφῶσι γὰρ αἱ τῶν ὀλιγαρχούντων): "But a supervisor of children and a supervisor of women and any other magistrates executing a similar kind of supervision are an aristocratic feature and not democratic (for how is it possible to prevent the wives of the poor from going out of doors?) nor is it oligarchic (for the wives of oligarchic rulers love luxury)."; see also 6,1323a 3-6.
135. τάς τε αὐλητρίδας καὶ τὰς ψαλτρίας καὶ τὰς κιθαριστρίας οὗτοι σκοποῦσιν ὅπως μὴ πλείονος ἢ δυεῖν δραχμαῖν μισθωθήσονται.
136. On a dedication to Peitho in this context see ch. 6.6.
137. See Busolt (1920), 494 with n. 1: evidence from Magnesia (supervised girls' schools), from Gambreion (appropriate attire controlled during funerals and the period of mourning for men and women), from Andania (responsible for clothing in festivals); evidence also for Miletus, Samos and Syracuse).
138. The inscription was first published by Croissant, Salviat (1966), 461f.; for the dating see 462; for more examples of magistral dedicatory inscriptions see Martin (1944-45), 158-61, nos. 3 and 4.
139. See Arist. *Pol.* 6,1322b39-1323a3; see on that also Martin (1944-45), 60.
140. στεφανοῦν actually means "crown with the badge of office" and is said of magistrates in office, see Demosthenes' speech *Meid.* (21,17) where Meidias is accused of having bribed the *archon* in office (ἐστεφανωμένον ἄρχοντα διέφθειρε). στεφανωθέντες ὑπὸ δήμου ("hon-

oured with a crown by the people") seems to be a formulaic expression, found also in Chios and Erythrae (so Graf (1985), 264).

141. On the name see Croissant, Salviat (1966), 462.

142. See Graf (1985), 264 with n. 43.

143. See *IDélos* 1810 (see also 1811): in 110-09 BC Dionysius the governor of Delos built a temple and dedicated a statue to Aphrodite and also repaired another temple of hers—presumably for the well-being of the people of Athens:

> Διονύσιος Νίκωνος Παλληνεὺς
> ἐπιμελητὴς γενόμενος Δήλου
> ἐν τῶι ἐπὶ Πολυκλείτου ἄρχοντος
> ἐνιαυτῶι, τὸν ναὸν κατασκευάσας
> καὶ τὸ ἄγαλμα ἐπισκευάσας ἐκ
> τῶν ἰδίων ἀνέθηκεν ὑπὲρ τοῦ
> δήμου τοῦ Ἀθηναίων Ἀφροδίτηι.

144. The other deity who is also associated particularly with these concepts seems to be Hermes: In a dedication (mid 3rd-century BC), three *agoranomoi* thank him for the fact that "everybody endeavoured to go to the market in harmony" (*IG* XI.4.1143); for a quotation see also W. Peek, "Weihung von Agoranomen", *Hermes* 76 (1941), 416:

> στῆσέ με Ἀθά[μβ]ητος παῖς Λυσιφάνους Ἀγοραίωι
> Ἑρμεῖ Πανταγόρας τ' Εὐδίκου υἱὸς ἐών
> τῶνδε μέτ' Ἀρχέπολις Λυσιξένου οἷς ὁμονοίαι
> νεῖσθαι ἀνεύθυνος πᾶς ἀγοράνδ' ἔρατο.

145. See Croissant, Salviat (1966), 462 on the statues.

146. See *SEG* ix 133: Ἀφρ<ο>δείταν Νομοφυλακίδα ἀνέθηκαν and *SEG* ix 135: Νομοφ[ύλ]ακες (...) Ὁμόνοια[ν - -] ἀν[έθηκαν]. For a dedication to Hermes for providing ὁμόνοια, see above, n. 144. On the cults of Homonoia see Thériault (1996).

147. Ναυαρχίς (*Corpus Inscriptionum Regni Bosporani* 30 and 1115); Ἐπιστασία (Pouilloux (1954), 233, no. 24): Ἀφροδίτηι ἐπιστασίηι (and then follow four names of the respective college); Συναρχίς: by *agoranomoi* on Delos *IG* XI.4.1146 (to Aphrodite alone; for the date (circa 200 BC) see Hicks (1890), 255-70, esp. 258); for dedications to Aphrodite and Hermes see also no. 1144 (2nd half of 3rd century BC) and no. 1145 (1st half of 3rd century BC); on their dating see Dürrbach (1902), 480-553, esp. 510 and 513. On the different locations see Graf (1985), 264.

148. Στρατηγίς (*IG* IX.1².256, from Thyreion); for the variant Στρατεία see *IE* 207.9f.; the same epiclesis Στρατεία was found in Mylasa and Iasos (see Graf (1985), 177 with n. 119 and esp. 262ff.).

149. See Sokolowski (1964), 6 and Graf (1985), 264 with n. 33 (Argos: Paus. 2,25,1; for a temple in Lato see Bousquet (1938), 386-408); see also ch. 2.3.

150. In an inscription on a small marble altar from Samos (circa 100 BC) the college of six *eisagogeis* make a dedication to Hermes and Aphrodite, since they "followed and understood each other in a pure and just manner": (list of names) συνπεριενεχθέντες ἑαυτοῖς ὁσίως καὶ δικαίως Ἑρμεῖ τῶι εἰσαγωγῶι καὶ Ἀφροδίτηι συναρχίδι. συνπεριφέρεσθαι actually means "have intercourse with", "adapt oneself to", "be conversant with"; the noun συνπεριφορά means "intercourse", "companionship", "society" (Polyb. 5,26,15; Phld. *De bono rege* 18,7 (82 Dorandi). Thus one could also translate "for keeping fair and just companionship" (during their period of office). The inscription was first published by Schede (1912), 216, no. 17 (see also L. Robert (1935), 485f.). The role of the magistrates is not clear: Schede argues that they were a jurisdictional college (so also in Athens, see Busolt (1920), 485), whereas Robert suggests a financial committee. Busolt (1920), 630 (= corrigenda et addenda ad p. 433) says that they dealt with the purchase of corn in Samos (so also Sokolowski (1964), 2).

151. For evidence see Sokolowski (1964), 6f.; Croissant, Salviat (1966), 465-71 and Graf (1985), 264.

152. *Hell.* 5,4,4: See the interpretations of Sokolowski (1964), 6f. and Croissant, Salviat (1966), 465-70.
153. For a discussion see ch. 3.4.
154. Apart from other Olympian gods such as Ares and Hermes.
155. See Thériault (1996), 183f.
156. In the Classical period, the *ekklesia* moved from the agora to the Pnyx.
157. See Paus. 9,35,1; 9,35,3. This is confirmed by a mid-6th-century inscription from Thera (cited in ch. 5.3). On the date range of the Charites' worship in Athens see also Sokolowski (1964), 5 and Hamdorf (1964), 45 and 103f. Also the *agoranomoi* dedicated to Peitho at Olynthus (see J. & L. Robert (1959), 230).
158. See *SIG*³.227a.14: ὁ δῆμος καὶ ἡ βουλὴ ἐπίσταται χάριτας ἀποδιδόναι τοῖς ἀεὶ λέγουσιν καὶ πράττου[σιν τὰ βέλτιστ]α ὑπὲρ τῆς βουλῆς καὶ τοῦ δήμου.
159. See ch. 5.1.
160. *IG* I³.776: hΕρμεί[αι τόδε] | ἄγαλμα [δίδος] | χάριν ἐν[θάδε ἔ]θηκεν Οιν[όβιο] | ς κῆρυχς μ[νεμ] | οσύνες hέ[νεκα]. For an interpretation see Pulleyn (1997), 40f.
161. *ICret.* I.XVI.24.

    σοὶ Διὸς ὑψίστοιο καὶ εὐπλοκάμοιο Διώνα[ς,
    Κύπρ[ι], ναὸν [π]ροπάροιθε Εὐνομίας ἔθεσαν
    οἵδε σὺν Αὐτίωνι· τίνες δ' ὅδε πέτρος ἐλέγχ[ει,
    πότνια, τοῖς σὺ δίδου πανδάματορ χάριτας,
    καὶ λιπαρὸν πρὸς τέρμα βίου γηραιὸς ἱκέσθαι
    πάντας ἀπημάντους, Κυπρογένεια θεά.

    The idea of χάρις in prayers also always implies the idea of an exchange of favours between gods and mortals; on this see Pulleyn (1997), 37; 40f. and 93f.
162. For evidence see J.&L. Robert (1959), 230 and Sokolowski (1964), 6.
163. See Shapiro (1995), 119. On the cult-association see ch. 7.2.
164. On a likely Eastern origin for Harmonia, see Astour (1965), 159-61.
165. The other passage where she appears in Aphrodite's erotic train is Aeschylus' *Danaids* (see n. 60 above).
166. Laks, Most (1997), 19: "Heavenly Aphrodite and Zeus . . . and Persuasion and Harmony are established as name for the same god (τῷ αὐτῷ θεῷ ὄνομα κεῖται)."
167. The most complete collection of evidence for cults of Aphrodite and Ares is still Burkert (1960), 133, n. 6.
168. See M.L. West (1966), 415.
169. The cults of Homonoia have recently been examined by Thériault (1996), *passim*. On the shifting and sharing of names by deities in the Derveni Papyrus see Obbink (1994), 111-35, esp. 121-25.

Chapter 3

1. Unless otherwise stated, *Homeric Hymn* indicates the so-called "major *Homeric Hymn*" (= *Hymn. Hom.* V). References to the "minor *Homeric Hymn*" (= *Hymn. Hom.* VI) will be explicitly indicated.
2. On the term προοίμιον see Thuc. 3,104, who introduces the quotation of the *Homeric Hymn to Apollo* in the following way: δηλοῖ δὲ μάλιστα Ὅμηρος ὅτι τοιαῦτα ἦν ἐν τοῖς ἔπεσι τοῖσδε, ἅ ἐστιν ἐκ προοιμίου Ἀπόλλωνος; see also Pind. *Nem.* 2,1ff.; for further examples see Lenz (1975), 9 with n. 1 and Graf (1997), 98f. Epic heroic themes are announced in *Hymn. Hom.* XXXI,18f.; *Hymn. Hom.* XXXII,32ff.; see also *Hymn. Hom.* VI,19f. On hymns in general see the overview by Wünsch (1916), 140-83, and now Furley, Bremer (2001). On the structure of the *Homeric Hymns* see Janko (1981), 9-24, esp. 10-6.
3. Formally: χαῖρε, ἵληθι are the form of address in both "genres", but in contrast to actual prayers, hymns do not normally request epiphany, see the prayer of the Elean women to

Dionysus (871 *PMG*) with a clear plea for epiphany: ἐλθεῖν ἥρω Διόνυσε / Ἀλείων ἐς ναὸν / ἁγνὸν σὺν Χαρίτεσσιν / ἐς ναὸν / τῶι βοέωι ποδὶ δύων, / ἄξιε ταῦρε, / ἄξιε ταῦρε); see similarly 879 *PMG* (καλεῖτε θεόν) and Sappho fr. 2 V. in which Aphrodite is asked for an epiphany. For an interpretation of these prayers see Patzer (1962), 91f. and 102f. For thematic links of hymns with actual cult songs, see Lenz (1975), 9-21; H. Meyer (1933). On nature, form on composition of Greek hymns, see Furley, Bremer (2001), 1-64.

4. So e.g. Lenz (1975), 12 with n. 3; Clay (1989), 152f.

5. So Herington (1985), 6; see also Herter (1981), 183-201, esp. 196: "essendo «proemia» non erano utilizzabili in qualsiasi maniera, ma destinati per determinate occasioni in certe feste, di cui glorificavano le divinità"; more cautious Parker (1991), 1-17, esp. 1; cf. Clay (1989), 152f. who points out the "absence of an overtly religious context".

6. So Parker (1991), 1.

7. See Parker (1991), 2.

8. See ch. 3.4.

9. On Pandora see Hes. *Theog.* 571-612; *Op.* 60-82; on Hera see *Il.* 14,166-86; on Aphrodite see fr. 4 Davies/Bernabé.

10. See Penglase (1994), 166ff.

11. See Burkert (1985), 9: "The importance of the myths of the gods lies in their connection with the sacred rituals for which they frequently provide a reason." However, we cannot decide with certainty which came first and prompted the other. Perhaps rituals were inspired by mythical features, so that in this case cult imitates myth.

12. Presumably actual cult images made exactly the same impression on worshippers, in the sense that they had something divine without being identical with the divinity. For a discussion of the relationship between deities and their images see now: Donohue (1997), 31-45, esp. 44f. arguing for an identity of artwork and god ("images looked like the gods and were treated accordingly"); similarly Elsner (1996), 515-31, esp. 529, but cf. earlier Vernant (1991), 151-63, esp. 154f. (on *xoana*) holding that they were never supposed to represent the deity; similarly Burkert (1985), 91f.: he supports his view that image and deity are not to be equated by pointing out that philosophers from Heraclitus (22 F 5 D.-K.) onwards warned against confusing the image with the god. This is also suggested by Aesch. *Eum.* 242 when Orestes addresses Athena: πρόσειμι δῶμα καὶ βρέτας τὸ σόν, θεά.

13. For a useful typology of the *Homeric Hymns* in general see Lenz (1975), 9-21: the common elements of the introductions are (1) the announcement of the song by terms like ἀείδω or similar expressions; (2) the theme to be displayed: the deity who will be praised; (3) praising epithets; (4) praising relative clause; see also Janko (1981). On similarities between the hymns see Allen, Halliday, Sikes (1936), 350; Lenz (1975), 51 with n. 1; Heitsch (1965), 38ff.

14. See Flückiger-Guggenheim (1984), 32ff. and 59ff.

15. The *Hymn to Demeter* provides an *aition* for the Mysteries at Eleusis; the *Hymn to Apollo* displays the history of the cults in Delphi and Delos.

16. See 58f.: ἐς Κύπρον δ᾽ ἐλθοῦσα θυώδεα νηὸν ἔδυνεν / ἐς Πάφον· ἔνθα δέ οἱ τέμενος βωμός τε θυώδης.

17. For the epiphany of a goddess surrounded by animals see the cultic ring made of gold in Vermeule (1974), 13 and Nilsson (1927), 353, pl. 162; Matz (1958), 14 with pl. 5.

18. See E. Meyer (1877), *passim*, followed by v. Wilamowitz (1916), 83 and Nilsson (1967), 522; see also Rose (1924), 11-6 and P. Smith (1981), 8f.; on the Asian Goddess in general (her Eastern origins and links with Aphrodite in particular) see Helck (1971), *passim*. On the syncretism of the Great Mother and Aphrodite in the Troad see Nilsson (1967), 522 f., Càssola (1975), 240; Burkert (1985), 154.

19. See v. Wilamowitz (1916), 83 with n. 1: the affair between Aphrodite and Anchises is the Greek version of that of Cybele and Attis in Asian myth; Nilsson (1967), 523, draws a parallel to the family of Cinyras at Paphos; like the Cinyrades the *Aineiadai* are seen as "priest-kings" who have their origins in Asia Minor. In the epic of Gilgamesh, the hero, after having

rejected Ishtar, enumerates all other mortals who have suffered harm from the union with her (for a discussion of this episode see ch. 2.3); Flückiger-Guggenheim (1984), 132, hints at Ishtar-Astarte and Tammuz and the Sumerian love-goddess Inanna and Dumuzi.

20. In the *Hymn to Apollo* much attention is given to Leto's troubles giving birth to Apollo; the *Hymn to Demeter* shows Demeter's sorrow before the foundation of her cults; Hermes, in his hymn, is displayed as a successful thief. On "conflict" as a typical element in the *Homeric Hymns* see Lenz (1975) 14f. In later hymns, for example Callimachus' *Hymns*, conflict is missing.

21. But the birth is mentioned in the other hymn to Aphrodite (*Hymn. Hom.* VI,1f.) which may be influenced by the Hesiodic version, where her connection with the islands of Cyprus and Cythera is also explained (see *Theog.* 192-200; ch. 1.4). Her actual dwelling places are mentioned in *Hymn. Hom.* VI and *Hymn. Hom.* X. In the *Iliad* (5,330; 422; 458; 760; 883) and the *Odyssey* (8,222 and 18,193) they are used as mere epithets.

22. This has been the *communis opinio* particularly in German scholarship, see Wilamowitz (1916), 83f.; similarly Jacoby (1933), 43. Reinhardt (1956), 1-14 even assumed that the hymn was written by the same hand which composed Aeneas' *aristeia* in *Il.* 20,302f. These views are challenged by P.M. Smith (1981), 17-58. He doubts the historicity of the only source which mentions the existence of a princely family for the Archaic period in the Troad, Strabo 13,1,52f. [607f.] (p. 25f.), and argues that the *Hymn to Aphrodite* and the passage in *Il.* 20,302f. do entirely square with their respective literary contexts and do not require extratextual reference to poetic audiences (p. 52). Before P.M. Smith, Lenz (1975), 266f. was also sceptical.

23. Contemporary with the *Iliad*: v. Wilamowitz (1916), 83f. (followed by Jacoby (1933), 42f. and Reinhardt (1961), 507f.). Since the hymn gives no internal information concerning its dating, investigations have often been based upon linguistic criteria, see Solmsen (1960), 1-13, who sees the hymn influenced by Hesiod's works, and Janko (1982), who argues that the *Hymn to Aphrodite*, the earliest hymn (around 675 BC), is later than Homer and was composed during Hesiod's lifetime (151-80; 181f.). Whereas Richardson (1974), 43, dates the *Hymn to Demeter* earlier, in the 7th century (similarly Càssola (1975), 250f.), Allen, Halliday and Sikes (1936), xcvi-cix conclude that the *Hymn to Apollo* is the oldest, followed by the *Hymn to Aphrodite* (date varying from 800-700 BC). For an early date see more recently Bickerman (1976), 229 and Penglase (1994), 169.

24. In comparison, in the narrative of the *Hymn to Demeter* the role of the priestly family seems to be relatively subordinated to more general topics. In Demeter's realm, the foundation of the Eleusinian Mysteries (in which, however, the family has a certain importance) and the donation of agriculture are the main themes: see Foley (1993). She argues for a Panhellenic audience and therefore a "de-emphasis" of the priestly family (142f.).

25. The "Amphitryon motif" in particular seems to have had repercussions for the self-definition of kings: see Flückiger-Guggenheim (1984), 133f. and Burkert (1965), 166-77. Herodotus gives an account of the Spartan king Demaratus, whose legitimacy was in doubt. His mother claims that the Spartan hero Astrabacus had slept with her in the shape of his father. On the topic in general see Scheer (1993).

26. *Il.* 2,820 and 5,313. See also Hes. *Theog.* 1008-10.

27. References to families also occur in the *Hymn to Demeter*, which praises the family of Eleusis, although this is less emphatic. The *Hymn to Apollo* gives clearer information about the background of its performance, presumably the background of a rhapsodic competition at a festival of Apollo at Delos. It mentions Δηλιάδες, a girls' chorus praising Apollo, Leto and Artemis (158); in 169 the speaker asks them for support.

28. Zeus, her most famous victim, appears later in 36f.

29. For Aphrodite's defeat, see also Clay (1989), 155 with n. 7.

30. See her etymology of Aeneas' name in 199.

31. Argued by Bickerman (1976), 229-54.

32. This aspect also comes to the fore in Aeschylus' *Danaids* (Radt, *TrGF* 3 (1985), fr. 44), and already in Hesiod's *Theogony* (194f.) when, immediately after her birth, the grass starts growing after she has put her feet on the earth for the very first time.

33. Helen does not suffer physically from her sexual desire, but feels ashamed and guilty for having given in to it. Proitus' wife Anteia, whose passion for Bellerophon was unrequited, takes revenge on him by twisting the situation and accusing him of attempted rape (*Il.* 6,160f.).

34. So P. Smith (1981), 5f., but he gives no details on the kind of audience.

35. See Clay (1989), 151-201, esp. 197-201.

36. Walcot (1991), 137-55, esp. 139.

37. The *Dios Apate* in *Iliad* 14 has been claimed to have its origins in such tales: see Burkert (1960), 132f. and ch. 2.3.

38. *Hymn. Hom.* IV (Hermes), 68f.: the theft of the cattle, see also *Hymn. Hom.* II, 202f.

39. Walcot (1991), 141.

40. See 2f.: ἥ τε θεοῖσιν ἐπὶ γλυκὺν ἵμερον ὦρσε / καί τ' ἐδαμάσσατο φῦλα καταθνητῶν ἀνθρώπων, / οἰωνούς τε διιπετέας καὶ θηρία πάντα; 36: καί τε παρὲκ Ζηνὸς νόον ἤγαγε τερπικεραύνου; 38: πυκινὰς φρένας ἐξαπαφοῦσα.

41. So Lenz (1975), 126.

42. When mortal women announce their desire in myth, this usually follows the "Potiphar's wife" motif. The best known examples are featured in Euripidean tragedy: Stheneboia (alias Anteia in *Il.* 6,160f.) in the play of the same name and Phaedra in the lost *Hippolytus*. In the hymn it is left to Zeus' initiative to cause Aphrodite's desire for Anchises: Ἀγχίσεω δ' ἄρα οἱ γλυκὺν ἵμερον ἔμβαλε θυμῷ (53). Compare the expression of 56f. τὸν δὴ ἔπειτα ἰδοῦσα φιλομμειδὴς Ἀφροδίτη / ἠράσατ' with *Il.* 3,446 (Paris' expression of desire for Helen).

43. See Walcot (1991), 142; similarly: Flückiger-Guggenheim (1984), 130f. arguing that the story does not influence later literature, as Aphrodite's behavior does not fit the Greek divine world, in which it is the gods who rape mortal women. A mortal woman's desire is typically not fulfilled in myth, as she is normally rejected. Even when a woman's love is requited, as in the case of Clytemnestra or Helen, she has to suffer for that reason. This may explain in part why even Aphrodite experiences pain in the hymn.

44. See P. Smith (1981), 43.

45. So P. Smith (1981), 42 (since Aphrodite is anointed with oil and brilliant with gold). The fact that the doors are shining (θύρας φαεινάς 60) anticipates a typical characteristic of divine epiphany: the deity, in particular his or her eyes are depicted as shining (see Pfister (1924), 277-323, esp. 315f. for numerous examples).

46. So Gladigow (1990), 98-121, esp. 99 with n. 14

47. P. Smith (1981), 41.

48. Hes. *Theog.* 513f.; *Op.* 72f.; for a discussion see ch. 6.3.

49. But she will add her specific powers, φιλότης and ἵμερος, subsequently on Hera's request to guarantee the success of Hera's seduction of Zeus. For a discussion of the contrasts and similarities between this scene and the *Homeric Hymn*, see P. Smith (1981), 113 with n. 36.

50. Himerius, for example, narrates the contents of such a hymn (or *paean*) composed by Alcaeus (= Himer. *Or.* 48, 10f. (200f. Colonna) = Alc. fr. 307c V. = R 3 (Rutherford)): after his birth, Apollo receives sceptre, lyre and chariot from Zeus, who sends him to Delphi and the Castalian spring, from where he is supposed to make prophecies about *dike* and *themis* to the Hellenes. After his departure to the Hyperborean fields, the Delphians compose *paianes* and perform dances in order to induce Apollo to appear (113ff.). On the genre see Rutherford (2001), 27f. and 91. On early iconographical evidence of epiphany on Minoan rings and gems, all dated around 1400 BC, see Vermeule (1974), 13f. (with Plates). On representations of epiphanies of Aphrodite on Athenian vases: Metzger (1965), 59-69, see also Simon (1959), 46-47; 36-38.

51. Apollo's epiphany as described in the *Homeric Hymn* (440-5) indicates that it happened in the *adyton*, the "innermost shrine"; the Dioskouroi appear on the sea after invocation (see *Hymn. Hom.* XXXIII,9). For other places of epiphany, see Gladigow (1990), 101. It is hard to imagine how epiphanies take place, i.e. how deities can become visible to human beings. Hägg distinguishes between an "ecstatic epiphany", during which the deity is perceived by the worshippers in a vision which can be caused by drugs, ecstatic dances, or incantations, and a "performed epiphany", in which a human being, usually a priest, appears in the disguise of the respective god and is venerated by the worshippers as if he or she were the real deity. The theory that such performed epiphanies existed is based on Hägg's analysis of Minoan temple architecture (1986), 41-62.

52. So Gordon (1979), 13; Gladigow (1990), 99; Donohue (1997), 44f.; Burkert (1997), 29 who argues that statues of Dionysus are especially inspired by cultic epiphany. Delivorrias (1984), II.1., 2-151, esp. 13f. (nos. 41-53) establishes a category of late Classical vase depictions displaying "Aphrodite in the shape of an Archaic cult image within hypaethral sanctuaries, accompanied by cultic scenes." On almost all of them Aphrodite is present in a double way. We see the goddess (in late Classical style) sitting next to her altar (no. 41) or a pillar (no. 43), and we are presumably meant to interpret this as the presence of the "real goddess" in a sanctuary. But, in addition, there is an Archaic cult image of the goddess. Furthermore, there are archaizing cult images of her alone (nos. 40 and 48). How can this twofold way of representation be explained? Maybe the Aphrodite in late Classical style is meant as a temporary and spontaneous epiphany in her sanctuary, while the cult image embodies an earlier appearance.

53. On the architecture see e.g. Dinsmoor (1973), 40; Mazarakis Ainian (1988), 105-19; Lawrence, Tomlinson (1996), 111 state that in the 8th century BC there was a possible influence from places such as Cyprus, where temple buildings had an even more ancient tradition since the Phoenicians had reused and reformed late Bronze Age buildings, the construction of which seemed to anticipate the stone buildings of Classical Greece.

54. See Romano (1980), 4: "Greek temples arose as a result of the origin of Greek cult images, with the need to provide a dwelling (a ναός) for these divine earthly surrogates."; see also Scheer (2000), 130-46 for multiple cult images in one temple.

55. See Bielefeld (1968), 3ff. on the ornaments. It has been pointed out, interestingly, by Boardman (1991), ad pl. 110 that the so-called "Lyons kore" from the Acropolis (dated to about 540 BC) has earrings of the same type as Hera in *Il.* 14,182f.

56. *Il.* 14,169 = *Hymn. Hom.* V,60; 172 = 63; 283 = 68; see P. Smith (1981), 113 with n. 36.

57. So Parker (1991), 3.

58. *Il.* 14,169 = *Hymn. Hom.* V,60.

59. In the *Odyssey*, Aphrodite retreats to Paphos after her erotic encounter; there are literal correspondences between the two texts: *Od.* 8,363-5 correspond to 59 and 61f. of the hymn; for a similar scene see also *Hymn. Hom.* VI,5f. and *Cypria* fr. 4 (Davies/Bernabé). For traditional elements of a woman's or goddess's toilet as a pattern in oral poetry, see P. Smith (1981), 114 with n. 38.

60. See fr. 4 (Davies/Bernabé); the lines of this fragment are transmitted in Athenaeus (15,682D-E) together with fr. 5 (Davies/Bernabé).

61. φέρουσ' ὥραι Bernabé ("such as the seasons bring"). Davies' φοροῦσ' is the version given in codd. indicating "to wear constantly", it is preferable to φέρουσ' of which it is the *verbum frequentativum*. I would prefer Davies' version φορουσ' Ὧραι (instead of the "seasons" which are not personified), also on contextual grounds, since the Horae are mentioned already in l.1 as the producers of garments.

62. With Bernabé, I read αἰθέσι, since "burning" (αἰθής) seems to be a suitable adjective to describe the color of the cups of the yellow narcissus; the duplication of the adjectives may seem too much of a good thing, but quite fits the pompous style of the whole passage. Davies prefers ἄνθεσι as in A, but this seems syntactically impossible: for ἄνθεσι

cannot stand in apposition to καλύκεσσιν. Moreover, καλλιρρόου, as transmitted in the mss., cannot be right: a flower is not likely to be "beautiful-flowing". Ludwich's correction καλλιπνόου is tempting since it differs from the transmitted version only in two letters; Meineke's καὶ λειρίου "and of the lily", which is accepted by Davies, requires much change. Ἀφροδίτη is established in the transmitted text and also in its position at the end of the line (see fr. 5,1 Davies/Bernabé). Ludwich's correction, which is accepted by Bernabé, is the only plausible suggestion since it satisfies the metrical requirements.

63. See Bernabé's extensive *apparatus criticus* and testimonia which provide numerous parallels and bibliographical notes on modern discussions. In the discussion of fr. 4 I use Bernabé's text as a basis; line 6 is undoubtedly badly preserved, but Aphrodite's name seems securely transmitted.

64. Athenaeus (15,682D-E), who cites them not within the context of an adornment scene or of the *Cypria* themselves, but within a discussion about flowers, more specifically about "flowers used in wreaths" (ἀνθῶν στεφανωτικῶν).

65. See the comment of Davies (1989), 35: "F 4 in particular has been deemed rather vacuously ornamental in comparison with the other epic instances of the motif of a goddess's self-beautification: the list of flowers meanders confusingly and the repetition of the word for "flower" (*anthos*) three times in five lines does not display the archaic device of emphasis through duplication at its most elegant." One may add that the doubling of her attendants is entirely consistent with the style and contents of these lines.

66. See Ath. 15,682F: οὗτος ὁ ποιητὴς καὶ τὴν τῶν στεφάνων χρῆσιν εἰδὼς φαίνεται δι' ὧν λέγει· Then he quotes our fragment: ἡ δὲ σὺν ἀμφιπόλοισι φιλομμειδὴς Ἀφροδίτη / πλεξάμεναι στεφάνους εὐώδεας, ἄνθεα γαίης, / ἂν κεφαλαῖσιν ἔθεντο θεαὶ λιπαροκρήδεμνοι, / Νύμφαι καὶ Χάριτες, ἅμα δὲ χρυσῆ Ἀφροδίτη, / καλὸν ἀείδουσαι κατ' ὄρος πολυπιδάκου Ἴδης. A lacuna after Ἀφροδίτη has been suggested by Meineke, but this has not been accepted by Bernabé. Apart from this, his text is the same as Davies'.

67. See Stinton (1965), 62.

68. For an emphasis of the garments, see also εἵματα καλά (64; 171), εἵματα σιγαλόεντα (85), πέπλον . . . φαεινότερον πυρὸς αὐγῆς (86); see also *Hymn. Hom.* II (Dem.), 277ff.

69. The link of Aphrodite's birth with the sea is probably inspired by the version given in Hesiod's *Theogony* which is discussed in ch. 1.4.

70. See Parker (1991), 2 and Penglase (1994), 166f. and 172f.

71. See Penglase (1994), 166f.

72. For a discussion of the hymn see Labat, Caquot, Sznycer and Vieyra (1970), 247ff.

73. For the source see Seux (1976), 39 (French translation quoted in Penglase (1994), 167 with n. 18).

74. See Penglase (1994), 167 with n. 17: "In-bi" means "sexual attractiveness and power".

75. See Penglase (1994), 172f. Compare the bestowal of Zas' robe to Chthonie (Pherecydes F 68 Schibli): Zas presents the robe not simply as a bridal gift to Chthonie; it transforms Chthonie into Ge and attributes to her the earth as her specific sphere of influence.

76. See ch. 3.2 for the historical background.

77. This has been pointed out by Scheer (2000), 57.

78. See Burkert (1997), 30 with n. 53. See similarly Kirk (1990) ad 87-94: "the details are important for the understanding of Greek cult: (i) Athena has a free-standing temple on the Acropolis; (ii) it is normally kept closed (note that this feature occurs as well in the *Homeric Hymn to Aphrodite* (60)); (iii) it contains a seated cult image large enough to receive a large πέπλος on its knees". Further examples of ritual dressing of images of other deities are discussed by Scheer (2000), 55f. She argues that performers of such rites often act, as if they treated the deities themselves ("Hierbei verhalten sich die Ausführenden häufig so, als würden sie der Gottheit selbst aufwarten.").

79. These rituals have been discussed in detail by Scheer (2000), 57f.

80. But cf. Mansfield (1985), 581 who prefers the idea that a ritual bridal bath took place; for the cleaning and bathing of images of other gods at different places in Greece, see 557-64 and 568-84.

81. It has been dated to the 2nd half of the 6th century BC. For the date and ancient sources see Simon, Bauchhenss (1984), II.1., no. 332; see also Boardman (1991), 89.

82. The expression κατὰ τὰ πάτρια is discussed by Parker (1996), 7f.

83. For the festivals see Deubner (1932), 17-22; Parker (1983), 26-8; Burkert (1985), 79 and 228; for washing as part of cult practice in general see Gladigow (1985-86), 114-33, esp. 116.

84. See Parker (1983), 27 with n. 45, who infers from the name "Kallynteria" that "sweeping clean" was related to the cleaning of the temple precinct, whereas at the Plynteria the cult image was bathed; on the Plynteria see Burkert (1985), 79 and especially 228.

85. According to Burkert (1985), 79 and 228, Athenian wives and virgins performed the rite. The *Palladion*, another image of Athena, also underwent washing rituals. It was carried to the sea by ephebes and afterwards put back in place in the law court: see Burkert (1985), 79.

86. On the latter see Parker (1983), 26f.

87. So Deubner (1932), 21.

88. *LSCG* 39; see also ch. 2.5 for a discussion of this decree.

89. So Deubner (1932), 215f.

90. The statues were of Aphrodite and Peitho, see *LSCG* 39; for ἕδος see Soph. *OT* 886 δαιμόνων ἕδη σέβων; *El.* 1373 ἕδη θεῶν. On the purple see Pfuhl (1900), 97.

91. But cf. Deubner (1932), 215, who does not think that this washing has the same significance as in the Plynteria.

92. This aspect, surprisingly, is completely neglected when Aphrodite comes to Anchises, but cf. *Hymn. Hom.* II (Dem.), 277 and, similarly, *Hymn. Hom.* VII (Dion.), 5f. Maybe the smell would have immediately revealed her divine identity to Anchises.

93. See Campbell (1967), 276, who points out that our two earliest references to frankincense offerings (λιβανωτός) to Aphrodite are found in fr. 2 and 44,30 V.

94. See Simon (1998), 209f.

95. See *IG* XI.2.161A.92-3 (dated to 279 BC) and 203A.38-39 (dated to 269/70 BC).

96. So *Hymn. Hom.* II (Dem.), 275f.; *Hymn. Hom.* III (Ap.), 267f.; *Hymn. Hom.* V (Aphr.), 174; *Hymn. Hom.* VI (Aphr.), 1f.

97. That is exactly what epiphanies normally cause. For fright see also e.g. *Il.* 24,170 (Priam and Iris). For further examples in the hymns see Pfister (1924), 317f.

98. Shine and brilliance are characteristics of the gods and come from their eyes (so of Athena in *Il.* 1,200 or of Aphrodite later in *Hymn. Hom.* V,181 etc.) or from their body (so *Hymn. Hom.* III (Ap.), 260f.; *Hymn. Hom.* II (Dem.), 189f.). Finally Aphrodite will regain her divine size (172f.).

99. On this, see Donohue (1997), 31-45, who argues that our idea of a "cult image" is alien to the Greeks, as they had no proper term for it. The idea that cult images existed with particular functions in worship and ritual is still widely accepted: see e.g. Romano (1980), esp. 2ff. for her definition; Burkert (1985) and Gladigow (1990) also use the term "cult image" or "Kultbild"; for a definition see also Funke (1981).

100. On the term *xoanon*, see Donohue (1988), esp. introduction and ch. 1. According to her, our idea of *xoanon*, an old wooden image of a god, is influenced by Pausanias. Although the word *xoanon* does not occur in the Hesiodic or Homeric texts it would be wrong to assume that images of gods were wholly absent from the life of Archaic Greece (see book 6 of the *Iliad*, where Athena's temple and seated image are mentioned). For an analysis of other Greek terminology for statues (ἄγαλμα, ἀνδριάς, βρέτας), see Scheer (2000), 8-34.

101. Aphrodite and Ares have both wooden images there; according to the local myth, they were dedicated by Polynices.

102. This is obviously an aetiology for a cult statue shown on Delos. It has no evidential value, since it cannot be dated.

103. See Romano (1980), 432f.
104. Aphrodite holds a *phiale* in the right and wears a *stephane*, together with a belted *peplos* and a cape (Beazley (1963), 1313/5). On another vase painting Aphrodite (accompanied by fluttering Erotes) wears a long-sleeved, brightly ornamented *peplos* and holds a *phiale* (1325/51). Delivorrias (1984), II.1., 13f. (nos. 41-53) categorizes late Classical vase-depictions of Aphrodite in the shape of an Archaic cult image (see above, n. 52).
105. See Boardman (1991), pl. 28: the so-called "Dame d' Auxerre" found on Delos is the earliest one of its kind and dated to 640-630 BC.
106. See e.g. Gladigow (1985-86), 115.
107. But cf. Mansfield (1985), 442 and 445, according to whom adorning of cult statues is not a ritual act, but part of the normal devotion to the gods as objects of worship; 443: weaving of garments for statues as a cult ritual is rare, but adorning them for ritual banquets is frequent.
108. Gladigow (1985-86), 118.
109. See Gladigow (1990), 100.
110. And so they are in 164 when Anchises undresses her.
111. This expression has an equivalent in a completely different context: a description of a military object (*Il.* 18,610: θώρηκα φαεινότερον πυρὸς αὐγῆς).
112. The exact meaning of the terms is unclear (see Bielefeld (1968), 3ff.). The wording of the hymn is probably based on the only scene in Homer where they occur. At *Il.* 18,401 Hephaestus tells Thetis that he has created ἕλικες and κάλυκες. ἕλικες, according to its literal meaning, signifies a curved or twisted ornament (enhanced by γνάμπται). The scholiasts, who obviously were not any more familiar with the terminology, suggest several meanings for ἕλικες: "hair ring" or "pendants for necklaces" (schol. ex./A ad *Il.* 18,401a (Erbse)). In inscriptions, for "earring" the term ἐνώτιον is used, but see also Ar. *Ran.* 102. κάλυξ actually means "cup" or "bud" of a flower and thus probably describes the shape of an ornament. Again, it is not clear which one exactly. For an analysis of both terms (without a final conclusion) see Hadaczek (1903), 121 (cited by Bielefeld (1968), 6 with n. 23).
113. ὅρμος means "cord" or "chain". Several chains form a necklace, therefore plural (also *Il.* 18,401; *Od.* 15,460).
114. In a more general context, it means the ornament or decoration of a woman, so e.g. Hes. *Op.* 76; in *Il.* 14,187 it denotes jewellery *and* clothing of a goddess, and so it does for cult statues. In Her. 5,92 it refers only to clothing: see Mansfield (1985), 507.
115. See Mansfield (1985), ch. 7 (438-587), who provides a useful catalogue for the adornment of statues.
116. For the inscription and its date ("Archaic"), see Blinkenberg (1941), esp. 178 with n. 34.
117. *SEG* xxviii 100.
118. *IDélos* 290.229-244: the term κόσμος occurs in lines 230,238,239-40 and refers to the metal ornaments of the statues.
119. See also *Hymn. Hom.* V,93 χρυσέη Ἀφροδίτη (also in Mimnermus fr. 1 W.).
120. See *IG* II/III².1424.14 (from 368/67 BC). On the history of the ancient statue of Athena see Mansfield (1985), ch. 3; on the inscriptions documenting the numerous pieces of jewellery, see 144ff.
121. *IDélos* 1417AII.1-3 (155/4 BC).
122. *IDélos* 1423Ba.18-19, from 150 BC. For further examples see Mansfield (1985), 514.
123. See *IDélos* 1417AI.49-53 (155/4 BC).
124. *IDélos* 313A.23-24.
125. This may prefigure the haloes of Christian saints.
126. For χρυσός and its compounds as epithets for gods, see also chs. 7.7 and 8.6.
127. *IDélos* 290.151-153, from 246 BC.
128. *IG* II/III².1534B.169.
129. *IG* XI.2.159A *passim*.

130. *IDélos* 313A.76-77. For further examples see Mansfield (1985), 506f.
131. See *Hymn. Hom.* V,1f., Sappho fr. 33 V. (for other goddesses see Hes. *Theog.* 136 (Phoibe)).
132. This expression always has a highly erotic connotation; it is a euphemism for having sex, or even defloration. In *Od.* 11,245 (Poseidon in the shape of Enipeus rapes Tyro), and in Theocritus (*Id.* 27,55) it describes a possessive and violent act by a man. But in Pindar (*Isthm.* 8,44f.) this metaphor has a different implication: women loosen their girdles themselves as a sign of being willing to make love. In *Anth. Pal.* 7,324 it is a metaphor for marriage and thus not markedly erotic. For the motif see Syndikus (1990), ad c. 61.
133. It is interesting that while a goddess seems to take off her divinity with her clothes, a mortal woman takes off her shame with her clothes, as Candaules' wife in Her. 1,8,3: ἄμα δὲ κιθῶνι ἐκδυομένῳ συνεκδύεται καὶ τὴν αἰδῶ γυνή. Raubitschek (1957), 139f. has argued that this idea goes back to a saying of Theano, the wife or disciple of Pythagoras (transmitted by Diogenes Laertius 8,43).
134. The text of line 173 requires discussion (mss: ἄρα] πὰρ Stephanus mss: εὐποιήτοιο] κεὐποιήτοιο Sikes: εὐποιήτου δὲ Ruhnken): the locative dative κλισίῃ (so mss.) seemed unusual and thus led scholars to follow Stephanus, who emended ἄρα the mss. by introducing the preposition πὰρ (this has not been accepted by Allen, Halliday, Sikes; see ad loc.). However, locative datives in a similar context can be found elsewhere (σταθμοῖσι "in the steading" 76; for more examples see Chantraine (1953), 78f., who, however, says that the locative dative is used "surtout dans des expressions de sens assez général"). Furthermore, "to stand by / near the hut" or "to be present at the hut" is less suitable than "she stood in the hut". The asyndeton makes the passage appear abrupt and may seem unusual considering the change of subject which is caused by the expression κῦρε κάρη (see *LSJ*, s.v. κυρέω whose translation I follow above). However, the hiatus (κλισίῃ, εὐποιήτοιο), which requires a pause, may be intended as a rhetorical feature increasing the surprise of the particular moment when Aphrodite dresses, stands up, regains her superhuman height and then touches the "well-wrought" beam. Therefore there is no need either to introduce a particle as Sikes (κεὐποιήτοιο) suggests or to even emend the text as Ruhnken (εὐποιήτου δὲ) does; similarly Càssola ad loc.: "eliminare l' asindeto, il che tuttavia non è necessario". Perhaps a correction is not only not necessary, but would even destroy the effect of the hiatus. κῦρε is only mentioned in M, but the same formula μελάθρου κῦρε κάρη also occurs in the *Hymn to Demeter* (188f.), which indicates that superhuman height is a regular feature in divine epiphanies. Allen, Halliday, Sikes (see ad loc.) point out that the other mss. (βυρε E T: ἠυρε L¹Πp: ἦρε At D: ἦρε ed. pr.) show the exchange between η and κ, which is found in the early period of minuscule.
135. This is a traditional motif of narrative epiphany, see n. 97 above.
136. Demeter, for example, appears in her superhuman height and thus in her fully divine identity at a considerably earlier stage of the mythical narration of the hymn (in 188f.).

Chapter 4

1. So e.g. in the title of Shapiro's monograph (1993), preferring the term "abstract concepts" to "abstraction", which is applied by other scholars (see M.L. West (1966), 31 and *passim*). On personifications see also Stoessl (1937), 1042-58; Pötscher (1972), 661-3: the category of "Person-Bereichsdenken" means that certain phenomena are conceived of as a person and a thing at the same time. Within this unity, the deity represents the personal aspect, whereas the phenomenon appears as the deity's particular province. Burkert's definition is discussed in ch. 4.3. On cult personifications see Nilsson (1952), 31-40; on the worship of personified virtues and their political significance see most recently Stafford (2000).
2. Nilsson (1952), 32 assumes that appearance in a myth is a necessary condition for cultic worship. But Peitho, for example, has early cults, but no specific myths (see ch. 6.2).

3. So particularly Webster (1954), 10-21, esp. 13f.; see also Shapiro (1993), 26f. with reference to Pottier (1889-90), 15-9.

4. This was probably the direction in which the development went in most cases (abstract first, then personification). But cf. Kretschmer (1924), 101-16, esp. 106, who assumes that the process went the other way round and speaks of "Abstraktifizierung von Dämonen". Stoessl (1937), 1043f. and Webster (1954), 11 deny that this can be decided. There are examples which suggest that both directions are actually possible: Aphrodite was first conceived of as a deity before her name was taken as an appellative to represent her sphere of interest ("sexual love", "pleasure"), so in *Od.* 22,444, or even earlier in the inscription on "Nestor's cup". Ares, however, is an ancient abstract noun meaning "throng of battle", "war" (so Burkert (1985), 169) which occurs in many formulaic expressions (see Mader (1973), 1246-65, esp. 1259-62). On the other hand, Ares is the god of war: Phobos and Deimos are his charioteers; he meets Athena in battle (*Il.* 21,391f.) and he has a special relationship with Aphrodite (*Il.* 5,355f.,21,416; *Od.* 8,267f.). In epic, both the war god and the abstract noun coexist. For a detailed survey of ancient and modern definitions of "personification" and of approaches in their interpretations, see Stafford (2000), 3-19.

5. See Erbse (1986), 10f. He argues that the personal aspect often becomes discernible only in specific contexts and situations; for example, when poets describe an event where the context suggests that something is being perceived as superhuman. This may be the reason why νέμεσις and ἔρως appear personified in Hesiod, but not in Homer.

6. But cf. Nilsson (1952), 31f.: Homer's personifications are "dichterisch". (…) "Dadurch, daß sie mythologisiert wurden, konnten Personifikationen erst zu Kultgottheiten werden." similarly Burkert (1985), 185: "Personifications appear first in poetry, move into the visual arts and finally find their way into the realm of cult."

7. See e.g. M.L. West (1966), 33, who lists them among the gods of cult.

8. Hypnos is discussed later in this chapter; Eros in Hes. *Theog.* 120 is simply called "the most beautiful" and in 201, together with "beautiful" Himeros, he "accompanies" (ὡμάρτησε) Aphrodite. The emphasis on their beauty and their ability to move may account for their personified features, but in any case they are less clearly described than Aphrodite, and we do not know their age or height or the way they act. War-demons like Eris could easily be imagined as animals or monsters, but in the *Iliad*, they regularly appear in a human shape.

9. These are characteristics scholars agree upon; see Petersen (1939), 1f.; Stoessl (1937), 1043; Webster (1952-1953), 29f. (personifications have a genealogy which couple them with a known individual or divinity; verbs or adjectives which describe them denote human activity); see also M.L. West (1966), 33. Pötscher (1959), 19ff. argues that the criterion for personified deities is not cultic veneration, but knowledge and will: "Persönliche Götter sind also solche, die sich die Menschen als Bewußtseinswesen (Wissen, Wille) vorgestellt haben. Diese Eigenschaft kann sich unmittelbar oder durch eine deutlich anthropomorphe Gestalt der Götter äußern." See also Shapiro's categories, (1993), 14 with references.

10. So Shapiro (1993), 14.

11. So already Deubner (1909), 2069f.; see especially the detailed discussion of the gender question within a sociological and iconographic context by Stafford (2000), 27-35.

12. See Stafford (2000), 34.

13. See Shapiro (1993), 110-24.

14. See Stafford (2000), 31f.

15. See Simon (1986a), 114f. on Kratos and Shapiro (1988), 180-82 on scenes with Heracles and Geras, who is depicted in a smaller scale, possibly because he is a personification. On personifications of neuter abstracts see also Stafford (2000), 33.

16. A survey based on the structure of the *Theogony* is given by M.L. West (1966), 31f.

17. See Webster (1954), 10f. However, the two groups cannot be clearly distinguished since phenomena like Eris, Eros or Neikos certainly affect individuals as well.

18. For the classification see Webster (1954), 13f.

19. See below, chs. 4.7, 7.3 and especially ch. 8.6: in Ibycus' imagery (287 *PMGF*) it is the personified Eros himself who, like a hunter, induces the poet to enter Aphrodite's "endless hunting net".

20. Nilsson (1952), 33 and 38 claims that cults of personifications were not established before the 4th century. But documents for their cults, independently from Aphrodite, are not rare in Archaic times: according to an inscription, the Charites had a cult in Thera at least as early as the mid-6th century (see ch. 5.3); Peitho had a cult in Thasos, probably transferred from Paros during the colonisation in 682/68 (see ch. 6.2); for more examples see Hamdorf (1964), 104 and 117; on cults of these goddesses see also chs. 5.3 and 6.2.

21. See Burkert (1985), 185; similarly, but less detailed before him: Fränkel (1951), 67f. See also Reinhardt (1960), 7-41, esp. 7ff.

22. Although ἵμερος is not a personified deity here, he is already emergent elsewhere, as a component of Aphrodite's κεστὸς ἱμάς in *Il.* 14,216 and already as her attendant in Hes. *Theog.* 201.

23. For the idea of this unity see Pötscher (1959), 14; for more vivid examples of "personifications" see id. (1978), 217-31; for a similar concept see Erbse (1986). In this monograph he discusses the nature of the deities in the *Iliad* and the *Odyssey* with special regard to those who are probably a poetic creation ("Nomen proprium und appellativum", esp. 9-54); see also the definition suggested by Shapiro (1993), 14: "when both occur side by side, the divinity is called a personification in that he/she was felt to embody the essence of the abstraction." See also Fränkel (1951), 85f. and Burkert's examples (1985), 185.

24. See Usener (1929), 279f. and 292f.

25. But cf. Kirk (1985), ad loc., p. 325.

26. See Pl. *Symp.* 202e.

27. See Reinhardt (1960), 20ff.

28. Nilsson (1952), 34; Deubner's definition is based upon this cultic phenomenon. He argues that a personification is an aspect of a deity which developed into an independent deity via a stage as a cult epithet, see (1909), 2068-169, esp. 2069f.

29. *Il.* 14,153-353.

30. *CEG* 454=*SEG* xiv 604; on the date see M.L. West (1995), 205 with n. 11.

31. So S. West (1994), 9-15, esp. 11, and similarly Faraone (1996), 77-112, esp. 78f., who both follow Dihle's interpretation: "Der Inhalt der Inschrift ist ohne Zweifel als ein—wie weit auch immer ernst zu nehmender—Liebeszauber zu verstehen." (see (1969), 257-61, esp. 261).

32. For other possible restorations of the lacuna, see Faraone (1996), 78 with n. 3.

33. Since the Rhodian vessel is fairly unassuming in comparison with the ornamental cup described in the epic, some scholars have suggested interpreting the inscription as a joke, a witty allusion to the *Iliad* for which it provides a *terminus ante quem* (see especially P.A. Hansen (1976), 25-43); cf. S. West (1994), 9-15 who argues that the source of inspiration need not be our *Iliad*. She relates the mighty cup to mythological tradition in general, not to an individual work of poetry. She assumes that the vessel played a significant role in the myth of Nestor; moreover, the motif of the mighty goblet itself has parallels in Ugaritic poetry current in 14th century BC (see M.L. West (1995), 205 with n. 13); see also Taplin (1992), 33 with n. 39.

34. Aphrodite's epithet has been assumed to presuppose not only the Iliad, but even the Odyssey, see Risch (1987), 1-9, esp. 8f.: according to him, καλλιστε.[φά]ν.ο : Ἀφροδίτες mimics Od. 8,267 ἀμφ' Ἄρεος φιλότητος ἐϋστεφάνου τ' Ἀφροδίτης and 288 ἰσχανόων φιλότητος ἐϋστεφάνου Κυθερείης; but cf. S. West (1994), 14 with n. 27: "But this resemblance is scarcely sufficient support for his attempt to argue that our Odyssey was already current by 725."

35. See de Jong (1989), 1194-95 for similar formulaic uses of ἵμερος in other, erotic and non-erotic contexts, and with other verbs such as ἐμβάλλειν or ὀρνύναι; for ἵμερος αἱρεῖ she counts eight epic occurrences; see also Rüter, Matthiessen (1969), 231-55, esp. 244. The

same formulaic line occurs in *Il.* 3,446 when Paris is overcome with desire for Helen. In *Hymn. Hom.* V,56f. Aphrodite is in the same way swiftly overcome by desire for Anchises: τὸν δὴ ἔπειτα ἰδοῦσα φιλομμειδὴς Ἀφροδίτη / ἠράσατ᾽, ἐκπάγλως δὲ κατὰ φρένας ἵμερος εἷλεν.

36. See Faraone (1996), 78 with n. 2.

37. See Faraone (1996), 81 with n. 13 for references: *Od.* 10,237 for the description of the immediate effects of Circe's magic; Sappho fr. 1,21-23 V. which imitates an erotic incantation; further references are made to later magical incantations. These can only be considered as parallels, of course, not as instances of direct borrowing.

38. So argued by Risch (1987), 1-9.

39. On this adornment scene see ch. 3.4.

40. The meaning "sexual love" is indicated in many other Homeric passages (often with the verb μίσγειν), see *Il.* 13,636; 14,163; 237; 353; *Od.* 8, 267; 288; *Hymn. Hom.* V,133; cf. Faraone (1999), 97 with n. 2 who takes φιλότης as poetic equivalent for φιλία and translates "affection".

41. ἵμερος, particularly in connection with a genitive of a person, means "longing for", not always with a sexual connotation (so e.g. in *Il.* 3,139f.), which ἔρως always seems to have. The images and metaphors associated with ἵμερος are peculiar: ἵμερος (not ἔρως) is often aroused or even "thrown into" a person by a god or somebody else: *Il.* 3,139: Iris "throws" ἵμερος (for her husband, home, and parents) "into" Helen's heart by words; in *Hymn. Hom.* V,45, Zeus "throws" ἵμερος (for Anchises) "into" Aphrodite's breast.

42. For the meaning "enchantment" see *Od.* 1,337 (of heroic lays); *Od.* 8,509 (of the wooden horse). The verb θέλγειν is used frequently in different contexts. In Homer its subject is usually the gods (18x), less often humans (only 6x) and abstracts (only 2x). It usually conveys the idea of "magically bewitching", often connected with the idea of rendering an organ inoperative, e.g. in battle contexts: *Il.* 12,255 of Zeus etc. Hermes puts people to sleep with his wand (*Il.* 24,445); Circe bewitches with her φάρμακα (*Od.* 10,290). For erotic contexts see *Od.* 18,212, where the suitors' mind is bewitched by desire for Penelope: ἔρῳ δ᾽ ἄρα θυμὸν ἔθελχθεν (note that here ἔρως, which is not part of the κεστὸς ἱμάς, functions as a θελκτήριον). Words are supposed to work in the same way: in *Od.* 1,57 Calypso "allures" Odysseus into forgetting Ithaca by "flattering words", in the same way as Aegisthus tries to persuade Clytemnestra (*Od.* 3,264).

43. For a discussion of of ὀαριστύς and πάρφασις as a means of erotic persuasion and their association with Peitho, see ch. 6.3.

44. See Faraone (1990), 219-29 and id. (1999), esp. 96-110.

45. See Faraone (1999), 102f. on a non erotic Neo-Assyrian egalkura spell.

46. See Faraone (1990), 222f. and (1999), 101-09 for details and also for other examples of magical, but non erotic spells which include the use of knotted cords. For a later example, see Theocritus (*Id.* 2): Simaetha applies magic to win her unfaithful lover's love back by performing an incantation (17-63), not by wearing a specific garment which would enhance her attraction and enable her to seduce him easily.

47. Faraone (1999), 103-10.

48. *PGM* XXXVI.275: χαριτήσιν μέγα πρὸς παρόντας καὶ πρὸς ὄχλους (the papyrus transmits χαριτήσιν, but the editors of *PGM* declare this an error and suggest the otherwise attested χαριτήσιον ("a means for gaining favour")).

49. *PGM* VII.390-393: Νικητικὸν δρομέως. γράψον ἐπὶ τοὺς μεγάλους | ὄνυχας αὐτοῦ γράφων χαλκῷ γραφείῳ τοὺς χαρακτῆρας | τούτους· (here follow two characters), γράφε 'δός μοι ἐπιτυχίαν, ἐπαφρο‹δι›σιαν, | δόξαν, χάριν ἐν τῷ σταδίῳ.' καὶ τὰ κοινά, ὅσα θέλεις.

50. See e.g. *PGM* VIII.923-925.

51. For examples see Winkler (1990), 82-91.

52. Faraone (1990), 227 interprets δός as an allusion to the standard end of a Greek prayer. Hera invokes Aphrodite for her favours in the same way as a mortal would do (see *PGM* VII.390-393, quoted above n. 49); for more examples see Faraone (1999), 107-09.

53. For a discussion of the influence of the Babylonian epic upon the *Iliad*, see Burkert (1992), 88-96; see also Brenk (1977), 17 with n. 1. For another Near Eastern myth which is paralleled in the *Iliad*, see ch. 2.3.

54. Aphrodite's presence in *Il.* 3 and the garment in *Il.* 14 have exactly the same effect on Paris' and Zeus' desire respectively.

55. See *Il.* 14,328: Zeus is seized by ἵμερος and so is Aphrodite herself in *Hymn. Hom.* V,57.

56. On this see Dickie (1995), 29-56.

57. Suggested by Bonner (1949), 1-6. He argues that the κεστὸς ἱμάς is to be identified with a special garment worn by an "Eastern goddess of fecundity" who may be identified with Ishtar-Astarte. It is an ornament which consists of two x-shaped bands, crossing between the breast and on the back. Hera is not meant just to put it in her κόλπος as an amulet, but to wear it properly (see Janko (1992) ad 219). For representations of the saltire from 3000 BC onwards, see Bonner (1949), 1 with n. 2. For Brenk, however, the κεστὸς ἱμάς is not the original saltire, but came to be thought of as the possibly embroidered chest necklace worn by Near-Eastern goddesses, see (1977), 17-20.

58. The verbal adjective κεστός has to be derived from κεντέω ("to prick", "to stitch"), see Chantraine (1970), 515. According to Beck (1991), 1391 in *LfgrE*, it refers to a pattern "pierced" or "stitched" into the leather. This suggests a soft material such as cloth or leather for the ornament rather than metal (but cf. Janko (1992) ad loc., who considers even gold).

59. For a discussion of the Latin cognate "centones" which seem to have been quilts, see Sider (1978), 41-4.

60. See Shapiro (1993), 19. He first argued this in a talk at the American Philological Association in 1975. His results are accepted by Brenk (1977), 17 and 19 ("it would be most apt if this piece (...) had embroidered in it the allegorical figures Love and Desire (...) much as the Sarpedon vase has the figures Sleep and Death."); cf. Bonner (1949), 4.

61. See Arn/A ad *Il.* 14,214a (Erbse): ἐλύσατο κεστὸν ἱμάντα: ὅτι κεστὸς ἐκ παρεπομένου ὁ ποικίλος, ἀπὸ τοῦ διὰ τὰς ῥαφὰς κεκεντῆσθαι, ἐμπεποικιλμένης τῆς φιλότητος καὶ ἱμέρου καὶ ὀαριστύος. καὶ οὐκ ἔστι κύριον ὄνομα ὡς ἔνιοι τῶν ἀρχαίων· διὸ καὶ ἐπ᾽ ἄλλου λέγει "ἄγχε δέ μιν πολύκεστος ἱμάς".

62. See *LSJ* s.v. "ποικίλος": "wrought in various colours of woven or embroidered stuffs", in the *Iliad* frequently of πέπλοι (e.g. *Il.* 5,735), see also Aphrodite's epithet ποικιλόθρονος in Sappho fr. 1 V. There is only one passage in epic with a similar expression: in *Il.* 3,371 the chin strap of Paris' helmet is called πολύκεστος ἱμάς, which has to be taken as simply a "decorated strap" (see Janko (1992) ad loc.).

63. So Janko, see (1992) ad loc.; Shapiro (1993), 19ff.

64. For the earliest iconography of Eris, see Giroux (1986), III.1.,846-50, esp. 847 and III.2., 608, no. 1.

65. It has been argued that lines 535-38 have been interpolated into the *Iliad*: see Lynn-George (1978), 396-405, followed by Edwards (1991), ad loc., who argue that these lines were originally composed for the *Aspis*. The arguments (the content suits the *Aspis* much better; the lack of parallels to the personifications' activities) are, however, not conclusive. I suggest that the depiction of the *Iliad* is original since the scene depicted matches the theme "the city at war" very well. Cf. *Iliad* 4,439f., which in a similar way displays the activities of "war-personifications". The description of *Aspis* is more modelled on Achilles' shield (see Fittschen (1973), 18ff. and M.L. West (1996), 700). In his *Iliad* edition (2000), M.L. West considers lines 535-38 as an interpolation.

66. In *Il.* 4,439f. they participate in the battle together with Eris; in *Il.* 15,199 they are Ares' charioteers. Edwards suggests that they will have been depicted as monsters with an apotropaic function to terrify the bearer's opponents ((1991), ad 14,200).

67. The artist's work is described as ἔτευξε (*Il.* 18,483) or ποίκιλλε (590) or ποίησε (573; 587). Fittschen (1973), 9, assumes that these formulas are to indicate the change from one circle of images to another. See Bonner (1949), 4, who does not believe that the verb suggests a representation of the powers.

68. See Fittschen (1973), N21; similarly Webster (1954), 14; for a bibliography on that topic, see Edwards (1991), 200f.

69. So Shapiro (1993), 22; according to him, this is the first source for personifications after the *ekphraseis* in the *Iliad*.

70. δηλοῖ μὲν δὴ καὶ τὰ ἐπιγράμματα, συνεῖναι δὲ καὶ ἄνευ τῶν ἐπιγραμμάτων ἔστι Θάνατόν τε εἶναι σφᾶς καὶ Ὕπνον καὶ ἀμφοτέροις Νύκτα αὐτοῖς τροφόν.

71. Two other scenes on the chest displayed Aphrodite in specific epic contexts, also without train. In 5,18,5, Aphrodite is led by Ares (identified by Ἐνυάλιος); in 5,19,5 Hermes is leading Hera, Athena and Aphrodite to Paris' judgement (with inscription).

72. So Shapiro (1993), 19.

73. For iconographical evidence see Hermary (1990), V. 1., 425f., section "Himeros directement associé à Aphrodite".

74. Hypnos, who is also necessary for the success of Hera's deception, is clearly personified and participates actively as well complementing the effect of the κεστὸς ἱμάς.

75. So in her own love affair with Anchises. By telling him her lie she pours sweet longing into him so that he is seized by desire: ὡς εἰποῦσα θεὰ γλυκὺν ἵμερον ἔμβαλε θυμῷ. / Ἀγχίσην δ' ἔρος εἷλεν (*Hymn. Hom.* V,143f.).

76. See *Hymn. Hom.* V,45: τῇ δὲ καὶ αὐτῇ (= Aphrodite) Ζεὺς γλυκὺν ἵμερον ἔμβαλε θυμῷ and *Il.* 3,139f.: Iris arouses Helen's desire for her former husband, her town, and her parents (ὡς εἰποῦσα θεὰ γλυκὺν ἵμερον ἔμβαλε θυμῶι / ἀνδρός τε προτέροιο καὶ ἄστεος ἠδὲ τοκήων).

77. Hypnos is featured in later literature not very frequently, but in both Phrynichus' and Euripides' *Alcestis*; in Eur. *Cyc.* 599ff. Odysseus invokes Hypnos and Hermes for help against the Cyclopes; see Wöhrle (1995), esp. ch. 2: "Hypnos, Thanatos und Eros" (24-41).

78. But Athena and Hermes can cause sleep in the *Odyssey* (20,54; 24,4).

79. ἔρως too is described as a substance in *Theog.* 910.

80. So e.g. Hölscher (1955), 385, where he argues that the relationship of Sleep and Death as brothers is certainly an old mythological explanation for sayings like ὕπνος (...) / (...) θανάτῳ ἄγχιστα ἐοικώς (*Od.* 13,79f.); for a discussion see also Erbse (1986), 18f. and Kullmann (1956), 30f.

81. Cf. Soph. *OC* 1574. Only here they are the children of Ge and Tartaros.

82. They are brothers in *Theog.* 756.

83. See *Il.* 14,243-62. On a previous occasion Hypnos, on behalf of Hera, had made Zeus fall asleep so that she could involve Heracles in a sea storm. As Zeus woke up earlier than expected, he punished Hypnos. The latter then had to flee to his mother Nyx, who rescued him from Zeus' wrath.

84. See Erbse's arguments (1986), 19f. He denies a link and thinks that the description of Hypnos is original with Homer (21). But even if Homer does not refer to an epic about Heracles, considering his developed personality, Hypnos may have already been a mythical figure.

85. In *Il.* 16,454f. and 671f. they are summoned to carry Sarpedon's body. For iconography see the Attic white-ground 5th-century *lekythos* which shows them carrying a dead woman's body (Vermeule (1979), 151, pl. 4.).

86. See M.L. West (1966), ad 267-70; note the following mythic correspondences: Hera meets Hypnos on Lemnos, the island which Hephaestus came to after Zeus sent him away. Both marry one of the Graces (see Janko (1992), ad 256-61). But the only cult of Hypnos is that at Troizen and he does not seem to have an original relationship with Lemnos.

87. The image is probably influenced by *Theog.* 756. See Hamdorf (1964), 41-4 for iconography.

88. See Bazant (1997), VIII.1. Suppl., 643-5, esp. 643 and (1994), VII.1., 904f. This motif appears on numerous Attic vases dated between 520-420 BC.
89. See commentary in Bazant (1994), VII.1., 904, no. 3 ("winged unless otherwise stated").
90. Wöhrle (1995), 23.
91. It is, however, unlikely that the Platonic idea of a winged soul is already anticipated here. For the soul at the moment of death is nowhere described as winged or "flying away" in the *Iliad*; see Bremmer (1983), 70-125, esp. 74ff.
92. Eros and Himeros look like youths, but in comparison with Aphrodite, who holds them, they are outlined in a smaller scale—perhaps because they are not considered equal to the Olympian goddess; for the iconographical representation of Eros and Himeros, see Plate 6.
93. In a similar way, Eris is the only goddess who is present at the brutal fighting (Ἔρις δ᾽ ἄρα χαῖρε πολύστονος εἰσορόωσα· / οἴη γάρ ῥα θεῶν παρετύγχανε μαρναμένοισιν *Il.* 11,73f.).
94. For examples of the gods' taking the shape of a bird, see Janko ad loc. and on *Il.*13,62-5: the examples listed here suggest that the deities transform themselves into birds when they come down from on high to earth.
95. Similarly Erbse (1986), 20f.
96. On the relationship between death and sex see Vermeule (1979), 145-78 ("On the Wings of The Morning: The Pornography of Death").
97. See e.g. Alcman's *partheneion* (fr. 3,61f. *PMGF*) where it is, however, πόθος which is more powerful than sleep and death: λυσιμελεῖ τε πόσωι, τακερώτερα / δ᾽ ὕπνω καὶ σανάτω ποτιδέρκεται ("with a limb-loosening desire she is looking (at me) more meltingly than sleep and death").
98. See the discussion in ch. 7.4.
99. On the similar role of Ate, who damages the senses and is therefore made responsible for Agamemnon's quarrel with Achilles, see Erbse (1986), 11-18. He considers her a creation of the poet of the *Iliad*. For a similar function of sleep and dream in the *Diapeira* (*Il.* 2), see Wöhrle (1995), 18.
100. On vases depicting Heracles killing Alcyoneus: Hypnos, as a winged boy, sits on the monster's face and represents an exterior force which causes the eyes to close. (Olmos, Balmaseda (1981), VII.1., 558-64, esp. 560, no. 7), see also Wöhrle (1995), 23: Hypnos is present in almost all scenes representing this motif.
101. For an interpretation of this image see Vox (1992), 375f. and Davies (1983), 496f.
102. See also *Il.* 14,236 (Hera to Hypnos: κοίμησόν μοι Ζηνὸς ὑπ᾽ ὀφρύσιν ὄσσε φαεινώ).
103. Slightly different is *Il.* 14,359.
104. Similarly *Il.* 14,294 (when Zeus sees Hera: ὡς δ᾽ ἴδεν, ὥς μιν ἔρος πυκινὰς φρένας ἀμφεκάλυψεν).

Chapter 5

1. For the personified Charites see the overviews in Schachter (1997), 1102f.; Harrison (1986), III.1., 191-203; see also Escher (1899), 2150-67. MacLachlan (1993) examines Charis and the Charites under erotic, social, cultic and political aspects in early poetry; for a brief introduction to the Charites in Greek literature, see Deichgräber (1971).
2. For the personified Charites, see *Ol.* 14; *Nem.* 4; *Isthm.* 8; similarly also in Stes. fr. 212 *PMGF*. For χάριτες applied to poetry, see *Ol.* 13,19.
3. Pind. fr. 123,14 M.; Thgn. 1319ff.
4. See ch. 8.6.
5. See Thuc. 2,41: μετὰ χαρίτων. On the political dimension of χάρις, see Meier (1985); see also ch. 5.3. On cult associations of Charis with Aphrodite in civic contexts, see chs. 2.4-2.7.
6. See Pind. *Ol.* 14,13f.; for other references, see Harrison (1986), III.1.,191. For genealogies of the Charites, see Appendix, Fig. 1a.

7. Similar to the Charites' role in Aphrodite's train, but less frequently depicted in the literary sources, is that of the Horae. They will therefore not be examined in detail. I refer to Erbse (1986), 41ff. and the bibliography mentioned in n. 1. For a distinction of the roles of the Charites (responsible for works of art) and the Horae (responsible for flowers) in Hes. *Op.* 63ff. and 72ff. see Rocchi (1979), 5-16, esp. 9ff.

8. In *Theog.* 945, Aglaea, the youngest of the Charites, is Hephaestus' wife; this role is taken by Charis in the *Iliad* (18,382). Pasithea is the prospective wife of Hypnos (*Il.* 14,276).

9. *Od.* 6,18; for a similar expression see Hes. fr. 215 M.-W.

10. *Il.* 17,51.

11. *Il.* 14,267f. ὁπλοτεράων cannot convey a comparative meaning. Otherwise one would have to assume that older Charites also exist. For numerous examples of the function of the suffix -τερος as indicating not a comparative, but a contrast see Wittwer (1969), 54-110, esp. 63f., who suggests that the meaning is "young", "youthful" and points to the Charites' young age. For her own purpose, Hera wants to describe Charis as most attractive and therefore stresses her youth.

12. Hes. *Op.* 65 and 73.

13. *Il.* 5,338: weaving; Cypria fr. 4 (Davies/Bernabé): dying.

14. As featured in *Od.* 8,266-366 and in the major *Homeric Hymn to Aphrodite* (58-63). For this role of the Charites, see also ch. 3.4.

15. In the *Odyssey*, however, it is Athena who pours χάρις on Telemachus (2,12ff.) and Odysseus (6,232ff.) in order to beautify them; in Alcman (fr. 3,71 *PMGF*) χάρις is clearly also imagined as a fluid: it is poured on hair (–κ]ομος νοτία Κινύρα χ[άρ]ις / ἐπὶ π]αρσενικᾶν χαίταισιν ἴσδει). In *Od.* 8,362f. and *Hymn. Hom.* V,58ff. it is the Charites themselves who bathe and anoint Aphrodite in order to give her χάρις.

16. During the Classical period they were venerated more often conjointly with other divinities, see MacLachlan (1993), 49.

17. See Burkert (1986), 121-32, who recognizes a systematic method behind Herodotus' mode of discussing the Egyptian origins of the Greek gods. Burkert, by analysing the philosophical implications of οὔνομα, argues that the term does not signify "name" in the sense of a pho-netical construct, but rather a system: "Es geht nicht um einzelne, punktuelle Entsprechung von Lautgebilden, sondern darum, dass ein System von Bedeutungen ein anderes eindeutig abbildet. Eben darum ist Herodot sogleich aufs sorgfältigste bemüht auszugrenzen, was keine Entsprechung hat, Dioskuren, Poseidon, Heroen." (see esp. 130).

18. Lloyd (1976), vol. 2, 232.

19. Lloyd, Fraschetti (1989), vol. 2, ad 2,50.

20. On the Herodotean conception of Πελασγοί in general see the detailed survey by Lloyd (1976), 232ff., who considers them "a figment of the Greek imagination": His conclusion is that for Herodotus, the people and, consequently, the names of their deities were pre-Dorian and non-Greek.

21. See (1976), 236.

22. See 9,34,1; 9,35,1; 9,35,3.

23. So Hamdorf (1964), 45 and Simon (1998), 207f., who interprets the numerous Cycladic idols dating from circa 2400-2200 BC as Charites.

24. Harrison (1986), III.1., 191.

25. See Harrison (1986), III.1., 193, no. 16; Jeffrey (1990), 226.

26. Κάριτες is the unaspirated version. The inscription was discovered and published first by Hiller v. Gärtringen (1899), 181-91, esp. 182; now re-published in *IG* XII.3ˢ.1312. According to Dr Wörrle who kindly helped me with the dating, the inscription cannot, as has been sug-gested, be much earlier than the mid-6th century BC.

27. On the relief see Harrison (1986), III.1., 195, no. 19.

28. Call. fr. 3 Pf. and Apollod. *Bibl.* 3,15,7.

29. On the location of the two reliefs see now esp. Harrison (1986), 194f., no. 16. For the inscriptions, see *IG* XII.8.358: a (for the relief of Apollo and the Nymphs): Νύμφηισιν κἀπόλλωνι Νυμφηγέτηι θῆλυ καὶ ἄρ– | σεν, ἄμ βοληι, προσέρδεν· οἶν οὐ θέμις οὐδὲ χοῖρον· | οὐ παιωνίζεται. b (for that of the Charites) Χάρισιν αἶγα οὐ θέμις οὐδὲ χοῖρον. On cults on Thasos in general, see Seyrig (1927), 178-233, esp. 179ff.

30. For the same sacrificial regulations in Thasos (no goat, no pig) see besides *IG* XII⁵.394 (= *SEG* ii 506) (Peitho): Πειθοῖ αἶγα οὐ | δὲ χοῖρον οὐ θέμ[ις] and *IG* XII.8.358b (Charites): Χάρισιν αἶγα οὐ θέμις οὐδὲ χοῖρον.

31. On the cult association of Peitho and the Charites in Paros (2nd century BC), see also *IG* XII⁵.206 (= Peek (1934), 60): Θρα[σ]ύξενος Θράσωνος | Πειθοῖ καὶ Χάρισιν. On the antiquity of the cults, see Rubensohn (1949), 1781-1872, esp. 1845f. and Pouilloux (1954), 333ff., who are followed by Hamdorf (1964), 45.

32. On this see Miller (1997), 259: "Eine wichtige Bindung an die Traditionen des Mutterlandes ergab sich für eine Kolonie normalerweise durch die Übernahme der in der Mutterstadt verehrten Gottheiten".

33. For the idea that the Charites are chthonic deities, see Rocchi (1979), 13f.; but cf. ch. 2.7.

34. For epigraphical, numismatic, and literary evidence of this cult see Schachter (1981), 140f.

35. Schol. Pind. *Ol.* 14 (389/390 Drachmann) = Hes. fr. 71 (M.-W.).

36. See Schachter (1981), 141 "the cult is undoubtedly an old one"; MacLachlan (1993), 44 suggests that the cult dates from the Bronze Age.

37. See Dornseiff (1965), 65.

38. See schol. ex/T ad *Il.* 9,381b¹ (Erbse) referring to the historian Ephorus: Ὀρχομενόν· τὸν τῆς Βοιωτίας φησίν, ὃν †μηνῦαι† κατῴκησαν· πολὺ γὰρ τούτῳ παράκειται πεδίον, εἰ πιστός ἐστιν Ἔφορος (=*FGrH* 70 F 152), πολλὰ δὲ καὶ ταῖς Χάρισι ταῖς αὐτόθι τιμωμέναις δῶρα πέμπεται. κἂν τὸν "πολύμηλον" (Β 605) δὲ λέγῃ, οὐδὲν ἧττον πλούσιον· φησὶ γοῦν "ἔν δ' ἄνδρες ναίουσι πολύρ<ρ>ηνες πολυβοῦται" (Ι 296); for the Charites' links with springs and more literary references on the fertility of the area see Schachter (1981), 141 with n. 2. That the ancient inhabitants were famous for their wealth is already mentioned in Hom. *Il.* 2,511, see Verdenius (1987) ad loc.

39. When Nymphs are born, fir trees and oaks grow with them (264f.) and these woods are called τεμένη ἀθανάτων. Although not immortal themselves, but only long-living, they do not seem to be very different from the Olympian gods since they eat ambrosia and dance with them (260f.).

40. On the Nymphs' worship in caves see *Od.* 13,347-8.

41. So Dowden (1992), 126f.; on nymphs see also Nilsson (1967), 244-55, esp. 244f.

42. See *Hymn. Hom.* V,95f.

43. See Burkert (1985), 174 (with reference to *Il.* 20,4-9); similarly Dowden (1989), 102ff., who argues that the Nymphs were considered the "mythic representatives" of girls about to be initiated. For the interpretation of male river-gods as personified deities and local gods, see Waser (1909), 2774-815. They appear in a human shape as early as in Homeric epic and are already depicted correspondingly in Archaic monumental architecture, as at the temple of Zeus at Olympia (the river-gods Alpheus and Cladeus). On this see also Webster (1954), 12, who argues that the great number of personifications which emerged in the 5th century BC were shaped according to the model of Nymphs of springs and mountains, who were traditionally established in ancient belief and could easily become city goddesses.

44. But cf. MacLachlan (1993), 44f., who interprets them as "wedding deities".

45. The Charites' relationship to these arts is also reflected in their proximity to the Muses, as displayed in Hes. *Theog.* 64.

46. See Dornseiff (1965), ad loc.

47. Dated between the 2nd and 1st centuries BC. See e.g. *IG* VII.3195: Μνασίνω ἄρχοντος, ἀγωνο | θετίοντος τῶν Χαριτεισίων | Εὐάριος τῶ Πάντωνος, τύδε | ἐνίκωσιν τὰ Χαριτείσια· (a list of victors follows); 3196: Νενικηκότες ἐν τοῖς Χαριτησίοις; similarly see also 3197.

For the other inscriptions, together with the most recent and detailed treatment of the Charitesia, see now Schachter (1981), 142f., and MacLachlan (1993), 47f. for a brief overview. On the Charitesia as a pan-Hellenic musical and dramatic festival, see also Tod (1934), 159-62. Schachter (1981), 144 and (1997), 1102f. links the Charitesia at Orchomenus with the Museia at Thespiae and suggests that there may have been a dancing competition between them. The tradition which locates Hesiod's tomb at Orchomenus may reflect the relationship between the places; Buckler (1984), 49-53, by adducing two new inscriptions, supports Schachter's assumption that the musical and dramatic competitions took place in the theatre of Dionysos.

48. Fr. 87 Powell. ἀφαρέσιν is conjectured by Pierson and means "without a pharos", "unclad", "naked" (see *LSJ*: ἀφαρής is attested only in Euphorion). It is not only accepted by Powell, but also by v. Groningen in his Euphorion edition (1977), fr. 91. The transmitted variants Ὀρχούμενον Χαρίτων φάρεσιν (? "with cloaks") in A and ἀφαίρεσιν ("taking away") in F make no sense.

49. *Leg.* 815c2-4: ὅση μὲν βακχεία τ' ἐστὶν καὶ τῶν ταύταις ἑπομένων, ἃς Νύμφας τε καὶ Πᾶνας καὶ Σειληνοὺς καὶ Σατύρους ἐπονομάζοντες, ὥς φασιν, μιμοῦνται.

50. Burkert (1985), 173f. *Thiasoi* are groups of worshippers of a god attested epigraphically no earlier than the Hellenistic period. Earlier literary evidence connects such gatherings with ecstatic cults of Demeter and Dionysus (see Parker (1996), 1513). The appearance of female *thiasoi* in Euripides' *Bacchae*, one of barbarian women (56; 604) and three of Theban women (680) who are called "bacchae" or "maenads", has been taken as the main literary source for discussing the links between myth and ritual; see also Seaford (1997), 35ff., esp. 36 with n. 39 for bibliography.

51. See Burkert (1985), 173 with n. 10. v. Wilamowitz (1889), 85 argued the other way round: the mythical *thiasos* is a reflexion of human gatherings in cult reality. The interdependence between mythical and historic ritual worshippers of a deity has also been a matter of interest in recent scholarship. The question whether ritual reflects myth or the other way round is, however, not exemplified by the Charites, but by the Maenads.

52. He refers to them simply as girls' choruses.

53. On this see Harrison (1986), III.1., 191.

54. The *peplos* was normally offered to the cult image in a ritual: see Burkert (1985), 92. *Peploi* as gifts for goddesses are frequently mentioned in literature, mainly for Athena: In *Il.* 6,87-95 and 286-311, Trojan women bring a *peplos* to the cult image of Athena; see Burkert (1985), 141 on the Panathenaea and 133 on the festival of Hera at Olympia.

55. Pind. *Paean* D3 (Rutherford); for an interpretation see Rutherford (2001), 275-80.

56. Paus. 2,32,5 and 9,35,8. On the dating, see Pfeiffer (1952), 20-32; see also MacLachlan (1993), 48 for further references.

57. See MacLachlan (1993), 49 for examples.

58. See Daux (1965), 81. For a detailed discussion of the cult association of Aphrodite and the Charites in its civic and political context, see also ch. 2.7.

59. Paus. 9,35,2 who mentions only two Charites; see further Farnell (1909), vol. 5,430.

60. See Rocchi (1980), 19-28, esp. 20ff., for an interpretation see also ch. 2.5.

61. *IG* II².2798: ἡ βουλὴ ἡ ἐπὶ Διονυσίου ἄρχοντος ἀνέθηκεν | Ἀφροδίτει ἡγεμόνει τοῦ δήμου καὶ Χάρισιν | ἐπὶ ἱερέως Μικίωνος τοῦ Εὐρυκλείδου Κηφισιέως | στρατηγοῦντος ἐπὶ τὴν παρασκευὴν Θεοβούλου τοῦ Θεοφάνου Πειραιέως.

62. For the political background in Athenian history, see ch. 2.5.

63. On the cult in Rhamnus, see Parker (1996), 272 with n. 72.

64. It is interesting that, in Peitho's case too, civic and political connotations, as reflected for instance in some genealogies, are probably more relevant for cult reality than her erotic function; see ch. 6.2.

65. See *IG* I³.1065. On this cult see Parker (1996), 233.

66. See Harrison (1986), 194; also MacLachlan (1993), 44 for the dating of the Charites' cult to the Bronze age.
67. Simon (1998), 206 (with Plates).
68. See 236 with n. 55.
69. See chs. 2.1 and 3.4.
70. See Hom. *Il.* 18,382; *Od.* 8,266f.
71. Hes. *Op.* 65 and 73.

Chapter 6

1. See Icard-Gianolio (1994), VII.1., 242-50; Voigt (1937), 194-217; Weizsäcker (1902-09), 1795-1813; Hamdorf (1964), 33-9 and 63f.; Shapiro (1993), 186-207, and most recently Stafford (2000), 111-45.
2. See Worthington (1994). Peitho in the tragedians is the main interest of Buxton (1982), who also provides two chapters on the meaning of the persuasive word in general (5-28), and an introduction into Peitho in cult, literature, and visual arts (29-47). For a discussion of various Latin and Greek passages see Gross' study (1985). In Thasos Peitho's veneration as a *polis*-goddess is documented by epigraphical evidence from the 5th century BC onwards (*IG* XII.8.360); this cult, however, like many others, seems to have been transferred from Paros, where it had been established earlier during the period of colonisation (682-68 BC). A cult decree from Paros mentions a sanctuary of Peitho which may have existed before the colonisation in Thasos: see Prott, Ziehen (1906), no. 119, Hamdorf (1964), 63f. and 117f.; cf. the sceptical view of Stafford (2000), 113-5.
3. According to Weizsäcker (1902-09), 1809, there are three of them: in Mylasa, Thasos (see above, n. 2) and Sicyon; for the one in Sicyon see also Pirenne-Delforge (1994), 130. On the possibility that an independent cult of Peitho existed at Athens, where she may have had a political or rhetorical meaning, see Parker (1996), 234. For genealogies of Peitho see Appendix, Fig. 1a.
4. See Hes. *Theog.* 349; on the progeny of Oceanus and Tethys in general see M.L. West (1966), 259f. and Buxton (1982), 36f.
5. On the cult association of Peitho with Aphrodite Πάνδημος at Athens, see Stafford (2000), 121-9.
6. Paus. 2,7,7f.
7. Musti, Torelli (1986), ad loc. are more optimistic since they consider it "una delle più notevoli tradizioni mitiche e rituali siconie".
8. So Musti, Torelli (1986) ad loc., who suppose that the image had been removed from the sanctuary ("che egli (Pausanias) vede privo della statua del culto"); cf. Stafford (2000), 119.
9. It has been argued by Buxton (1982), 43 that the idea of Peitho as a goddess of "general" persuasion could also be reflected in some Presocratic writings. However, the underlying concept is different from the one implied in the cult-*aition*: in Parmenides' fragment about knowledge (28 B 2,3ff. D.-K.) the path of Peitho is undoubtedly linked with the truth (the "is-and-cannot-not-be") which Peitho can convey: ἡ μὲν ὅπως ἔστιν τε καὶ ὡς οὐκ ἔστι μὴ εἶναι, / Πειθοῦς ἐστι κέλευθος (Ἀληθείηι γὰρ ὀπηδεῖ). In Empedocles (31 B 133,3 D.-K.) the meaning is also different, as Peitho is associated instead with appearance and probability: the deity cannot be perceived by hands and eyes, paths on which the power of persuasion invades the senses of human beings.
10. When Democritus (68 B 51 D.-K.) says that for persuasion the word is often more valuable than gold, this may point to forensic contexts implying that words are more efficient than bribery.
11. According to Pirenne-Delforge (1994), 154, there is, however, no epigraphical evidence for Peitho's cultic role at Argos.

12. According to the scholium on Eur. *Or.* 1246 (211 Schwartz) she is the wife of Phoroneus, the founder of the political order. This mythic version implies her relationship with politics, which we find e.g. in the cult association of Aphrodite Πάνδημος and Peitho in Athens.
13. *FGrH* 244 F 113.
14. Dem. *Proem.* 54; Isoc. *Antid.* 249.
15. Cf. Parker (1996), 234, who argues that, considering the political and rhetorical implications of the sacrifice, it is more likely that Demosthenes and Isocrates refer to the cult Peitho shared with Aphrodite Πάνδημος; for a discussion see also Stafford (2000), 127f.
16. *IG* II².4583: Πειθοῖ, Καλλίμα[χος] τήνδ᾿ ἀνέθηκε Σολεύς.
17. Εὐνομίας <τε> καὶ Πειθῶς ἀδελφὰ / καὶ Προμαθήας θυγάτηρ; on the fragment, see particularly Buxton (1982), 41f., who interprets these personifications as political concepts, comparing Pind. *Ol.*13,6f. and Anacreon 384 *PMG*; see also Hdt. 8,111,2.
18. See Calame (1983), 500. For the genealogy, see Appendix, Fig. 1a.
19. So e.g. also in Hdt. 3,36; Pind. *Nem.* 11,46; *Isthm.* 1,40; Aesch. *Supp.* 178 etc.; the personified Prometheia is attested in *IG* I².84.37 and *IG* II².1138.11.
20. See Calame (1983), 500: he refers to *Od.* 17,487.
21. See Welcker (1863), 204: "Denn neben dieser (Eunomia) kann sie (Peitho) nur die durch weises Zureden und wohlmeinende Verständigung den guten Gesetzen von den Vorstehern geleistete Hülfe bedeuten."
22. Aesch. *Supp.* 516-23.
23. Pind. *Ol.* 13, 1-10.
24. There is no evidence for an independent cult of Peitho at contemporary Athens (see Parker (1996), 234).
25. In the *Dios Apate* it is sleep which is poured on the eyes: *Il.* 14,165 and 251f.
26. Peitho is coupled with Charis also in Pind. fr. 123,14 M., where they are said to reside in the beloved boy Theoxenus. The idea that Peitho is identical with Aphrodite in the passage in the *Works&Days* has been suggested by C. Robert (1914), 17-38. The presence of Peitho is probably due to the fact that there were cults of Aphrodite and Peitho in which Peitho was not understood as an independent goddess, but occupied part of Aphrodite's sphere.
27. The words are seductive probably not only in the sense that somebody is flattered, but also that the recipients have to give in to love even if they do not want to at first.
28. See the scholium on 73a (39 Pertusi): ὅρμους δὲ χρυσείους Πειθώ λέγεται <θεῖναι> ἐπειδὴ ἡ γυνὴ κεκοσμημένη πείθει τὸν ἄνδρα πρὸς συνουσίαν τάχος. On the persuasion of gods by gifts see fr. 361 M.-W. (δῶρα θεοὺς πείθει).
29. *Hymn. Hom.* IV,13: (Μαῖα) καὶ τότ᾿ ἐγείνατο παῖδα πολύτροπον, αἱμυλομήτην. The image of Hermes as a god of trickery, deception and theft is a standard pattern in the famous myth of the god stealing Apollo's cattle (for the earliest literary reflexion see *Hymn. Hom.* IV,69f.). It is also recalled in *Il.* 24,24, when the gods ask him to steal Hector's body from Achilles' camp, or when Aphrodite pretends that she was snatched by Hermes (*Hymn. Hom.* V,117) from the crowd of nymphs. Cult epithets such as Δόλιος (at Pellene) or Κλέπτης (at Chios) also attest these specifications. For cults and myths of Hermes see Baudy (1998), 426-32, and Siebert (1990), V. 1., 285-387. The idea of Hermes as the god of speech is closely associated with his typically epic function as a messenger-god, but he is not called λόγιος until quite late: see Roscher (1886-90), 2342-434, esp. 2366: his role as a patron of orators is not attested in the Archaic period and therefore is a more recent development.
30. The effect of ὀαριστύς and πάρφασις as contained in Aphrodite's κεστὸς ἱμάς is similar.
31. Hermes and Peitho appear together in Aphrodite's train with different functions in Cornutus (*Theol. Graec.* 24): (Ἀφροδίτη) παρέδρους δὲ καὶ συμβώμους τὰς Χάριτας ἔχει καὶ τὴν Πειθὼ καὶ τὸν Ἑρμῆν διὰ τὸ πειθοῖ προσάγεσθαι καὶ λόγῳ καὶ χάρισι τοὺς ἐρωμένους ἢ διὰ τὸ περὶ τὰς συνουσίας ἀγωγόν. Peitho seems to embody persuasion in a more general way, whereas Hermes stands more for witty, but maybe calculating speech. λόγῳ καὶ χάρισι implies a certain intellectual and artistic quality.

32. For similar contexts in which a woman fails to seduce a man see *Od.* 7,258: Odysseus gives an account of Calypso's attempt to keep him on her island: ἀλλ' ἐμὸν οὔ ποτε θυμὸν ἐνὶ στήθεσσιν ἔπειθεν.
33. See *Hymn. Hom.* V,7: τρισσὰς δ' οὐ δύναται πεπιθεῖν φρένας οὐδ' ἀπατῆσαι.
34. Janko (1992), ad *Il.* 14,216 simply translates ὀαριστύς with "love-talk"; see also Faraone (1999), 97.
35. For the derivation from ὄαρ = "wife", see Chantraine (1968), 771: "rencontre amoureuse"; for the verb ὀαρίζειν, see examples in Mader (1997), 481.
36. See also *Hymn. Hom.* XXIII,3.
37. On the term πάρφασις see Janko (1992), ad 14,217.
38. In epic πάρφασις means "encouragement", "coaxing", "persuasion", see *Il.* 11,793; *Od.* 16,286; 19,5f. The verb παράφημι means: "to speak gently to", "to advise"; "to persuade", "appease" (in its middle form). It may have the notion of deceit, so in Pind. *Ol.* 7, 66; *Pyth.* 9,43: "speak deceitfully"; "to beguile" (Pind. *Nem.* 5,32).
39. On this see Mader (1997), 482.
40. The attribution to Theocritus is doubtful, as is the originality of the current title of the poem. It is likely to have been a later addition derived from the *Dios Apate* in the *Iliad*, see Gow (1950), 485 on Theoc. *Id.* 27.
41. Buxton's statement (1982), 31 that Peitho's province should be the "alluring power of sexual love" is too general.
42. In an inscription from Sappho's hometown Mytilene (*IG* XII.2.73), Peitho is merely an epithet of Aphrodite. On the inscription see Stafford (2000), 115f.
43. See Appendix, Fig. 1a and 2.
44. See also Aesch. *Supp.*1041, where Aphrodite is mother of Pothos and Peitho; see also Sappho's and Alcaeus' different parentages of Eros in Appendix, Fig. 2. They are discussed in ch. 7.7.
45. Campbell (1982), vol. 1., 115 therefore translates "nursling (i.e. a child) of Cythereia", rejecting the suggestion "nurse of Cythereia" (meaning either: she nursed Aphrodite or: she raised Aphrodite's children for her), which has been made by other commentators. The goddesses Aphrodite, Peitho, and the Charites nurture the mortal Euryalus in Ibycus fr. 288 *PMGF*.
46. = fr. inc. 23 V.
47. See Hamm (1957), 157 § 242a: transmitted is χρυσοφάη which can easily be changed into χρυσοφάην. Otherwise we have to assume synizesis.
48. More cautious about Sappho's authorship are Lobel and Page ("fort. recte") and Voigt, who therefore quote the fragment amongst those which are *incerti auctoris*.
49. The restoration is accepted by Broger (1996), 249.
50. See v. Wilamowitz (1913), 46 with n. 2.
51. He thinks that it refers to Hecate, whom the philosopher discusses just before.
52. Musso (1976), 37-9.
53. So in fr. 53 V. and fr. 128 V.; Himerios, *Or.* 9,4 (p. 75s. Colonna = fr. 194 V.) says that Sappho, in her *epithalamia*, "introduces Aphrodite on the chariot of the Charites and also a chorus of Erotes" (ἄγει καὶ Ἀφροδίτην ἐφ' ἄρμα<τι> Χαρίτων, καὶ χορὸν Ἐρώτων συμπαίστορα). Here only the Charites are mentioned. Since the plurality of Erotes is not attested before Pindar, it may therefore not be originally Sapphic, but the projection of a more recent development into her poems.
54. *Anth. Pal.* 7,14 = 11 G.-P.
55. See Obbink (1996), 73 for examples.
56. First suggested by Nauck.
57. The earliest reference according to *LSJ* is Herodotus (3,134).
58. Also θεράπων indicates a mortal: according to Schmidt (1989), 1015-19, esp. 1019, it denotes either mortal attendants (or servants) of mortal masters in epic (for different types of such relationships, see 1016-19), or human servants of a deity, but never divine attendants

of another god of a higher rank (1019: the Greeks are called θεράποντες Ἄρηος in numerous passages; Pelias and Neleus are τὼ κρατερὼ θεράποντε Διὸς μεγάλοιο in *Od.* 11,255; the poet is Μουσάων θεράπων in Hes. *Theog.* 100).

59. χρυσοφαής, as it appears in Euripides, is the more current form (see *LSJ*); the Sapphic χρυσοφάη is Aeolic barytonesis; on the form see Hamm (1957), 157 §242a.

60. See e.g. *Hymn. Hom.* VI,1: χρυσοστέφανος and *Hymn. Hom.* V,16 χρυσηλάκατος (of Artemis).

61. See fr. 379 *PMG*: ὥστε ἰσχὺς μὲν καὶ τάχος καὶ κάλλος καὶ ὅσα σώματος ἀγαθὰ χαιρέτω καὶ ὁ Ἔρως ὁ σός, ὦ Τήιε ποιητά, ἐσιδών με, / (a) ὑποπόλιον γένειον χρυσοφαέννων, εἰ βούλεται, / (b) πτερύγων †ἢ ἀετοῖς† παραπετέσθω, / καὶ ὁ Ἱπποκλείδης οὐ φροντιεῖ.

62. Transmitted by Pollux (*Onom.* 10,124): πρώτην δέ φασι χλαμύδα ὀνομάσαι Σαπφὼ ἐπὶ τοῦ Ἔρωτος εἰποῦσαν.

63. The idea of the winged Eros is more likely to be original for several reasons: his image is modelled on that of Hypnos and Thanatos, who are depicted with wings from a very early stage in art. In Alcaeus (327 V.) Eros may also have been imagined as having golden wings since he is called the son of Zephyrus and Iris, whose golden wings are attested from the *Iliad* onwards (on this genealogy see ch. 7.7 and Appendix, Fig. 1a and b).

64. On winged gods in epic and early vase painting see Dunbar (1995), ad 572-6.

65. It has been much discussed whether in a corrupt passage of one of Sappho's most famous poems (1 V.) the last term of line 18 is the verb πείθω (then connoting the workings of Aphrodite), or even the name of the goddess Πειθώ (see Saake (1971), 54ff., who gives a list of 38 versions of the text which have been suggested). This is hard to decide, since the following line 19 is badly preserved. Considering that the mss. in line 19 have μαισαγηνεσσαν (P) or καισαγηνεσσαν (cett.) it is perhaps more likely that πείθω / μαι ("obey") was the original version (suggested by Saake (1971), 40 and 61). Moreover, πείθεσθαι occurs in Sappho (see Hamm (1957), 215 (index)) and can be combined with the transmitted version of the text. No emendation is required if we take σ' as a dative and keep the infinitive.

66. See the two other famous depictions of the myth of Medea: Euripides in two tragedies (*Peliades* and *Medea*) and Apollonius Rhodius in *Argonautica*, book 3.

67. Cf. Johnston (1995), 177-206, esp. 203f.

68. See M.L. West (1965), 188-202, esp. 199f.

69. See S. West (1994), 11 with n. 9.

70. See Faraone (1993), 1-19 and (1999), 55-69; cf. the critical views of Johnston (1995), 203 and O'Higgins (1997), 103-26.

71. See Faraone (1999), 61f.; on the common Greek idea that desire is a form of madness see e.g. Padel (1995) *passim*.

72. For elements of torture in erotic spells and rituals, see Faraone (1999), 65-7.

73. See Johnston (1995), 184-9 for more examples; furthermore, she supports her argument by offering cognates of ἴυγξ, ἰύζω ("shout", "cry out"), ἰυγμός ("shout", "cry") and ἰυκτής ("singer"). However, if we consider the meanings of these terms in their contexts, this is not quite convincing. They suggest a strong emotional, sometimes even violent utterance: ἰύζω, for instance, means to "scare beasts" in epic (so in *Il.* 17,66 and *Od.* 15,162). In Pindar' works, in fact elsewhere in this very ode (*Pyth.* 4,237), it means "to yell from grief or pain" or "cry out" (said of Aietes when he sees Jason coping with the bulls: ἴυξεν δ' ἀφωνήτῳ περ ἔμπας ἄχει / δύνασιν Αἰήτας ἀγασθείς). ἰυγμός is a shout of joy in *Il.* 18,572, but a cry of pain in the parodos of Aesch. *Cho.* 26, where the chorus forebodes gloom and pain (δι' αἰῶνος δ' ἰυγ- / μοῖσι βόσκεται κέαρ). For similar contexts in Aeschylus see *LSJ*. Her third example ἰυκτής, "singer", does not occur until Theocritus (*Id.* 8,30). In myth, Iynx, daughter of Echo and Peitho, was a nymph who seduced Zeus or helped Io to seduce him. She was transformed into a bird by Hera (Call. fr. 685 Pf.).

74. For examples of instruments of torture in *agoge* spells see Faraone (1999), 60f. and (1993), 9; cf. Johnston (1995), 189-91, who takes μάστιξ not literally, but considers it simply the

"chord" which sets the *iynx* in motion. The literary evidence for that is not convincing since we find neither the meaning "chord" for μάστιξ, nor is it made explicit that the *iynx* was set in motion by it. The epigram (*Anth. Pal.* 5,205,5=35 G.-P.) does not mention a μάστιξ, but a soft thread (θρίξ), by which the *iynx* is "hung", not "set in motion": Ἴϋγξ ἡ Νικοῦς . . . πορφυρέης ἁμνοῦ μαλακῇ τριχὶ μέσσα δεθεῖσα.

75.   Ἔρος δηὖτέ μ᾽ ὁ λυσιμέλης δόνει, / γλυκύπικρον ἀμάχανον ὄρπετον.
76.   Cf. Johnston (1995), 190.
77.   For Peitho as a concept of persuasive speech in contrast to violence, see ch. 6.2 above.
78.   In the *Dios Apate*, Peitho has to be linked with ὀαριστύς and πάρφασις, two components of Aphrodite's κεστὸς ἱμάς.
79.   Johnston (1995), 190 attributes the *iynx* to Peitho.
80.   See Faraone (1993), 4f. and (199), 61-3; cf. Johnston (1995), 189, who argues that the "*iynx's* voice" is connected with the sort of persuasion that forces its victim into doing something against his or her natural judgement.
81.   For examples referring to the skills of poets and musicians, see Pind. *Ol.* 1,9; *Pyth.* 1,42; 3,113; Soph. (Radt, *TrGF* 4 (1977), fr. 88,10): γλώσσῃ σοφόν; for rhetorical skills of sophists Pl. *Ap.* 20a, *Prot.* 309d.
82.   See Braswell (1988), ad loc. He refers to Hes. *Theog.* 31f. Here the Muses are said to have inspired Hesiod (ἐνέπνευσαν δέ μοι αὐδήν / θέσπιν).
83.   The immediate effect of the erotic spell is that, before they promise each other a κοινὸν γαμόν (223f.), she first of all prepares Jason for the fight against the bull by making up a remedy, an ointment, to protect him from severe pain (220f.). That the verb φαρμακόειν is linked with medical healing rather than with magic in this case is clearly indicated by ἀντίτομον, which here means a remedy against the pains the bull could inflict on him, not implying magic powers: καὶ τάχα πείρατ᾽ ἀέθ᾽λων δείκνυεν πατρωΐων· / σὺν δ᾽ ἐλαίῳ φαρμακώσαισ᾽ / ἀντίτομα στερεᾶν ὀδυνᾶν / δῶκε χρίεσθαι (220-2). Magic powers, however, are likely to be implied when Jason is said not to be affected by the fire during the fight (233: πῦρ δέ νιν οὐκ ἐόλει παμ– / φαρμάκου ξείνας ἐφετ᾽μαῖς). ἐφετμαίς (= "commands") are to be understood as instructions on how to cope with the bull rather than as prayers.
84.   But it is in Ap. Rhod. *Argon.*, book 3.
85.   See *PGM* XIXa.50-4: μὴ ἐάσῃς (sc. κύριε δαῖμον) αὐτὴν τὴν Κάρωσα, ἣν ἔτεκεν Θελώ, μὴ [ἰδίῳ] ἀνδρὶ (read: [ἰδίου] ἀνδρὸς) μνημονεύειν, μὴ τέκνου, μὴ ποτοῦ, ἀλλὰ ἔλ[θῃ τη] κομένη τῷ ἔρωτι καὶ τῇ φιλίᾳ καὶ συνουσίᾳ; see Faraone (1993), 7f. and (1999), 59-61.
86.   On Peitho's involvement in the seduction of Helen on Athenian vases see Stafford (2000), 129-35.
87.   On the meaning of ποθεινός see Braswell (1988), ad loc. for similar examples with the participle ποθούμενος (also present); see also Faraone (1993), 9 with n. 24 for examples in which participles of ποθεῖν are used in magical formulae. Hellas is very closely linked with Jason, since it is only because of him that she wants to go there (but cf. O'Higgins (1997), 119). The idea that a person in love is "burning with desire" is a frequent image in Archaic lyric poetry (see e.g. Sappho fr. 48 V. ἦλθες, †καὶ† ἐπόησας, ἔγω δέ σ᾽ ἐμαιόμαν, / ὂν δ᾽ ἔψυξας ἔμαν φρένα καιομέναν πόθωι). On the idea of love in general in Sappho's poems, see M.L. West (1970a), 307-30. Eros' attribute, the torch, is a further development of this idea. Presumably this literary motif is influenced by magical spells which aim at torturing a victim by fire so that she/he leaves her/his home and comes to the performer of the spell; for such erotic incantations see the examples in Faraone (1993), 6ff.
88.   Pind. *Ol.* 13 (*epinikion*); fr. 122 M. (*skolion*, referred to in line 14: σκολίου).
89.   See esp. 13,573E-F: ὑπάρχοντος οὖν τοῦ τοιούτου νομίμου περὶ τὴν θεὸν Ξενοφῶν ὁ Κορίνθιος ἐξιὼν εἰς Ὀλυμπίαν ἐπὶ τὸν ἀγῶνα καὶ αὐτὸς ἀπάξειν ἑταίρας εὔξατο τῇ θεῷ νικήσας. Πίνδαρός τε τὸ μὲν πρῶτον ἔγραψεν εἰς αὐτὸν ἐγκώμιον, οὗ ἡ ἀρχὴ <τρισολυμπιονίκαν ἐπαινέων οἶκον> (= *Ol.* 13), ὕστερον δὲ καὶ σκόλιον τὸ παρὰ τὴν

θυσίαν ἀσθέν, ἐν ᾧ τὴν ἀρχὴν εὐθέως πεποίηται πρὸς τὰς ἑταίρας, αἳ παραγενομένου τοῦ Ξενοφῶντος καὶ θύοντος τῇ Ἀφροδίτῃ συνέθυσαν.

90. Ath. 13,573C: when the Corinthians were praying to Aphrodite about matters of great importance, they customarily "invited" or "took in as assistants" as many *hetairai* as possible (συμπαραλαμβάνεσθαι πρὸς τὴν ἱκετείαν τὰς ἑταίρας ὡς πλείστας). We learn that they contribute to the citizens' supplications to the goddess and are also present at the sacrifices (ταύτας προσεύχεσθαι τῇ θεῷ καὶ ὕστερον ἐπὶ τοῖς ἱεροῖς παρεῖναι); Athenaeus refers to Chamaeleon's book Περὶ Πινδάρου (fr. 31 Wehrli=fr. 37 Giordano) as his source. For Theopompus' and Timaeus' testimonies see Conzelmann (1967), 247-61, esp. 255f.

91. 8.6.20 [378]: ἱεροδούλους ἑταίρας; for a discussion of this testimony see Pirenne-Delforge (1994), 124ff.

92. In defence most recently Vanoyeke (1990), 29-31 and Kurke (1996), 49-75.

93. The existence of ritual temple prostitution was refuted by Conzelmann (1967), 247-61, who convincingly argues that, apart from the latest source (Strabo 8,6,20 [378]), no author explicitly mentions sacred prostitution at the temple of Aphrodite at Corinth. He is followed by Pirenne-Delforge (1994), 110-27, who argues that a dichotomy between sacred and non-sacred *hetairai* cannot be inferred from any textual evidence; see similarly Saffrey (1985), 359-74. The value of the testimony of Strabo (about 64 BC-24 AD) is in question; in view of the radical discontinuity in Corinth following the Roman destruction 146 BC it is doubtful whether Strabo can be expected to have had any trustworthy knowledge of religion and cults of earlier times. On the deficiencies of the examination of the geographical and historical material in Strabo see Syme (1995).

94. Meineke's emendation is presumably inspired by the fact that Athenaeus, when referring to the context of the *skolion*, uses ἀπάγειν. But ἐπάγειν is the version given by the mss. which cite the *skolion*, see v. Groningen (1960), 44f. who supports the idea of sacred prostitution ("ἀπάγειν appartient au vocabulaire du culte"); similarly Schmitz (1970), 30 with n. 50. They are followed by Kurke (1996).

95. Indicated by the last lines of the *skolion* (see fr. 122,17-20 M.) and Ath. 573F: (the *hetairai*) αἳ παραγενομένου τοῦ Ξενοφῶντος καὶ θύοντος τῇ Ἀφροδίτῃ συνέθυσαν.

96. Suggested in Ath. 13,573C.

97. On the *skolion* as a literary genre in general, see Reitzenstein (1893); for a discussion of the definition given by Dicaearchus (= schol. ad Pl. *Gorg.* 451e: σκόλιον· λέγεται ἡ παροίνιος ᾠδή), see 3ff. Dicaearchus differentiates between three types of after-dinner-songs (τρία γένη ἦν ᾠδῶν): (a) the kind of song performed by all guests (τὸ ὑπὸ πάντων ᾀδόμενον), (b) that which is sung by each guest in turn (<τὸ δὲ ὑπὸ πάντων μὲν ᾀδόμενον οὐχ ὁμοῦ δέ, ἀλλὰ> καθ᾽ ἕνα ἑξῆς; for the supplement see Reitzenstein, 4) and finally (c) the *skolion* which was performed not by all guests, but only by those who were most able (τὸ δὲ ὑπὸ τῶν συνετωτάτων, ὡς ἔτυχε τῇ τάξει. ὃ δὴ καλεῖσθαι διὰ τὴν τάξιν σκόλιον). Reitzenstein points out that Pindar's *skolia* belong to the third category (11). Furthermore he argues (43) that Dicaearchus' account describes the nature of the genre not only in 5th century Athens, but also elsewhere in Greece.

98. See Ath. 573F, who names it a σκόλιον τὸ παρὰ τὴν θυσίαν ἀσθέν.

99. For an interpretation of the inscription see Robinson (1933), 602-4.

100. Διάγραμμα: τὸ μίσθωμα. διέγραφον γὰρ οἱ ἀγορανόμοι, ὅσον ἔδει λαμβάνειν τὴν ἑταίραν ἑκάστην.

101. On this see Stafford (2000), 117.

102. On the performance of Archaic lyric see ch. 8.

103. Peitho is not restricted to heterosexual relationships, as Pind. fr. 123,14 M. shows: Peitho and Charis are said to reside in the beloved boy Theoxenos. Here Peitho seems to indicate the boy's seductive charm. This fragment is very similar in phraseology to Ibycus (fr. 288 PMGF), where the beauty and charm of Euryalus is expressed by the idea that the Charites, Aphrodite, Peitho and the Horae were his nurses; for an interpretation see ch. 8.6.

104. So Buxton (1982), 32.

Chapter 7

1. See Appendix, Fig. 1 and 2.
2. Scholars usually distinguish between the Hesiodic cosmogony and the so-called Orphic cosmogonies, although they have some characteristics in common, see e.g. Kirk, Raven, Schofield (1983), 33.
3. So e.g. Hamdorf (1964), 9 and 75f. and Fasce (1977), 15-39 ("I luoghi di culto").
4. Soph. *Ant.* 781-805; Eur. *Hipp.* 525-64.
5. For an interpretation of this fragment (327 V.) see ch. 7.7.
6. See Barrett (1964), 261; Broneer (1932), 31-55; id. (1933), 329-417; id. (1934), 109-88. Simon (1983), 40f. identifies this sanctuary with that of "Aphrodite in the Gardens" which is mentioned by Pausanias (1,19,1f.) who, however, does not mention Eros in this context.
7. They are both quoted in Broneer (1932), 43f. and have been re-published as *IG* I³.1382 a and b; for the dating, see Broneer (1932), 44ff. He argues that the date of inscription a is the middle of the 5th century BC, basing his assumption on particular features of the letters. He says that the letter forms are almost identical with those of an inscription (= *IG* I².394) which is securely dated to the year 446/5 BC. The dramatic setting of Plato's *Symposium* (Agathon's first tragic victory in the dramatic contest of the Lenaea in 416 BC) cannot be related to the establishment of the cult itself or the inscription. The date is mentioned in Ath. 217A-B, coming from the Athenian official record of the festivals (see Dover (1980), 9).
8. No literary evidence, see Pirenne-Delforge (1994), 72.
9. The Attic inscription (*IG* I³.255a.5; dated to ca 430 BC) recording a sacrifice to Eros is, however, not conclusive evidence of an independent worship of Eros either, since he is mentioned along with many other deities.
10. See Deubner (1932), 215f. and Fasce (1977), 33ff.
11. But according to Pausanias (3,26,4) he did so at Leuktra: he records a temple and a grove there and describes a miracle: the rain in spring, however strong, cannot remove the leaves that have fallen from the trees. The place, the reference to spring, and the association leaves-water suggest that this was a fertility cult. On this see Fasce (1977), 21ff., who infers that the cult must be ancient, given the way Eros is said to have been worshipped there as a god of fertility. But no other source refers to this cult. I would agree that in any case it represents one of Eros' aspects, namely that of growth and reproduction (which is in accordance with his cosmic role as well), but it need not necessarily have been Archaic.
12. Fasce (1977), *passim*, but 113-30.
13. See Knigge, Rügler (1989), 81-99, esp. 84f., pl. 4: ΕΡΟΤΟΣ ΙΕΡΟΣ.
14. E.g. in an epigram by Leonidas (*Anth. Pal.* 6,211=3 G.-P.): Aphrodite is offered a little silver Eros; on the date, see Gutzwiller (1998), 88.
15. See Broneer (1933), 416f.
16. See Fasce (1977), 30f., but cf. Lasserre (1946), 69.
17. Paus. 1,30,1: πρὸ δὲ τῆς ἐσόδου τῆς ἐς Ἀκαδημίαν ἐστὶ βωμὸς Ἔρωτος ἔχων ἐπίγραμμα ὡς Χάρμος Ἀθηναίων πρῶτος Ἔρωτι ἀναθείη. The present tense suggests that Pausanias could actually still see the altar himself. On Charmos and the Pisistratids, see Parker (1996), 73f.
18. *FGrH* 323 F 15 (= Ath. 13,609D, citing the 4th-century historian Cleidemus): συνέβη δέ, ὥς φησι, τὸν Χάρμον ἐραστὴν τοῦ Ἱππίου γενέσθαι καὶ τὸν πρὸς Ἀκαδημία Ἔρωτα ἱδρύσασθαι πρῶτον, ἐφ' οὗ ἐπιγέγραπται. Plutarch (*Sol.* 1,7), by contrast, wrongly makes Pisistratus the lover of Charmos and says that it was the former who dedicated a statue to the god (λέγεται δὲ καὶ Πεισίστρατος ἐραστὴς Χάρμου γενέσθαι, καὶ τὸ ἄγαλμα τοῦ Ἔρωτος ἐν Ἀκαδημεία καθιερῶσαι); on this see Parker (1996), 74 with n. 26.
19. For a similar style, see e.g. Simonides (575 *PMG*), who makes Eros the wicked child of Aphrodite and Ares, for a discussion of the fragment, see p. 168.

20. See also the famous account in Thucydides (6,55f.). He connects Harmodius' and Aristogeiton's murder of the Pisistratid Hipparchus with a love affair: the reason was that Hipparchus had tried several times to seduce Harmodius, the darling of Aristogeiton. The assumed importance of the Pisistratids in the formation of cults at Athens has recently been denied by Parker (1996), 75 with n. 30.

21. So e.g. Waser (1907), 484-542, esp. 489f.; conceded also by M.L. West (1966), ad 120, see also Barrett (1964), 261. For the point of view that Eros is the youngest god, see e.g. Pl. *Symp.* 195c1 (speech of Agathon).

22. So e.g. v. Wilamowitz (1880), 131 ("die Theogonie des Hesiodos, die ganz in den Vorstellungen des Eros von Thespiae fußt"); similarly also Jacoby (1926), 158-91, esp. 166f. and Kern (1926), 251.

23. See Schachter (1981), 216-8.

24. For the examples of Apollo, Hermes and Dionysos, see Nilsson (1967), 201-07; see also de Visser (1903), esp. 21f.; an aniconic image of Aphrodite in the shape of a cone is discussed in Delivorrias (1984), II.1., 9. On the worship of stones at Athens, see Xenophon (*Mem.* 1,1,14) and Theophrastus (*Char.* 16); on the meteorite see *Marm. Par.* (*FGrH* 239 A 57) and Plut. *Lys.* 12,2f.

25. See Schachter (1981), 217 with n. 2.

26. An inscription mentioning both deities was first published by Jamot (1903), 195-9.

27. Karouzos (1934), 39, pl. 135. More hesitant in identifying the figures is Schild-Xenidou (1972), 65, pl. 75.

28. See Schachter (1981), 217f.; on the sculpture see Knoepfler (1997), 17-39.

29. Pausanias (9,27,3) records that Praxiteles' famous marble Eros at Thespiae had been carried off by Nero to Rome, where it was destroyed in a conflagration. It was then replaced by Lysippus' statue of Eros. Pausanias himself, however, saw at Thespiae a marble statue of Eros sculptured by the Athenian Menodoros imitating Praxiteles' masterpiece. It was placed next to Praxiteles' statue of Aphrodite and Phryne which were still visible in Pausanias' time (Paus. 9,27,4f.); concerning Phryne, see also Plut. *Mor.* 753F (= *Amatorius*): ἡ δὲ σύνναος μὲν ἐνταυθοῖ καὶ συνίερος τοῦ Ἔρωτος, ἐν δὲ Δελφοῖς κατάχρυσος ἑστῶσα μετὰ τῶν βασιλέων καὶ βασιλειῶν, ποίᾳ προικὶ τῶν ἐραστῶν ἐκράτησεν; see also the (however fictitious) letter from Phryne to Praxiteles in Alciphron 4,1.

30. See e.g. Antipater of Sidon *Anth. Pal.* 16,167; Meleager *Anth. Pal.* 12,56; 12,57 (=110; 111 G.-P.).

31. One may, however, argue that a public cult of Eros would be a likely place to dedicate the statue. On the other hand, it is also possible that an originally private dedication in an already existing sanctuary entailed a public veneration of the god Eros by the mid-4th century BC.

32. So called by the comic poet Poseidippus (Kassel-Austin *PCG* 7 (1989), fr. 13) soon after her death (cited in Ath. 13,591E-F).

33. See Galen, *Protr.* 10.

34. See Ath. 13,585E: when she was offered some wine of excellent quality, but small in quantity, by a friend who explained that it was ten years old, she is said to have replied: "Small indeed, considering how many years old it is" (μικρὸς ὡς πολλῶν ἐτῶν). When a cheap client called her "Praxiteles' little Aphrodite" (Ἀφροδίσιον Πραξιτέλους), she said to him "you are Pheidias' Cupid" (Ἔρως Φειδίου), "Praxiteles" implying "exacting a price", "Pheidias" meaning "saving one's money".

35. According to Ath. 13,590F; see the critical view of Havelock (1995), 42-9 on the historicity of this relationship.

36. See fr. 171-80 Jensen (*In Defence of Phryne*); the historicity of their love affair has been questioned by Cooper (1995), 307-12. On the trial see Trampedach (2001), 137-55, esp. 142-4.

37. See the slightly diverging versions in Ath. 13,590E and ps.-Plut. Mor. 849E (= *Vitae decem oratorum*). The disrobing of Phryne became a *topos* in works of rhetoric, see Quint. *Inst.* 2,15,9.

38. On this and the historicity see Rosenmeyer (2001), 243-5 with n. 14 who compares the sexual power of Helen's uncovered bosom over Menelaos in Eur. *Andr.* 629f.; cf. the skeptical arguments of Cooper (1995), 312-8. He argues that the biographer Idomeneus of Lampsacus (source of Athenaeus and Plutarch) invented the disrobing scene due to a false interpretation of the *peroratio* of Hyperides' speech. The famous provocative stratagem of uncovering Phryne's bosom may have been simply a rhetorical device to plea for the pity of the jury, i.e. a standard strategy in courtroom oratory comparable to the introducing of women and children into court. On Phryne's breast-baring see also Engels (1993), 67-70.

39. See e.g. Peitho's cult at Sicyon (2,7,7).

40. *IG* VII.1785 (date unknown); for a similar inscription see also *IG* VII.4240b. Both inscriptions and four further literary testimonies referring to this context are quoted in the edition by Jacoby (1930), 133.

41. So the title of Lesky's book *Vom Eros der Hellenen* (1976); for the most recent publications on this topic see Calame (1996), there Chapter Two: "L' Eros des Poèmes Epiques" is concerned with "love" in Homeric epic; see also the title of Thornton's monograph *Eros. The Myth of Ancient Greek Sexuality* (1997); Carson's monograph *Eros the Bittersweet* (1986) focuses on desire in general.

42. Exceptions are the *LfgrE* article by Nordheider (1987), 714f. and Kloss (1994), 24-39 and 78-85. For causes, effects and different aspects of the non-personified ἔρως see Müller (1981). This doctoral thesis provides a useful collection and literary interpretation of relevant passages from epic to Euripidean tragedy according to special motifs.

43. In Homeric epic two forms are found: ἔρως (e.g. *Il.* 3,442; acc. ἔρωτα not before *Hymn. Hom.* IV,449) and ἔρος (e.g. *Il.* 14,315; acc. ἔρον as in the formula: αὐτὰρ ἐπεὶ πόσιος καὶ ἐδητύος ἐξ ἔρον ἕντο). Hesiod also applies both forms ἔρως (fr. 298 M.-W.) and ἔρος (personified *Theog.* 120; non-personified *Theog.* 910; fr. 266a,8 (= 266c,1) M.-W.). As the latter form has been considered an Aeolic variant by the scholiasts, I will use ἔρως since it is the usual spelling for the non-personified phenomenon imitating φιλότητος ἔρον in *Il.* 13,636f., as well as for the deity in subsequent literature, see schol. Hrd./AbT ad *Il.* 1,469 (Erbse) and schol. D; schol. ad Ap. Rhod., *Argon.* 1,609-19c (53f. Wendel); see also Chantraine (1958), vol. 1, 211. Archilochus no longer distinguishes between the two forms when he says φιλότητος ἔρως (191 W.). It has been claimed by Lasserre (1946), 21ff. that there is a difference in meaning between ἔρως and ἔρος in epic. It is interesting that in the *Iliad* and the *Odyssey* the form ἔρως is only used in erotic contexts and only without a genitive supplement (see e.g. *Il.* 3,442: ἔρως ἀμφεκάλυψεν and *Il.* 14,315f. ἔρος γυναικός), but I do not think that this differentiation can be maintained given that Hesiod (*Theog.* 120 and 201) twice calls the god Ἔρος (but cf. Kloss (1994), 28). Moreover, the fact that ἔρως is found only before consonants (see Chantraine (1958), vol. 1., 211) suggests that the use of ἔρως and ἔρος is a question of metre rather than of meaning. Janko (1992), ad *Il.* 14,294 claims that ἔρως is a more recent form, replacing Aeolic ἔρος.

44. See e.g. also the formula αὐτὰρ ἐπεὶ πόσιος καὶ ἐδητύος ἐξ ἔρον ἕντο, which occurs not only in the *Iliad*, but also in Hes. fr. 266a,8 (=266c,1) M.-W.

45. See the linguistic examination by Kloss (1994), esp. Chapters One and Two.

46. Also formulaic: Priam is ready to be murdered by Achilles once he has appeased his desire for mourning over his dead son Hector (αὐτίκα γάρ με κατακτείνειεν Ἀχιλλεύς / ἀγκὰς ἑλόντ' ἐμὸν υἱόν, ἐπὴν γόου ἐξ ἔρον εἵην).

47. A good example of this is *Od.* 5,491-3: τῷ δ' ἄρ' Ἀθήνη / ὕπνον ἐπ' ὄμμασι χεῦ', ἵνα μιν παύσειε τάχιστα / δυσπονέος καμάτοιο, φίλα βλέφαρ' ἀμφικαλύψας.

48. See the examples in *Il.* 10,2; 14,353; 24,678; *Od.* 7,318; 13,119; 15,6.

49. I think that there is no difference in meaning between θυμός and φρένες in these similar erotic contexts. They both seem to be responsible for intellectual rather than emotional perception (for a detailed examination of both terms, see Kloss (1994), 168f.).

50. This does not mean, however, that the experience of love is always positive in the *Iliad*, as the example of Helen in book 3 shows.

51. Further references are Archilochus 196 W. and Sappho 130 V.

52. Cf. Kirk (1985), ad 4,467-9. He counts eight different variants "used of these martial deaths".

53. γυῖον and μέλος are used as synonyms in epic (cf. Capelle (1889), 131).

54. Formulaic, see also 23,343.

55. Mader (1991), 1724 cites no passage where λυσιμελής is an epithet of death. The first reference is Eur. *Supp.* 47 according to *LSJ*.

56. Next in time in Sappho in fr. 31 V. and 130 V.

57. The concrete (and very strong) meaning of πεπαρμένος (πείρειν) is "to pierce through", which implies the use of a pointed instrument in different contexts: so in *Il.* 7,317 of meat pierced by sticks. Then, more frequently, of weapons piercing through the body of an enemy (21,577 περὶ δουρὶ πεπαρμένη). With lethal consequences: see *Il.* 4,457ff. where Antilochus captures a Trojan soldier (ἕλεν) and kills him as follows: πέρησε δ᾽ ἄρ᾽ ὀστέον εἴσω / αἰχμὴ χαλκείη (460-1).

58. See Boisacq (1923), 375f., and Chantraine (1970), 363 and 464, where he links ἵμερος with ἱμείρειν.

59. On this see Kloss (1994), 44-66, esp. 47ff.

60. ὣς εἰποῦσα θεὰ γλυκὺν ἵμερον ἔμβαλε θυμῶι / ἀνδρός τε προτέροιο καὶ ἄστεος ἠδὲ τοκήων.

61. So argued by Kloss (1994), 47ff.

62. See *Il.* 3,441-6 and 14,294-6 and 315-28.

63. See M.L. West (1966), ad *Theog.* 120.

64. So e.g. Hölscher (1953), 391ff.; cf. Rudhardt (1986), 13ff., who argues that Eros' activity is present throughout the whole *Theogony*.

65. Alcaeus fr. 327 V. may belong to a hymn to Eros (see Page (1955), 269f.) since it conveys a distinctive constituent of a hymn: a genealogy of Eros. On the number of genealogies and their basis in poetic fiction rather than in mythic or cultic tradition, see ch. 7.7; see also Appendix, Fig. 1 and 2.

66. See e.g. Hölscher (1953), 397.

67. See the hymn to Zeus at the beginning of *Works&Days*, the praise of Hecate (*Theog.* 404ff.), and also the examples of the *Homeric Hymns*.

68. See *Hymn. Hom.* II,276 (περί τ᾽ ἀμφί τε κάλλος ἄητο); *Hymn. Hom.* V,174f. (κάλλος δὲ παρειάων ἀπέλαμπεν / ἄμβροτον).

69. M.L. West (1966), ad. loc., points out that beauty is one of the love-god's most constant attributes. However, epic focuses on the activities and effects of the phenomenon rather than on the development of a physical appearance of Eros. In this Eros differs from Aphrodite. His looks seem to have been more important in another genre, namely that of lyric poetry. The reasons for that are examined in Chapter Eight.

70. For other typical elements (not found here) see ch. 3.2.

71. Although Homer explains its meaning with λύων μελεδήματα, two other passages confirm that the actual meaning of the term is λύων τὰ μέλη: *Od.* 4,794 (= 18,189), both of Penelope: εὗδε δ᾽ ἀνακλινθεῖσα, λύθεν δέ οἱ ἅψεα πάντα; see also *Od.* 18,212 above. For further references see M.L. West (1966), ad 120.

72. See Mader (1991), 1724.

73. See Norden (1923), 168f. on this hymnic feature.

74. See fr. 191 W. and fr. 193 W. (of πόθος) cited earlier.

75. See e.g. Lasserre (1946), 24ff. and Fasce (1977), 80ff. Presupposing that there were two different traditions of Eros, Fasce argues that Hesiod assimilated the divine generative principle to a "better-known divinity": the Thespian "cult god Eros", who in her view stands for

fecundity and reproduction, and, referring to *Theog.* 201f., "Eros, the love-god", Aphrodite's attendant. On the idea of two different traditions, see below ch. 7.6.

76. See Calame (1996), 201f.: "Contrairement à l'hypothèse souvent avancée quant à l'existence de deux traditions parallèles, le role cosmique d'un Eros élevé au rang de démiurge et les développements philosophiques qu' il a connus s'inscrivent dans la ligne même du désir divinisé et constructeur de relations sociales tel qu' il est défini par les poètes."

77. The most extensive overview is probably Schwabl (1962), 1433-589, which includes Greek as well as non-Greek, particularly Near-Eastern theogonies. For a more concise survey see also M.L. West (1966), 1-13.

78. The poet of the *Iliad* seems to have known a different cosmic genealogy when he makes Oceanus and Tethys the primordial parents of the gods in *Il.* 14,201-7, see M.L. West (1997), 383.

79. For Indian cosmogonies see for example Schwabl (1962), 1497f. and more recently M.L. West (1994), 289-307 who also discusses different Phoenician versions.

80. Some of these myths can be traced back to the 2nd millennium BC, but they will not have been introduced to Greece much before 700BC (see M.L. West (1994), 289). Thus Hesiod can be supposed to have known them; for a discussion of similarities see most recently M.L. West (1997), 276ff.

81. For a text and translation of the *Song of Kumarbi* see Güterbock (1952); detailed parallels have been drawn by Hölscher (1953), *passim*; see also M.L. West (1966), 20ff. and id. (1997), 279f. with n. 5 for bibliography.

82. For the most recent translations of Near-Eastern epics see Dalley (1989); for correspondences see M.L. West (1997), 280f., esp. 282f.

83. There is only one from an unknown number of tablets preserved (see M.L. West (1997), 278)—but as it is the first one, there seem to be no extant tablets narrating the beginning of the world.

84. Similarities have been discussed by M.L. West (1966), 27; Kirk, Raven, Schofield (1983), 7ff.; Hölscher (1953), 392ff.

85. See e.g. by Schwabl (1962), 1506, who considers not only Greek and Near-Eastern, but also Iranian and Indian cosmogonies ("die Liebe (Sehnsucht) als kosmogonischer Gedanke sitzt ganz fest"); similarly M.L. West (1994), 304.

86. For more examples see M.L. West (1966), 193; also Schwabl (1962), 1506.

87. On the phenomenon, see Burkert ((1992), 5f.; 88-127 and id. (2003), 28-78)). He posits a direct literary influence of Near-Eastern texts in the "orientalizing period".

88. See M.L. West (1994), 302-4, where he provides a construction of an archetype from the Greek and Phoenician cosmogonic accounts, as well as an overview of motifs which are shared by Greek and Phoenician versions.

89. Damascius, Περὶ τῶν πρώτων ἀρχῶν, vol. 3, 166 (ed. by Westerink, Combès (1986-91)) = Eudemus fr. 150 Wehrli.

90. Also in Damascius, vol. 3, 166f. I will omit this one since no primeval element equivalent to Eros or Pothos appears here.

91. For the relevant text we depend on Eusebius' *Praeparatio Evangelica* 1,10,1-5 (= FGrH 790 F 2), where major passages from Philo's work are cited (= FGrH 790 F 2).

92. See M.L. West (1994), 289-307, esp. 289f. on Orph. fr. 66a/b Kern.

93. See M.L. West (1994), 305.

94. See M.L. West (1994), 304.

95. See Orph. fr. 66a/b Kern; FGrH 790 F 2. On the meaning of "Chaos" see Baumgarten (1981), 106ff.

96. I disagree with Baumgarten (1981), 110f.: "Figures similar to Pothos are not found in Near-Eastern cosmogonies". He therefore favours the idea that the Sidonian cosmogony and Philo's were borrowing from Greek sources, Hesiod in particular, but see Clapham (1969),

46ff., who in my opinion rightly insists that Pothos is not taken from Hesiod (quoted in Baumgarten (1981), 132ff.), but goes back to Phoenician sources.

97. See the survey given by Baumgarten (1981), 1-7; 106f.

98. Maybe one could also approach this question from the opposite angle. If the Phoenician cosmogonic tradition was already known to Hesiod's contemporaries in Greece, it seems likely that the cosmic Desire was named Πόθος. Then one would have to assume that Hesiod deliberately chose the different appellation Ἔρος in order to delimit his concept from the one conveyed by Phoenician tradition. Hesiod's concept is different in so far as his Ἔρος is not merely related to the creation of the cosmos, see below, ch. 7.6.

99. See Damascius 3,165f.; on Eudemus' informants see M.L. West (1994), 291: the location of Rhodes makes it likely that he received his information from Phoenician travellers and merchants, who themselves drew their knowledge from oral tradition. Hebrew "Sidonian" is the current term for "Phoenician", see M.L. West (1994), 291.

100. On the defective character of Eros and Chaos in Hesiod and their insufficient integration into the cosmic context see M.L. West (1966), 192; similarly Hölscher (1953), 397f. Attempts have also been made to describe and work out the way Eros is active in the cosmogony (see Bonnafé (1985), esp. 9f. and 25f. and Rudhardt (1986), *passim*). I think that Rudhardt in particular overinterprets the role Hesiod had intended for Eros, considering that the poet nowhere explicitly says how he actually becomes active. Rudhardt states that Eros has a double function in unfolding and "making visible" what is inside Gaia (he relates this idea to the Orphic Phanes) and in coupling the male with the female element. He then develops this interpretation further and ascribes to him a cosmic, political and theological meaning. However, Eros in Hesiod is simply poorly developed in his activity.

101. Our knowledge of the Greek source is based on fragments given by Eusebius in his *Praeparatio Evangelica*, where he cites long passages from Philo's work (see especially 1,9,20-1,10,53); the fragments are collected in *FGrH* 790 F 2. Thus our text is that of Eusebius quoting Philo and, as M.L. West (1994), 295f. has shown, Porphyrius' quotations of Philo's text. Philo claims to translate Sanchuniathon, who purports to recount a cosmogony by Thoth, the (mythical) inventor of the art of writing (see *FGrH* 790 F 1). On Philo and his work see M.L. West (1966), 24ff. and id. (1983), 177ff., see also Hölscher (1953), 393ff.

102. See M.L. West (1997), 285 for motifs which are not Hesiodic and therefore may stand for an original Phoenician tradition: so, e.g. the eventual king has three predecessors in the *Phoenician History*, whereas Zeus has only two etc. On the dating see e.g. Hölscher (1953), 393. He argues that the way Philo treats the contents paralleled in the epic of Kumarbi suggests that he is also a reliable source for the *Phoenician Theogony*. He claims on the basis of the cosmogony's poetic form, which he compares with that of *Genesis* among others, that the cosmogony is not influenced by Greek speculation (see 141f.); see also Schwabl (1962), 1487; M.L. West (1994), 293f. and (1997), 284 is more careful: he concedes that there is an authentic Phoenician source behind Philo's work, but it may be from the Hellenistic period. The authenticity has been completely denied by Kirk, Raven, Schofield (1983), 41 with n. 1.

103. Baumgarten (1981), 5ff.; 100ff. and 130f.

104. For the sequence, see M.L. West (1966), 25f. and M.L. West (1994), 295ff.

105. I follow M.L. West (1994), 295f. in assuming that the expression ἢ πνοὴν ἀέρος ζοφώδους is an alternative phrasing to ἀέρα ζοφώδη καὶ πνευματώδη, which reflects the fact that Eusebius was quoting from two versions: Philo's text and Porphyrius' comment on Philo.

106. See Kloss (1994), 39f. for examples and also *LSJ*, s.v. ἐράω and ποθέω.

107. Quoted also by Damascius 3,165f.: Αἰθὴρ ἦν τὸ πρῶτον καὶ Ἀήρ, αἱ δύο αὗται ἀρχαί. Αἰθὴρ means "Sky" here; but for the meaning αἰθήρ = "air", see Empedocles (31 B 100,5 D.-K.); for Ἀήρ, see Empedocles (31 B 17,18 D.-K.).

108. See M.L. West (1994), 292.

109. On the correspondence of Chaos in Hesiod and Philo, see M.L. West (1994), 297.

110. See F 72 Schibli (7 B 3 D.-K.): ὁ Φερεκύδης ἔλεγεν εἰς Ἔρωτα μεταβεβλῆσθαι τὸν Δία μέλλοντα δημιουργεῖν (on this passage see also Schibli (1990), 55ff.).

111. Self-fructification itself is a motif in most ancient cosmogonic accounts: see the masturbation of the sun god in Egyptian myth (Hölscher (1953), 396).

112. See Hölscher (1953), 395f.; for details on this and other parallels see also M.L. West (1994), 297; see also Clapham (1969), 46f.

113. On this motif see Clapham (1969), 46f. and Baumgarten (1981), 132. Both interpret this as a sexual assault; the connection between desire and wind has a strongly Semitic implication since the term "*rûah*" can mean both (see M.L. West (1983), 201).

114. Clapham (1969), 37ff. (cited in Baumgarten (1981), 131ff.); see also M.L. West (1994), 304.

115. See Clapham (1969), 37f.; Gordon (1965), 95: The root "rs" means "desire".

116. The demiurgic function is paralleled in Indian and Iranian cosmogonies, see M.L. West (1994), 304.

117. According to the categories set by Brisson (1995), I 389-420, esp. 390ff. ("Les Théogonies Orphiques et le Papyrus de Derveni"). He distinguishes between the "version ancienne", the "discours sacrés en 24 rhapsodies" and the "théologie de Hiéronymos et d' Hellanicos"; also M.L. West (1983), 111 considers the parody an early transmission of an Orphic theogony. On the cosmogony in the Derveni papyrus, see Calame (1997), 69.

118. Dunbar (1995), esp. 437f.

119. See Appendix, Fig. 1 for the genealogy.

120. On the role of Νύξ see M.L. West (1983) *passim* and Brisson (1995), I 399.

121. *Enûma Elish's* description of the primordial state begins as follows: "when skies above were not yet named, nor Earth below pronounced by name"; for an orphic cosmogony see e.g. fr. 66b (Kern): οὐδέ τι πεῖραρ ὑπῆν, οὐ πυθμήν, οὐδέ τις ἕδρα.

122. Dunbar (1995), ad loc. also considers the translation "filled with longing" possible.

123. See schol. ad 3,26b (216 Wendel): αὐτὰρ Ἔρωτα Χρόνος καὶ πνεύματα πάντ' ἐτέκνωσε.

124. See e.g. M.L. West (1983), 225, who points out the Hellenistic style of fr. 86 Kern.

125. See Dunbar (1995), ad 697.

126. See Anacreon fr. 379 *PMG*. In Eur. *Hipp.* 1268-75 it is the "golden-shining" Eros who flutters around with his colourful wings. On the golden shining wings of Aphrodite's companions, see also ch. 6.4.

127. See M.L. West 1966, 157ff..

128. M.L. West (1994), 290.

129. See M.L. West (1983) *passim*.

130. See Ibycus, fr. 286,6-13. *PMGF*: ἐμοὶ δ' ἔρος / οὐδεμίαν κατάκοιτος ὥραν. / †τε† ὑπὸ στεροπᾶς φλέγων / Θρηίκιος Βορέας / ἀίσσων παρὰ Κύπ'ριδος ἀζαλέ- / αις μανίαισιν ἐρεμνὸς ἀθαμβής / ἐγκρατέως πεδόθεν †φυλάσσει† / ἡμετέρας φρένας and Sappho fr. 47 V.: Ἔρος δ' ἐτίναξέ <μοι> / φρένας, ὡς ἄνεμος κὰτ' ὄρος δρύσιν ἐμπέτων; on Zephyrus' role as Eros' father see ch. 7.7.

131. See Lasserre (1946), 77ff.

132. Fasce (1977), 77: "Era naturale, cioè, identificare il dio principio generativo, così poco percepito ed inteso nel suo preciso carattere, per assimilarlo ad una divinità più nota, come quella di Tespie o come quella del corteggio di Afrodite, la cui funzione principale implicava appunto un' opera promotrice della fecondazione."

133. Pherecydes F 72-3 Schibli (7 B 3-4 D.-K.) and Parmenides 28 B 13 D.-K.

134. Cf. Calame (1996), 201f. He suggests that the cosmic Eros elevated to the rank of a demiurge acts on the universe in the same way as the Eros of the poets operates on social relations.

135. See Appendix, Fig. 1 and esp. 2.

136. Lasserre (1946), 135 similarly distinguishes between "two genealogical traditions": one related to Eros as a "chthonic" god, the other to Eros as related to Aphrodite. I find the former tradition, in which he wants Eros to be understood as "Urgott" (see n. 2), vague: I assume

that Lasserre here links Eros to a sort of old cult god whose sphere of interest is related to nature and fertility.

137. See e.g. the comments in the scholium on Ap. Rhod. *Argon.* 3,26 (216 Wendel) or the beginning of Theoc. *Id.* 13.

138. Pl. *Symp.* 178b2-11; Hes. *Theog.* 116ff.; Parm. 28 B 13 D.-K.; Acus. *FGrH* 2 F 6a.

139. However, this does not mean that all cosmic contexts feature Eros (or his personified or non-personified equivalents) without parentage when his reproductive aspect is not emphasized. In Philo, for example, πόθος is the result of the wind's self-fructification and in Aristophanes' parody of an Orphic theogony Eros also hatches from the wind egg which Night has brought forth (see ch. 7.5).

140. Fr. 198 V.

141. See schol. on *Id.* 13,1/2 b (258 Wendel): after enumerating several pedigrees of Eros, he finally adds: καὶ ἄλλοι ἄλλων, implying that there were even more.

142. = fr. 198 V.: Σαπφὼ δὲ (τὸν Ἔρωτα) Γῆς καὶ Οὐρανοῦ (γενεαλογεῖ).

143. = fr. 198 V.: ἀμφιβάλλει, τίνος υἱὸν εἴπῃ (sc. Theoc.) τὸν Ἔρωτα . . . Ἀλκαῖος Ἴριδος (Gaisf., Ἔριδος cod.) καὶ Ζεφύρου (Alc. 327 V.), Σαπφὼ Ἀφροδίτης (cod: Γῆς Blomfield) καὶ Οὐρανοῦ.

144. See e.g. Schwabl (1962), 1478.

145. So e.g. in Philo and in the parody of an Orphic theogony in Aristophanes' *Birds*; for more examples see the visualized schemes of different Orphic versions in Brisson (1995), I 391f.

146. See Page (1955), 269ff.; for further references, see testimonia in Voigt (1971), p. 306f.

147. See *Il.* 17,547, see also *Il.* 11,27. Eros' cloak in Sappho fr. 54 V. has the same colour, but πορφύριος, when describing cloths, means "purple" (so *LSJ*).

148. *Il.* 2,786 and 5,353 &c.; *Il.* 8,409 &c.; see also *Il.* 8,399 &c.: ἴθι, Ἶρι ταχεῖα.

149. *Il.* 8,398 = 11,185; cf. Broger (1996), 216, who relates all epithets to the messenger-goddess's swiftness.

150. See Kossatz-Deissmann (1990), V. 1., 741-60, esp. 744 and id. (1990), V. 2., 485 (s.v. Iris I.4.).

151. See Anacreon fr. 379 *PMG*.

152. On the personified wind god Boreas, see *Il.* 20,223f. For the myth in which he seizes Oreithuia, the daughter of Erechtheus, see ch. 2.4.

153. See *Hymn. Hom.* VI,1-4: strong Zephyr's "moist breath" (Ζεφύρου μένος ὑγρὸν ἀέντος) conveyed Aphrodite to Cyprus; see also *Od.* 14,458: αἰὲν ἔφυδρος ("always rain bringing").

154. See Hes. *Theog.* 379; 870: ἀργεστής ("brightening"); *Hymn. Hom.* III,433: αἴθριος ("bright", "fair").

155. See Silk (1974), 159f. For a more detailed discussion of χρυσοκόμης, see ch. 8.6.

156. The epithets ἠύκομος and καλλίκομος are exclusively applied to goddesses and women: Leto (*Il.* 1,36), Demeter (*Hymn. Hom.* II,297,315), Helen (*Il.* 3,329; 7,355).

157. For a discussion of this fragment, see also ch. 8.6.

158. See Broger (1996), 216f.

159. This fragment is transmitted in schol. ad Ap. Rhod. *Argon.* 3,26 (216 Wendel); for the same parentage of Eros in Simonides, see also schol. ad Theoc. *Id.* 13,1/2 (258 Wendel).

160. (i) δολομηχάνωι in line 2 ("contriving wiles") which is transmitted by the codd., is, apart from here, only attested in a Hellenistic source (Theoc. *Id.* 30,25); (ii) as an epithet of Ares it seems strange since it does not fit his character and mythical role; (iii) cod L. attests a similar-sounding epithet δολόμηδες ("wily", "crafty") in line 1, and this kind of doubling may seem unusual. Therefore some scholars, assuming an error in line 2, emended δολομηχάνωι into κακομαχάνωι ("evil-contriving") (Bergk) or θρασυμαχάνωι ("bold in contriving") (Wilamowitz). Page in *PMG* assigns a crux to δολομηχάνωι. If we defend the transmitted δολόμηδες in line 1, it has to be taken as a vocative and related to Eros (so e.g. Giangrande (1969), 147-49, who defends the reading δολομηχάνωι describing Ares as a "destroyer of marriages"). Davies (1984), 114ff. rejects δολόμηδες and accepts Rickmann's conjecture δολομήδεος since otherwise Eros would be given a second epithet (in addi-

tion to σχέτλιε in line 1), while his mother Aphrodite has none. He emends, however, the transmitted δολομηχάνωι to δολομήχανον and thus relates it to Eros (the only other passage in extant literature is in fact Theoc. *Id.* 30,25, where it is applied to Eros; Gow (1950) translates "crafty"). Independently, Marzullo (1984/85), 15 suggested the same text as Davies. I find Davies' stylistic argument convincing and would therefore accept the conjecture δολομήδεος as an epithet of Aphrodite (see e.g. Sappho fr. 1 V., where she is δολοπλόκος). However, I am inclined to accept the transmitted δολομηχάνωι as an epithet of Ares for the following reasons: it need not refer to the war-god as a "destroyer of marriages", although it is clear that Eros is the product of the mythical adultery committed by Ares and Aphrodite. Perhaps Aphrodite and Ares had to apply wiles in order to outwit the goddess's husband Hephaestus so that they could carry on their erotic encounters. On the other hand, of course, "contriving wiles" does not quite describe the activity of the god of war in myth. Yet given that both parents are "wily" or "crafty", or "contriving wiles", Eros would receive a "double portion" of δόλος, which would perfectly fit the image of the god of love not only in Archaic lyric poetry, but also tragedy and Hellenistic poetry. Considering this possibility, Davies' emendation δολομήχανον is not necessary. Perhaps Theocritus called Eros δολομήχανος as an allusion to Simonides, where the god had a δολομήδης mother and a δολομήχανος father.

161. On the cultic and mythic origins of the story of the love affair between the goddess of love and the god of war see Burkert (1960), 130-44, esp. 132f.: "Der Götterschwank als Form scheint uralt zu sein" (…) "Die Verbindung von Ares und Aphrodite zwar ist offenbar in Kult und Sage fest verwurzelt, sehr zweifelhaft dagegen ist dies für die Ehe von Aphrodite und Hephaistos."; see also ch. 2.3.

162. See app. crit. ad fr. 324 *PMGF*.

Chapter 8

1. So e.g. Pellizer (1990), 177-84, esp. 180: "Eros and the pleasures of love figure amongst the most characteristic subjects of the logos sympotikos."

2. On the term and its implications see M.L. West (1981), 73-142, esp. 73ff.

3. The fragment (696 *PMG*) which is cited by Pausanias (4,4,1; 4,33,2) belongs to a *prosodion* for a chorus of Messenian men; according to M.L. West (1995), 218 it suits the time of the revolt from Sparta (i.e. circa 660 BC).

4. For the dating, see M.L. West (1981), 103: Alcman was active in the late 7th century BC, about one generation after Tyrtaeus.

5. For the distinction see Pellizer (1990), 181 and Rossi (1983), 41-50, esp. 42.

6. See Latacz (1990), 240f. for a detailed overview; for a definition of the two genres and their background see e.g. Latacz (1991), 318ff. and 362ff.

7. See Graf (1997), 113ff. for references to ritual; also Herington (1985), 186f.; for the participation of adolescents, see Buxton (1994), 24f. and 31; Herington (1985), 24f. and 228 with ns. 41 and 50.

8. See Gentili (1988), 72ff. and also Calame (1977a), *passim*; for examples see Alcman fr. 10,17 *PMGF* (also Pind. *Ol.* 10,12-77); fr. 1 and 3 *PMGF*.

9. Polybius 4,20; for an interpretation see also Buxton (1994), 23ff.

10. Herington (1985), 21 has called this "dramas that represent the performance and even the rehearsal of lyrics".

11. Pindar, who represents the culmination of this genre, is present in the *epinikia*, but he generally ascribes to himself only the role of poet and laudator (see e.g. *Ol.* 8,54f.; 9,80 etc.). Only once, as it seems, are the performers mentioned. The poet addresses the chorus leader, Aeneas, to encourage them (*Ol.* 6,87f.: ὄτρυνον νῦν ἑταίρους, Αἰνέα). There is a current debate whether Pindar was choral. On this, see Lefkowitz (1991), 191-201 who suggests that the victory odes were sung as solos.

12. On this see Hutchinson (2001), 77.
13. Scholars have situated Alcman's *partheneion* (fr. 1 *PMGF*) in a variety of different performance contexts: Buxton (1994), 26, referring to the praises of beauty, considers an occasion like a "Derbyshire Well Dressing" as probable. Dover (1978), 181, thinks that it may have been a beauty contest of the kind which is attested on Lesbos or Sicily. It has been argued by Calame that the young women praise their feminine qualities in order to make themselves attractive to men as future wives, in a sort of public context involving initiation rites (Calame, (1977a), ch. 4). Gentili (1988), 73-7 assumes that the *partheneion* is an *epithalamium* written for ritual performance within the girl's community, not for an ordinary marriage-ceremony, but for an initiation within the *thiasos*, for which the girls then sing this song. Kannicht ((1989), 48f.) assumes that the song accompanied a ritual ceremony, but he, probably rightly, does not interpret it as connected with initiation activities. He sees in the praising of Hagesichora and Agido rather a contest between this chorus and another one. He therefore suggests that, integrated into the background of cultic activities, the *partheneion* reflects poetic *Kallisteia*, a sort of poetic *agon* in praising the beauty of the most beautiful girls.
14. Here, however, its meaning is relatively marginal since the story about Heracles' enemies, the murderous sons of Hippocoon, does not seem to be told for its own sake, but rather to illustrate the gnomic statement about justice. It seems to have been included in order for the performing girls to demonstrate their knowledge of local Spartan mythology and to warn themselves and their rival chorus against the dangers of overweening ambition in competition.
15. Hymnic performances normally do not allow additional information about the singers. The only reference to the singer is normally given at the end of the hymn, when he invokes the relevant deity for support in the competition. Thus, for instance, in the formulaic verses: χαῖρ' ἑλικοβλέφαρε γλυκυμείλιχε, δὸς δ' ἐν ἀγῶνι / νίκην τῷδε φέρεσθαι, ἐμὴν δ' ἔντυνον ἀοιδήν. / αὐτὰρ ἐγὼ καὶ σεῖο καὶ ἄλλης μνήσομ' ἀοιδῆς (*Hymn. Hom.* VI,19ff. (Aphrodite)).
16. This is suggested by her name and the prayers addressed to her: see M.L. West (1965), 199f.; but cf. Gentili (1988), 73 (following Giangrande (1977), 156ff.), who interprets her as a confidante, an authority whom the girls address and tell of their loves.
17. For an introduction and commentary see Hutchinson (2001), 76-102.
18. See e.g. Hes. *Theog.* 384: καλλίσφυρος (of Nike); similarly: Hom. *Il.* 24,607: καλλιπάρηος (of Leto); *Hymn. Hom.* IV,57: καλλιπέδιλος (of Hermes); *Od.* 5,390; 20,80: ἐϋπλόκαμος (of Eos and Artemis).
19. See *Hymn. Hom.* III,260f.; *Hymn. Hom.* II,189f. *Hymn. Hom.* V,181.
20. On this see Herington (1985), 23.
21. See e.g. the simile of the two horses and the comparison with the doves (lines 59 and 60). On the metaphor of girls as young horses and its association with marriage, see Calame (1977a), 412ff. For parallels in the erotic language in Sappho and Alcman, see Gentili (1988), 73 and 258 with n. 3.
22. On the question whether these are actual relationships or the reflexion of an "atmosphere of emotional intimacy" between chorus-members of the same sex, see Calame (1977a), 27f.; see also Hutchinson (2001), 73. Institutionalized homoerotic relationships before marriage are attested for Archaic Sparta by Plut. (*Lyc.* 18,9); on parallels with Lesbos see Calame (1977a), 433ff. and Gentili (1988), 73. On the homoerotic feelings of the girls, see Calame (1977b), 86ff.
23. For a collection of the iconographical evidence showing monodic poets (especially Anacreon) on Athenian works of art, mainly vase painting, see Herington (1985), App. V, 198ff.; for Sappho, see McIntosh Snyder (1997), 108-19.
24. See Rösler (1980); this phenomenon is documented also in a volume of collected essays: Vetta (1983); see esp. Vetta's introduction, XIIIff.; important also Latacz (1990) and for the reflexion in vase painting, see Herington (1985), 36: identifiable poets (Sappho, Alcaeus and

Anacreon) on vase painting are depicted in the context of the symposium, see also n. 23 above.

25. So Lissarrague (1987), 119f. in his study of the "mental world" of the symposium: he draws a parallel between the poems and the wine which both move round at the symposium.

26. Symposiastic eroticism has received increasing interest particularly from Italian scholars: see Gentili in Vetta (1983), 83-94 and Gentili (1988), chapter "The ways of love in Thiasos and *Symposium*"; see also Pellizer (1990), 180 on erotic motifs in general.

27. See e.g. Murray (1990), esp. his introductory chapter "Sympotic History" with bibliography, 3-13; for a more recent collection of essays not merely on the Greek symposium, but also on oriental feasts and Roman convivia see W.J. Slater (1991); the public aspect of symposia is explored by Schmitt-Pantel (1992).

28. So Bremmer (1990), 142-5 and Shapiro (1981), 133-43.

29. The earliest winged Erotes are all in red-figure and belong to the last two decades of the 6th century BC: this is the view of Greifenhagen (1957), 71ff., who is followed by Shapiro (1995), 121f.

30. I use the term "symposium" here as well, since it originally also implied that not only, as one would infer from the meaning of the word itself, drink, but also food was served: Bremmer (1990), 144 recently interpreted as a sign of decadence the fact that around 510 BC solid food disappeared from the tables.

31. See Murray (1983a), 195f. Latacz (1990), 227f. has differentiated the type of the Archaic symposium, which flourished until down to 500 BC, from the earlier Homeric type, the δαίς, and the later symposium of Classical times, to which Plato (*Symp.* 172b2 and *passim*) refers as σύνδειπνον. The Archaic symposium has been seen, under a social aspect, as the continuation of the Homeric δαίς since both institutions were meeting places for the male aristocracy (on that see Murray (1983a), 195-9, esp. 196, and Buxton (1994), 28).

32. On the meaning of the surplus see Murray (1990), 3f.

33. See Bremmer (1990), 143 and 145: banquet and warrior scenes are frequently depicted together on Archaic vessels.

34. See Buxton (1994), 28.

35. See Murray (1983a) and (1983b); cf. Bremmer (1980), 279-98; id. (1990), *passim*; see also Shapiro (1981), 136ff.

36. *Il.* 1,470: κοῦροι μὲν κρητῆρας ἐπεστέψαντο ποτοῖο (formulaic also in *Il.* 9,175; *Od.* 1,148; 3,339; 21,271); *Od.* 15,141: οἰνοχόει δ' υἱὸς Μενελάου κυδαλίμοιο.

37. For examples in art see Fehr (1971), 44 and 49; see also Dentzer (1982), 89, 98, 117, 128, 252f.; see also schol. ex/bT ad *Il.* 4,2b1 (Erbse) and schol. ex/T ad 20,234 d (Erbse); Bremmer (1990), 139 n. 28 also mentions Eustathius 438,42; see n. 57 below.

38. For evidence of the boys' presence in the company of adult men, see besides Ephorus *FGrH* 70 F 149: the Cretan lawgiver commanded "the boys to attend the troops" (τοὺς μὲν παῖδας εἰς τὰς ὀνομαζομένας ἀγέλας κελεύσας φοιτᾶν) "and that from childhood onwards they should grow up accustomed to arms and toils" (πρὸς δὲ τὸ μὴ δειλίαν ἀλλ' ἀνδρείαν κρατεῖν ἐκ παίδων ὅπλοις καὶ πόνοις συντρέφειν). In Pyrgion (*FGrH* 467 F 1) we learn that during meals the sons sat below their fathers' chairs and received only half of the portion of food (ἀπονέμουσι δὲ καὶ τοῖς υἱοῖς κατὰ τὸν θᾶκον τὸν τοῦ πατρὸς ὑφιζάνουσιν ἐξ ἡμισείας τῶν τοῖς ἀνδράσι παρατιθεμένων); see also Dosiadas *FGrH* 458 F 2; for the meaning of Apollo Delphinius for the ephebes in Cretan initiation rites see Graf (1979), 2-22, esp. 13 and id. (1982), 157-85, esp. 160f., where he refers to wine pouring in ancient Greek rituals in general.

39. See Critias 88 B 33 D.-K.: in Sparta, boys function as wine pourers (ὁ δὲ παῖς ὁ οἰνοχόος <ἐπιχεῖ> ὅσον ἂν ἀποπίηι), on this see also Xen. *Lac.* 5,5 and Plut. *Lyc.* 12; for a short description of the procedure of a symposium, see v. der Mühll (1957), 80-109.

40. See Bremmer (1990), 142 with n. 39 for relevant bibliography; see also Halperin (1990), 54ff. and 75ff.

41. See Semonides fr. 1 W; Alcaeus fr. 366 V. On the didactic character of this sort of poetry addressed to boys see Rösler (1980), 244. Dover (1978), 195 points out that there are no implications of homosexuality distinguishable in elegiac and iambic poetry of the 7th century BC.

42. So Dover (1978), 195f.

43. The couplet is contemporary with the first preserved homoerotic scenes on black Attic vase painting (see Dover (1978), 196).

44. So Shapiro (1981), 136.

45. So Murray (1983b), 257-72, esp. 263.

46. See Murray (1983a), 195-9, esp. 198.

47. See Latacz (1990), 241.

48. But cf. Buxton (1994), 28 and Murray (1983a), 198, who says that, in spite of the privatization of the institution, political and social aspects remained, and takes Alcaeus' political poems as proof that public life was still dominated by the aristocratic males, who feasted together even though they had actually lost their power. This balance seems to have differed from place to place.

49. See Bremmer (1990), 142ff.

50. The *kalos*-inscriptions have been recently interpreted within the context "of the culture of fame" in the 6th and 5th centuries BC. It has been argued by N.W. Slater (1998), 143-61 that the *kalos*-inscriptions which appear on symposiastic vessels are not just a means of communication between ostensible sender and recipient of the vessel within the erotic pursuit. The former does not only want to woo, but he also wants a third party, the other symposiasts, to watch to whom he offers the vessel and to witness whether he is successful. Slater interprets this goal as a means of self-definition and an attempt to create fame among contemporaries (see esp. 150f. and 160); on *kalos*-inscriptions see also ns. 54 and 129 below.

51. See Bremmer (1990), 144; these changes were observed earlier by Fehr (1971), 100ff. and Dentzer (1982), 109f.; on the reflexion of these changes in red-figure vase painting, see also Schmitt-Pantel, Schnapp (1982), 57-74, esp. 71.

52. See Shapiro (1981), 133-43. The first to collect these courtship scenes on vases was Beazley (1947), 3-31. He categorized them in three different groups: *alpha* encompasses courtship scenes in which the ἐραστής, often with bent knees, approaches the ἐρώμενος, e.g. by touching the boy's skin, both are usually naked (most frequent type); *beta* depicts the giving of love gifts (cocks, hares, lyres); *gamma* shows ἐραστής and ἐρώμενος physically involved with each other, the man rubbing his penis between the thighs of the boy. Further vase paintings have been collected by Schauenburg (1965), 849-67. The black-figure bowl he describes shows an ithyphallic ἐραστής standing in front of the ἐρώμενος with knees bent, touching the boy's chin; on gifts, see 864f. The chronological analysis by Frel (1963), 60-4, esp. 61f., has shown that 12 belong to the second quarter of the 6th century BC, 50 to the third, 57 to the last; from then on, there are only 9 after 500 BC, the latest being around 470 BC. For a more recent collection and interpretation of early homoerotic courtship scenes within their social background see Reinsberg (1989), 163-215 and Kilmer (1997), 36-49.

53. See Hipponax fr. 13 W.; Anacreon fr. 356 and fr. 360 *PMG*.

54. It is also interesting that in vase painting we find not only *kalos*-inscriptions, but also some ὁ παῖς καλός inscriptions. The inscriptions on vessels also point to the symposiastic environment, see Lissarague (1999), 359-73, esp. 365f.

55. Pointed out also by Nisbet, Hubbard (1970), 421: within the context of Horace's symposiastic poetry, they interpret these young Greek wine pourers generally as slaves ("the address to an attendant slave was a common and natural device in Greek sympotic lyric and epigram").

56. See *LSJ* s.v. διάκονος. The *skolion* is transmitted in Arist. *Ath. Pol.* 20, see Bremmer (1990), 140 with n. 30.

57. Schol. ex/AbT ad *Il.* 1,470a (Erbse): κοῦροι μὲν κρητῆρας: ἀρχαῖον ἔθος οἰνοχοεῖν τοὺς νέους; in addition b(BCE³E⁴)T say: οἰνοχόει δ' υἱὸς Μενελάου (*Od.* 15,141). Ab(BCE³E⁴)T

have: διὸ καὶ παῖδας μέχρι τοῦ νῦν τοὺς δούλους φαμέν (see similarly schol. ex/bT ad *Il.*
4,2b1 (Erbse): <***> Διὸς οἰνοχόος· ἢ ὅτι περὶ Ἰλίου ὁ λόγος, ἵνα μὴ λυπῇ τὸ συμπόσιον.
νέων δὲ τὸ ὑπηρετεῖν, ὡς καὶ Μεγαπένθης. ὅθεν καὶ παῖδας τοὺς δούλους φαμέν; men-
tioned, but not further interpreted by Bremmer (1990), 140 with n. 32. Normally expres-
sions like this have to be viewed with caution, since the Greeks are inclined to consider
everything ancient and Archaic. In this case, however, the example of Menelaus' son is taken
from the *Odyssey* and thus really is "Archaic".

58. See also Schmitt-Pantel, Schnapp (1982), 69f. and Dentzer (1982), 108f.: they set serving
     boys among the new figures who appear at the symposium after 510 BC.

59. *Il.* 20,232-5; on the homoerotic component in this myth see below ch. 8.6.

60. So also Dover (1978), 195.

61. See Shapiro (1981), 133-6.

62. So M.L. West (1970b), 205-15, esp. 207f.; for a critical discussion of the identity of Polycrates
     see Hutchinson (2001), 231-3.

63. Suda I 80 (2,607,16 Adler): (Ibycus came to Samos) ὅτε αὐτῆς ἦρχεν ὁ Πολυκράτης τοῦ
     τυράννου πατήρ. M.L. West (1970b), 208 argues that this sentence is "not Greek" and cor-
     rects into Πολυκράτους (following a suggestion made by Schmid); cf. Barron (1964), 210-
     29, who keeps the original Suda entry and takes it as "Polycrates the father of the tyrant".
     Among others, he takes this passage as a proof that there were two Polycrates, the famous
     one and his father. He tries to show that the older tyrant reigned for more than 30 years and
     that it was he who invited Ibycus and Anacreon to the court; cf. Hutchinson (2001), 232
     with n. 6.

64. Fr. 491 *PMG*: ἦν Πολυκράτης ἔφηβος· . . . . ὁ δὲ . . . Πολυκράτης ἦρα μουσικῆς καὶ μελῶν,
     καὶ τὸν πατέρα ἔπειθε συμπρᾶξαι αὐτῷ πρὸς τὸν τῆς μουσικῆς ἔρωτα· ὁ δὲ Ἀνακρέοντα τὸν
     μελοποιὸν μεταπεμψάμενος δίδωσιν τῷ παιδὶ τοῦτον τῆς ἐπιθυμίας διδάσκαλον ὑφ' ᾧ τὴν
     βασιλικὴν ἀρετὴν ὁ παῖς διὰ τῆς λύρας πονῶν τὴν Ὁμηρικὴν ἔμελλε πληρώσειν εὐχὴν τῷ
     πατρί.

65. This is the view of e.g. M.L. West (1970b), 208 and Gentili (1988), 127; but cf. Barron
     (1964), 223ff. and id. (1969), 119-49, esp. 136f., who assumes in accordance with his theory
     that there were a father and a son both called Polycrates, and that the eulogy was composed
     for Polycrates the elder, i.e. the father of the famous one. The political background is men-
     tioned in Hdt. 3,39,3ff.; 3,120,3f.

66. It has been argued that the tyranny actually began in 590 BC; see Mitchell (1975), 75-91,
     and Shipley (1987), 68-73.

67. See M.L. West (1970b), 208.

68. On the archaeological evidence attesting the wealth of the island of Samos, see Hutchinson
     (2001), 232f.

69. See Hdt. 3,131,2; 3,60,3.

70. *FGrH* 539 F 2 (=Ath. 12,540D-F).

71. See Percy (1996), 149f.

72. So Dover (1978), 197. The poem is transmitted in the scholium on Ap. Rhod. *Argon.* 3,114-7
     (220 Wendel) (= fr. 289 *PMGF*): διὰ τούτων τῶν στίχων παραγράφει τὰ εἰρημένα ὑπὸ Ἰβύκου
     ἐν οἷς περὶ τῆς Γανυμήδους ἁρπαγῆς εἶπεν ἐν τῇ εἰς Γοργίαν ᾠδῇ· καὶ ἐπιφέρει περὶ τῆς Ἠοῦς
     ὡς ἥρπασε Τιθωνόν. Dover bases his argument on the fact that the scholiast puts this relation-
     ship in the same context as Eos' rape of Tithonus, which has a traditional erotic connotation.
     However, one may also consider *Hymn. Hom.* V,202-6 and 218, where both couples are also
     mentioned together and ask oneself whether this does not also imply a sexual relationship
     between Zeus and Ganymedes.

73. See *Il.* 20,232-5: καὶ ἀντίθεος Γανυμήδης, / ὃς δὴ κάλλιστος γένετο θνητῶν ἀνθρώπων· /
     τὸν καὶ ἀνηρέψαντο θεοὶ Διὶ οἰνοχοεύειν / κάλλεος εἵνεκα οἷο, ἵν' ἀθανάτοισι μετείη.

74. On *kalos*-inscriptions, see e.g. Shapiro (1995), 120 and 124; see also ns. 50, 54 and 129; on
     graffiti see n. 113.

75. See Kaempf-Dimitriadou (1979), 7-12.
76. So Bernardini (1990), 69-80, esp. 76ff.
77. See Bremmer (1990), 141 with n. 36.
78. Radt, *TrGF* 4 (1977), T 75 (= Ath. 13,603E-604F).
79. Fr. 360 *PMG*; fr. 396 *PMG*.
80. See fr. 402c *PMG*: ἐμὲ γὰρ †λόγων εἵνεκα παῖδες ἂν φιλέοιεν· / χαρίεντα μὲν γὰρ ἄιδω, χαρίεντα δ' οἶδα λέξαι.
81. See e.g. Latacz (1991), 428ff. and also Gentili (1988), 89ff. On the playful polyptoton of these lines, see Pfeiffer (1968), 12f.
82. But cf. Labarbe (1960), 45-58. He thinks that "gaze at" is too weak compared with the other verbs and suggests the following (in my opinion not necessary) emendation for the 3rd line: Κλεόβουλον Διὸς ἐκκλινέω. For the effect of "looking", see also Sappho (fr. 31 V.).
83. As noted just above, Anacreon and Polycrates were rivals in courtship, see Anacr. fr. 414 *PMG*.
84. Schol. Pind. *Ol*. 7,5 (200 Drachmann) = fr. 407 *PMG*.
85. See similarly M.L. West (1970b), 207 on fr. S151 *PMGF*.
86. See above, n. 52: Beazley (1947), 3ff. has collected this type of homoerotic love scene under group *gamma*.
87. Goddesses too are described in more detail, see fr. 348 *PMG*; fr. 390 *PMG*; fr. 418 *PMG*.
88. See fr. 471 *PMG* (= Max. Tyr. 37,5); fr. 402 *PMG* (= Max. Tyr. 18,9).
89. According to an epigram by Antipater of Sidon (*Anth. Pal.* 7,27=15 G.-P.), the Thracian Smerdies who was famous for his curls.
90. For love's painful side see e.g. fr. 286 *PMGF*.
91. So *Suda* I 80 (2,607,16 Adler); see also Cic. *Tusc*. 4,33,71.
92. On Ibycus' innovations of style and composition in his love-poetry see Gentili (1988), 99-102; 267 with n. 128.
93. For metrical reasons, some scholars noted a lacuna after θάλος in line 1 (see Davies' apparatus: lacunam post θάλος notant Hermann, Schneidewin, ne claudicent numeri). The rhythm "limps" at the end of line 1 without a supplement since we would receive a cretic in the last foot within a dactylic metre. A metrical analysis gives the following structure:

line 1 (without lacuna):	3da + cret.
line 2:	4da (da in last foot)
line 3:	7da (spondee in last foot)

    It is the cretic in the last foot which makes the metre "limp". We can eliminate the cretic by supplementing Ὡρᾶν, as has been suggested by Bergk, who is backed by Page. Then we receive a metrical structure for line 1 which is in harmony with the subsequent lines:

line 1 (lacuna assumed):	5da (spondee in last foot)

    Very probably one has to postulate a lacuna not only for metrical, but also for syntactic reasons, since, in an entirely asyndetic sequence, the Charites would be assigned two adjectives. Moreover, it is hard to imagine that Euryalus would be called both θάλος and μελέδημα of the Charites. Thus a supplement required for metrical reasons is also supported by the meaning of the fragment as a whole. I find Bergk's suggestion (θάλος, <Ὡρᾶν> καλλικόμων) convincing in view of Hes. *Op.* 73ff., to which Page has drawn attention: it is the adornment scene in which Pandora receives all kind of gifts from Aphrodite and her traditional train, to which, in addition to the Charites and Peitho, the "beautiful-haired" Horae also belong: Χάριτές τε θεαὶ καὶ πότνια Πειθώ / ... ἀμφὶ δὲ τήν γε / Ὡραι καλλίκομοι στέφον ἄνθεσι. In any case, the Horae would have the epithet καλλίκομοι in both passages.
94. So e.g. also Bernardini (1990), 69-80; for the imagery see Davies (1986), 404f.
95. I read γλαυκέων (so in codd. A and C of Athenaeus' text and accepted by Bergk and in *PMG* and *PMGF*); some scholars consider this passage corrupt—see Jacobs' conjecture γλυκέων and Schneidewin's γλυκεῶν or γλυκεᾶν, which have been made for metrical reasons (see the

preceding note). The context in which the fragment is transmitted in Athenaeus is relevant for the discussion whether γλαυκέων can be kept. It is clear that his source had γλαυκέων, which he then related to the Charites' eyes. He says that Philoxenus Cytherius' (435-380 BC) Cyclops, who is in love with Galatea, has a premonition of his own blindness and thus praises everything but Galatea's eyes, preferring not to be reminded of the organ of sight, when he says: "Galatea with the lovely face, with golden tresses, with a gracious voice, child of the Erotes." Athenaeus refers to the poem in a sort of *enallage* as a "blind praise" (τυφλὸς ὁ ἔπαινος)—since it is without praise of the beauty of the eyes—and contrasts the poem by Philoxenus with that of Ibycus, which is then subsequently quoted (τυφλὸς ὁ ἔπαινος καὶ κατ᾽ οὐδὲν ὅμοιος τῶι Ἰβυκείωι ἐκείνωι). The context makes clear that Athenaeus "read" γλαυκέων, which he then related to the Charites' eyes (but cf. the conjectures of Jacobs et al.). Γλαυκός is originally without any notion of color and means simply "gleaming" (see Hes. *Theog.* 440 and Hom. *Il.* 16,34). Later, it denotes a colour: "light blue", "grey", "blue-grey", "blue-green" in poetic use, so Beck (1982), 160; see also Gow (1950), 148f. (ad Theoc. *Id.* 20,25) where he translates γλαυκός, which he considers as a synonym to γλαυκῶπις, as "grey-eyed" (of Athena's eyes), see also vol. 2,367 ad loc. Page (see ad fr. 288 *PMG*) is not convinced that γλαυκός denotes "blue-eyed" in poetry: "sunt qui γλαυκέων de caeruleis oculis dictum putent (cf. Wilam. *Pind.* 510): scimus ita locutos esse Herodotum Hippocratem Aristotelem, exempla apud poetas frustra quaerimus". Gulick (1937), translates "blue-eyed" (see ad loc.).

96. On this image see Treu (1955), 285. He interprets the roses as a first step towards the peak of physical beauty.

97. See Gentili (1988), 113.

98. Similarly v. Wilamowitz (1913), 125: the beloved and Eros are blended into a composite picture; Lasserre (1946), 57 is more careful: "Il risque en outre une image plus libre en personnifiant dans Eros le regard de l' éromène: C'est Eros qui l' a regardé."; similarly also Bowra (1961), 263. But cf. Davies (1980), 255-7, who argues that the feature of a personified Eros would be unique here, and he therefore rejects this idea.

99. See Hutchinson (2001), 107f.:"The language depicts a violent assault on the consciousness of the person in love."

100. However, I cannot agree with Gentili (1988), 103, who considers the dark eyelashes as the attribute of a mature man, "someone of an age to command and control" since in *Il.* 1,528 Zeus' brows are also κυάνεοι and so is Odysseus' beard (*Od.* 16,176). In Ibycus, however, the color has nothing to to do with age, but with aesthetics and sensuality.

101. See chs. 4.7 and 7.3 for an interpretation of this imagery.

102. See e.g. Gentili (1988), 127.

103. See Hutchinson (2001), 255: "Polycrates is not compared to the supreme Troilus, but to all three beauties". Cyanippus and Zeuxippus have been supplemented by Barron (1969), 131 and (1961), 185-7.

104. See Barron (1969), 131. This version requires an additional ἐστίν in 46.

105. See Gentili (1988), 129 with n. 34.

106. Suggested by Hutchinson (2001), 255.

107. See Gentili (1988), 113.

108. Transmitted in the scholium on Pind. *Isthm.* 2,1b (213 Drachmann): Ἀνακρέοντα γοῦν ἐρωτηθέντα, φασί, διατί οὐκ εἰς θεοὺς ἀλλ᾽ εἰς παῖδας γράφεις τοὺς ὕμνους; εἰπεῖν, ὅτι οὗτοι ἡμῶν θεοί εἰσιν.

109. Pointed out by v. der Mühll (1976), 493; cf. Hutchinson (2001), 273f.

110. For gifts in general see Dover (1978), 92; for gifts in vase painting, see n. 52.

111. Tyrt. fr. 4 [2] W.; Pind. *Ol.* 6,41; 7,32; *Isthm.* 7,49.

112. So Silk (1974), 159f. An overview of the use of the term χρυσοκόμης is given by Lorimer (1936), 14-33, esp. 15f. who examines also epithets with "gold" applied to divine beings; Hutchinson (2001), 275 points out that it is "always used of gods".

113. The graffiti are published and analyzed by Garlan, Masson (1982), 3-22; on the date see esp. 13.

114. The most frequent is καλός (12), which is also found regularly on vase painting; further popular attributes are: ἡδύς (8); εὔχαρις (4); χρυσός (see *LSJ*: χρυσός as an adjective is first attested in Pind. *Nem.* 7,78) (3); εὐπρόσωπος (2); others are: ἄργυρος, ἀστεροπρόσωπος, εὔρυθμος, εὐσχήμων, καλλιπρόσωπος, φιλόκωμος, φιλός, ὡραῖος.

115. But cf. Gentili (1988), 94.

116. In the second line I follow the translation by M.L. West (1993), 35.

117. This supplement—suggested by Bentley—looks certain and has been accepted in *PMG* and *PMGF*; see Easterling (1974), 37.

118. See e.g. Lasserre (1946), 30: he interprets the fragment within the context of a wedding. Thus the "galingale" is the donation of a young bride to Hera, the goddess of the Laconian virgins, and μάργος denotes the bride's aversion to love. Smyth (1921), 196 suggests that the fragment belongs to a love song in which a girl compares herself to flowers.

119. Easterling (1974), 37-43, esp. 40.

120. See Easterling (1974), 38ff.; see also M.L. West's translation. κυπαιρίσκος is a *hapax legomenon* and therefore hard to identify. As a diminutive of κύπαιρος it was very probably closely related to "Cyperus longus" or "galingale", a flowerless plant which was very suitable for being bound into a garland.

121. See Greifenhagen (1957), 71 for a survey of Eros on red-figure vases of the Archaic and early Classical period; Kilmer (1993) on erotica on Attic red-figure vases. Boardman (1974), 219 points out that "Eros is to be the darling of red-figure [begins after 530 BC], not black-figure"; he is followed by Shapiro (1995), 121, who, however, does not relate the emergence of Erotes to the poets Anacreon and Ibycus or to the literary interests of the Pisistratids; see also Boardman (1975), 226.

122. See Greifenhagen (1957), 14 with pl. 7 (= Hermary, Cassimatis, Vollkommer (1986), III.2., no. 748b).

123. See Greifenhagen,15, pl. 8; 16, pl. 9; 17, pl. 10; 18, pl. 11; 23, pl. 18; 27, pl. 20; 29, pl. 22 Eros with a lyre and a drinking-vessel 23, pl. 18; Hermary, Cassimatis, Vollkommer (1986), III.2., e.g. nos. 661 and 663.

124. See also Hermary, Cassimatis, Vollkommer (1986), III.2., nos. 600-06.

125. It is also interesting that, with the disappearance of homoerotic courtship scenes in the middle of the 5th century, Eros appears for the first time frequently in wedding and marriage scenes (see Hermary, Cassimatis, Vollkommer (1986), III.2., nos. 639-49).

126. See Pl. [Hipparch.] 228c1-2.

127. See examples in Herington (1985), Appendix V, esp. 198-9. He refers to numerous instances and describes five in detail, see e.g. a *kylix* (62f., no. 86 in Beazley (1963)): Anacreon (inscription) is depicted in a dancing posture, playing the lyre (dated to circa 515 BC); for more images of Anacreon on Attic vases, see Kurtz, Boardman (1986), 35-70; see also S.D. Price (1990), 133-75.

128. ποικιλοσάμβαλος ("with broidered sandals") of a girl in fr. 358 *PMG*.

129. It is probably no coincidence that *kalos*-inscriptions which appear in the third quarter of the 6th century celebrate in a similar way the ideal ἐρώμενος, see Shapiro (1995), 123 and most recently Lissarague (1999), 359-73: he points out that the *kalos*-inscriptions are an almost exclusively Athenian phenomenon (so 361)—which also confirms that the cult of beautiful boys seems to be peculiar to Athenian aristocracy. These *kalos*-acclamations, together with depictions of Eros, also reach a peak in number in the early red-figure period (see 362); for the meaning of *kalos*-inscriptions, see also N.W. Slater (1998), 143-61 (see n. 50 above).

130. For the borrowing of the motifs (knucklebones and ball) from Anacreon, see Hunter (1989), 109f. and 113.

131. Cf. Rosenmeyer (1951), 11-22, esp. 18-20 who translates "love-experiences". He concedes that Pindar's Eros is the "pederastic ephebe of the Dorians", but does not establish a link

between the beloved boys and the plurality of Erotes. He sees in the pluralization a "domestication and prettification of the symbol of Love" a reflection of the poet's emotional side which is "perhaps the least impressive of his attributes".

132. For a plurality of Erotes in iconography, see e.g. Greifenhagen (1957), 31, pl. 25.

133. For other genealogies of Eros, see Appendix, Fig. 2.

Genealogies of Aphrodite & Erotic Personifications

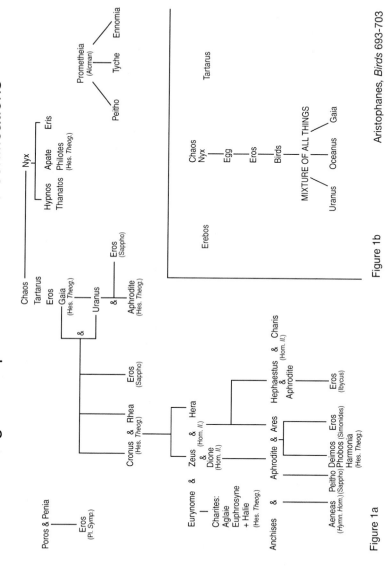

Figure 1a

Figure 1b

Aristophanes, *Birds* 693–703

Figure 1

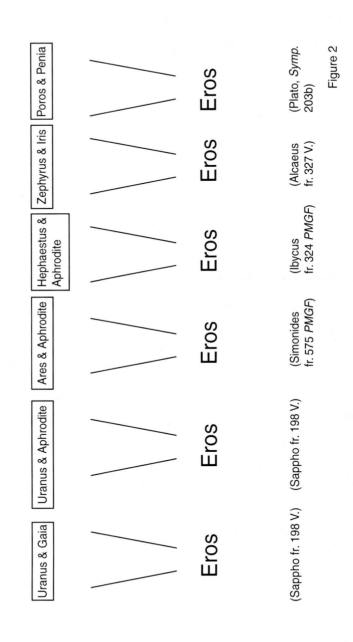

Figure 2

Bibliography

Principal Texts

Hesiodi Opera: Theogonia, Opera et Dies, Scutum (ed. F. Solmsen); *Fragmenta Selecta* (ed. R. Merkelbach, M.L. West), Oxford ³1990
Homeri Ilias (ed. M.L. West), Stuttgart 1998-2000
Homeri Odyssea (ed. P. v. der Mühll), Leipzig ³1961
Homeri Opera (ed. T.W. Allen), vol. 5, Oxford 1946 (= ed. of 1912 repr. with corrections)

Collections of Fragments, Papyri, and Scholia

Bergk, Th., *Poetae Lyrici Graeci*, 3 vols., Leipzig 1878-82
Bernabé, A., *Poetarum Epicorum Graecorum Testimonia et Fragmenta*, vol. 1, Leipzig 1987
Calame, C., *Alcman* (ed. with introduction, text, translatin, testimonies and commentary), Rome 1983
Campbell, D.A., *Greek Lyric*, 5 vols., Cambridge (Mass.) 1982-93
Davies, M., *Epicorum Graecorum Fragmenta*, Göttingen 1988
— *Poetarum Melicorum Graecorum Fragmenta*, vol. 1, Oxford 1991
Diels, H., Kranz, W., *Die Fragmente der Vorsokratiker*, 3 vols., Berlin ⁶1952
Drachmann, A.B., *Scholia Vetera in Pindari Carmina*, 3 vols., Leipzig 1903-27
Erbse, H., *Scholia Graeca in Homeri Iliadem*, 5 vols. + index vols., Berlin 1969-87
Jacoby, F., *Die Fragmente der griechischen Historiker*, Berlin/Leiden 1923-58
Kassel, R., Austin C., *Poetae Comici Graeci*, 8 vols., Berlin/New York 1983-95
Kern, O., *Orphicorum Fragmenta*, Berlin 1922
Kirk, G.S., Raven, J.E., Schofield, M., *The Presocratic Philosophers. A Critical History with a Selection of Texts*, Cambridge ²1983
Lloyd-Jones, H., Parsons, P.J., *Supplementum Hellenisticum*, Berlin 1983
Lobel, E., Page, D.L., *Poetarum Lesbiorum Fragmenta*, Oxford 1955
Maehler, H., *Pindari Carmina cum Fragmentis,* vol. 2 (Fragmenta, Indices), Leipzig 1989
Nauck, A., *Tragicorum Graecorum Fragmenta*, Leipzig ²1889 (Suppl. by B. Snell (1964))
Page, D.L., *Poetae Melici Graeci*, Oxford 1962
Preisendanz, K., Henrichs, A., *Papyri Graecae Magicae: Die griechischen Zauberpapyri*, Stuttgart ²1973-74
Snell B., *Pindari Carmina cum Fragmentis*, vol. 1 (Epinicia), Leipzig ⁸1987 (rev. H. Maehler)
Snell, B., Kannicht, R., Radt, S., *Tragicorum Graecorum Fragmenta*, 4 vols., Göttingen 1971-85 (vol. 1: Göttingen ²1986)
Voigt, E.-M., *Sappho et Alcaeus*, Amsterdam 1971
Wendel, C., *Scholia in Theocritum Vetera*, Leipzig 1914
— *Scholia in Apollonium Rhodium Vetera*, Leipzig 1935
West, M.L., *Iambi et Elegi Graeci ante Alexandrum cantati*, Oxford ²1989-92

Collections of Inscriptions

Blinkenberg, C., *Lindos. Fouilles de l' Acropole* 1902-1914, II.1., Berlin/Copenhagen 1941
Corpus Inscriptionum Graecarum, Berlin 1828-77
Dittenberger, W., *Sylloge Inscriptionum Graecarum*, Leipzig ³1915-24
Dürrbach, F. et al., *Inscriptions de Délos*, Paris 1923-72
Engelmann, H., Merkelbach R., *Die Inschriften von Erythrai und Klazomenai*, Bonn 1972-74
Halbherr, F., Guarducci, M., *Inscriptiones Creticae*, Rome 1935-50
Hansen, P.A., *Carmina Epigraphica Graeca Saeculorum VIII-V a.Chr.n.*, Berlin 1983
Inscriptiones Graecae, Berlin 1873-
Jeffrey, L.H., *The Local Scripts of Archaic Greece*, Oxford ²1990 (rev. ed. with Suppl. by A.W. Johnston)
Peppa-Delmousou, D., Rizza, M.A., (eds.) M. Segre. *Iscrizioni di Cos*, 2 vols., Rome 1993
Prott, H., Ziehen, L., *Leges Graecorum Sacrae*, 2 vols., Leipzig 1896-1906
Sokolowski, F., *Lois Sacrées de l' Asie Mineure*, Paris 1955
— *Lois Sacrées des Cités Grecques* Suppl., Paris 1962
— *Lois Sacrées des Cités Grecques*, Paris 1969
Solmsen, F., Fraenkel, E., *Inscriptiones Graecae ad Inlustrandas Dialectos Selectae*, Stuttgart ⁴1966
Supplementum Epigraphicum Graecum, Leiden 1923-

Dictionaries, Grammars, and Lexica

Boisacq, E., *Dictionnaire Etymologique de la Langue Grecque*, Paris 1923
Cancik, H., Schneider, H. (eds.), *Der Neue Pauly. Enzyklopädie der Antike*, Stuttgart/Weimar 1996-
Capelle, C., *Vollständiges Wörterbuch über die Gedichte des Homeros und der Homeriden*, Leipzig ⁹1889
Chantraine, P., *Dictionnaire Etymologique de la Langue Grecque*, Paris 1968-80
— *Grammaire Homérique*, 2 vols., Paris 1958-63
Hamm, E.-M., *Grammatik zu Sappho und Alkaios*, Berlin 1957
Hornblower, S., Spawford, A. (eds.), *The Oxford Classical Dictionary*, Oxford/New York ³1996
Klauser T., Dassmann E. (eds.), *Reallexikon für Antike und Christentum. Sachwörterbuch zur Auseinandersetzung des Christentums mit der antiken Welt*, Stuttgart 1941-
Lexicon Iconographicum Mythologiae Classicae, 9 vols. in 18 pts., Zurich/Munich 1981-99 (part 1 of each volume = commentary; part 2 of each volume = Plates)
Lexikon des frühgriechischen Epos, Göttingen 1955-
Liddel, H.G., Scott, R., rev. Jones, H.S., *A Greek-English Lexicon*, Oxford 1996 (9th edn. with a rev. Suppl. 1996)
Smith, W. (ed.), *Dictionary of Greek and Roman Geography*, London 1878
Wissowa, G., Kroll, W., Mistelhaus, K. (eds.), *Pauly's Real-Encyclopädie der classischen Altertumswissenschaft*, Stuttgart 1893-1972

Modern Studies

Albright, W.F., "Syria, the Philistines, and Phoenicia", in: *The Cambridge Ancient History*, vol. 2, part 2, Cambridge ³1975, 507-36
Allen, T.W., Halliday, W.R., Sikes, E.E., *The Homeric Hymns* (ed. with introduction and commentary), Oxford ²1936
Andreae, B., Flashar, H., "Strukturäquivalenzen zwischen den Homerischen Epen und der frühgriechischen Vasenkunst", *Poetica* 9 (1977), 217-65 (= M. Kraus (ed.), *H. Flashar, Eidola. Ausgewählte Kleine Schriften*, Amsterdam 1989, 7-55)

Arrighetti, G., *Poeti, Eruditi e Biografi: Momenti della Riflessione dei Greci sulla Letteratura*, Pisa 1987
— "Hesiod", in: *Der Neue Pauly* 5 (1998), 506-10
Asheri, D., Antelami, V., *Erodoto. Le Storie* (ed. with introduction and commentary), vol. 1, Milan 1989
Astour, M.C., *Hellenosemitica*, Leiden 1965
Barrett, W.S., *Euripides. Hippolytos* (ed. with introduction and commentary), Oxford 1964
Barron, J.P., "The Son of Hyllis", *CQ* n.s. 11 (1961), 185-7
— "The 6th Century Tyranny at Samos", *CQ* n.s. 14 (1964), 210-29
— "Ibycus: To Polycrates", *BICS* 16 (1969), 119-49
— "Bacchylides, Theseus and a Woolly Cloak", *BICS* 27 (1980), 1-8
Baudy, G., "Hermes", in: *Der Neue Pauly* 5 (1998), 426-32
Baumgarten, A.I., *The "Phoenician History" of Philo of Byblos. A Commentary*, Leiden 1981
Bazant, J., "Thanatos", in: *LIMC* VII.1. (1994), 904-8
Beazley, J.D., "Some Attic Vases in the Cyprus Museum", *ProcBritAc* 33 (1947), 3-31
— *Attic Red Figure Vasepainters*, Oxford ²1963
Beck, W., "γλαυκός", in: *LfgrE* (1982), 160
— "κεστός", in: *LfgrE* (1991), 1391
Bernardini, P.E., "La Bellezza dell' Amato: Ibico frr. 288 e 289 P.", in: *Lirica Greca e Latina. Atti del Convegno di Studi Polacco-Italiano, Poznan 2-5 Maggio 1990 = AION (filol)* 12 (1990), 69-80
Bernhardt, M., *Aphrodite auf griechischen Münzen*, München 1934
Bertman, S., *Climbing Olympus. What you can learn from Greek Myth and Wisdom*, Naperville 2003
Beschi, L., "Contributi di Topografia Ateniese", *ASAA* 45-46 (1967-68), 511-36
Bethe, E., *Homer. Dichtung und Sage*, vol. 2, Berlin 1922
Bickerman, E.J., "Love Story in the Homeric Hymn to Aphrodite", *Athenaeum* 54 (1976), 229-54
Bielefeld, E., *Schmuck*, Göttingen 1968 (=*Archaeologia Homerica*, vol. 1, ch. C)
Boardman, J., *Athenian Black Figure Vases*, London 1974
— *Athenian Red Figure Vases. The Archaic Period*, London 1975
— *The Greeks Overseas*, London ²1980
— *Greek Sculpture. The Archaic Period*, London ²1991
Boedeker, D., *Aphrodite's Entry into Greek Epic*, Leiden 1974 (= *Mnemosyne* Suppl. 32)
Bonnafé, A., *Eros et Eris*, Lyon 1985
Bonner, C., "ΚΕΣΤΟΣ ΙΜΑΣ and the Saltire of Aphrodite", *AJPh* 70 (1949), 1-6
Bonnet, C., *Astarté. Dossier Documentaire et Perspectives Historiques,* Rome 1996 (= *Contributi alla Storia della Religione Fenicio-Punica* 2)
Bonnet, C., Pirenne-Delforge, V., "Deux Déesses en Interaction: Astarté et Aphrodite dans le Monde Egéen", in: C. Bonnet, A. Motte (eds.), *Les Syncrétismes Religieux dans le Monde Méditerranéen Antique. Actes du Colloque International en l' Honneur de Franz Cumont à l' Occasion du Cinquantième Anniversaire de sa Mort. Rome, Academia Belgica, 25-27 Septembre 1997*, Brussels 1999, 249-73
v. Bothmer, D., "Sarpedon", in: *LIMC* VII.1. (1994), 696-700
Bousquet, J., "Le Temple d' Aphrodite et d'Arès à Sta Lenika", *BCH* 62 (1938), 386-408
Bowie, E., "Early Greek Elegy, *Symposium* and Public Festival", *JHS* 106 (1986), 13-35
Bowra, C.M., *Greek Lyric Poetry,* Oxford ²1961
Brand, H., *Griechische Musikanten im Kult*, Würzburg 1987
Braswell, B.K., *A Commentary on the Fourth Pythian Ode of Pindar*, Berlin 1988
Bremmer, J.N., "An Enigmatic Indo-European Rite: Pederasty", *Arethusa* 13 (1980), 279-98
— *The Early Greek Concept of the Soul*, Princeton 1983
— (ed.), *Interpretations of Greek Mythology*, London 1987
— "Adolescents, Symposion, and Pederasty", in: Murray (1990), 135-48

— *Götter, Mythen und Heiligtümer im antiken Griechenland*, Darmstadt 1996 (= German translation of *Greek Religion*, Oxford 1994 by K. Brodersen)

Brenk, F.E., "Aphrodite's Girdle. No Way to Treat a Lady (*Iliad* 14. 214-223)", *CB* 54 (1977), 17-20

Brisson, L., *Orphée et l' Orphisme dans l' Antiquité Gréco-Romaine*, Aldershot 1995

Broger, A., *Das Epitheton bei Sappho und Alkaios*, Innsbruck 1996

Brommer, F., *Theseus. Die Taten des griechischen Helden in der antiken Kunst und Literatur*, Darmstadt 1982

Broneer, O., "Eros and Aphrodite on the North Slope of the Acropolis in Athens", *Hesperia* 1 (1932), 31-55

— "Athens. Excavations on the North Slope of the Acropolis in Athens 1931-1932", *Hesperia* 2 (1933), 329-417

— "Athens. Excavations on the North Slope of the Acropolis 1932-1934", *Hesperia* 3 (1934), 109-88

Buckler, J., "The Charitesia at Boiotian Orchomenus", *AJP* 105 (1984), 49-53

Burkert, W., "Das Lied von Ares und Aphrodite. Zum Verhältnis von Odyssee und Ilias", *RhM* 103 (1960), 130-44

— "Demaratos, Astrabakos und Herakles. Königsmythos und Politik in der Zeit der Perserkriege (Herodotus 6,67-69)", *MH* 22 (1965), 166-77

— "Kekropidensage und Arrhephoria. Vom Initiationsritus zum Panathenäenfest", *Hermes* 94 (1966), 1-25

— "Das hunderttorige Theben und die Datierung der Ilias", *WS* 10 (1976), 6-21

— *Structure and History in Greek Mythology and Ritual*, Berkeley/Los Angeles /London 1979

— "Götterspiel und Götterburleske in altorientalischen und griechischen Mythen", *Eranos* 51 (1982), 356-8

— *Greek Religion. Archaic and Classical*, London 1985 (= Engl. translation of *Griechische Religion der archaischen und klassischen Epoche*, Stuttgart/Berlin/Cologne/Mainz 1977 by J. Raffan)

— "Herodot über die Namen der Götter: Polytheismus als historisches Problem", *MH* 42 (1986), 121-32

— "Herodot als Historiker fremder Religionen", in: O. Reverdin, B. Grange (eds.), *Hérodote et les Peuples non Grecs*, Vandœuvres-Genève 1990, 1-32 (= *Entretiens sur l' Antiquité Classique. Fondation Hardt* 35)

— "Homer's Anthropomorphism. Narrative and Ritual", in: D. Buitron-Oliver (ed.), *New Perspectives in Early Greek Art*, Washington 1991, 81-91

— *The Orientalizing Revolution. Near Eastern Influence on Greek Culture in the Early Archaic Age*, Cambridge (Mass.) 1992 (= Engl. translation of *Die orientalisierende Epoche in der griechischen Religion und Literatur* (= SHAW 1984.1.), Heidelberg 1984 by M.E. Pinder and W. Burkert)

— "From Epiphany to Cult Statue: Early Greek *theos*", in: A.B. Lloyd (ed.), *What is a God?*, London 1997, 15-34

— *Die Griechen und der Orient*, Munich 2003 (= German translation (with an additional chapter) of *Da Omero ai Magi. La Tradizione Orientale nella Cultura Greca*, Venice 1999 by W. Burkert)

Bury, R.G., *The Symposium of Plato* (ed. with introduction, critical notes and commentary), Cambridge 1973

Busolt, G., *Griechische Staatskunde* (= *Handbuch der klassischen Altertumswissenschaft* vol. 4, part 1), Munich ³1920

Buxton, R.G.A., *Persuasion in Greek Tragedy*, Cambridge 1982

— *Imaginary Greece*, Cambridge 1994

Calame, C., *Les Choeurs de Jeunes Filles en Grèce Archaïque*, vol. 1, Rome 1977 (= 1977a)

— *Les Choeurs de Jeunes Filles en Grèce Archaïque. Alcman*, vol. 2, Rome 1977 (= 1977b)

— *Thésée et l' Imaginaire Athénien*, Lausanne 1990

— *L' Eros dans la Grèce Antique*, Paris 1996

— "Sexuality and Initiatory Transition", in: A. Laks, G.W. Most (1997), 65-80

Campbell, D.A., *Greek Lyric Poetry*, London 1967

Carson, A., *Eros the Bittersweet*, Princeton 1986

Càssola, F., *Inni Omerici* (ed. with introduction, text, translation and commentary), Milan 1975

Chadwick, J., *The Decipherment of Linear B*, Cambridge ²1970

Clapham, L.R., *Sanchuniathon: The First Two Cycles*, Harvard University 1969 (PhD dissertation)

Clarke, M.E., Coulson, W.D.E., "Memnon and Sarpedon", *MH* 35 (1978), 65-73

Clay, J.S., *The Politics of Olympus. Form and Meaning in the Major Homeric Hymns*, Princeton 1989

Connor, W.R., "Theseus in Classical Athens", in: A.G. Ward (1970), 143-74

Conzelmann, H., "Korinth und die Mädchen der Aphrodite: Zur Religionsgeschichte der Stadt Korinth", *NGG* 8 (1967), 247-61

Cook, A.B., *Zeus. A Study in Ancient Religion*, 2 vols., New York 1964-5

Cooper, C., "Hypereides and the Trial of Phryne", *Phoinix* 49 (1995), 303-18

Croissant, F., Salviat, F., "Aphrodite Gardienne des Magistrats: Gynéconomes de Thasos et Polémarques de Thèbes", *BCH* 90 (1966), 460-71

Dakaris, S., *Dodona*, Athens 1993

Dalley, S., *Myths from Mesopotamia*, Oxford 1989

Daux, G., "Inscriptions de Thasos", *BCH* 52 (1928), 57-8

— "Deux Stèles d'Acharnes", in: Χαριστήριον εἰς Ἀναστάσιον Κ. Ὀρλανδον, vol. 1, Athens 1965

— "Chronique des Fouilles et Découvertes Archéologiques en Grèce en 1967", *BCH* 92 (1968), 711-1135

Davidson, J.N., *Courtesans and Fishcakes*, London 1997

Davies, M., "The Eyes of Love and the Hunting Net in Ibycus 287 P", *Maia* 32 (1980), 255-7

— "The Judgement of Paris and *Iliad* Book XXIV", *JHS* 101 (1981), 56-62

— "Alcman 59ᴬ P.", *Hermes* 111 (1983), 496-7

— "Simonides and Eros", *Prometheus* 10 (1984), 114-6

— "Symbolism and Imagery in the Poetry of Ibycus", *Hermes* 114 (1986), 404-5

— *The Epic Cycle*, Bristol 1989

— *Sophocles. Trachiniae* (ed. with introduction and commentary), Oxford 1991

Deichgräber, K., *Charis und Chariten, Grazie und Grazien*, Munich 1971

Delcourt, M., *Hermaphrodite. Mythes et Rites de la Bisexualité dans l' Antiquité Classique*, Paris 1958

Delivorrias, A., "Aphrodite", in: *LIMC* II.1. (1984), 2-151

Dentzer, J.-M., *Le Motif du Banquet Couché dans le Proche-Orient et le Monde Grec du VIIème au IVème Siècle avant J.-C.*, Paris 1982

Deubner, L., "Personifikation abstrakter Begriffe", in: W.H. Roscher, *Ausführliches Lexikon der griechischen und römischen Mythologie*, vol. 3, part 2, Leipzig 1909, 2068-169

— *Attische Feste*, Berlin 1932

Dickie, M., "The Geography of Homer's World", in: O. Andersen, M. Dickie (eds.), *Homer's World*, Bergen 1995, 29-56

Dihle, A., "Die Inschrift vom Nestor-Becher aus Ischia", *Hermes* 97 (1969), 257-61

Dillon, M.P.J., Garland, L. (eds.), *Ancient Greece*, London 1994

Dillon, M.P.J., "Post-nuptial Sacrifices on Kos (Segre, *ED* 178) and Ancient Greek Marriage Rites", *ZPE* 124 (1999), 63-80

Dinsmoor, W.B., *The Architecture of Ancient Greece*, New York ²1973

Donohue, A.A., *Xoana and the Origins of Greek Sculpture*, Atlanta 1988

— "Greek Images of the Gods: Considerations on Terminology and Methodology", *Hephaistos* 15 (1997), 31-45

Dornseiff, F., *Pindars Dichtungen*, Munich 1965

Dover, K., *Greek Homosexuality*, London 1978

— *Plato. Symposium* (ed. with introduction and commentary), Cambridge 1980

Dowden, K., *Death and the Maiden. Girls' Initiation Rites in Greek Mythology*, London 1989
— *The Uses of Greek Mythology*, London/New York 1992
Dunbabin, T.J., *The Greeks and their Eastern Neighbours*, London 1957
Dunbar, N., *Aristophanes. Birds* (ed. with introduction and commentary), Oxford 1995
Dunkel, G., "Vater Himmels Gattin", *Die Sprache* 34 (1988/90), 1-26
Dürrbach, F. "Fouilles de Délos", *BCH* 26 (1902), 480-553
Easterling, P.E., "Alcman 58 and Simonides 37", *PCPhS* n.s. 20 (1974), 37-43
— *Sophocles. Trachiniae* (ed. with introduction, text and commentary), Cambridge 1982
Edwards, C.M., "Aphrodite on a Ladder", *Hesperia* 53 (1984), 59-72
Edwards, M.W., *The Iliad: A Commentary, Vol. 5, Books* 17-20, Cambridge 1991
Elsner, J., "Image and Ritual", *CQ* n.s. 46 (1996), 515-31
Engels, J., *Studien zur politischen Biographie des Hypereides*, Munich ²1993
Enmann, A., "Kypros und der Ursprung des Aphroditekults", *Mém. de l' Acad. de St. Petersburg* 34
    (1886), XIII
Erbse, H., *Untersuchungen zur Funktion der Götter im Homerischen Epos*, Berlin/New York 1986
Ermatinger, E., *Die Attische Autochthonsage bis auf Euripides*, Berlin 1897
Escher, J., "Charis, Charites", in: *RE* III.2. (1899), 2150-67
Faraone, C.A., "Aphrodite's ΚΕΣΤΟΣ and Apples for Atalanta: Aphrodisiacs in Early Greek Myth
    and Ritual", *Phoenix* 44 (1990), 219-43
— *Talismans and Trojan Horses*, Oxford 1992
— "Erotic Magic in Pindar *Pythian* 4, 213-19", *CJ* 89.1. (1993), 1-19
— "Taking the 'Nestor's Cup Inscription' Seriously: Erotic Magic and Conditional Curses in the
    Earliest Inscribed Hexameters", *CA* 15 (1996), 77-112
— *Ancient Greek Love Magic*, Cambridge (Mass.) 1999
Faraone, C.A., Obbink, D. (eds.), *Magica Hiera. Ancient Greek Magic and Religion*, Oxford 1991
Farnell, L.R., *The Cults of the Greek States*, 4 vols., Oxford 1896-1909
Fasce, S., *Eros. La Figura e il Culto*, Genova 1977
Fauth, W., *Aphrodite Parakyptusa*, Mainz 1966
Fehling, D., *Herodotus and his "Sources": Citation, Invention and Narrative Art*, Leeds 1989 (=
    Engl. translation (with addenda) of *Die Quellenangaben bei Herodot*, Berlin/New York 1971
    by J.G. Howie)
Fehr, B., *Orientalische und griechische Gelage*, Bonn 1971
Fittschen, K., *Bildkunst, Teil 1: Der Schild des Achilleus*, Göttingen 1973 (= *Archaeologia Homerica*,
    vol. 2, ch. N)
Flemberg, J., *Venus Armata. Studien zur bewaffneten Aphrodite in der griechisch- römischen Kunst*,
    Stockholm 1991
Flückiger-Guggenheim, D., *Göttliche Gäste. Die Einkehr von Göttern und Heroen in der
    Griechischen Mythologie*, Bern/Frankfurt/New York 1984 (=*Europäische Hochschulschriften*
    237)
Foley, H.P., *The Homeric Hymn to Demeter* (ed. with translation, commentary and interpretive
    essays), Princeton 1993
Foucart, P., "Le Temple d'Aphrodite Pandemos", *BCH* 13 (1889), 156-78
Franke P.R., Hirmer M., *Die griechische Münze*, Munich ²1972
Fränkel, H., *Early Greek Poetry and Philosophy. From Homer to Pindar*, New York 1975 (= Engl.
    translation of *Dichtung und Philosophie des frühen Griechentums*, Munich ²1962 by M.
    Hadas, J. Willis)
Fraschetti, A., Lloyd, A.B., *Erodoto. Le Storie* (ed. with introduction, text, commentary and trans-
    lation), vol. 2, Milan 1989
Frel, J., "Griechischer Eros", *Listy Filologicke* 86 (1963), 60-4
Friedrich, P., *The Meaning of Aphrodite*, Chicago 1978
Friis Johansen, H., Whittle, E.W., *Aeschylus. The Suppliants* (ed. with bibliography, introduction,
    text and commentary), 3 vols., Copenhagen 1980

v. Fritz, K., "Das Prooem der hesiodischen Theogonie", in: H. Erbse (ed.), *Festschrift B. Snell*, Munich 1956, 29-45

Funke, H., "Götterbild", *RAC* 11 (1981), 659-828

Furley, W.D., Bremer J.M., *Greek Hymns. Selected Cult Songs from the Archaic to the Hellenistic Period*, 2 vols., Tübingen 2001 (vol. 1: *The Texts in Translation* (=2001a); vol. 2: *Greek Texts and Commentary* (= 2001b)).

Garlan, Y., "Etudes d'Histoire Militaire et Diplomatique", *BCH* 102 (1978), 97-108

Garlan, Y., Masson, O., "Les Acclamations Pédérastiques de Kalami", *BCH* 106.1. (1982), 3-22

Garland, R., *Introducing New Gods*, Cornell 1992

Gartziou-Tatti, A., "L' Oracle de Dodone. Mythe et Rituel", *Kernos* 3 (1990), 175-84

Gentili, B. "Eros nel Simposio", in: M. Vetta (1983), 83-94

— *Poetry and its Public in Ancient Greece*, Baltimore 1988 (= Engl. translation of *Poesia e Pubblico nella Grecia Antica: da Omero al V Secolo*, Rome/Bari 1985 by A.T. Cole)

George, A., *The Epic of Gilgamesh*, London 1999

Giangrande, G., "Simonides and Eros", *AC* 38 (1969), 147-9

Giroux, H., "Eris", in: *LIMC* III.1. (1986), 846-50

Gladigow, B., "Präsenz der Bilder — Präsenz der Götter", *Visible Religion* 4-5 (1985-86), 114-33

— "Epiphanie, Statuette, Kultbild. Griechische Gottesvorstellungen im Wechsel von Kontext und Medium", *Visible Religion* 7 (1990), 98-121

Gomperz, Th., *Philodem über Frömmigkeit*, Leipzig 1866 (= *Herkulanische Studien, Heft 2*)

Gordon, C.H., *Ugaritic Textbook*, Rome 1965

Gordon, R.L., "The Real and the Imaginary. Production and Religion in the Greco-Roman World", *Art History* 2 (1979), 5-34

Gow, A.S.F., *Theocritus* (ed. with translation and commentary), 2 vols., Cambridge 1950

— Page, D.L., *The Greek Anthology. Hellenistic Epigrams*, 2 vols., Cambridge 1965

Graf, F., "Apollon Delphinios", *MH* 36 (1979), 2-22

— "Culti e Credenze Religiose della Magna Grecia", in: *Megale Hellas. Nome e Immagine. Atti del Ventesimo Convegno di Studi sulla Magna Grecia 2-5 Ottobre 1981*, Tarent 1982, 157-85

— "Women, War, and Warlike Divinities", *ZPE* 55 (1984), 245-54

— *Nordionische Kulte. Religionsgeschichtliche und epigraphische Untersuchungen zu den Kulten von Chios, Erythrai, Klazomenai und Phokaia*, Rome 1985

— "Religion und Mythologie im Zusammenhang mit Homer", in: J. Latacz (ed.), *200 Jahre Homer-Forschung*, Leipzig/Stuttgart 1991, 331-62

— *Griechische Mythologie*, Zurich ⁴1997

— "Epiphanie", in: *Der Neue Pauly* 3 (1997), 1150-2

Greifenhagen, A., *Griechische Eroten*, Berlin 1957

v. Groningen, B.A., *Pindare au Banquet*, Leiden 1960

— *Euphorion*, Amsterdam 1977

Gross, N.P., *Amatory Persuasion in Antiquity*, Newark/London 1985

Güterbock, H., *The Song of Ullikummi*, New York 1952

Gutzwiller, K.J., "The Nautilus, the Halcyon, and Selenaia: Callimachus's Epigram 5 Pf. = 14 G.-P.", *CA* 11 (1992), 194-209

— *Poetic Garlands. Hellenistic Epigrams in Context*, Berkeley/Los Angeles/London 1998

Habicht, C., *Studien zur Geschichte Athens in hellenistischer Zeit*, Göttingen 1982 (= *Hypomnemata* 73)

— *Athens from Alexander to Anthony*, Cambridge (Mass.) 1997 (= Engl. translation of *Athen in hellenistischer Zeit*, Munich 1994 by D.L. Schneider)

— "Neue Inschriften aus Kos", *ZPE* 112 (1996), 83-94

Hägg, R., "Die göttliche Epiphanie im Minoischen Ritual", *MDAI* 101 (1986), 41-62

Hall, E., "Lawcourt Dramas: the Power of Performance in Greek Forensic Oratory", *BICS* 40 (1995), 39-58

Halliday, W.R., "A Note on Herodotus vi. 83 and the Hybristica", *BSA* 16 (1909-10), 212-9

Halperin, D., *One Hundred Years of Homosexuality*, New York/London 1990

Hamdorf, F.W., *Griechische Kultpersonifikationen der vorhellenistischen Zeit*, Mainz 1964

Hansen, P.A., "Pithecusan Humour. The Interpretation of 'Nestor's Cup' Reconsidered", *Glotta* 54 (1976), 25-43

Harden, D.B., *The Phoenicians*, London 1962

Harrison, E.B., "Charis, Charites", in: *LIMC* III.1. (1986), 191-203

Havelock, C. M., *The Aphrodite of Knidos and Her Successors*, Ann Arbor 1995

Heitsch, E., *Aphroditehymnos. Aeneas und Homer*, Göttingen 1965 (= *Hypomnemata* 15)

Helck, W., *Betrachtungen zur großen Göttin und den ihr verbundenen Gottheiten*, Munich/Vienna 1971

Henrichs, A., "Greek Maenadism from Olympias to Messalina", *HSPh* 82 (1978), 121-60

— "Changing Dionysiac Identities", in: B.F. Meyer, E.P. Sanders (eds.), *Jewish and Christian Self-Definition*, vol. 3, London 1982, 137-60

— "Die Götter Griechenlands. Ihr Bild im Wandel der Religionswissenschaft", in: H. Flashar (ed.), *Auseinandersetzungen mit der Antike*, Bamberg 1990, 115-62

Herbig, R., "Griechische Harfen", *AM* 54 (1929), 164-93

Herington, J., *Poetry into Drama. Early Tragedy and the Poetic Tradition*, Berkeley/Los Angeles/London 1985

Hermary, A., Cassimatis, H., Vollkommer, R., "Eros", in: *LIMC* III.1. (1986), 850-942

Hermary, A., "Himeros", in: *LIMC* V. 1. (1990), 425-6

Herter, H., "Theseus der Athener", *RhM* 88 (1939), 244-326

— "L' Inno Omerico a Hermes alla Luce della Problematica della Poesia Orale", in: C. Brillante, M. Cantilena, C.O. Pavese (eds.), *I Poemi Epici Rapsodici non Homerici e la Tradizione Orale*, Padova 1981, 183-201

Heubeck, A., *Die Homerische Frage*, Darmstadt 1974

Hicks, E.L., "The Collection of Ancient Marbles at Leeds", *JHS* 11 (1890), 255-70

Hiller v. Gärtringen, F., "Neue Ausgrabungen auf Thera", *AA (Beiblatt)* 14 (1899), 181-91

Hobsbawn, E., Ranger, T. (eds.), *The Invention of Tradition*, Cambridge 1983

Hölscher, U., Review of: W. Schadewaldt, *Von Homers Welt und Werk*, Stuttgart ²1951, *Gnomon* 27 (1955), 385-99

— "Anaximander und die Anfänge der Philosophie", *Hermes* 81 (1953), 257-77; 385-418 (= H.G. Gadamer (ed.), *Um die Begriffswelt der Vorsokratiker*, Darmstadt 1968, 95-176)

Hommel, F., "Aphrodite-Astarte", *NJPhP* 125 (1882), 176

Hunter, R., *Apollonius of Rhodes, Argonautica. Book* 3 (ed. with introduction, text and commentary), Cambridge 1989

Hutchinson, G.O., *Greek Lyric Poetry. A Commentary on Selected Larger Pieces*, Oxford 2001

Huxley, G.L., *Kythera. Excavations and Studies*, London 1972

Huxley, G., "The Date of Pherecydes of Athens", *GRBS* 14 (1973), 137-45

Icard-Gianolio, N., "Peitho", in: *LIMC* VII.1. (1994), 242-50

Jacoby, F., "Hesiodstudien zur Theogonie", *Hermes* 61 (1926), 158-91

— *Hesiodi Carmina. Theogonia* (ed. with text, introduction and testimonies), vol. 1, Berlin 1930

— "Homerisches", *Hermes* 68 (1933), 1-50

— "ΓΕΝΕΣΙΑ. A Forgotten Festival of the Dead", *CQ* 38 (1944), 65-75

— "The First Athenian Prose Writer", *Mnemosyne* 13 (1947), 13-94

Jamot, P., "Deux Petits Monuments. Relatifs au Culte de Déméter en Béotie", in: *Mélanges Georges Perrot. Recueil de Mémoires Concernant l' Archéolgie Classique, la Littérature et l' Histoire Anciennes, dédie à Georges Perrot*, Paris 1903, 195-9

Janko, R., "The Structure of the *Homeric Hymns*: A Study in Genre", *Hermes* 109 (1981), 9-24

— *Homer, Hesiod and the Hymns. Diachronic Development in Epic Diction*, Cambridge 1982

— *The Iliad: A Commentary, Vol. 4, Books 13-16*, Cambridge 1992

Johnston, S.I., "The Song of the *Iynx*: Magic and Rhetoric in *Pythian* 4", *TAPA* 125 (1995), 177-206 de Jong, I.J.F., " ἵμερος", in: *LfgrE* (1989), 1194-5

Kaempf-Dimitriadou, S., *Die Liebe der Götter in der attischen Kunst des 5. Jahrhunderts v. Chr.*, *AntK* 2 Suppl. (1979), 7-12

— "Boreas", in: *LIMC* III.1. (1986), 133-42

Kannicht, R., "Thalia", in: W. Haug, R. Warning (eds.), *Das Fest*, Munich 1989, 47-52

Kantor, H.J., "A Bronze Plaque with Relief Decoration from Tell Tainat", *Journal of Near Eastern Studies* 21 (1962), 93-117

Karouzos, Ch., Τὸ Μουσεῖο τῆς Θήβας. Ὁδηγός, Athens 1934

Kearns, E., "Theseus", in: *OCD* (³1996), 1508-9

Kendrick Pritchett, W., *Pausanias Periegetes*, Amsterdam 1998 (= ΑΡΧΑΙΑ ΕΛΛΑΣ, vol. 6)

Kern, O., *Die Religion der Griechen*, vol. 1, Berlin 1926

Kilmer, M.F., *Greek Erotica on Attic Red-Figure Vases*, London 1993

— "Painters and Pederasts: Ancient Art, Sexuality, and Social History", in: M. Golden, P. Toohey (eds.), *Inventing Ancient Culture. Historicism, Periodization, and the Ancient World*, London/ New York 1997, 36-49

Kirk, G.S., *The Iliad: A Commentary, Vol. 1, Books 1-4*, Cambridge 1985

— *The Iliad: A Commentary, Vol. 2, Books 5-8*, Cambridge 1990

Kloss, G., *Untersuchungen zum Wortfeld 'Verlangen/Begehren' im frühgriechischen Epos*, Göttingen 1994 (= *Hypomnemata* 105)

Knigge, U., Rügler, A., "Die Ausgrabungen im Kerameikos 1986/87", *AA* (1989), 81-99

Knoepfler, D., "*Cupido ille propter quem Thespiae visuntur*. Une Mésaventure Insoupçonnée de l' Eros de Praxitèle et l' Institution du Concours des *Erôtideia*", in: id. (ed.), *Nomen Latinum. Mélanges de Langue, de Littérature et de Civilisation Latines Offerts au Professeur André Schneider à l' Occasion de son Départ à la Retraite*, Neuchâtel 1997, 15-39

Kossatz-Deissmann, A., "Iris I", in: *LIMC* V. 1. (1990), 741-60

Kretschmer, P., "Dyaus, Zeus, Diespiter und die Abstrakta im Indogermanischen", *Glotta* 13 (1924), 101-16

Kron, U., "Demos, Pnyx und Nymphenhügel. Zu Demos-Darstellungen und zum ältesten Kultort des Demos in Athen", *AM* 94 (1979), 49-75

Kullmann, W., *Das Wirken der Götter in der Ilias*, Berlin 1956

— *Die Quellen der Ilias*, Wiesbaden 1960

Kurke, L., "Pindar and the Prostitutes, or Reading Ancient "Pornography"", *Arion* 4.2. (1996), 49-75

Kurtz, D., Boardman, J., "Booners", in: J. Frel (ed.), *Greek Vases in the J. Paul Getty Museum*, vol. 3, Malibu 1986, 35-70

Labarbe, J., "Anacréon Contemplateur de Cléobule?", *RBPh* 38 (1960), 45-58

Labat, R., Caquot, A., Sznycer, M., Vieyra, M. (eds.), *Les Religions du Proche-Orient Asiatique*, Paris 1970

Laks, A., Most, G.W. (eds.), *Studies on the Derveni Papyrus*, Oxford 1997

Lasserre, F., *La Figure d' Eros dans la Poésie Grecque*, Lausanne 1946

Latacz, J., *Zum Wortfeld "Freude" in der Sprache Homers*, Heidelberg 1966

— "Die Funktion des Symposions für die entstehende griechische Literatur", in: W. Kullmann, M. Reichel (eds.), *Der Übergang von der Mündlichkeit zur Literatur bei den Griechen*, Tübingen 1990, 227-64

— *Die griechische Literatur in Text und Darstellung. Archaische Periode*, vol. 1, Stuttgart 1991

— "Neuere Erkenntnisse zur epischen Versifikationstechnik", in: F. Graf, J. v. Ungern-Sternberg, A. Schmitt (eds.), *J. Latacz. Erschließung der Antike. Kleine Schriften zur Literatur der Griechen und Römer*, Stuttgart/Leipzig 1994, 235-55

— *Homer, der erste Dichter des Abendlandes*, Munich ³1997

— "Homeros", in: *Der Neue Pauly* 5 (1998), 686-99

Launey, M., "Inscriptions de Thasos", *BCH* 57 (1933), 410

Lawrence, A.W., Tomlinson, R.A., *Greek Architecture*, New Haven ⁵1996

Lefkowitz, M.R., *First-Person Fictions. Pindar's Poetic "I"*, Oxford 1991

Leigh, M., "Wounding and Popular Rhetoric at Rome", *BICS* 40 (1995), 195-212

Lendle, O., *Die "Pandorasage" bei Hesiod*, Würzburg 1957

Lenz, L.H., *Der Homerische Aphroditehymnos und die Aristie des Aeneas in der Ilias*, Bonn 1975

Lesky, A., *Vom Eros der Hellenen*, Göttingen 1976

Lissarrague, F., *Un Flot d' Images. Une Esthétique du Banquet Grec*, Paris 1987

— "Publicity and Performance: *kalos*-Inscriptions in Attic Vase Painting", in: S. Goldhill, R. Osborne (eds.), *Performance, Culture and Athenian Democracy*, Cambridge 1999, 359-73

Lloyd, A.B., *Herodotus. Book 2* (ed. with introduction and commentary in 3 vols.), Leiden 1975-88

Lonsdale, S.H., *Ritual Play in Greek Religion*, Baltimore/London 1993

Lorimer, H.L., "Gold and Ivory in Greek Mythology", in: C. Bailey, E.A. Barber, C.M. Bowra, J.D. Denniston, D.L. Page (eds.), *Greek Poetry and Life. Essays Presented to Gilbert Murray*, Oxford 1936, 14-33

Lynn-George, J.M., "The Relationship of Σ 535-540 and Scutum 156-160 Re-examined", *Hermes* 106 (1978), 396-405

MacLachlan, B., *The Age of Grace*, Princeton 1993

Mader, B., " Ἄρης", in: *LfgrE* (1973), 1246-65

— "λυσιμελής", in: *LfgrE* (1991), 1724

— "μαχλοσύνη", in: *LfgrE* (1993), 49

— "μίσγω", in: *LfgrE* (1993), 225-9

— "ὀαρίζω", in: *LfgrE* (1997), 481

— "ὀαριστύς", in: *LfgrE* (1997), 482

Mansfield, J.M., *The Robe of Athena and the Panathenaic Peplos*, Berkeley 1985

Martin, R., "Fouilles de Thasos", *BCH* 68-69 (1944-45), 158-61

Marzullo, B., "Simon. fr. 575 P.", *MCr* 19-20 (1984-85), 15

Matz, F., *Göttererscheinung und Kultbild im minoischen Kreta*, Mainz 1958

Mazarakis Ainian, A.J., "Early Greek Temples: Their Origin and Function", in: R. Hägg, N. Marinatos, G.C. Nordquist (eds.), *Early Greek Cult Practice*, Stockholm 1988, 105-19

McIntosh Snyder, J., "Sappho in Attic Vase Painting", in: A.O. Koloski-Ostrow, C.L. Lyons (eds.), *Naked Truths*, London/New York 1997, 108-19

Meier, Ch., *Politik und Anmut*, Berlin 1985

Merkelbach, R., "Volksbeschluß aus Erythrai über den Bau eines Tempels der Aphrodite Pandemos", *EA* 8 (1986), 15-8

Metzger, H., *Recherches sur l' Imagerie Athénienne*, Paris 1965

Meyer, E., *Geschichte von Troas*, Leipzig 1877

Meyer, H. *Hymnische Stilelemente in der frühgriechischen Dichtung*, Würzburg 1933

Mikalson, J.D., *Religion in Hellenistic Athens*, Berkeley/Los Angeles/London 1998

Miller, T., *Die griechische Kolonisation im Spiegel literarischer Zeugnisse*, Tübingen 1997

Mills, S., *Theseus, Tragedy and the Athenian Empire*, Oxford 1997

Miranda, E., "Osservazioni sul Culto di Euploia", *MGR* 14 (1989), 123-44

Mitchell, B.M., "Herodotus and Samos", *JHS* 95 (1975), 75-91

v. der Mühll, P., "Das Griechische Symposion", in: G.P. Landmann, *Xenophon. Das Gastmahl*, Berlin 1957, 80-109 (= id., *Ausgewählte Kleine Schriften*, Basle 1976, 483-505)

Müller, H.M., *Erotische Motive in der griechischen Dichtung bis auf Euripides*, Hamburg 1981 (= Hamburger Philologische Studien 50)

Murray, O., "The *Symposium* as a Social Organisation", in: R. Hägg, N. Marinatos (eds.), *The Greek Renaissance of the Eighth Century B.C.*, Stockholm 1983, 195-9 (=1983 a)

— "The Greek Symposion in History", in: E. Gabba (ed.), *Tria Corda. Scritti in Onore di A. Momigliano*, Como 1983 , 257-72 (=1983b)

— (ed.), *Sympotica. A Symposium on the Symposium*, Oxford 1990

Musso, O., "Un Verso dell' Inno Omerico a Demetra e un Frammento di Saffo", *ZPE* 22 (1976), 37-9

Musti, D., Torelli, M., *Pausania. Guida della Grecia. Libro II: La Corinzia e l' Argolide* (ed. with text, translation and commentary), Naples 1986

Niemeyer, H.G., "Die Phönizier und die Mittelmeerwelt im Zeitalter Homers", *JRGZM* 31 (1984), 3-94

Nilsson, M.P., *Griechische Feste von religiöser Bedeutung*, Leipzig 1906
— *The Minoan-Mycenean Religion and its Survival in Greek Religion*, Lund 1927
— "Kultische Personifikationen", *Eranos* 50 (1952), 31-40
— *Geschichte der Griechischen Religion*, vol. 1, Munich ³1967

Nisbet, R., Hubbard, M., *A Commentary on Horace: Odes Book 1*, Oxford 1970

Norden, E., *Agnostos Theos*, Berlin 1923

Nordheider, H.W., "ἔρος, Ἔρος, ἔρως", in: *LfgrE* (1987), 714-5

Obbink, D., "A Quotation of the Derveni Papyrus in Philodemus' *On Piety*", *CErc* 24 (1994), 111-35
— *Philodemus. On Piety* (ed. with text and commentary), Oxford 1996

Oberhummer, E., "Urania", in: *RE* IX.A1. (1961), 931-42

O' Higgins, D.M., "Medea as a Muse: Pindar's Pythian 4", in: J.J. Clauss, S. Iles Johnston (eds.), *Medea. Essays on Myth, Literature, Philosophy and Art*, Princeton 1997, 103-26

Oliver, J.H., *Demokratia, the Gods and the Free World*, Baltimore 1960

Olmos, R., Balmaseda, L.J., "Alkyoneus", in: *LIMC* I.1. (1981), 558-64

Otto, W.F., *Die Götter Griechenlands*, Bonn 1947

Padel, R., *Whom Gods destroy*, Princeton 1995

Page, D.L., *Alcman. The Partheneion*, Oxford 1951
— *Sappho and Alcaeus*, Oxford 1955

Parca, M., "Sappho 1.18-19", *ZPE* 46 (1992), 47-50

Parke, H.W., *The Oracles of Zeus. Dodona, Olympia, Ammon*, Oxford 1967

Parker, R., *Miasma. Pollution and Purification in Early Greek Religion*, Oxford 1983
— "Myths of Early Athens", in: J.N. Bremmer (ed.), *Interpretations of Greek Mythology*, London 1986, 187-214
— "The *Hymn to Demeter* and the *Homeric Hymns*", *G&R* 38 (1991), 1-17
— *Athenian Religion. A History*, Oxford 1996
— "Attic Cults and Myths", in: *OCD* (³1996), 212
— "thiasos", in: *OCD* (³1996), 1513

Parker, R., Obbink, D., "Aus der Arbeit der «Inscriptiones Graecae» VI. Sales of priesthoods on Cos I", *Chiron* 30 (2000), 415-47

Patzer, H., *Die Anfänge der griechischen Tragödie*, Wiesbaden 1962

Peek, W., "Griechische Inschriften", *AM* 59 (1934), 35-80
— "Weihung von Agoranomen", *Hermes* 76 (1941), 416

Pellizer, E., "Outlines of a Morphology of Sympotic Entertainment", in: O. Murray (1990), 177-84

Penglase, C., *Greek Myths and Mesopotamia*, London 1994

Percy, W.A., *Pederasty and Pedagogy in Archaic Greece*, Illinois 1996

Petersen, L., *Zur Geschichte der Personifikation*, Würzburg 1939

Petrakos, B., "Ἀνασκαφὲς (Ραμνους)", Τὸ Ἔργον 39 (1992), 1-7
— "Ἀνασκαφὲς (Ραμνους)", Τὸ Ἔργον 42 (1995), 13-20

Pfeiffer, R., *Callimachus*, 2 vols, Oxford 1949-51
— "The Image of the Delian Apollo and Apolline Ethics", *JWI* 15 (1952), 20-32
— *History of Classical Scholarship. From the Beginnings to the End of the Hellenistic Age*, Oxford 1968

Pfister, F., "Epiphanie", in: *RE* Suppl. 4 (1924), 277-323

Pfuhl, E., *De Atheniensium Pompis Sacris*, Berlin 1900

Pirenne-Delforge, V., *L' Aphrodite Grecque*, Liège 1994 (= *Kernos* Suppl. 4)
— "Aphrodite", in: *Der Neue Pauly* 1 (1996), 838-43

Pötscher, W., "Das Person-Bereichdenken in der frühgriechischen Periode", *WS* 72 (1959), 5-25
— "Personifikation", in: *Der Kleine Pauly* 4 (1972), 661-3

— "Person-Bereichdenken und Personifikation", *Literaturwissenschaftliches Jahrbuch* n.s. 19 (1978), 217-31

Pottier, E., "Les Représentations Allégoriques dans les Peintures de Vases Grecs", *Monuments Grecs* 17-18 (1889-90), 15-9

Pouilloux, J., *Recherches sur l' Histoire et les Cultes de Thasos*, vol. 1, Paris 1954

— "Trois Décrets de Rhamnonte", *BCH* 80 (1956), 57-75

Powell, B., "Homer and Writing", in: I. Morris, B. Powell (eds.), *A New Companion to Homer*, Leiden/New York/Cologne 1997, 3-32

Powell, I.U., *Collectanea Alexandrina*, Oxford 1925

Price, S., *Religions of the Ancient Greeks*, Cambridge 1999

Price, S.D., "Anacreontic Vases Reconsidered", *GRBS* 31 (1990), 133-75

Puccioni, G., "La Poesia di Saffo", *Antiquitas* 3 (1948), 84-111

Pulleyn, S., *Prayer in Greek Religion*, Oxford 1997

Putnam, M.C.J., "Throna and Sappho I,1", *CJ* 56 (1960), 79-83

Rapp, A., "Die Mänade im griechischen Cultus, in der Kunst und Poesie", *Rassegna Monetaria* 27 (1972), 1-22

Raubitschek, A.E., "Die schamlose Ehefrau (Herodot 1,8,3)", *RhM* 100 (1957), 139-40 (= D. Obbink, P.A. Vander Waerdt (eds.), *The School of Hellas*, Oxford 1991, 330-1)

Reinhardt, K., *Das Parisurteil* (= *Wissenschaft und Gegenwart*, vol. 11), Frankfurt 1938 (= id., *Von Werken und Formen*, Godesberg 1948, 11-36 and id., *Tradition und Geist*, Göttingen 1960, 16-36)

— "Zum homerischen Aphroditehymnus", in: H. Erbse (ed.), *Festschrift B. Snell*, Munich 1956, 1-14

— "Personifikation und Allegorie", in: id., *Vermächtnis der Antike. Gesammelte Essays zur Philosophie und Geschichtsschreibung*, Göttingen 1960, 7-41

— *Die Ilias und ihr Dichter*, Göttingen 1961 (ed. by U. Hölscher)

Reinsberg, C., *Ehe, Hetärentum und Knabenliebe im antiken Griechenland*, Munich 1989

Reitzenstein, R., *Epigramm und Skolion*, Giessen 1893

Richardson, N.J., The *Homeric Hymn to Demeter*, Oxford 1974

— *The Iliad: A Commentary, Vol. 6, Books 21-24*, Cambridge 1993

Risch, E., "Zum Nestorbecher aus Ischia", *ZPE* 70 (1987), 1-9

Riis, P.J., "The Syrian Astarte Plaques and their Western Connections", *Berytos* 9 (1949), 69-90

Robert, C., "Pandora", *Hermes* 49 (1914), 17-38 (= id., in: E. Heitsch (ed.), *Hesiod*, Darmstadt 1966, 342-66)

Robert, J.&L., *Bull. épigr.* 72 (1959), 229-30

— *Bull. épigr.* 75 (1962), 195-6

Robert, L., "Inscriptions de Lesbos et de Samos", *BCH* 59 (1935), 471-88

— "Les colombes d' Aphrodisias et d' Ascalon", *JS* (1971), 91-7

Robinson, D.M., "A New Inscription from Macedonia", *AJA* 37 (1933), 602-4

Rocchi, M., "Contributi allo Culto delle Charites (I)", *StudClas* 18 (1979), 5-16

— "Contributi allo Culto delle Charites (II)", *StudClas* 19 (1980), 19-28

Romano, I.B., *Early Greek Cult Images*, Pennsylvania 1980 (PhD dissertation)

Roscher, W.H., "Hermes", in: *ML* I.2. (1886-90), 2342-434

— "Selene", in: *ML* I.2. (1886-90), 1885-1910

Rose, H.J., "Anchises and Aphrodite", *CQ* 18 (1924), 11-6

Rosenmeyer, P.A., "(In-)Versions of Pygmalion: The Statue Talks Back", in: A. Lardinois, L. McClure (eds.), *Making Silence Speak: Women's Voices in Greek Literature and Society*, Princeton/Oxford 2001, 240-60

Rosenmeyer, T., "Eros-Erotes", *Phoenix* 5 (1951), 11-22

Rösler, W., *Dichter und Gruppe. Eine Untersuchung zu den Bedingungen und zur historischen Funktion früher griechischer Lyrik am Beispiel Alkaios*, Munich 1980

Rossi, L.E., "Il Simposio Greco Archaico e Classico come Spettaculo a se stesso", in: *Spettacoli Conviviali dall' Antichità Classica alle Corti Italiane del '400: Atti del VII Convegno di Studio*, Viterbo 1983, 41-50

Rubensohn, O., "Paros", in: *RE* XVIII.2c. (1949), 1781-1872

Rudhardt, J., *Le Role d' Eros et d'Aphrodite dans les Cosmogonies Grecques*, Paris 1986

Rüter, K., Matthiessen, K., "Zum Nestorbecher von Pithekussai", *ZPE* 2 (1969), 231-55

Rüter, K., Schmidt, M., "γάμος", in: *LfgrE* (1984), 119-20

Rutherford, I., *Pindar's Paeans. A Reading of the Fragments with a Survey of the Genre*, Oxford 2001

Saake, H., *Zur Kunst Sapphos. Motiv-analytische und kompositionstechnische Interpretationen*, Paderborn 1971

Saffrey, H.D., "Aphrodite à Corinthe. Réflexions sur une Idée reçue", *RBi* 92 (1985), 359-74

Schachter, A., *Cults of Boiotia*, vol. 1, London 1981 (= *BICS* Suppl. 38.1.)

— "Charites", in: *Der Neue Pauly* 2 (1997), 1102-3

Schauenburg, K., "Erastes und Eromenos auf einer Schale des Sokles", *AA* (1965), 849-67

Schede, M., "Mitteilungen aus Samos", *Athenische Mitteilungen* 37 (1912), 199-218

Scheer, T.S., *Mythische Vorväter. Zur Bedeutung griechischer Heroenmythen im Selbstverständnis Kleinasiatischer Städte*, Munich 1993

— *Die Gottheit und ihr Bild. Untersuchungen zur Funktion griechischer Kultbilder in Religion und Politik*, Munich 2000 (= *Zetemata* 105)

Schibli, H.S., *Pherecydes of Syros*, Oxford 1990

Schild-Xenidou, W., *Boiotische Grab- und Weihreliefs Archaischer und Klassischer Zeit*, Munich 1972

Schmidt, M., "θεράπων", in: *LfgrE* (1989), 1015-9

Schmitt-Pantel, P., *La Cité au Banquet. Histoire des Repas Publics dans les Cités Grecques*, Rome 1992

Schmitt-Pantel, P., Schnapp, A., "Image et Société en Grèce Ancienne: Les Représentations de la Chasse et du Banquet", *Rev. Arch.* 1 (1982), 57-74

Schmitz, H., *Hypsos und Bios. Stilistische Untersuchungen zum Alltagsrealismus in der archaischen griechischen Chorlyrik*, Bern 1970

Schwabl, H., "Weltschöpfung", in: *RE* Suppl. 9 (1962), 1433-1589

Seaford, R., "The Tragic Wedding", *JHS* 107 (1987), 106-30

— Review of M. Détienne, *Dionysos at Large*, Cambridge/London 1989, *CR* 40 (1990), 173-4

— *Euripides. Bacchae* (ed. with introduction, translation and commentary), Warminster 1997

Seidl, U., Wilcke, C., "Inanna/Ishtar (Mesopotamien)", in: *Reallexikon der Assyriologie*, vol. 5, Berlin/New York 1976-80, 74-89

Seux, M.-J., *Hymnes et Prières aux Dieux de Babylonie et d'Assyrie*, Paris 1976

Seyrig, H., "Quatre Cultes de Thasos", *BCH* 51 (1927), 178-233

Shapiro, H.A., "Courtship Scenes in Attic Vase Painting", *AJA* 85 (1981), 133-43

— "Geras", in: *LIMC* IV. 1. (1988), 180-2

— *Personifications in Greek Art. The Representation of Abstract Concepts 600-400 B.C.*, Kilchberg 1993

— "Eros and Aphrodite: Love and the Polis", in: id., *Art and Cult under the Tyrants in Athens, Suppl.*, Mainz 1995, 118-24

Shear, T.L., "The Athenian Agora: Excavations of 1980-1982", *Hesperia* 53 (1984), 24-32, 38-40

Sherwin-White, S.M., *Ancient Cos*, Göttingen 1978

Shipley, G., *A History of Samos 800-188 BC*, Oxford 1987

Sider, S., "On Stuffing Quilts", *AJP* 99 (1978), 41-4

Siebert, G., "Hermes", in: *LIMC* V. 1. (1990), 285-387

Silk, M.S., *Interaction in Poetic Imagery*, Cambridge 1974

Simon, E., *Die Geburt der Aphrodite*, Berlin 1959

— "Aphrodite Pandemos auf attischen Münzen", *Schweizerische Numismatische Rundschau* 49 (1970), 5-19
— *Festivals of Attica*, Wisconsin 1983
— "Bia et Kratos", in: *LIMC* III.1. (1986), 114-5 (=1986a)
— "Dione", in: *LIMC* III.1. (1986), 411-3 (=1986b)
— "Neues zu den Mythen von Aineias, Sarpedon und Itys in der Etruskischen Kunst", *AA* (1992), 233-42
— *Die Götter der Griechen*, Munich ⁴1998
Simon, E., Bauchhenss G., "Apollo", in: *LIMC* II.1. (1984), 183-464
Slater, N.W., "The Vase as Ventriloquist: *kalos*-Inscriptions and the Culture of Fame", in: E.A. Mackay (ed.), *Signs of Orality*, Leiden 1998, 143-61
Slater, W.J. (ed.), *Dining in a Classical Context*, Ann Arbour 1991
Smith, P., *Nursling of Mortality. A Study of the Homeric Hymn to Aphrodite*, Frankfurt 1981
Smith, P.M., "Aineidai as Patrons of *Iliad* XX and the *Homeric Hymn to Aphrodite*", *HSCP* 85 (1981), 17-58
Sokolowski, F., "Aphrodite as Guardian of Greek Magistrates", *HThR* 51 (1964), 1-8
Solmsen, F., "Zur Theologie im großen Aphroditehymnus", *Hermes* 88 (1960), 1-13
Sourvinou-Inwood, C., "The Myth of the First Temples at Delphi", *CQ* n.s. 29 (1979), 231-51
Stafford, E., *Worshipping Virtues. Personification and the Divine in Ancient Greece*, London 2000
Stinton, T.C.W., "Euripides and the Judgement of Paris", *JHS* Suppl. 11 (1965), 2-77 (= id., *Collected Papers on Greek Tragedy*, Oxford 1990, 17-75)
Stoessl, F., "Personifikationen", in: *RE* XIX.1. (1937), 1042-58
Syme, R., Birley A. (eds.), *Anatolica. Studies in Strabo*, Oxford 1995
Syndikus, H.P., *Catull. Eine Interpretation. Die großen Gedichte*, vol. 2, Darmstadt 1990
Taplin, O., *The Stagecraft of Aeschylus*, Oxford 1977
— *Homeric Soundings*, Oxford 1992
Thériault, G., *Le Culte d' Homonoia dans les Cités Grecques*, Lyon 1996
Thompson, D' A.W., *A Glossary of Greek Birds*, Oxford ²1936
Thornton, B.S., *Eros. The Myth of Ancient Greek Sexuality*, Boulder 1997
Tod, M.N., "Greek Inscriptions at Cairness House", *JHS* 54 (1934), 159-62
Trampedach, K., "'Gefährliche Frauen'. Zu athenischen Asebie-Prozessen im 4. Jahrhundert v. Chr.", in: R. von den Hoff, S. Schmidt (eds.), *Konstruktionen von Wirklichkeit. Bilder im Griechenland des 5. und 4. Jahrhunderts v. Chr.*, Stuttgart 2001, 137-155
Travlos, J., *Bildlexikon zur Topographie des antiken Attika*, Tübingen 1988
Treu, M., *Von Homer zur Lyrik*, Munich 1955
Tsakos, K., "Θησαυρός Ἀφροδίτης Οὐρανίας· ἡ ἐπιγραφή", *Horos* 8-9 (1990-1), 17-28
Tudor, H., *Political Myth*, London 1972
Usener, H., *Götternamen. Versuch einer Lehre von der religiösen Begriffsbildung*, Bonn 1929
Vanoyeke, V., *La Prostitution en Grèce et à Rome*, Paris 1990
Ventris, M., Chadwick, J., *Documents in Mycenean Greek*, Cambridge ²1972
Verdenius, W.J., *Commentaries on Pindar*, vol. 1, Leiden 1987 (= *Mnemosyne* Suppl. 97)
Vermeule, E. T., *Götterkult*, Göttingen 1974 (= *Archaeologia Homerica* vol. 3, ch. V)
— *Aspects of Death in Early Greek Art and Poetry*, Berkeley 1979
Vernant, J.P., "From 'Presentification' of the Invisible to the Imitation of Appearance", in: F. Zeitlin (ed.), *Mortals and Immortals*, Princeton 1991, 151-63
Versnel, H.S., "What did Ancient Man see when he saw a God? Some Reflections on Greco-Roman Antiquity", in: J. van der Plas (ed.), *Effigies Dei*, Leiden 1987, 42-55
— *Ter Unus. Isis, Dionysos, Hermes: Three Studies in Henotheism*, Leiden 1990 (= *Studies in Greek and Roman Religion* 6)
Vetta, M. (ed.), *Poesia e Simposio nella Grecia Antica. Guida Storica e Critica*, Bari 1983
Visser, E., *Homerische Versifikationstechnik*, Frankfurt/Bern/New York 1987
de Visser, M.W., *Die nicht menschengestaltigen Götter der Griechen*, Leiden 1903

Voigt, F., "Peitho", in: *RE* XIX.1. (1937), 194-217

Vox, O., "On Love as a Fluid", *Hermes* 120 (1992), 375-6

Walcot, P., "Hesiod's Hymns to the Muses, Aphrodite, Styx and Hecate", *Symbolae Osloenses* 34 (1958), 5-14

— "The Homeric Hymn to Aphrodite. A Literary Appraisal", *G&R* 38 (1991), 137-55

Ward, A.G. (ed.), *The Quest for Theseus*, London 1970

Waser, O., "Flussgötter", in: *RE* VI.2. (1909), 2774-815

Webster, T.B.L., "Language and Thought in Early Greece", *Memoirs of the Manchester Literary and Philosophical Society* 94 (1952-1953), 17-38

— "Personification as a Mode of Greek Thought", *JWCI* 17 (1954), 10-21

v. Wees, H., "The Homeric Way of War: The *Iliad* and the Hoplite Phalanx (I)", *G&R* 41 (1994), 1-18, 131-55

Weizsäcker, P., "Peitho", in: *ML* III.2. (1902-09), 1795-813

Welcker, F.G., *Griechische Götterlehre*, vol. 3, Göttingen 1863

Welter, G., "Datierte Altäre in Athen", *AA* 54 (1939), 23-38

Welz, K., "Die Tauben der Aphrodite", *GNS* 34 (1959), 33-7

West, M.L., "Alcmanica", *CQ* n.s. 15 (1965), 188-202

— *Hesiod. Theogony* (ed. with prolegomena and commentary), Oxford 1966

— "Burning Sappho", *Maia* 22 (1970), 307-30 (=1970a)

— "Melica", *CQ* n.s. 20 (1970), 205-15 (= 1970b)

— "Cynaethus' Hymn to Apollo", *CQ* n.s. 25 (1975), 161-70 (=1975a)

— *Immortal Helen*, inaug. lecture, London 1975 (=1975b)

— *Hesiod. Works & Days* (ed. with prolegomena and commentary), Oxford 1978

— "Melos, Iambos, Elegie und Epigramm", in: E. Vogt (ed.), *Neues Handbuch der Literaturwissenschaft. Griechische Literatur*, vol. 2, Wiesbaden 1981, 73-142

— *The Orphic Poems*, Oxford 1983

— *Greek Lyric Poetry*, Oxford 1993

— "Ab Ovo", *CQ* n.s. 44 (1994), 289-307

— "The Date of the *Iliad*", *MH* 52 (1995), 203-19

— "Hesiod", in: *OCD* (³1996), 700

— *The East Face of Helicon*, Oxford 1997

— "The Name of Aphrodite", *Glotta* 76 (2000), 133-8

West, S., Heubeck A., Hainsworth, J.B., *A Commentary on Homer's Odyssey*, vol. 1, Oxford 1988

West, S., "Nestor's Bewitching Cup", *ZPE* 101 (1994), 9-15

v. Wilamowitz-Moellendorff, U., *Aus Kydathen*, Berlin 1880

— *Euripides. Herakles*, vol. 1, Berlin 1889

— *Sappho und Simonides*, Berlin 1913

— *Die Ilias und Homer*, Berlin 1916

— *Der Glaube der Hellenen*, 2 vols., Berlin 1931-32

Wilson, V., "The Kouklia Sanctuary", *AA* (1975), 446-55

Winkler, J.J., "Double Consciousness in Sappho's Lyrics", in: id., *The Constraints of Desire*, New York/London 1990, 162-87

— "The Constraints of Eros", in: id., *The Constraints of Desire*, New York/London 1990, 71-98 (= C.A. Faraone, D. Obbink (eds.), *Magica Hiera. Ancient Greek Magic and Religion*, Oxford 1991, 214-43)

Wittwer, M., "Über die kontrastierende Funktion des griechischen Suffixes -τερος", *Glotta* 47 (1969), 54-110

Wöhrle, G., *Hypnos der Allbezwinger. Eine Studie zum literarischen Bild des Schlafes in der griechischen Antike*, Stuttgart 1995 (=Palingenesia 53)

Worthington, I. (ed.), *Persuasion: Greek Rhetoric in Action*, London/New York 1994

Wünsch, R., "Hymnos", in: *RE* IX (1916), 140-83

Index

Index of Ancient Authors and Passages

A

Acusilaus
  FGrH 2 F 30: 209, n. 74; *FGrH* 2 F 31:
    209, n. 74; *FGrH* 2 F 6a:
    245, n. 138
Aeschylus
  Cho. 26: 235, n. 73
  Eum. 242: 215, n. 12
  Supp. 119; **178:** 233, n. 19; **516-23:** 119;
    233, n. 22; **1034-42:** 29; 208,
    n. 60; 234, n. 44
  PV 69
  fr. 44 (*Danaids*): 118; 217, n. 32; **fr.**
    281: 209, n. 74
Alcaeus
  fr. 307c: 218, n. 50; **fr. 327:** 140; 142;
    166ff.; 189; 241, n. 65; 245,
    n. 143; **fr. 366:** 179; 249, n.
    41
Alciphron
  4,1: 239, n. 29
Alcman
  fr. 1: 128; 173-6; 246, n. 8; 247, n. 13; **fr.**
    3: 173f.; 176; 186f.; 228, n.
    97; 229, n. 15; 246, n. 8; **fr.**
    10: 246, n. 8; **fr. 38:** 174f.; **fr.**
    39: 174f.; **fr. 58:** 189ff.; 253,
    n. 118; 253, n. 120; **fr. 59a:**
    191; **fr. 64:** 119; 233, n. 17
Alexis
  FGrH 539 F 2:183; 250, n. 70
Anacreon
  fr. 348: 251, n. 87; **fr. 356:** 181; **fr. 357:**
    185; 189; **fr. 358:** 168; 189f.;
    193f.; 253, n. 128; **fr. 359:**
    184; **fr. 360:** 181; 184; 251,
    n. 79; **fr. 379:** 126; 161; 167;

244, n. 126; 245, n. 151; 235,
n. 61; **fr. 384:** 233, n. 17; **fr.**
390: 251, n. 87; **fr. 396:** 184;
251, n. 79; **fr. 398:** 189; **fr.**
402: 184f.; 251, n. 80; 251,
n. 88; **fr. 407:** 185; 251, n.
84; **fr. 414:** 184f.; 251, n. 83;
fr. 417: 189; **fr. 418:** 251, n.
87; **fr. 428:** 190; **fr. 471:** 185;
251, n. 88; **fr. 491:** 182; 250,
n. 64
Anth. Pal.
  5,177 (Meleager): 165; **6,211** (Leonidas):
    238, n. 14; **7,14** (Antipater):
    125; 235, n. 54; **7,27**
    (Antipater): 185; 251, n. 89;
    7,324: 222, n. 132; **9,320:**
    207, n. 40; **9,321:** 207, n. 40;
    12,56 (Meleager): 239, n. 30;
    12,57 (Meleager): 239, n.30;
    16,167 (Antipater): 239, n.
    30; **16,171:** 207, n. 40
Anth. Pal. App. **1,31:** 141; 193
Apollodorus
  FGrH 244 F 113: 118; 210, n. 97; *FGrH*
    244 F 114: 203, n. 82
  Bibl. 1,9,4: 208, n. 72; **2,4,7:** 208, n.
    72; **3,5,8:** 108; **3,14,8:** 209,
    n. 73; **3,15,1:** 208, n. 72;
    3,15,7: 108; 230, n. 28
Apollonius Rhodius
  Argon. 3: 236, n. 84; **3,114-40:** 193
  schol. *Argon.* **1,609-19c:** 240, n. 43;
    3,26: 160; 165; 169; 244, n.
    123; 245, n.137; 245, n. 142;
    245, n. 159; **3,114-7:** 250, n.
    72